Love Me Tender

Books by Susan Fox

Caribou Crossing Romances
Caribou Crossing
Home on the Range
Gentle on My Mind
Stand by Your Man
Love Me Tender

Wild Ride to Love Series
His, Unexpectedly
Love, Unexpectedly
Yours, Unexpectedly

Stand-Alone
Body Heat

Writing as Susan Lyons
Sex Drive
She's on Top
Touch Me
Hot in Here
Champagne Rules

Anthologies
The Naughty List
Some Like It Rough
Men on Fire
Unwrap Me
The Firefighter

Love Me Tender

SUSAN FOX

ZEBRA BOOKS
KENSINGTON PUBLISHING CORP.
http://www.kensingtonbooks.com

Chapter One

At five-thirty A.M., Dave Cousins eased open his daughter's door to check that all was well. Eleven-year-old Robin didn't stir from what he'd be willing to bet was a horsy dream. Merlin, their black poodle, raised his head from where he lay curled on the rug beside the bed. At Dave's silent gesture, his head went back down. Robin would take the dog out once she rose. Until then, it was Merlin's job to guard her while Dave, the owner of the Wild Rose Inn, went downstairs to do some work.

He cast one more loving glance at her face, so sweet and relaxed in sleep, and the tumbled chestnut hair that by day was always pony-tailed. He sure did like the days Robin stayed with him, rather than with Jessie and Evan. His ex-wife and her new husband lived outside town, surrounded by horses. In many ways, they had so much more to offer Robin. So far, luckily, that fact didn't seem to trouble the girl. Dave loved her to pieces, and she seemed to reciprocate.

When Robin wasn't around, his life, no matter how busy, felt empty. Lonely.

If Anita hadn't died, things would be so different.

The thought brought a surge of pain, anger, guilt, and

desolation, that nasty thundercloud of emotions. He swallowed against the ache that choked his throat, and forced back the feelings.

This was why he tried not to think of the fiancée who had been the love of his life.

Briskly he walked to the door of the two-bedroom owner's suite on the top floor of the Wild Rose and pulled on his cowboy boots, then let himself out. As he ran down the four flights of stairs, he was already looking forward to returning in a couple of hours to have breakfast with Robin.

When he entered the lobby, lit by early morning sun, the Wild Rose worked her—he always thought of the inn as "her"—magic on him, and he felt a sense of peace and satisfaction. He had rescued a lovely but ramshackle historic building that was destined for destruction and restored her, creating a haven for travelers and a gathering place for locals.

The décor featured rustic yet comfortable Western furniture accented with photographs and antiques honoring Caribou Crossing's gold rush history. Behind the front desk, Sam, the retired RCMP officer who handled the inn overnight, frowned into space through his horn-rims.

"Morning," Dave greeted him. "Words not flowing?" Sam was writing a mystery novel and it came in fits and starts.

"Got distracted." Sam scratched his balding head. "By the woman in twenty-two."

"Someone who checked in last night?" Twenty-two had been one of only three empty rooms at the beginning of the man's shift. "I take it she's pretty?" Sam had never married and had an eye for the ladies, which translated into a rough charm that suited the Wild Rose's ambience.

"For sure. Once she got some color back in her cheeks." Sam paused, a born storyteller confident that he'd hooked his audience.

"Go on."

The night manager leaned forward, his pale gray eyes bright even after a night awake. "It's past eleven when she staggers into the lobby. Mid- to late twenties, slim build, some Latina blood. Jeans and a top that's too light for the nights this time of year." June in Caribou Crossing featured warm, sunny days but the temperature cooled when the sun went down.

"Staggers?" Pale and staggering; that didn't sound good.

"Those white cheeks of hers, they weren't just from the cold. It's more like she's done in, on her last legs. She stumbles across to the desk, backpack weighing her down. I get up to go take her pack, but before I reach her, what does she up and do?" His shaggy gray eyebrows lifted.

"What does she up and do?"

"Faints dead away."

Dave frowned, worried. "Did you call nine-one-one?"

The storyteller was probably incapable of giving a simple yes-or-no answer. "I bend down, make sure she has a pulse, and by then she's stirring. So I whip into the bar and fetch a shot of rye. The Caribou Crossing Single Barrel. Figure if our hometown drink doesn't fix her up, I'll call for help."

Dave didn't know whether to groan or grin. "Did she drink it?"

"I wave it under the gal's nose, and she snorts and jumps back like a horse when it sees a snake. She sits up, grabs the glass, downs it in one swallow, and says, 'Damn, that's good.'"

Surprised and relieved, Dave laughed and Sam joined in.

"I did offer to call a doc," Sam assured him, "but she says no, she's just exhausted and hungry. Been hitchhiking all day, up from Vancouver, hasn't had much to eat. Says she came in to ask if there's a hostel in town. That whisky put some color back in her cheeks and she's trying to be all bright and cheery. But under all that, she looks like a nag that's been rode hard and put up wet. I tell her she'll stay here; she starts to argue; I tell her I won't take no guff. Give her a key, carry her pack up to twenty-two, then I heat up some beef stew and biscuits from the kitchen and take it up." He shrugged. "After that, I don't hear another peep out of her."

"Hmm." Dave glanced at the ceiling, still concerned. "I'd feel better if a doctor had taken a look at her." A few of the doctors had an arrangement through an answering service: one was always on call, and they made house calls.

"She said she wasn't going to waste a doctor's time. The gal was pretty damned firm about it." He gave his balding head a shake. "Put me in mind of old Ms. Haldenby. You know?"

The retired schoolteacher was a fine—and intimidating— woman who definitely knew her own mind. "There's no arguing with someone like that," Dave agreed. "It sounds like you did all you could. Good work, Sam."

"See if you still say that when I tell you I didn't get a credit card or even a name. Figured it could wait till she was feeling better."

"Yeah. Even if she skips, it's no big loss." Dave was more worried about the woman's health. But Sam was a smart, observant guy. If he'd thought their visitor really was sick, he'd have overridden her objections, as he had when he'd given her a room.

"Anyhow," Sam said, "the damned woman took my mind right out of my book. Got me thinking about her story, and I bet it's a good one."

Dave rolled his eyes. "You and your overactive imagination. She's a hitchhiker who didn't have the sense to rest when she needed to. She'll be up and on the road, hopefully paying her bill before she goes."

* * *

Around eleven, Dave was at the front desk relieving Deepta, the receptionist who worked week days from six-thirty to two-thirty. He was trying to book opera tickets in Vancouver for guests who were heading there tomorrow, but the online system kept glitching. Frustrated, he took a deep breath, unsnapped the cuffs of his Western shirt and rolled them up his forearms, and gave the system another go. It stalled again.

"Hi there," a cheerful female voice said. "Anywhere around here I can get a good capooch?"

He looked up and his eyes widened in appreciation. This had to be the guest in twenty-two, and yeah, she sure was pretty. Medium height, slim, nice curves shown off by shorts and a purple tank worn over something that had pink straps. He saw the Latina in her olive-toned skin and the shiny black hair cut in a short, elfin cap. Her black-lashed eyes were blue-gray and sparkling, matching her white smile. She was the picture of health, he was relieved to see.

And that smile was irresistible. He smiled back. "That translate to cappuccino?"

Humor warmed her eyes. "What else?"

"Thought maybe you were talking about some weird mixed-breed dog," he drawled.

Her burble of laughter was musical and infectious. "No, it's caffeine I need right now." She yawned widely without covering her mouth.

It should have been unattractive but he had trouble imagining that anything this woman did would be unattractive. Something stirred inside him, a warm ripple through his blood. "Caffeine does come in handy now and then."

"A double-shot capooch sure would." She stuck a hand out. "I'm Cassidy. Cassidy Esperanza."

With guests, he aimed for the personal touch, so he came out from behind the desk and extended his hand. "Dave Cousins."

He spotted a tattoo on the cap of her right shoulder: a Canada goose flying across the moon. Striking, almost haunting.

Cassidy's hand was like the rest of her: light brown, slender, attractive. Her shake was full of vitality. He shook a lot of hands in the course of a day, but this one felt particularly good in his—and now the ripple in his veins was a tingle of awareness. No, more than awareness; he was *aware* of lots of appealing women. This was attraction.

His heart—the part of it that could fall in love—had died three years ago. His body hadn't, but he had zero desire to follow up on any hormonal stirrings.

So why was it so difficult to free his hand from his guest's? "Best coffee in town's right here." A couple of the coffee shops did a fine job too, but for some reason he wanted to keep Cassidy Esperanza at the Wild Rose. "Good food too, if you're hungry."

"Cool." She gave another of those huge yawns, stretched her arms up, and raked her fingers through that cap of hair, ruffling it. Normally, he preferred long hair on women, but the pixie cap suited Cassidy's slightly exotic face.

"I'm awake," she said with a quick laugh, eyes dancing as she studied his face. "I swear I am. Got a good sleep too. Don't know why I'm yawning." Her face sobered. "Before I do anything, I need to have a talk with the manager."

"Let me guess, you're twenty-two."

"Twenty-two?" She shook her head slightly, looking confused. "No, I'm twenty-seven. What a weird question."

"Sorry, I mean room twenty-two. The woman who came in last night and . . ." He paused, curious to see what she'd say.

"Did a face plant?" She raised her brows ruefully. "You heard about that? Yeah, that's me. Totally embarrassing. But the guy on the desk was great. Only problem is . . ." She pressed her full, pink lips together, then released them. "Can I confide in you? Maybe you can give me some advice."

He dragged his gaze from her lips. "Uh, sure."

"The nice guy gave me a room last night, and food, but the thing is, I don't have the money to pay. I came in to get warm and see if someone could point me toward a hostel, and next thing I knew I was on the floor and this guy was"—she broke off and grinned with the memory—"waking me up with a whiff of whisky. Which tasted delicious, and I guess I owe for that too, now that I think of it."

"Look—"

"No, I realize I owe for the room and everything, and this is a classy place so it won't be cheap. But the thing is, I'm pretty much broke."

Oh, great.

He opened his mouth, but she rushed on again. "I swear I won't cut out on you. I was going to look for a job in Caribou Crossing anyway, and as soon as I get one and have some money, I'll pay up. But it might take a few days and I'd sure understand if the manager was mad. So if you could give me any tips on how to deal with him, I'd really appreciate it."

As best he could tell, she was sincere. "Tell him the truth. And you did. I'm the owner of the Wild Rose."

"Oh! My gosh, I didn't realize. Wow. You don't look old enough."

He'd heard that before. "Just turned thirty."

She studied him again, lips curving. "Gotta love a hotel where the owner wears jeans and cowboy boots."

"It's part of our ambience."

She glanced around the lobby. "Yeah, it's kind of a cool blend of Old West and Santa Fe. That room—twenty-two—is awesome. That four-poster canopy bed with all the ruffles and flounces, the stool to climb up into it. I worried when I saw the chamber pot, but then I realized it was for decoration and there was a real bathroom. Claw-foot tub and all."

Canopy bed. Claw-foot tub. Slim, vibrant, sexy Cassidy. Physical stirrings below the belt had him giving a mental head-shake. He would never fool around with an inn guest. In the past three years, he'd pretty much figured he'd never fool around again. If he wanted female companionship, he had platonic friends. Casual sex wasn't his thing, and love wasn't going to happen. Anita had been the love of his life. His heart belonged to her, and always would.

And there he went, thinking of her again. The familiar sense of desolation threatened, but somehow the grin Cassidy tilted toward him countered it.

"So, Dave Cousins, Mr. Owner, want to have breakfast with me? I'll run my tab even higher and you can tell me where I might find work."

Though he liked being friendly and informal with guests, he kept it professional. Occasionally, he joined them for a drink or a coffee, but not often. This time he was tempted—against his better judgment. There was something about Cassidy that made him feel . . . lighter.

Chapter Two

Cassidy studied the man in front of her. He was handsome in a way that snuck up on you. At first, he'd just been a tall, rangy guy with regular features. But the longer she looked, the more she took in. The leanness of hip and length of leg in nicely faded jeans belted with braided leather. The flex of muscles in his tanned forearms and beneath the gentle drape of his sage green Western-style shirt. The way his thick sandy brown hair framed the strong lines of his face and flopped engagingly over his forehead; the direct gaze of hazel eyes flecked with green and gold; the tiniest suggestion, when he smiled, that a dimple might want to break through.

Easy on the eyes. The expression had been made for Dave Cousins.

"Easy" wasn't the word to describe his effect on other parts of her body. He most definitely sent a tingle through all her girly parts. It had been a while since she'd felt so attracted.

Unfortunately, Dave was shaking his head. "Sorry, I need to stay on the desk until the receptionist gets back."

Cassidy was about to respond when her attention was caught by a Native Canadian woman striding into the lobby.

She looked to be twenty or so, and was striking with long, shining black hair falling past the shoulders of a crisp white Western shirt. Cassidy checked the footwear below her slim-fitting dark jeans: red cowboy boots that gave her a rare case of shoe envy.

"Hey," Dave greeted her. "Madisun, this is Cassidy Esperanza, one of our guests. Cassidy, Madisun Joe is my assistant manager."

And young for such responsibility. Clearly, Madisun had career ambitions and drive. Unlike Cassidy, who was all about new places, new people, new experiences.

"It's nice to meet you," Cassidy said.

"Welcome to the Wild Rose, Cassidy," Madisun said. She turned to Dave, setting silver feather-shaped earrings dancing against her neck. "I have the final plans for Karen and Jamal's wedding reception, whenever you want to take a look."

"Thanks." He glanced at Cassidy, then back to Madisun. "Would you mind taking the desk until Deepta comes back?"

"No problem."

Excellent! Thank you, Madisun.

"Great," Dave said. "And could you book two tickets for the Vancouver Opera's *Carmen* at the Queen Elizabeth, Wednesday night, for Mr. and Mrs. Grunewald? The online system kept glitching, so you may have to make a call."

"Sure."

"If you need me, I'll be in the restaurant with Cassidy."

Madisun's brown eyes widened slightly. "Okay."

Smiling, Cassidy crossed the lobby at Dave's side. As they were about to enter the dining room, a female instinct made her dart a glance over her shoulder. Madisun stood rooted to the spot, staring after them. Hmm. What was up with that?

Inside the restaurant, Dave said hello to a female server. The young blonde's long burgundy velvet dress was flattering, but the style was old-fashioned, as was her upswept hairdo held in place with sparkly combs. Glancing past her, Cassidy noted a male server in a buttoned vest, bow tie, and brimmed hat. The servers and the décor, featuring dark wood and gleaming brass, had the feel of a classy saloon from a Western movie set back in the 1800s.

The Wild Rose Inn was impressive, and so was its owner. Cassidy peeked at Dave's ring finger, which was bare. If he was single, a hot guy like him, a business owner, had to be one of the most eligible bachelors in this small town. Which meant that, if he was *still* single, he likely wasn't marriage minded. And that meant he and Cassidy had something important in common. Marriage was a crap shoot, the odds of failure higher than those of success. She'd learned that from her parents. And when marriages failed, families were torn apart. Hearts got broken.

Even if she felt an occasional twinge of envy for couples and families who did seem happy, she always reminded herself that their odds of staying that way were slim. Seemed to her, it was crazy to set yourself up for heartbreak. Much better to have a little short-term fun, both partners knowing exactly what they were doing, then move on. Not that she was a slut or anything. Fun was great, but the guy had to be special, and she had to feel not just lust but a real sense of connection. That hadn't happened for eight or nine months, but already she sensed potential in Dave Cousins.

She'd come to Caribou Crossing for riding, fresh air, a healthy lifestyle. Add a sexy guy with potential, and life didn't get much better.

The server seated them in a window booth. After Cassidy had ordered her capooch and Dave had asked for plain black coffee, she grinned at the man seated across from her. "Nice place you've got here. It's like a saloon in *Butch Cassidy and the Sundance Kid*—which, by the way, I'm not named after."

"Who are you named after?"

"My gramps. James Cassidy. He was the best guy in the world."

"Nice." He nodded approvingly. "Anyhow, yes, the dining room is modeled on an upscale gold rush saloon."

"Oh yeah, this must have been a gold rush town, right? I saw those old pictures in the lobby." She'd noticed sepia photos of miners and cowboys.

"Yup. Caribou Crossing was on the Cariboo Wagon Road. A couple of miners struck gold in a big way in the early 1860s and a town sprang up. When the gold ran out, a few enterprising miners decided not to follow the lure of gold elsewhere, but to start ranching. The land was ideal for it. And now Caribou Crossing is also a tourist town, playing up both our gold rush history and the Western ranching theme."

"That's why I came. For the horses."

"I'm curious. But you're hungry." He gestured to the menu lying on the table. "Order some food; then tell me what brings you here."

Confident that she'd find a job and pay Dave back, she wouldn't choose the cheapest meal. Miners' flapjacks served with bacon, maple syrup, and strawberries sounded delicious.

She gratefully accepted the cappuccino the server brought her, then placed her order. "Fuel for job hunting," she said cheerfully.

While Dave added his order for a side of biscuits, she savored the first hot, frothy, delicious sips of coffee and glanced out the window. Last night, the town had been dark and she'd been too dog-tired to take in any details. She'd honed in on the light coming from the Wild Rose's windows and stumbled toward it, with that stupid bum leg going numb on her.

Now, in late morning sunlight, she saw what a picturesque town it was. Across the street were small shops: a toy store, a women's clothing boutique, an arts and crafts shop, a drugstore. Attractive and well maintained, each had its own style, yet they fit together comfortably.

The people on the street were like that, too. A woman in a business suit, carrying a briefcase, strode briskly past a family of four who'd stopped to peer in the window of the toy store. A striking brunette in an RCMP uniform chatted with a middle-aged couple in Caribou Crossing T-shirts bearing a logo similar to a pedestrian-crossing sign but with a stylized caribou.

"What do you think?" Dave asked.

She turned from one appealing view to another and saw curiosity in those gorgeous eyes of his. "Nice town you have here."

"Thanks. We like it." He gave a rather smug grin that she found enormously sexy.

Actually, pretty much everything he did, from the easy, athletic way he moved, to the relaxed way he chatted with his staff, to the way he raised his coffee mug with his strong hand, was sexy. Her body hadn't felt so alert and alive in a long time—and it wasn't from the caffeine.

He went on. "So you were saying you came here for the horses? You're a rider?"

"Kind of." She savored another sip of coffee, closing her eyes to enhance the pleasure. When her lashes drifted upward, she caught him gazing at her with obvious male interest.

Quickly, he glanced away. "Go on."

"I was waitressing at a sports bar in Vancouver and the job itself was fun, especially when Canucks games were playing on the wide screen." She grinned, remembering the cheers when the home team scored, not to mention the good tips.

"But the manager kept coming on to me, wouldn't take no for an answer." The memory sent a sour twinge through her stomach. "Sunday night, he crossed the line. I got away from him, but it was totally obvious I couldn't keep working there."

Dave frowned. "That's terrible. You should report the jerk."

"Yeah, well . . ." It was easier to just move on. "I also wasn't getting along with my roommate. I'd moved into her place and was paying half the rent, but I sure didn't get equal rights. She filled the fridge with her crap, hogged the bathroom, always had her friends in the living room, even stored some of her stuff in my bedroom. We fought all the time."

Their food arrived. Dave's steaming biscuits were the same kind she'd savored last night along with that rich beef stew. This morning they came with butter, honey, and strawberry jam. Her own flapjacks formed a golden-brown stack surrounded by crisp bacon and sliced strawberries. The server placed a ceramic jug of maple syrup on the table.

"Mmm, thank you." Cassidy's nose twitched at the delicious scent of bacon.

For a few minutes, she ate happily. Dave tackled his biscuits, apparently content to wait for her to pick up her story when she was ready. She liked that. Most guys filled any silence with talk about their jobs, their cars, their favorite sports teams.

She also liked the intentness with which he'd listened to her, and the indignation in his eyes when she'd told him about her former boss. A nice guy, this Dave Cousins, on top of being a hottie. She got a vibe that he was attracted to her too, but it was a subdued one, as if he had reservations.

Or perhaps a wife or girlfriend, which made him total taboo for her.

After downing half her meal, she carried on. "I was tired of Vancouver. I love cities and it's a great one, but I was ready for something different. I'd been there four months and I rarely stay anywhere much longer than that."

His brow furrowed as if he wasn't sure he'd heard correctly. Lots of people didn't relate to her gypsy lifestyle. For her, "a new day, a new adventure" was a much more rewarding way to live than all that planning, saving, thinking about the future stuff that so many people invested themselves in. For God's sake, who knew if you were even going to have a future? Look at her mom's mom, who fell down the steps and broke her neck at the age of twenty-eight.

Cassidy went on with her story. "This woman I met when I was getting my hair cut, she was saying how much fun she had last summer at a resort ranch near Caribou Crossing."

"The Crazy Horse?"

"Right." She accepted the server's offer of a second cappuccino, then told Dave, "I've done a little riding and I have a craving to do it again. And to breathe nice fresh country air." City days were long and demanding, what with work, friends, partying. She was only twenty-seven, but she'd been feeling run-down. And then there was that stupid thing with her left leg. She must have strained it, because a week or so ago it had gone tingly, then numb. The numbness went away after two or three days, though since then she still got occasional pins and needles and numbness. Like last night, when that crazy-long day had culminated in her embarrassing face plant.

She'd strained her leg, and she was run-down. That's all it was. It was nothing like what had happened to her great-grandmother. GG had ended up unable to walk, unable to speak properly, incontinent—

No, she wasn't going to think about her mom's grandmother. No way did she have GG's debilitating disease.

"So," Cassidy resumed the story, "yesterday morning I told my roomie I was leaving. She said I owed rent because I wasn't giving notice, so I gave her the few hundred dollars I had and kept twenty for myself. I should've kept at least a hundred, but she was yelling and I couldn't wait to get out of there. I tossed my belongings in my backpack and hit the road."

Dave frowned, like she wasn't making sense. "You must have money in the bank, though."

Must? Like it was some kind of rule? She shook her head. "I've never been big on saving. Life's for living, right?"

"But you have to think about tomorrow, next month, next year."

All those strings people wove around themselves, tying them down like they were in prison. "Not me. Tomorrow comes, I'll decide what I want to do. Next month, I'll decide where to go. Next year"—she shrugged—"I could be in India, Albuquerque, or Cuba."

Now he was looking at her like she'd descended from outer space. "Where's your home?"

She was tempted to say Alpha Centauri but figured the truth would freak him out enough. "Wherever I hang my backpack."

"But you must come from somewhere."

"Born in Victoria, but I haven't lived there since I was seventeen."

"Your parents are there?"

"No, they're in Acapulco right now. But that won't last." Marriage number three—to each other—was as doomed to failure as the previous two. Her parents never learned.

"Why not?"

"Long story." Talking about her parents was depressing.

She polished off the last of her late breakfast. "That was delicious."

"You have no home, no savings, and everything you own is in your backpack?" His face bore a glazed expression, like she'd laid too much on him too quickly. The guy probably lived in the same town he'd been born in, next door to his parents. Hard to believe a man like that wouldn't be married. Why not find out?

"That's me. Now how about you? You own the Wild Rose, you were probably born in Caribou Crossing . . ." She paused, collected his nod. "Married to your high school sweetheart?"

He blinked. "Uh, kind of. We're divorced."

"Ah." He didn't go on to say he was engaged or dating someone seriously. Chances were, a smart guy like Dave had figured out, as she had, that it was crazy to invest your heart in a relationship that would likely crash and burn.

The server began to clear their empty plates. Cassidy said, "Bring me the bill for both of us, please."

The woman whipped it out of the small ruffled apron she wore over her velvet dress. It was a typical hotel bill with space to put your room number. Cassidy added a 25 percent tip and wrote "22" for the room number.

Dave glanced at the bill. "You're a generous tipper."

"Good service deserves it."

"It does. Thought you didn't have any money." He eyed her quizzically.

"I'll pay the hotel bill the moment I get my first paycheck."

"Uh-huh."

Okay, he wasn't convinced. But she was telling the truth. She hated being in anyone's debt. "I need to pick your brain about where I might find work. You think the Crazy Horse might be hiring?"

"I doubt it, but I'll give you Kathy and Will's phone number. What kind of job are you looking for?"

"Whatever. Server, bartender, salesclerk, cashier. Receptionist, clerk, admin person. Nanny, companion, housekeeper, chambermaid. Flag girl, shelf stocker, dishwasher. Basically, anything that doesn't call for a degree, I can do. Oh, and I have up-to-date first aid certification."

Again seeing skepticism on his face, she said, "I swear I'm good. And I don't just up and leave jobs—I give fair notice. Unless the boss harasses me, like at the sports bar."

"Mmm."

Clearly, she still hadn't convinced him. And she needed to, not only so he'd help her find work, but because his opinion mattered. She was fine with him not "getting" the whole gypsy lifestyle thing, but she didn't want him thinking she was some irresponsible flake. "It's summer and you said this is a tourist town. Businesses must be taking on extra staff, right?"

"You have references?"

"Sure. On my flash drive. I need to find a place to print the file."

He studied her, his brow furrowed. "You really are good at all those things? Waiting tables, bartending, cashier, receptionist, chambermaid?"

She nodded eagerly. "I've worked across Canada, the States, Europe, Asia. I speak fluent Spanish—learned from my dad—and a bit of French, German, and Italian."

"Huh." His eyes had an inward look.

She tilted her head. "Huh?"

That almost-dimple flickered. God, he was so cute. She'd love to coax that dimple out of hiding. A ripple of sexual desire quivered through her body.

"The Wild Rose could use a fill-in person. For when the receptionist takes a break, or we need to turn over a bunch of rooms fast, or a server or bartender is on holiday or calls in sick."

"Oh!" She hadn't expected that. "A jill-of-all-trades?" She leaned forward. "You bet! I'm totally flexible about what hours I work. How about I run upstairs and get my flash drive? I should check out anyhow so I'll grab my backpack. Then we can print out my resume and references and you can take a look."

Cassidy liked everything she'd seen of the Wild Rose. Plus, Dave Cousins didn't seem like the kind of boss who'd sexually harass anyone. More likely the female staff came on to him.

Would he date an employee? She sure hoped that wasn't against his rules, because the more she got to know him, the more potential she saw for the two of them having a lot of fun.

Chapter Three

Late Friday afternoon, Robin burst through the door of Dave's office, beaming. "School's over! It's summer!"

His slim, vibrant daughter was dressed in jeans and boots, her chestnut hair pony-tailed under a straw Resistol hat. As usual, she'd ridden her mare the eight miles from Jessie and Evan's, stabling the horse a few blocks away at the same place where Dave kept his gelding.

Merlin, who'd been sleeping on the rug, bounced to his feet and rushed to greet her. She hugged and patted the more than fifty pounds of happily squirming black poodle. Last Christmas Dave had picked the young rescue animal as a gift for Robin, who'd been begging for them to have a dog at the Wild Rose. The pair had bonded immediately.

Dave had to admit that Robin had been right. The dog was a good companion for him when his daughter wasn't around. The poodle was smart and sweet-tempered, loved the outdoors, and didn't require much exercise other than a long walk or run every day. His short-clipped curly coat didn't shed and he didn't provoke allergies, important qualities for a hotel dog.

"Hey, how about me?" Dave said in a mock-grumbly voice. "Don't I get a hug too?" He was so happy to have his daughter back with him. He and Jessie each took her three or four nights a week and were flexible about adjusting to each other's—and of course Robin's—needs.

The girl laughed, rose, and came to throw her arms around him. "Hi, Dad."

He hugged her back. "Happy summer, sweetheart."

"It's going to be a great one!"

I just hope it's a safe one. His daughter lived life to the fullest. He appreciated her exuberance, but her tomboy ways often made him fear for her safety. If he lost Robin—

No, he wouldn't even think it.

"Mom's going to pay me to work at Boots!"

"I know. We discussed it."

His daughter had been riding and caring for horses since she was tiny. In Jessie's family, with their ranching background, it was tradition for children to pull their weight in terms of doing chores. Robin loved it, especially when, as at Jessie's Riders Boot Camp, it involved horses. Maybe paying her wasn't strictly kosher in terms of child labor laws, but there'd be no stopping her from helping out, her work did have value, and she deserved to be rewarded for it.

She was pretty amazing, his Robin.

A glance at the clock on the wall had him asking his daughter, "Is Kimiko still coming for dinner and a sleepover?"

"Uh-huh. She should be here soon." Robin flopped into a chair and Merlin sat, resting his chin on her knees as she stroked his head. "Can we make pizza? And watch movies and have popcorn?"

"Sure." The pizza would be Hawaiian. Not his favorite, but the girls loved it. There'd be a horsy movie for Robin and a girly one for Kimiko. Then the kids and Merlin would retire to Robin's bedroom and the suite would echo with giggles and squeals until they finally fell asleep.

Dave would treasure every minute, though the life he

offered Robin couldn't really compare with what her mom had going on. Not only was there Boots, but last Christmas, when Dave had given his daughter a dog, her mom had given her a baby brother. Not to mention, Jessie was now married to Evan.

Evan. Robin's biological father. A fact that no one knew except Dave, Evan, and of course Jessie.

Evan was a good guy and a terrific stepfather—which was great for Robin, and should make Dave happy. It was petty to feel twinges of jealousy. Hell, it wasn't a competition.

He focused on his daughter. "Happy-face pancakes for breakfast?" Ever since she was tiny, she'd loved the pancakes with blueberries dotted into the batter to make smiley faces. He dreaded the day that she'd be too "cool" to eat them.

"Yes, please! Then when Kimiko goes home, I'll ride back to Boots and go to work."

"What about our usual Saturday afternoon ride?" It was a tradition he'd hate to lose.

"Well, duh. Of course we'll go. Mom and I worked out my schedule so I have Saturday afternoons off."

"Good. I love our rides. Besides, Malibu and I haven't had enough exercise this week."

"You miss having basketball practice."

"Kind of." He volunteered as coach of the high school basketball team; back in the day, he'd been team captain. But basketball season was over, tourist season had begun, and he'd been too busy for much exercise other than taking Merlin for a run once or twice a day.

Thank heaven for Madisun, who was home from university for the summer and had moved ably into her job as assistant manager. Cassidy was proving to be a godsend as well.

On Tuesday, he and Madisun had looked over Cassidy's

resume, Madisun had interviewed her, and they'd hired her. Since then, she had filled in without complaint wherever they needed her. She cleaned rooms as fast as their best chambermaid, she'd taught the regular bartender a few new drinks, and several guests had commented on how helpful she'd been.

Not to mention, she was vivacious, genuine, and fun, with a sparkle that levelheaded Madisun, seven years her junior, lacked. Madisun had learned responsibility early; a tough family life hadn't bowed her shoulders—it had made them rigid. As for Cassidy, Dave had feared that she might be erratic and unreliable, but so far she'd proved him wrong.

His only complaint—and it was his fault, not hers—was that she distracted him. Her curves really weren't any different from those of a dozen women he knew, yet they drew his eye when she moved briskly around the Wild Rose. As did her face, with that exotic combination of olive skin and blue-gray eyes framed by a pixie cap of hair. He'd felt sexual attraction to other women and pretty easily tamped it down, yet he couldn't manage to do that with Cassidy. Why now? Why her?

And what was he going to do about it? Nothing. She was completely the wrong woman for him, not to mention being his employee. Besides, sex without emotion wasn't his style. And his heart had been shattered by Anita's death, spilling all the poison of pain, anger, guilt—

"Dad? Dad?"

He shook his head to banish the dark cloud and put on his "I'm fine" face. "What, Rob?"

"You were frowning. What's wrong?"

"Nothing. Sorry." What had they been talking about?

"How about we ask Cassidy to come riding with us?"

"You've met Cassidy?"

"She was on the desk today when I came in, and we got to talking. I told her I'd ridden over and she said she was going to book a trail ride at Westward Ho! tomorrow, her day off. But wouldn't it be fun if she came with us instead? I could give her some pointers, like I did with Ani—" She broke off abruptly, the animation on her face replaced by guilt.

Anita. People knew better than to mention her around Dave. Pretending he hadn't heard his daughter's slip, he said, "I don't think that's the best idea."

"Why not?" she asked, a little subdued. "I like Cassidy. Don't you?"

That was a complicated question. It was hard not to like Cassidy. Hard not to watch Cassidy. She was a nice addition to the Wild Rose's staff. And that's all she should be. "Sure. But she's staff."

"Madisun hangs out with us and the rest of the family sometimes."

"She was your mom and Evan's friend before I hired her." A couple of years ago, Jessie had worked as the dude wrangler at the Crazy Horse, and Madisun had assisted her. That's where Evan had met the teen and offered to mentor her, getting her away from an abusive father and helping her attend university in Vancouver, where she studied business and the hospitality industry. When she came back to Caribou Crossing for summer break last year, Dave had hired her. She'd done so well that this summer he'd offered her the job of assistant manager.

"Cassidy's new in town," Robin said. "We're supposed to be friendly here, aren't we?"

Amused at her blatant attempt at manipulation, he said, "You really want to invite her?" He'd prefer not to share his "Robin time," but he did like to make his daughter happy. Fortunately, she was good about not taking advantage of his softheartedness, or at least not taking advantage too often.

When she nodded vigorously, he said, "Okay, let's do it."

"Cool! Thanks, Dad." She jumped up and gave him a boisterous hug. "I'll go ask her."

As she ran out of the room, Dave shook his head ruefully. The truth was, he wouldn't mind one bit if Cassidy accepted the invitation. Yes, she was an employee and that was all she'd ever be. But as Robin had said, what was wrong with making a newcomer feel welcome?

When Dave hugged Robin good-bye on Saturday morning, he said, "When you're at Westward Ho! would you book a gentle horse for Cassidy for this afternoon?" The stable on the outskirts of town organized trail rides for tourists, rented horses to locals who rode occasionally, and stabled horses for several townspeople, like Dave, who owned their own.

"Sure. I'll see both of you later."

He settled in for a day's work, breaking in the early afternoon to eat a ham and Swiss panini at his desk with Merlin dozing on the floor beside him. After, he whipped upstairs to change his shirt, jeans, and boots to well-worn versions of the same and clapped his straw hat on his head. Then he headed back down to collect Merlin, who leaped up in excitement on recognizing the riding clothes.

Dave had arranged to meet Cassidy in the lobby. Given that she'd arrived in town with only a backpack, he guessed she wouldn't have proper riding gear. So when he saw the profile, backlit by sunshine, of a woman in Western gear and her own straw hat chatting to Nora at the reception desk, he didn't recognize her. But his dog ran over, and she turned with a bright smile.

Cassidy made one fine-looking cowgirl, he thought as he returned her smile.

"Hey, Merlin." She patted the poodle's back and said to

Dave, "I'm so excited. It was kind of you and Robin to invite me."

"You'll have a great time," Nora said, darting a considering gaze at Dave.

No doubt she wondered at his atypical behavior. It was on the tip of his tongue to point out that this was Robin's doing, but that might sound rude. Besides, it'd be a lie. It had been all too easy for his daughter to talk him into it.

"Let's get going." He gestured toward the door, and then as Cassidy moved in that direction, he opened it for her.

As she started through, the eager dog got in her way and threw her off balance so she bumped into Dave.

He caught her upper arm to steady her—and that simple touch of his bare palm to her shirt-sleeved arm definitely did not have a steadying effect on his pulse.

They headed down the sidewalk, Merlin on his leash, pacing along with his springy gait. On this summer Saturday afternoon, the main street was an active, cheerful place. Dave nodded a greeting to one of the town's pharmacists, tipped his hat to the woman who'd taught Robin in third grade, and grinned at a couple of kids licking madly as they tried to keep pace with rapidly melting ice cream cones.

"I didn't figure you'd have boots and a hat," he said to Cassidy.

"Maribeth at Days of Your is really nice."

"She is." So Cassidy had bought her gear at the thrift shop. That explained the comfortable, broken-in look.

"She wanted to get her hair and nails done for a date, so I looked after the shop on my lunch break yesterday. She gave me the hat and boots as a thank-you."

"Huh." That was nice of Cassidy—and enterprising. "Sounds like you're starting to fit in here."

She tilted her head up to him, eyes sparkling irresistibly under her hat brim. "It's a great place. People are so warm and friendly." She winked. "Guess I can see why you live here."

He chuckled. "Like I've ever had a choice?" That was pretty much the truth, but it was also true that Caribou Crossing was the only place in the world he could imagine living.

An RCMP car pulled up beside them and Karen MacLean rolled down the window. "Hey, Dave." She was in uniform, her striking features set off by the neatly pulled back brown hair and police cap.

"Hey, Karen." Amused at the inquisitive expression in his friend's golden-brown eyes, he stopped and Cassidy did the same. Merlin jumped up to rest his paws against the window frame and collect pats.

"Karen," he said, "meet the Wild Rose's newest employee, Cassidy Esperanza. Cassidy, this is Sergeant Karen MacLean, second in command of our RCMP detachment."

After the two women exchanged smiles and greetings, Dave said, "Cassidy wanted to go riding, and Robin couldn't pass up the opportunity to give her a few pointers."

"You couldn't have a better teacher," Karen said. Then, to Dave, "Madisun went over the final details with Jamal and me. It's going to be great."

"You getting nervous?"

"Just eager. Can't wait for it to be official. Well, I don't want to hold you up. Have a great ride. Nice to meet you, Cassidy. I'm sure I'll be seeing you around."

"You bet. If you come over to the Wild Rose when I'm working in the restaurant, I'll shoot you a complimentary cappuccino." She winked. "Just don't tell the boss."

Dave rolled his eyes.

When Karen had driven away, Cassidy asked, "She's getting married?"

"Next month. Neither she nor Jamal are church people, so they're doing it in the town square. Hoping for clear skies, but they've got tents on standby. The reception's at the Wild Rose. And Karen's family will be staying at the inn, so we want to be extra nice to them."

"Is Jamal's family here in town?"

"I gather he doesn't have family. Or many friends. He's RCMP as well, and worked undercover for a lot of years. It's not exactly a stable life."

"No, I bet it isn't. Is he still doing it?"

Dave shook his head. "Now he's head of the Williams Lake RCMP detachment. He and Karen bought a house and a little chunk of land between Caribou Crossing and Williams Lake."

Before Jamal entered the picture, Dave and Karen used to get together for an occasional dinner or movie, just as friends, but now they only saw each other for lunch every few weeks. He missed her company but was glad she'd found a good guy; she wanted all that home and family stuff and deserved to have it.

He just wished she hadn't joined the ranks of the females in his life who pushed him to date. How many times had some well-intentioned relative or friend told him he needed to dip his toe in the dating waters, get back in the game, yada yada? He rejected their efforts at matchmaking and suffered through the curious gazes they gave to every female he even spoke to.

Didn't they get it? He couldn't imagine ever loving again. Besides, he'd been by Anita's side from the time she got the diagnosis of terminal brain cancer until the day she died. Never, ever again, would he let himself be vulnerable to the shattering pain of loss. To the bitter anger against the world, himself, even the woman he loved but couldn't save.

His heart clenched, the ache rose in his throat, and—

"Dave? You okay?" Warm fingers brushed his forearm,

bare below the rolled-up sleeve of his lightweight denim shirt.

Cassidy. He breathed in, fresh air cleansing his throat, his chest.

"Yeah, sorry," he said brusquely. Her voice, her touch had beaten back the darkness.

And now that he was back in the real world, he realized how disconcertingly good those soft fingers felt against his skin.

They'd reached the outskirts of town, which gave him an excuse to raise his arm so that her hand dropped. He pointed ahead. "That's Westward Ho!—where I keep my horse." The well-maintained wooden stable housed a couple dozen horses. Beside it was a red-roofed barn, and two white-railed paddocks provided space for the horses to stretch and socialize.

"That's so cool, that you have your own horse."

He shrugged. "Can't imagine my life without a horse."

"You've been riding since you were little?"

"Yeah, though I wasn't a ranch kid, or into rodeo, like some of my friends. When I married Jessie, horses became a bigger part of life, and Robin lives and breathes them."

"Handy that you can keep your horse in town."

"Uh-huh," he said as they walked into the stable. "I try to get out on Malibu at least every couple of days. When I can't, Robin or one of the staff here exercises him for me."

Dave greeted Eddy, the teenage girl whose dad owned the business, and introduced Cassidy. Leaving the two of them to deal with Cassidy's paperwork, he and Merlin went out to the paddock to call Malibu. The palomino gelding came over, bobbing his head eagerly.

Dave went through the familiar ritual: tie his horse with cross ties, groom him and pick his hooves, then saddle and bridle him. By the time he was finished, Eddy'd got Cassidy up on the back of a pinto mare and given her refresher instructions on how to position her body, hold the reins, and give basic cues to her horse.

"You're all set," Eddy said. "Have fun."

"Absolutely." Cassidy beamed at the girl, then at Dave. "Lead on."

Her smile really did have a way of lighting the day. And warming his blood.

They headed out on a quiet dirt road that led out of town, their horses walking side by side with Merlin springing happily along beside them. Cassidy looked relaxed and comfortable in the saddle. Did she fit in this easily wherever she went?

She bent forward to stroke her horse's neck, the motion snugging her jeans even tighter against her firm butt. "This is Cherry Blossom, if you can believe it," she said. "Eddy says she prefers to be called Cherry, and I can see why. You said your palomino is Malibu?"

"Yes. Named by the woman who owned him before me."

"Suits him. Such a pretty boy." Her gaze skimmed up from his horse to move across Dave's torso and end up on his face, a hint of suggestive mischief in her eyes.

"Thanks." He added quickly, to make it clear he wasn't flirting, "On his behalf."

Her lips squeezed together like she was holding back a smile. "How long will it take us to get to . . . what did Robin call it? Riders Boot Camp?"

"Yes, that's the place her mom runs. It's about ten miles by highway, only eight by the back roads and trails. It usually takes Robin and me about half an hour, but we move fast. Don't know how much speed you're up for." He cocked an eyebrow.

"I'm up for pretty much anything." Her striking blue-gray eyes danced, and he got the sense she didn't just mean riding.

"Uh," he said awkwardly, "we should let the horses warm up first." The moment he said those words, he wondered if they could be taken sexually too. He was about to clarify, then figured that would only make things worse.

"Sure," she said. "My muscles could use a little warming up too."

Riding muscles, right?

Best to change the subject.

Chapter Four

Cassidy gazed at Dave, who looked the total cowboy this afternoon. It was fun getting him flustered, though frustrating trying to sort out his mixed signals.

"You're settling in okay in Caribou Crossing?" he asked.

So he had retreated to safety, had he? She'd go along. For now. "I sure am."

She stroked Cherry's neck again, enjoying the rhythm of the horse's body under her, the warmth of the sun on her shoulders, the scent of wild roses from a bush growing along a sagging wooden fence. They were out of town now, on a wide dirt track fenced on both sides and dotted with occasional piles of manure, which Merlin neatly avoided. A field of hay blew gently in the breeze on one side, and on the other cattle grazed, a few lifting their heads to watch her, Dave, and the well-behaved black poodle.

Riding, fresh air, gorgeous scenery, these were the reasons she'd come to Caribou Crossing. The handsome man on his pretty horse was an unexpected bonus.

Her old jeans and cotton shirt were comfy and the thrift shop boots fit as if she'd been wearing them for years. The cream straw cowboy hat sat lightly on her head, and its brim shaded her face from the brightest of the sun's rays. Oh yes, life was good.

Caribou Crossing had been a brilliant choice and she blessed the silver lining of her Monday exhaustion that had landed her on the floor of Dave's hotel lobby.

"Madisun said you got a room at Ms. Haldenby's. She's a, uh, interesting woman." Dave's mouth gave a wry twist.

She chuckled, thinking of her white-haired landlady: efficient, brisk, opinionated, yet warmhearted underneath it all. "Very interesting. I hear she was your fourth-grade teacher." Dave must have been a cute kid. The sandy hair that flopped boyishly over his forehead would have been lighter then. His greenish brown eyes and full mouth would have been carefree rather than, as now, often shadowed by some internal burden.

"Yup. You meet someone in Caribou Crossing between the ages of twenty-five and sixty, chances are she taught them."

"She has stories," she teased.

"I hate to think."

"D'you recall a frog you brought to school to try to scare her? Silly boy, thinking an experienced teacher like her would be frightened by a frog."

"Actually, it escaped. I didn't bring it for her; it was for Jessie."

"Aha! You were trying to scare a cute little girl?" The one he'd later married; Robin's mom.

He snorted. "You haven't met Jessie."

She was curious about his ex-wife. "She wasn't the typical little girl?"

"She loved nature. Horses and dogs especially, but basically any living thing. I found the frog in the garden at home. It had unusual markings and I figured she'd like it."

"You were in love with her even back in fourth grade?" She had to wonder what had broken them up in the end.

He shook his head. "Jessie was a pal, a buddy. A tomboy. A lot like Robin is now."

"So you fell for her in your teens? You must have married when you were awfully young. Robin's what? Eleven, twelve?"

"We got married a few months after high school graduation. Robin came along the next year. She's eleven now."

She wondered how long he and his ex had been divorced. Long enough for her to have fallen for another man, married him, and had a baby. Robin had mentioned a baby brother.

"Want to try a trot, see how it goes?" Dave asked.

"You bet." Though Cassidy wasn't into long-term planning, likely she'd stay in Caribou Crossing through the summer, so there'd be time to find out more about this intriguing man. Who knew, some of that learning might even come from pillow talk!

He eased his horse forward and hers followed along, the dog running beside them.

It took a few bone-rattling moments to get the feel of the trot, but she did better with the lope and let out a whoop of exhilaration. When Dave slowed the pace, she said, "This is exactly what I needed. A real change of pace."

"You're not talking about going from a trot to a lope, are you?"

"Vancouver to Caribou Crossing. Sports bars and clubbing to horses and sweet-smelling wild roses." A scuzzy boss to a good man like Dave. A bunch of metrosexual guys she didn't find sexy to an effortlessly masculine one like the rider atop the gorgeous palomino.

"Welcome to my world." He gestured expansively.

"It's lovely." Gazing ahead to where rolling hills rose to rocky outcroppings, she sucked in a deep breath of air that smelled of grass, sunshine, horse, dust.

"I couldn't imagine living anywhere else. But you, I gather you've got a gypsy spirit?"

"Totally. There's so much to see and do. I grew up in Victoria, spent some time in Toronto. After high school—when you were getting married—I was in Europe. My mom was there with her latest guy." She wrinkled her nose, remembering his high-handed ways. "I didn't get along with him, so I left and traveled around on my own."

"On your own in Europe? At what, seventeen, eighteen?"

"Just turned eighteen when I left Mom's house."

"If Robin tried to do that, it'd kill me." He snorted. "Or she'd kill me, because I'd make her call me three times a day."

"Control freak?"

"Only when it comes to her safety."

"Gramps was a bit like that." He'd worried about her, made her report in. It had felt like he didn't trust her to look after herself. But when he said he did it because he loved her, it was hard to get too resentful. In fact, after he died when she was fifteen, she'd missed his fussing. Missed him. A lot. "But my parents liked me and my brother to be independent." They loved her and JJ in their own way, but their personal dramas always came first.

"Traveling Europe on your own is pretty independent."

"Man, was it amazing. All these new experiences! Places, people, languages, food. I loved it. Eventually I came back to North America, but I kept up with the traveling. I've been across Canada and I've visited lots of the States."

He shook his head bemusedly. "You figure on ever settling down?"

"Nah." Anytime she'd thought she'd had a home, it had proved to be an illusion—and learning that had hurt. No, she wasn't destined to set down roots, so she found joy in variety. She tilted her head to glance sideways at him. "Do you ever get itchy feet? Imagine living somewhere else, or even just visiting?"

He shrugged. "Not really. Oh, it's nice to go to Vancouver occasionally, eat in a different restaurant, go to the theatre or a game. But"—another of those wry grins—"even though it makes me sound like a total stick in the mud, everything I want is here."

"Everything?"

One of those mysterious shadows crossed his face. "Robin's here," he said slowly. "My family, friends. The inn."

No mention of a woman. Surely he'd dated since his divorce. Cassidy wasn't pushy, but she didn't like to pussyfoot around either, so she said, "No special woman?"

He didn't look at her, nor respond. After a long moment of silence, he said, "No." Then, "You okay if we lope again?"

She couldn't force him to expand on that if he didn't want to. "You bet."

His horse speeded up, taking the lead. Merlin was at the palomino's heels and Cherry followed. Cassidy found her balance. She studied Dave's denim-clad back, so strong and athletic, imagining how it would feel to wrap her arms around him, to run her hands up under his shirt and feel those muscles flex.

He was clearly attracted to her, but he was holding back. Why, if he wasn't dating anyone else? Had Jessie broken his heart?

Cassidy didn't believe that human beings were designed for monogamy. Take her parents and her brother as prime examples. People should be sensible enough to recognize it, and not invest their hearts in all that soppy romantic stuff. On the other hand, few people were designed to be totally solitary beings. It was good to have friends and great to have sex. The smart thing to do was hook up, have fun, then move on, hopefully with no hard feelings. Sure, you missed out on the romance of being in love—something she'd never come close to experiencing herself—but you also got to skip the angst of a broken heart.

Dave was too sweet a guy to carry a torch for a woman who'd long ago moved on. Someone should make it her mission to shake that sweet guy out of his blues. To coax that dimple out of hiding.

And who better than Cassidy?

Was he worried about the fact that she worked for him? Maybe that was why he held back. She'd learned, during training by Madisun, that there was no rule against staff dating as long as they behaved professionally on the job. In fact, the chef, Mitch, and the bartender, Roy, had been a couple for the past year. But they were colleagues, not boss and employee.

Her instincts, which were usually reliable, told her Dave would never harass or pressure a staff member. Maybe he figured that coming on to one was inappropriate. Hmm. What if she seduced him and promised it wouldn't affect their work relationship? Would he say no? She mulled that notion over as Dave maintained the lead, trotting now, on a narrower trail.

Best not to get ahead of herself. He had included her in a family outing. Yeah, Robin had instigated it, but he could have said no. It seemed he was open to at least being friends. It wasn't a bad start. She'd enjoy the eye candy and his company, and see where things went from there.

Trees arched overhead, letting dappled sunlight sift through their branches. Birds chirped and a distinctive song trilled. She searched for the red-winged blackbird and found him perched on a fence post. She breathed in the pure, grassy country air and, exhilarated, let out her own corny rendition of the bird's call.

Dave glanced over his shoulder, laughing, and she grinned back.

A couple of minutes later, he slowed Malibu to a walk, and shortly afterward they turned into a neat stable yard. Robin had mentioned that Riders Boot Camp was less than two years old, and the buildings did look much newer than those at Westward Ho!

The girl's head poked out of the barn door, and Merlin ran over to greet her. She called, "Evan, they're here," and, with the dog at her side, came to meet them. A moment later, a man in jeans and a tee followed her.

He studied Cassidy with obvious interest, and she reciprocated. Evan actually looked a little like Dave: a lean, rangy build and easy on the eyes. Evan was a couple of inches shorter, at maybe six feet, his brown hair had sun streaks, and his eyes were a striking greenish blue. Oh yeah, Jessie did know how to pick them.

From Cherry's back, she held out her hand to him. "Hi. Cassidy Esperanza."

"Evan Kincaid. Welcome to Riders Boot Camp. Want to hop down and take the tour?"

"Love to." She dismounted, holding her breath that her stupid left leg wouldn't choose this moment to go numb. But no, it behaved just the way it was supposed to. She smiled with relief. Caribou Crossing was good for her health.

While Robin tied Cherry's and Malibu's reins to a hitching rail, Evan and Dave greeted each other. Cassidy expected awkwardness between the two men, but instead they acted like friends. Maybe they'd buried the hatchet, in Robin's best interests.

"Where's your mom?" she asked Robin, hoping to meet the intriguing woman.

"Out on a trail ride." She caught Cassidy's hand and tugged. "Come on. Most of the horses are out, but I'll show you the few that are left. And the barn, the tack room, the ring, the guest cabins. We're not fancy like the Crazy Horse, with a restaurant and a spa. We're no frills, intensive, all about horses and riding, and that's what folks come for."

Evan, Dave, and Merlin joined them and they strolled around Riders Boot Camp. The layout had obviously been well thought out, and the place was attractive in an appropriately rustic way. As each of her companions chipped in bits of information, she realized how closely they'd all been involved in setting up this operation. She also realized how mature Robin was for her age, which was obviously something her family encouraged.

"This is really impressive," Cassidy told them as they passed a couple of bunkhouses and several cute log cabins with wooden lounge chairs and flower boxes on the porches.

"We haven't even told you the best part," Robin said. "We've got a scholarship program. You guys fill her in. I'm going to get Concha." To Cassidy, she said, "That's my mare."

After she ran off, the dog at her heels, Evan said, "We set Boots up as a charitable foundation. Jess wanted to offer our riding experience to disadvantaged people who would benefit."

"That's a terrific idea. So you what, run on donations?"

"We do have donors. A few are on our board and some get the option of staying at Boots for a week or two themselves. We also have paying guests on a sliding scale based on what they can afford. Word's getting out and, sadly, we now have to turn people away."

"Your wife had a brilliant idea."

Evan glanced at Dave and they exchanged what looked like fond grins. Weird. Although she, personally, thought jealousy was a stupid emotion, it surprised her that there was so little tension between these two men.

"She did," Dave said, "but it took a village to make it happen."

"Luckily, Jess had that village," Evan agreed.

Cassidy prided herself on making her own way in the world. And yet she almost envied the woman who had a village behind her to make her dream come true. The woman who had such fantastic qualities that two amazing men had fallen in love with her. The woman who'd given birth to and raised a terrific daughter and now had a baby boy as well.

A touch on the back of her shoulder brought her out of her thoughts. She knew from the tingle of awareness that it was Dave behind her. "Ready to continue our ride?" he asked.

"Sure." She wanted to lean back against him, feel his arm come around her, but instead he dropped his hand and stepped away.

Flanked by the two lean, handsome men, she returned to where the horses were tied, Cherry and Malibu now joined by a sleek bay horse that Robin was saddling.

"Are you coming riding with us, Evan?" Cassidy asked.

He shook his head. "I've got the month-end accounts to attend to."

"You're an accountant?"

"Investment counselor, but I do handle the accounts for Boots."

"He's the money guy," Robin said, swinging lightly into the saddle. "When Mom and I want to spend money, he tells us we can't. Right, Evan?"

"Someone's got to keep this place in the black," he joked back. "Have a good ride and have fun at your grandparents' tonight. Say hi to Sheila and Ken for me." He patted her leg, then stepped back. "Want a leg up, Cassidy?"

"I wouldn't say no." Rarely used muscles were tightening up. It was a good feeling, though, for an active person like her.

He boosted her into the saddle, then untied the reins and handed them to her. "I'll see you again soon, I'm sure. Maybe tomorrow night at the Wild Rose, if you're working then."

Remembering the Wild Rose's schedule, she asked, "For the line dancing?"

"If we can get a sitter for Alex, our baby."

"Me!" Robin said. "You can bring him up to Dad's and my apartment and I'll look after him. Gramma Brooke and Jake could bring Nicki too."

"Thanks, Robin. I'll talk to your mom and gramma, and let you know."

Dave had untied his palomino and swung into the saddle. "Hope to see you then."

As Cassidy rode out of the stable yard between Robin and Dave, with Merlin trailing them, she tried to sort out the family relationships. "Sheila and Ken are your parents, Dave?"

"That's right."

Robin spoke up. "I have three sets of grandparents. It's cool!"

"I guess you do. Your dad's parents, your mom's parents, and Evan's parents."

"Yeah, except that Evan's mom, Gramma Brooke, isn't married to his dad."

A common-law relationship? She wasn't about to ask.

Dave said, "Evan's father's been out of the picture for a long time. Brooke remarried last year. Her husband, Jake, is in charge of the Caribou Crossing RCMP detachment. He works with Karen MacLean, who you met earlier this afternoon, Cassidy."

"And Gramma Brooke is a beauty consultant at Beauty Is You," Robin said.

"I've seen that salon."

"If you need a haircut, go there," the girl told her. "She's the best."

As the three horses left the dirt track and headed onto a long stretch of rolling grassland, Robin went on. "Gramma Brooke and Jake have this adorable baby girl, Nicki."

Cassidy wrinkled her brow. "Your mom and Evan have a baby, and his mom and Jake have a baby?"

"Isn't it cool?" The girl's face was bright with excitement. "Except that it's pretty weird that Nicki's my aunt. I'm her babysitter!"

"When Nicki's older," Cassidy said, "if she ever tries to lord it over you that she's your aunt, remind her that you used to change her diapers."

"Great idea! You're smart, Cassidy. I'm really glad you came riding. Aren't you, Dad?"

"Way to put your dad on the spot," Cassidy teased. "It's okay, Dave, you don't have to answer that." But she glanced at his face to read his reaction.

He met her gaze and lifted his hand to the brim of his hat in a gesture of acknowledgment. "I'm glad." Yet his expression wasn't so much pleased as uncertain.

Apparently Robin heard—or chose to hear—only the words themselves, because she said, "Cassidy, you should come to dinner with us. Meet Grandma Sheila and Grandpa Ken and the rest of Dad's family. It'll be barbecue, and my cousins will be there, and the dogs all play together, and it's so much fun!"

"That's really nice of you, Robin, but . . ." *But you should have asked your father first.* "It's not fair to your grandparents to invite someone without them knowing."

"No, honest, it's okay," she said earnestly. "They cook loads, and they always tell us we can bring our friends. You're our new friend, so you should come."

"Maybe Cassidy has other plans," Dave said. His tone

was neutral and his expression guarded. Did he want her to say she had other plans?

"But she's only been here a few days," his daughter protested. "How can she have other plans already?" She turned her big brown eyes on Cassidy. "You don't, do you?"

Feeling like she was at a tennis match, gazing between Dave on her right and Robin on her left, she turned back to Dave with a "tell me what to do" look.

The tension around his eyes and mouth softened. "It would be nice if you came."

Chapter Five

Saturday evening, Dave stood beside his father at the giant barbecue on the back patio of the home he'd grown up in, inhaling the tangy scent of grilling sweet-and-spicy ribs.

He was glad his parents hadn't moved when their kids flew the nest. This sprawling rancher-style house on two acres of benchland north of town held so many happy memories of growing up with his sister and two brothers. It was still the family's heart, with regular Saturday night dinners, out-of-town relatives coming for visits, and monthly sleepovers for the next generation. Robin and her cousins—the Cousins cousins, as they called themselves—loved those sleepovers, which featured home-baked treats from Dave's mother and gold rush ghost stories spun by Pops. No one could tell a ghost story as well as his old man.

Nor, he thought as he watched his father deftly turn the thick country-style ribs, did anyone's hand match his when it came to the barbecue.

Pops gestured toward three women sitting in lawn chairs. "Seems like a nice girl."

Cassidy, tonight dressed in beige capris and a smoky blue tee, with a lightweight purple hoodie tied around her shoulders, sat with his mom and younger sister, Lizzie.

"Yeah." Some strange momentum was under way and he was doing nothing to stop it. When Robin had issued the dinner invitation, Cassidy had consulted him in a wordless glance. If he'd given a tiny head shake, then explained later that it was family time, he was sure her feelings wouldn't have been hurt. But he hadn't. He enjoyed her company.

And what was the big deal? He had women friends: Karen MacLean, Sally Ryland, Brooke Brannon. Cassidy could be another friend.

The afternoon ride had been fun, with Robin deciding that Cassidy needed to see the view from atop Whisky Mountain, but he felt bad for not realizing the expedition would be too long for someone who hadn't ridden much. When they'd dismounted at Westward Ho! Cassidy's leg had given her trouble. She'd been a good sport, saying ruefully that riding used new muscles.

Hobbling back to the Wild Rose, she had leaned on him for support. She'd fit neatly against him, his arm around her shoulders, hers around his waist. He'd been aware of her. The unfamiliarity of her slender, curvy body and the light flowery scent that overpowered the smell of horse that clung to both of them.

Sunday nights at the Wild Rose, he danced with lots of women, holding them in his arms, feeling the sway of their hips as they followed his lead, smelling each one's distinctive feminine scent. It was pleasant, but kind of impersonal. Supporting Cassidy's slight weight had felt personal. Arousing. In a way that was more than just a hormonal physical response. She wasn't just a pretty woman with a killer body seen passing on the street. He liked Cassidy; she provided valuable assistance at the Wild Rose; she was terrific with his daughter. But then he could say the same about Madisun. There was just something . . . personal about his feelings for Cassidy.

Did he want to be friends with a woman who aroused him, or was it better to impose some distance?

"Son?"

"Hmm? What did you say, Pops?"

"Cassidy fits in like she belongs."

"Yeah." She had that knack. Maybe it came from traveling so much.

Since they'd arrived an hour ago, she had tossed balls with kids and dogs, fetched a lemonade for white-haired Great-aunt Joan, and exchanged teasing comments with some of the guys and gals before his mom and Lizzie cornered her.

"Son, your mom's so distracted by your lady friend—"

"She's not my lady friend."

Pops cocked an eyebrow. "Okay, the female you and Robin spent the afternoon with. Anyhow, what I was going to say is that the ribs are almost done and your mom hasn't brought out the salads. Want to get them out of the fridge, then let everyone know dinner's ready?"

"Sure."

Dave brought out potato salad, three bean salad, tossed green salad, and several loaves of French bread. When he'd set everything on a picnic table, he rounded people up. His sister and mom bustled away to help serve the food, and then Cassidy rose. She tested her left leg before putting weight on it. When he and Robin had picked her up earlier, she'd said that a cool shower and a nap had fixed her up, but muscles did tighten when you sat.

"Giving you trouble again?" His gaze focused on her ankles, bare below her capris, and her slim feet in sandals. Her toenails were painted a rosy pink. Sexy feet. Sexy ankles.

"It's fine now. I'm sure this helped." She hoisted a brown bottle. "Caribou Crossing does great beer."

Forcing his thoughts away from her sexiness, he said,

"Yeah, the local brewery's only been in business two years, but it's a real asset to the community." He and Cassidy strolled up the lawn in the wake of adults and half a dozen kids, ranging from toddlers to adolescents.

"Four different beers, and they're all popular," she said. "I've seen that the couple of times I've worked in the Wild Rose's bar. Speaking of which, I'm working there tomorrow night. Roy says the joint really hops on line-dancing night."

"It sure does." He cleared his throat, feeling a little awkward talking about work here in his parents' yard with this woman who was an employee, maybe a new friend, and a hormone inducer. "You're doing a good job at the Wild Rose. I'm glad we hired you."

"Me too."

They lined up for spare ribs and all the trimmings. The patio was crowded, with adults occupying a motley collection of chairs, and kids parked up and down the steps to the garden. Lizzie beckoned Cassidy to a chair she'd saved. Dave got himself a Pale Ale and, with all the chairs now taken, put the bottle on the porch railing and leaned against it. As usual, he was content to listen more than talk.

That was typical of the men in his family. The womenfolk always seemed to have more than enough to say. They covered the subject of his sister-in-law's pregnancy, moved on to Karen and Jamal's wedding next month, then turned to the town's planned celebrations for Canada Day on Monday.

Cassidy mostly listened attentively, eating with obvious enjoyment and occasionally chipping in a comment or asking a question. Dave's mom asked her where she'd been last year for Canada Day, and she said she'd celebrated the Fourth of July instead, eating pancakes in the plaza in Santa Fe. The women asked about her travels, and she told a few stories.

Darkness fell and some people drifted away to get

dessert and coffee; parents checked on children; Pops went off with Robin and a couple of her cousins. His mom stayed talking to Cassidy. And Dave, even though there were now empty chairs, continued to lean against the patio railing and listen.

A baby's cry broke into one of Cassidy's stories and Dave's cousin Andrea approached, rocking the little one in her arms. "Time for us to head home and tuck the brood into bed."

His mom rose to hug her and kiss the baby. "I didn't realize it was so late."

Once Andrea and her family started the migration, others followed. Robin came over. "Dad, we can stay a while, can't we?"

Dave glanced at Cassidy. "Okay with you, or are you tired out?"

"I'm fine and I'd love to stay."

"Of course you'll stay," his mom said. "We've been so busy talking, we haven't even had dessert. Let's get some cherry cobbler and coffee."

Cassidy, Dave, and his mom all served themselves. The two women headed back to their chairs and Dave hovered, wondering if he should make himself scarce. He had enjoyed Cassidy's stories, the animation on her face, the glimpse of a different kind of life even if it wasn't one he'd ever choose. Enjoyed, too, the mellow buzz of not exactly arousal—his mom's presence ruled that out—but male awareness. On the other hand, if Mom and Cassidy were going to talk girl talk, he didn't want to hang around.

"Sit down, son," his mom said, and he obeyed.

After tasting the cobbler, Cassidy said, "Mmm, this is delicious."

His mother gave a self-deprecating smile. "All this traveling you've done, I bet you've tasted far fancier desserts."

"Fancier maybe, but not better."

"Well, thanks very much." She cocked her head. "With those itchy feet of yours, I'm guessing you grew up in a military family?"

"Actually, my dad was a Realtor. In Victoria."

"Did he grow up there?"

"No, my mother did. Luis—my dad—is from Mexico." She finished the last bite of cobbler and put the bowl down.

"You call him Luis?"

She nodded. "And my mom's Justine."

Often when Cassidy talked, she fell into the rhythm of a natural storyteller, giving interesting details, injecting humor, throwing out teasers so the listener was drawn in and asked a question. Now, though, her words were brief and almost without inflection. Seemed like her folks weren't her favorite subject.

That didn't stop his mom. "How did they meet?"

After a sip of coffee, Cassidy said, almost reluctantly, "Justine was a university student. She and a couple of girlfriends went to Acapulco at Christmas break. Luis was this charming, gorgeous, sexy Mexican who worked at the excursion desk at the hotel. They both fell hard."

His mother nodded. "Every girl's holiday dream."

"I guess. Anyhow, he came back to Canada with her."

"I imagine your grandparents weren't entirely thrilled," Dave's mom said dryly.

Cassidy's lips twitched. "No, though there was only Gramps. Justine's mother had died when she was young. Gramps had a fair bit of money—he was a successful Realtor—and he spoiled her to bits. She had all the lessons, toys, clothes. She was his princess. Gramps figured Luis was after her money, or was using her to get Canadian citizenship."

Dave leaned forward, curious. "And?"

"Actually, he wasn't. He really did love her." She paused, then added, with a cynicism that surprised him, "Or, you know, they were young people in lust and they thought they were in love. Anyhow, Luis was smart and ambitious, and he'd probably have done well in Mexico, but he had no reason to stay there. His parents were dead and he wasn't close to the rest of his family. Once he was in Victoria, he studied real estate and actually impressed Gramps. He went to work for him, he and Justine got married, and she promptly got pregnant with me. She dropped out of university—art and drama—and stayed at home to raise me."

"It sounds like things worked out well for all of you," Dave's mom said.

"Yeah, for a while." There was a rare wistful note in Cassidy's voice. "A couple years later my brother came along. JJ—James Junior, named after Gramps. Yes, we were happy. Justine and Luis both had a flair for drama. They made everyday stuff into something special." Her smile faded and her lips twisted. "They loved, they fought, they made up. And then they didn't make up, and got divorced."

His mom reached over to touch her arm. "I'm sorry to hear that. How old were you?"

Cassidy puffed out air. "The first time or the second?"

"What?" The word popped out of Dave's mouth.

She turned to him. "Oh yeah. They've done it twice. So far."

So far? Before he could ask, she went on. "They divorced when I was seven. Luis went to the south of France with a sexy former client. JJ and I stayed with Justine. She dated a lot, finally got together with this guy and we moved to Toronto; then that broke up. Luis split with the south-of-France woman. And—can't you just hear the swell of violin strings?—he and Justine realized that it had all been a big mistake and they loved each other madly."

"They remarried," his mom said.

"Yeah, when I was ten. It lasted about six years. This time it was Justine who took off to Europe—with a jet-setter guy who flattered and fascinated her—leaving my brother and me with Luis. Gramps was dead by then . . ." A grimace suggested she'd been close to him. "Luis was working and dating, JJ hung out with a couple of buddies, and I bided my time waiting to finish high school and get out of there."

As Dave listened to her, heard an undertone of pain in her voice, his eyes widened. Her parents sounded self-centered, like their love lives were more important than their children. He glanced at his mom, grateful for her and Pops. She gave him an understanding smile, then said softly, "Cassidy, I'm sorry you and your brother had to go through that."

Cassidy shrugged. "When I graduated, I went to Greece, where Justine and her guy were living. I stayed with them a couple of months but I didn't get along with him. Besides, there was a whole world out there to explore."

She glanced at Dave with a smile. "That's when I learned to toss all my worldly belongings in a backpack and go wherever the mood took me."

And her parents were too self-absorbed to worry about her. No wonder she was so independent.

"We're glad you ended up in Caribou Crossing," Dave's mom said.

"Thanks, but this isn't the end of the road for me."

"Do you see an end to your road?" Dave asked, trying to get his home-centered head around her lifestyle.

"I don't think in those terms. Every day's a new beginning. That's as far ahead as I want to see."

"Huh." In a weird way, that almost made sense. If he thought ahead—to Robin growing up and getting her own place, marrying and starting a family; to his life being even more empty than it was now . . . No, that end to his road wasn't one bit appealing.

Forcing that thought away, he remembered something Cassidy had said earlier. "You said your parents have been divorced twice so far. D'you mean they got back together again?"

"Yeah, marriage number three was three years ago. They live in Acapulco, because that's"—she made air quotes—"'where their passion for each other truly flowers.'"

Dave caught his mom's amused glance and suppressed an eye roll.

"Maybe it'll be third-time lucky," his mom said tactfully. "Sometimes it takes people a while to grow up and figure out what they really want."

Dave leaned forward to squeeze her shoulder. "Says the woman who's been married to her high school sweetheart for thirty-five years."

"Thirty-six, but who's counting?" She shrugged. "Ken and I knew from the beginning and we've never had any doubts. But that's not how it works out for everyone." Her gray eyes met Dave's with a look of compassion. "That doesn't mean you should give up, though."

He frowned at her. She knew how Anita's illness and death had gutted him. No way would he go through that again.

Cassidy gave one of her musical burbles of laughter. "It's not giving up if you never chase the dream in the first place."

Dave realized that she'd thought his mom's comment had been addressed to her. And who knows, maybe his mother had been talking to both of them.

Cassidy went on. "I'm happy for you and Ken, Sheila. But you've been sprinkled with some kind of magic dust, to beat the odds the way you have."

"You don't believe in true love?" His mother sounded more than a little shocked.

Dave did believe in it. If he hadn't, he wouldn't have been so furious at fate when Anita was diagnosed. He wouldn't have been so angry that she couldn't beat the disease, that the power of his love couldn't somehow cure her. His heart wouldn't have shattered when she died.

"It's not my place to speak for other people," Cassidy said. "For me, no, I don't believe in it. I believe in being independent, respecting others, living life to its fullest. Not chasing unrealistic dreams."

"Love's not always the best thing," Dave said grimly.

He could see the effort his mother put into forcing a smile and saying lightly, "You kids today. I don't know what the world's coming to."

Chapter Six

While Madisun bent over her spreadsheet, Cassidy surreptitiously ran a hand over her left thigh, trying to massage out the pins and needles. The two women were in the Wild Rose's dining room on Saturday afternoon, preparing for Karen MacLean and Jamal Estevez's wedding reception. They wore white cotton short-sleeved shirts and pants, as did all the staff who would work the reception. Madisun's long hair was pulled back into a sleek knot at her nape.

Cassidy forced back a yawn. She felt tired and draggy, but there were hours to go before her workday would be done. She'd been in Caribou Crossing for a month and loved it, but unfortunately, healthy living hadn't cured her fatigue or healed her leg. She'd assumed that she'd strained it and it would heal with time, but now she wondered if it might be a pinched nerve.

The normally cool and collected Madisun wasn't in fantastic shape at the moment either. Color flushed her cheeks and her fingers trembled as she checked items off and scribbled notes.

Cassidy, who'd come to like and respect the younger woman, touched her hand. "Calm down. Everything's going to be wonderful."

"Perfect." Madisun's eyes widened with what looked almost like panic. "Everything has to be perfect. Dave put me in charge."

Cassidy had played a role in that. Dave, a close friend of the bride's, had been invited to the wedding, which was currently getting under way in the town square half a block away. He'd mentioned that he couldn't attend because he had to oversee reception preparations. The man could be a control freak, but so was Madisun. Cassidy had persuaded him to leave his assistant manager in charge, so he wouldn't hurt Karen's feelings by not seeing her get married.

She patted Madisun's arm. "Because he knows you'll do a great job." Quickly, she amended, "A *perfect* job, I mean. Now, what's next on the list?"

"The bar."

"Tick it off. I just checked with Roy. And Mitch has the food and the servers under control. And the décor looks fabulous." She gestured around the room. The dark wood and brass were tempered with peach and white table settings and vases of ivory-colored orchids blended with pink, orange, and peach freesias. The sweet, fresh scent of the freesias perfumed the air. "All that's left is putting the place cards on the tables, right? And you have the seating chart."

Madisun took a deep breath. "Okay, that sounds right." She fumbled the seating chart out from under the spreadsheet. "Oh God, I've lost the place cards!"

"They're here." Cassidy grabbed the stack off a nearby table. "I sorted them by table, but we should double-check as we put them out. Starting with the easiest, the head table. Read me the names on the seating chart." She and Madisun knew this table by heart, but it might calm the younger woman to get a process going.

Obediently, Madisun read from the chart. "Karen and Jamal, of course. The best man, Jake, and the matron of honor, Brooke."

"Who, conveniently, happen to be husband and wife." She put cards on the table.

"The maid of honor, Lark Cantrell, who doesn't have a plus one. Karen's parents and her brother and his wife." She looked up. "It's too bad Jamal has no family. He's outnumbered."

"At least he has Jake." The two men, both RCMP officers, were good friends.

Cassidy and Madisun moved on, table by table. The bride and groom had kept things small. There were RCMP colleagues, local friends, and a handful of Karen's relatives from Ontario.

At the final table, Madisun read, "Jess and Evan, Dave and Sally, and—"

"You're really sure that's a good idea?" Cassidy asked.

The younger woman frowned. "We discussed this before."

"I know, but it still seems strange."

Over the past weeks, Cassidy had learned a lot about the intriguing Dave Cousins. Not much from the man himself, as he tended to be closemouthed about his personal life, but from staff at the Wild Rose; her landlady, Ms. Haldenby; Dave's family; and other townspeople. Having experienced small towns before, she wasn't surprised that people minded each other's business. In the nicest possible way.

She'd found out that she had guessed wrong about Jess breaking his heart. In fact, their marriage had split up because he had fallen in love with Anita, a recently arrived teacher. That surprised Cassidy; it seemed so out of character for him. And, oddly, people didn't censure him. He was Caribou Crossing's fair-haired boy who could do no wrong. She'd lost track of the number of times someone had referred to him as the nicest guy in town, and told her about some problem he'd solved or generous act he'd bestowed.

According to the rumor mill, Dave and Anita had nobly

tried to deny and resist their mutual attraction. But Jess noticed that Dave seemed stressed and miserable, and she forced him to tell her the truth. Then she—Caribou Crossing's fair-haired girl despite her chestnut locks—nobly freed him from their marriage. It seemed that although Jess and Dave did love each other it wasn't that "once in a lifetime" kind of love, as Maribeth at Days of Your put it. So Jess freed Dave to find that kind of love with Anita, and she later found it herself with Evan, who'd been her best friend as a kid but had left Caribou Crossing for ten years.

Tragically for Dave, he and Anita had barely announced their engagement when she was diagnosed with terminal brain cancer. She'd undergone every possible treatment, with Dave steadfastly at her side, but had died in a few short months. That had been three years ago. Now Cassidy understood the sadness in the man's eyes, and why his dimple had gone into hiding.

"You've seen them all together," Madisun said. "Dave gets along great with Evan and Jess. He and Jess are like, you know, best friends."

That did seem to be true. But didn't Madisun see the occasional tinge of envy in Dave's hazel eyes? How must he feel, having lost his love to brain cancer, then seeing his ex-wife so happy with her new husband? Though, of course, she reminded herself, he was dating Sally Ryland, a widow who lived out at Ryland Riding, giving lessons and boarding horses.

The first afternoon Cassidy had ridden with Dave, he'd said there was no special woman in his life. It turned out that he was being discreet. She'd heard about him dating Sally from a number of people. Apparently the two of them were taking things slow and Dave even pretended they were just friends. Still, he was out at her place almost every Sunday. And today, she was his date for the wedding and reception.

The news about Dave and Sally's relationship had put an end to Cassidy's tentative plan to liven up his sex life. Now she knew why Dave, who sometimes seemed attracted to her, never acted on it. She respected that. Though she was a firm believer in casual sex, she didn't respect people who cheated on their partners.

Nor did she believe in sex for the sake of sex; there had to be some kind of connection. She hadn't felt that with any of the half dozen or so guys who'd asked her out. Yeah, she'd have a coffee or beer with them and chat, but it never got more serious than that. None of them measured up to Dave, nor turned her on the way he did. She sighed. Lucky Sally.

Cassidy hadn't met the woman yet, and was definitely curious. "How about Sally?" she asked as she distributed the last place cards. "She gets along with Jess?"

"Jess gets along with everyone." Madisun's tense expression lightened for a moment. "She's a lot like you, that way."

"Thanks." Cassidy had spoken to Jess a couple of times on line-dancing nights, but since she'd been working there hadn't been time for a real conversation. From what she'd seen, Jess was natural, outgoing, sensible, and definitely pretty, with her sleek chestnut hair and even features. She was also clearly very much in love with Evan.

"But I haven't seen her with Sally," Madisun said. "I haven't even seen Dave with Sally."

For some reason, Cassidy had trouble thinking of him dating Sally. Was it because she hadn't seen them together either? Or because she really wished he was single and available for a little fun? Or because he didn't seem like a happy man? His dimple never popped. He laughed, but it was never a belly laugh. Sometimes a shadow crossed his face, and then she did her best, with a touch or a light comment, to bring him back from whatever memory disturbed him.

"Sally hardly ever comes to town," Madisun went on.

"She and her husband moved here a while back, and set up Ryland Riding. It was like their own little world. Then he died of a massive heart attack when he was only thirty."

"I heard about that. It's so sad." And another reason to not buy into the notion of happily ever after relationships.

"She still keeps to herself—except for her students, of course. I don't know if she's snotty, or shy, or what. Dave goes out and helps her with stuff, and they have dinner or, you know, whatever." Madisun flashed a quick, conspiratorial grin, and then the grin turned to a frown. "I'm just not sure she's right for him. He's such an amazing guy, he deserves someone special."

"I know" She studied the striking Native Canadian woman. "You're not, uh, interested in him yourself, are you?"

"Me?" Madisun shook her head quickly. "No way. He's like Evan. They're mentors."

"And friends. It's obvious you're close to both of them."

"I guess." Her smile was self-deprecating. "It's kind of hard to believe that a girl like me can be friends with men like them."

Madisun, like Dave, was closemouthed about her personal life. Still, the gossip mill had enlightened Cassidy. She knew that the young woman's father drank and had trouble keeping a job. Her mom hadn't finished high school and was raising Madisun's eight younger siblings.

"You're hardworking, smart, and nice," Cassidy said. "You're exactly the kind of woman they'd like and respect."

Madisun's only flaw, as far as she could see, was that she could be too serious. On a whim, Cassidy went over to one of the large flower arrangements on a sideboard and tugged off a few freesia blossoms from where the loss would never be noticed. She tucked a couple of pink blossoms into the left pocket of Madisun's shirt, a bright, almost mischievous touch against the stark white uniform. Into her own pocket she tucked a couple of peach-colored blossoms.

Then, hearing excited voices from outside, she said, "The hordes are descending. Karen and Jamal are married."

"May they have many happy years together." Madisun's tone was dead serious.

"Uh, yeah." Who knew, maybe the newlyweds would be like Sheila and Ken Cousins, or the white-haired dance teachers Jimmy B and Bets, rather than like Cassidy's parents or her brother and his ex-wife. Sprinkled with magic dust, as she'd said to Sheila. An odd wistfulness sent a pang through her heart, but she shook it off, reminding herself she was the realistic one who didn't believe in chasing crazy dreams that might end up breaking your heart.

She and Madisun hurried toward the bar to help Roy and his staff.

The next hour went by in a whirl as staff served drinks to guests. Adrenaline overrode Cassidy's fatigue as she worked with Madisun and assisted the other staff.

The excited chatter stopped dead when the bridal party, fresh from being photographed in the town square, arrived with bright smiles. Karen looked stunning and glowed with happiness. Tall and shapely, she wore an off-the-shoulder ivory gown with lace and seed pearls. Her glossy dark brown hair was caught up in an artfully simple style, accented with a headpiece that matched the dress. Robin had said that her gramma Brooke was doing Karen's hair.

Jamal, a striking man with a smile that wouldn't quit, was her perfect match. He wore a light gray suit, a crisp white dress shirt, and a silver-and-black-striped tie. He was, Cassidy had learned, half African American and half Puerto Rican American. The clothing looked great against his beautiful skin, which was the color of dark coffee.

Madisun stepped forward with a tray of flute glasses filled with the bubbly passion fruit drink that Karen had chosen for the party, and served the bride, groom, then the rest of the wedding party.

The bride and groom had wanted an informal celebration and decided against a receiving line. Instead, they began to circulate around the room, chatting with their guests.

Cassidy checked that the wedding photographer was on the job, moving around unobtrusively and snapping informal shots. Then she picked up another tray of flutes filled with the peachy-gold punch. The drink was nonalcoholic, because Jamal, Brooke, and two or three others were recovering alcoholics. The guests who really wanted booze could get drinks at the bar.

She greeted Karen's family, who were staying at the Wild Rose, and said hi to townspeople she knew, refilling her tray as needed and trying to ignore the pins and needles in her leg. A fresh tray in hand, she gazed across the room at Dave, who looked great but slightly uncomfortable in a dark gray suit, cream shirt, and striped tie. He stood talking to Brooke and Jake Brannon, who were holding hands. The woman by his side must be Sally Ryland.

As Cassidy walked toward them, she checked out the other woman. Sally was attractive, with short, strawberry blond hair curling loosely around an oval-shaped face, greenish gray eyes, and freckles she hadn't bothered to conceal with make-up. In low-heeled pumps, she was a couple inches taller than Cassidy in her flats. Her build was toned and lean, on the thin side. Her short-sleeved green dress was flattering, but understated. In fact, there was something about the way Sally stood, a little round shouldered, close to Dave but not touching him, that almost made her look like she'd rather not be noticed. Not snobby, Cassidy thought, but perhaps shy.

Cassidy stepped up with her tray. "Would anyone like another glass of passion punch?"

As Brooke and Sally reached for glasses, Dave smiled

warmly. "Hey, Cassidy. Things are going well, don't you think?"

His smile was a magnet, tugging on something inside her. Making her want to move closer, to touch him, to press her lips to his smiling ones. Why did he have to be dating Sally?

She gave him a carefully professional smile. "Absolutely. Madisun's got everything spreadsheeted to death, along with Plan Bs and Plan Cs in case of glitches." She said hi to Brooke and Jake, who she'd met before.

Dave said, "Cassidy, this is Sally Ryland. Sally, say hello to Cassidy Esperanza. She's Madisun Joe's right-hand assistant."

The two women murmured greetings. Seeing Sally's face up close, Cassidy realized that she had to be several years older than Dave, just as Brooke was older than Jake.

When Dave gazed at Sally, Cassidy read fondness in his expression, and protectiveness. But not passion. And Sally mostly looked nervous. Was the woman so shy that it bothered her to attend a wedding reception with her boyfriend?

As Cassidy continued on with her tray of drinks, her mind was still on Dave and Sally. They had both lost the partners they loved deeply. Maybe they were a perfect match, but as Madisun and one or two other people had suggested, perhaps Sally wasn't right for Dave. Maybe each of them was stuck in the grieving stage and couldn't move on. The only person in Cassidy's life who had died—aside from her great-grandmother, when Cassidy was only six— was Gramps. She'd loved him so much and he'd been the only stability in her life. His death, when she was fifteen and her parents were breaking up for the second time, had shaken her to the core.

But you had to move on. Lighten up, loosen up, get on with life.

And speaking of moving on, a quick check of her watch told her it was almost time to herd the group into the dining room for a light dinner. Later, they'd return to the bar for dancing.

She loved dancing. She'd really like to dance with Dave. On line-dancing nights, she'd seen him dance with Karen, Brooke, Jess, and others while she'd been busy serving drinks.

Tonight, again she'd be staff. And—hah!—dancing? She just hoped her tingly left leg didn't go numb. It was tough keeping her balance when she couldn't feel one leg.

During her normal workdays, she would sneak into a vacant room during her breaks, curl up on the bed for a catnap, then smooth the bedspread and return to work refreshed. Tonight, all the rooms were full and she likely wouldn't get any breaks anyhow.

No, she wouldn't be dancing tonight. She'd be lucky if she could stumble the four blocks home to Ms. Haldenby's.

Chapter Seven

It was after midnight when Dave, tired but satisfied, walked from the dining room into the lobby and headed over to talk to Sam, at the desk.

"Everyone's cleared out?" the night manager asked.

Dave nodded. "Except for a couple of staff doing the final tidy-up." With a sigh of relief, he peeled off his unaccustomed jacket and tie, and stretched. "The guests have all gone and the bride and groom are tucked up in the luxury suite. They've got a gourmet room service breakfast on order, then they'll head to the airport to fly to Maui." He undid buttons at the neck of his dress shirt, then also undid the cuffs and rolled them up. Now he felt more like his normal self.

"Honeymooning in Hawaii," Sam mused. "Romantic."

"Yeah." From the way the newlyweds looked at each other, Dave figured they'd be just as happy spending their entire honeymoon up in their suite at the Wild Rose.

He and Jess had never had a honeymoon. Never even had sex until after Robin was born. But then, their marriage hadn't exactly been the usual sort from the get-go. And that was a secret known only to him, Jess, and Evan—and Anita, but she was gone now.

"I'm glad Karen's going to keep working in Caribou Crossing," Sam said. "She's a damned fine cop. She sure made a beautiful bride too." He had stopped into the bar for a glass of punch before he'd gone on shift, and taken a whirl around the dance floor with Karen.

"She did." Dave couldn't help imagining how Anita would have looked as a bride. She'd been traditional, so the ceremony would have been in a church. That would have suited Dave just fine, seeing her dressed in white lace walking down the aisle toward him. But then he'd have married her anywhere, anytime, and been the happiest man in the world.

After she'd been diagnosed, he'd kept trying to get his fiancée to marry him, even when she was so sick she couldn't leave her hospital bed. She'd turned him down, though. For some reason, she seemed to think it would be harder on him to lose a wife than a fiancée.

Crazy woman didn't seem to realize that, whatever the type of ring on her finger, she was the love of his life. Losing her wasn't *hard*; it was soul destroying.

"Dave?"

He forced his "I'm fine" face back in place. "Sorry. I was drifting. It's been a long day." Sad, of course, in making him think of what he'd lost. But happy, too, to see his good friend Karen so confident and excited about her future with Jamal. He'd try to hang on to the happy.

"Go on up to bed. The inn's in good hands."

Dave nodded and headed across the lobby to the corridor that led to his office, the back stairs, and the door out to the parking lot. Though he was tired and, yeah, a little melancholy, he was also still energized from the reception. Even though he'd let Cassidy persuade him to put Madisun in charge so he could play the role of guest, he'd kept an eye on how things were going. His assistant manager and the rest of his staff had come through beautifully. He'd be sure to thank them, and give Madisun a bonus. Mitch too, and Roy, and perhaps Cassidy.

She'd been a good hire. He only hoped her wanderlust didn't kick in before the busy tourist season ended. In the fall, Madisun would return to university in Vancouver. Likely Cassidy would head off somewhere too. He remembered what she'd said during their first conversation: India, Albuquerque, or Cuba.

He'd miss the two women. Madisun had become his right hand. Cassidy had become . . . what, exactly? A friend, for sure. Her bright smile warmed his workday, her rides with him and Robin were highlights of his week, and on the couple of occasions she'd mingled with his family and friends she'd fit in like she belonged there. Fit in, even though she was so different from anyone else he knew, with her crazy philosophy of life.

She was capable, but in an effortless way that made it look like she wasn't trying. She was fun; she'd say outrageous things; she was generous and occasionally quite insightful.

And why was he cataloguing her virtues? She was his employee. He didn't want a relationship. Nor did she, at least not with him. She'd stopped with the teasing, double entendre comments. He'd seen her out with other guys and she'd no doubt found someone who interested her more than he did. Which was good. It was crazy to feel a twinge of jealousy.

He stopped at the door to his office. Madisun and Cassidy had taken the unopened wedding gifts there for safekeeping. Brooke and Jake would pick them up tomorrow and hold on to them until the honeymooners returned and could open them.

Wanting to verify that they'd remembered to lock up, he tested the knob. It turned in his hand. He opened the door and glanced in. The room was dark, illuminated only by light from the hallway. He checked that the gifts were stacked in a massive pile in one corner, and was about to close and lock the door when something white on the couch caught his eye.

He flicked the light switch. And saw a slender form in white pants and shirt curled up, her back toward him. Cassidy. That black pixie haircut gave her away.

The light must have woken her because she stirred, stretched like a cat, then lazily rolled over. The moment she saw him, she jerked to a sitting position, then hastily rose. Her hands busily tidied her hair and smoothed her shirt and pants. She slipped her feet into black flats. "Sorry, Dave. When I brought in the last of the presents, I was tired and thought I'd sit down for a minute." She glanced at her watch. "Oops. That was more like an hour than a minute."

"Don't worry about it."

"I'll go help the others tidy up." She headed for the door.

He touched her upper arm to stop her. Then, because it felt too good, he let go. "They'll be finished and gone. Cassidy, you've put in a long day and you did a great job. Go on home."

"Right." She gazed at him and there was something soft, almost wistful, in her blue-gray eyes. "I'm going." She turned away.

Leaving him shaken. Damn it, this was the thing about Cassidy. One look like that, and he wanted to smooth the hair off her face, brush his fingers across her cheek, touch his lips to hers. That urge was so much harder to resist than a case of simple physical lust.

After she went through the door, he followed and locked it. They both headed toward the lobby, where Sam clacked away at the computer keyboard and didn't even look up.

Cassidy walked toward the main entrance door slowly, as if she was as tired as Dave was. He knew she was strong and active, yet right now her white-clad back looked almost fragile. She veered to the left, toward the dining room. "There's a light on in the bar."

Through the darkened dining room, he saw a glowing light. He followed her.

In the bar, the tables and chairs had been restored to normal, leaving an area of floor space clear for dancing. Someone had turned off the main lights, but not the light over the bar, which glinted off sparkling glasses and made liqueur bottles glow like jewels.

Karen and Jamal's music—the CD of their favorite songs that had played when the band took breaks—was still on, low enough that Sam couldn't have heard it in the lobby. Faith Hill was telling her lover to just breathe.

Cassidy turned to Dave. "I saw Sally leave early. I thought you'd go with her, or head over after the reception."

Wondering what had made her think of Sally, he responded, "She's not big on social stuff, nor much of a night owl."

"But the two of you, uh . . . you're dating, right?"

Dave huffed. "Why are people so determined to make two friends into a couple?"

Something sparked in her eyes. "You're really not dating?"

"No. She's a nice woman who tries too hard to be self-sufficient, and isolates herself from the community. She's my friend and I persuaded her to come to the reception because I thought she might like to get to know some more townspeople."

"That's nice of you." Cassidy moved a step closer.

One of the peach-colored blossoms she'd worn tucked in her pocket had fallen out somewhere, and the other was wilted and crumpled. Her clothing was wrinkled, there were shadows under her eyes, and yet her eyes gleamed with life.

Something indefinable had changed. Now, rather than fragility, he sensed vitality. And, God help him, it was sexy.

"You're a nice guy," she said. "Everyone turns to you when there's a problem. You help people, you fix things."

He shrugged. He didn't know if it was nice, so much as part of who he was. If someone was hurting, in trouble, had a problem, he was driven to help.

"But what do you do for you?" she asked. "What do you do for fun?"

Holding her would be fun. So would kissing her. His throat was dry and he had to swallow before he managed to say, "Hang out with Robin. See my family and friends."

"You dance sometimes. I've seen you on Sunday nights."

"I do dance sometimes." He barely knew what he was saying.

Cassidy was no more than five feet six compared to his six two, and she stood at least a foot away from him. And yet her presence overwhelmed him. Was it his overactive imagination, or was something going on here? His heart belonged to Anita. But the rest of him wanted to grab Cassidy and hang on to her.

"I like to dance," she said softly. "But I'm always working."

He swallowed. He was vaguely aware that Faith Hill had given way to Elvis Presley singing "Love Me Tender."

"I'm not working now," she said, tugging his jacket and tie away from him, then tossing them over the back of a chair.

When he didn't say anything, she prompted, "This is where you say, 'Cassidy, would you like to dance?'"

Was she flirting, or did she just want to dance? Though the need to hold her in his arms was painful, he couldn't shape the words or even move toward her.

That didn't discourage her. "And then I say, 'Thank you, Dave, I'd love to.'"

She stepped forward and some muscle memory or instinct or pure blind need had him raising his arms so she could step into them.

As Cassidy raised her arms and twined her hands around the back of his neck, as she pressed the front of her body lightly against him, his blood stirred. Oh God. Small, firm breasts lightly brushing his chest. Curved hips swaying gently as he and she shuffled in place. The heat of her back through wrinkled cotton, the total femininity of a bra strap under his fingers.

Arousal was fierce. Inevitable, irresistible, powerful, and now he had a full-blown erection. No way could he disguise it, with the way her pelvis shimmied against him.

Shit. How junior high. How mortifying. Cassidy was his friend. She worked for him; she'd been sexually harassed at her last job. She would be disgusted, embarrassed; she would . . . press seductively closer, shifting back and forth to rub against him, making him even harder.

His heart thundered against his rib cage and he held his breath, losing himself in this amazing, impossible moment.

Until she faltered, stumbled, like her leg—the one that gave her occasional trouble—had given way. "Shit," she muttered.

He tightened his grip, steadying her. Gazing down into her face, that exotic, elfin face, a slight frown of annoyance creasing her brow, he asked, "Are you okay?"

She shook her head, rueful humor chasing the annoyance away. "That wasn't how I wanted this to go."

He swallowed. "How did you want—"

She silenced him by rising on her toes—her leg must be steady again—and touching her lips to his.

Oh God, what soft, tender lips. He was so shocked, he couldn't even respond. Her lips were parted slightly, warm peach-scented breath caressing his mouth as she slid kisses across it. Open-mouthed kisses, with the damp inner side of her lips moistening and tugging his skin, her tongue giving tiny, darting licks. The sensations were so delicious, so foreign, he simply savored them, standing there like a dummy, not kissing her in return.

She eased back in his arms and broke the connection. Mouth pouty now, she teased, "Hey, mister, I'm trying to seduce you, in case you didn't notice."

Seduce him? So that meant she wasn't dating some other guy? This vibrant, sexy woman actually wanted *him*? Before he could fully process that thought, her lips were back on his. This time, his mouth caught up with the arousal that raged through the rest of his body, and he kissed her back. Not lightly and teasingly, but with all the need and passion that had lain banked deep inside him for more than three years.

He plundered her mouth, diving deep, his tongue dueling with hers, his lips claiming hers. She gave back just as greedily, as demandingly. His hips thrust against her firm belly; his erection strained against his fly. God, he wanted her, needed her, had to have her. Now.

Still kissing her fiercely, he released his grip on her slim torso and reached between them, fumbling for the button at the waist of her pants. She came down off her toes, lost her balance, and stumbled backward, her hip banging one of the tables. "Ouch," she grumbled.

That brought Dave to his senses. He caught her arm to steady her. Feeling totally unsteady himself, he ran his free hand through his hair. "Jesus. What just happened?"

Cassidy sank into a chair and grinned up at him. "Not enough, but it was a good start. To be continued, somewhere private?"

Sex. She meant sex. He could have sex with this captivating woman.

But no, that would be wrong. For a whole bunch of reasons he was having trouble recalling at the moment. "Look, it's not that I'm not attracted to you, but, uh . . ."

She rolled her eyes. "Translation: my dick wants to jump your bones but my brain has reservations."

He hated that kind of talk, but his erection apparently liked it, pulsing painfully against his fly. "D'you have to be so crude?"

"Oh, did you want to be romantic?" she teased.

"No! I don't want to be romantic. I don't want sex, either." Though the aching organ behind his fly sure as hell did. "We can't have sex," he said, as much to his erection as to her.

"Why not?"

He knew there were reasons, if only he could get his brain to work. Oh yeah, right. He waved his arm around the room. "You work for me."

"This has nothing to do with work. It's personal." She almost purred the last word. "Very personal."

Of course it was. That was the problem. "Look, uh, the thing is . . ." He searched for words, then finished clumsily, "My heart belongs to someone else. I lost my fiancée." He never talked about Anita, and it took an effort to force out those few words.

"I know, and I'm so sorry." The compassion in her eyes looked genuine. "But it's not your heart I want, Dave. We like each other, we're attracted, so why not have some fun?"

"I'm not that kind of guy." Despite his earlier thought that fun would be kissing her.

"But I think you could be, and I'd like to prove it."

And what did a guy say to that? The offer was so tempting. Before he could figure out how to respond, he heard footsteps approaching. He grabbed his jacket from the chair and held it casually in front of his aroused body before turning to face the door.

Sam stepped into the dimly lit room. "Hey there, you two. I thought you'd gone home long ago, Cassidy. And didn't I say good night to you a while back, Dave?"

"You were buried in your novel when we came through the lobby," Cassidy said. "We noticed the bar light and came in to turn it off."

"Yup, I finished writing a chapter, got up to stretch, and saw the light as well."

The three of them turned and stared at the light over the bar. Dave forced his feet into motion, first stopping the music and ejecting the CD, then clicking off the light.

"Okay," Sam said, heading back toward the glowing light from the lobby.

Cassidy paused to glance at Dave, then followed.

He brought up the rear, noticing that she limped slightly. "I'll give you a ride home."

She glanced over her shoulder. "I can walk. I do it all the time." It wasn't a yes or a no, more like she was trying to guess his intentions. Sam had interrupted before they'd resolved the issue between them. The *personal* issue.

In the lobby, Dave glanced around at the familiar surroundings. Several of the items there, as in the rest of the hotel, were refurbished antiques from the gold rush days. He and Anita had picked them up at collectibles shops and garage sales. She'd loved browsing for slightly battered treasures and giving them a new life.

Anita had valued tradition, stability. The woman had been the opposite of the rootless Cassidy. A newly graduated teacher, she had moved to Caribou Crossing to take a job at the high school. She'd joined the Heritage Committee, which was dedicated to preserving the town's history and historic buildings, a committee that Dave chaired. From the moment he met her, she'd owned his heart. And she still did.

But Cassidy said she didn't want his heart and he believed her. Unlike most women, she shunned any hint of permanence.

Sam's voice tugged him out of his thoughts. "Cassidy, it's after midnight. You're tired and it's chilled off out there. Let the man give you a ride."

"If you insist," she said to Sam, then turned to Dave, her dark eyebrows arched.

"Right. The Jeep's parked out back."

After a round of good nights, he and Cassidy went out to the parking lot. When they'd climbed into the Jeep with the Wild Rose logo on the side, she said, "Well? I have my own entrance at Ms. Haldenby's. Want to come in and finish what we started?"

"No." He grimaced at the brusqueness of his rejection. "I mean . . . Well, yes, but no."

She snorted. "You know I'm going to ask why not."

That was another difference between her and Anita. His fiancée had been subtle. Persistent, but subtle. Cassidy was more "in your face."

"As if there's an easy answer," he said ruefully.

She cocked her head. "I bet there's a one-word answer: Anita."

"That's certainly one reason."

"I bet she wouldn't want you to spend the rest of your life being miserable."

How many times had he heard that from well-meaning friends? He even believed it. His mind told him that having sex with someone else, even falling in love, wouldn't mean being disloyal to Anita. But his heart had died. Oh yes, it had the capacity to love Robin, Jessie, his family, and his close friends, but the part of it that could sing with love for a life mate had shattered. And he was glad, because it meant he could never suffer that particular agony again.

Trying to be polite, he said to Cassidy, "Look, no offense, but I don't talk about Anita."

"So people say, but I'm not sure it's healthy."

Dave gritted his teeth. Of course Cassidy, being Cassidy, wouldn't be warned off the way *considerate* people were.

She went on. "Gramps died when I was fifteen. I was closer to him than to anyone else."

Her words distracted him briefly from his annoyance. She talked more about her grandfather than about her parents. Dave gathered that he'd been the one person who had always let her know that she mattered and was loved.

"When he died, it helped to talk about him with JJ and my parents," she said. "It kept him close. Don't you think maybe—"

"Anita's in my heart," he burst out. "She'll always be there. And talking hurts." Even thinking about her dredged up those horrible dark feelings of anger, guilt, desolation.

After a moment, Cassidy said, "Okay. We're all different."

Dave breathed a sigh of relief. "Thank you." Now she'd leave him alone. He turned the key in the ignition.

Chapter Eight

Cassidy studied Dave's profile. The Wild Rose parking lot was illuminated only by security lights, but there was enough light to see that the tense line of his jaw had relaxed.

She lowered the window on the passenger side. The nights had warmed up since she'd arrived in Caribou Crossing, but the air still had a refreshing touch of coolness.

He drove out of the parking lot. It was only four blocks to Ms. H's house. Should she leave the poor guy alone? Usually, when she could tell that his thoughts had gone to a dark place, she tried to cheer him up. But that was like sticking a bandage on a wound that wasn't healing. It was obvious he was stuck. She'd bet everything she owned— which wasn't much, but did include the battered Winnie-the-Pooh that Gramps had given her when she was a toddler—that Anita would hate to see Dave like this.

And so did she.

She clicked off the radio. "The gossip mill thinks you're dating Sally."

His jaw clenched again and he didn't speak.

"They think the two of you are taking it slow but likely will end up together." Though he seemed to be trying to ignore her, she went on. "Some people aren't sure if that's a good thing."

"Huh?" He cast a quick glance in her direction. "Everyone's been after me to date. Now they don't think it's a good thing?"

"It's Sally. No one dislikes her, but they don't know her. She holds herself apart." Maybe it was shyness, but it made the woman hard to relate to.

He snorted. "Seems to me there's something to be said for that. As compared to being a busybody."

She chuckled. "I refuse to take offense. People mind each other's business because they care." And she did care about Dave Cousins. He'd become a friend and she wanted him to be happy. To unstick himself, loosen up, let that dimple break free. To lighten up on being so protective of his daughter, his inn, anyone and anything he cared for. To have fun.

To have sex, for God's sake! With her, preferably.

When he didn't respond, she urged, "Think about it. Let's take—oh, how about Mr. Dave Cousins, for example?"

He shook his head, clearly confused. "What are you on about now?"

"He could mind his own business and leave Sally alone, struggling to keep things going since her husband died. But no, he pokes his nose in, helps her out every week."

"We're friends."

"And he gives Madisun Joe a summer job."

"Madisun's a damned fine employee."

"Absolutely. But she's going back to university in the fall, which means Dave'll have to hire and train another assistant manager, or do without. And, let's see, he gives Karen a huge discount on her wedding reception, and—"

"It's my wedding present to her and Jamal."

"Of course it is. Then there's the way he gives his staff

extra time off when they have family issues to deal with, or how there always happens to be a seniors special when Mr. Bertuzzi comes for a meal. Or remember last month, how he hired this drifter who turned up on his doorstep, and fronted her the first two weeks' pay so she could find a place to stay?"

While she'd been talking, Dave had pulled the Jeep up in front of Ms. H's green rancher, with its neatly kept garden. He didn't turn off the engine. "Good night, Cassidy."

Undeterred, she said, "It's good to get involved with people, to try to help those you care about—the way you do, and the way I'm trying to, if you'd let me."

"I don't need help, damn it."

"Did Sally say the same thing when you first messed around in her life?"

His mouth, which had been tight with anger, opened in a silent "oh."

Point made. "You care about everyone else, but you need to care more about yourself." She touched his arm below the rolled-up sleeve of his white shirt. "Dave, you're stuck and you're not doing anything to fix yourself."

His Adam's apple worked as he swallowed. He stared down at her hand, which she didn't remove. Finally he lifted his arm, shut off the Jeep engine, then put his hand back on the steering wheel. When he spoke, the words grated out. "Fine, I'm stuck. But I get through every day. That's the best I can do."

She'd felt that way once—when Gramps had died, her parents had split up for the second time, and her father had barely noticed she was alive. JJ had thrown himself into activities with his buddies, but she'd withdrawn. She'd gotten through each day, counting them until she could break free and strike out into the world. The solution for Dave Cousins clearly wasn't to go explore the world, because that would mean leaving everyone and everything he loved, but he did deserve a happier life.

Gently she squeezed his arm, feeling the tension of rock-hard muscles. "It's not fair to you. Not fair to Robin or the others who care about—"

"Robin?" He jerked his arm off the wheel, away from her, and glared at her. "You're saying I'm not a good father?"

"Of course you are. But she sees how sad you are. Everyone sees it. They tiptoe around it; they try to cheer you up."

Dave had turned to stare out the front window again. His face was so still that he could have been a statue.

"Your daughter's eleven. She should be having fun with her dad, not having to be careful what she says to him."

After a moment, he said slowly, "What do you mean?"

Cassidy bit her lip. She was hurting him. And if she kept going, she might lose his friendship, not to mention her job. But there were things he needed to hear. "She loved Anita too. You lost the woman you were going to marry and Robin lost the woman who was going to be her stepmom. She can talk to the rest of us about Anita, but you two were the closest to her. She told me she can't even say Anita's name to you, and that's tough on her."

A muscle twitched in his cheek. As if weighing each word, he said, "Robin talks to you about Anita?"

"Yes. She told me about—"

"No!" He held up a hand. "I don't want to hear."

"Ask yourself this," she said quietly. "For three years, you've avoided talking about Anita. Maybe even tried to hold back the memories. Has it made you feel any better?"

He didn't answer. She hadn't expected him to. At least he had let her have her say without throwing her out of the Jeep.

Suddenly, fatigue swamped her. As she reached for the door handle, she realized that her left leg had gone numb.

Determined not to let Dave see her weakness, she opened the door and turned her body sideways to face out. Keeping a tight hold on the door, she slid to the ground, letting her right leg take her weight until she got her balance.

"Thanks for the ride," she said, then closed the door.

She stood on the sidewalk and waited until he drove away. Then, moving slowly and cautiously with her gaze fixed on the path in front of her, she made her way to the side door that led to her studio apartment. It was tough walking when one foot didn't feel the ground, but she was getting used to it.

Inside, she paused in the tiny kitchen area to drink a glass of cold water. She noticed that one of the freesia blossoms had fallen out of her pocket somewhere. The other was half wilted, still sweet smelling when she held it to her nose. She filled a smaller glass with water and stuck the poor thing in it.

Tonight, she couldn't be bothered removing her make-up or brushing her teeth. It was all she could do to unfold the hide-a-bed and pull off her clothes before sliding between the sheets.

"Night," she murmured to Pooh Bear, who sat on the end table.

She didn't set the alarm on her cell. Thank heavens Madisun had given her the day off on Sunday. A good rest would get her healed up and reenergized.

On Monday she'd find out if she still had a job.

Sunday, Cassidy woke to the sound of firm knocking on the door of her apartment. Not the outside door, but the one that led into Ms. Haldenby's house.

"Coming!" She rolled out of bed, warily testing her left leg, which now behaved just fine. Sunlight filtered through the blinds and she hummed as she grabbed her robe from a hook and wrapped it around her.

"Good morning," she said as she opened the door.

Her white-haired landlady, dressed in a blue-and-white-striped shirt tucked into a blue skirt, greeted her with a frown. "Are you sick? There's no excuse for lying in bed past nine o'clock unless you're sick."

Ms. H had a brusque manner, a keen intellect, a soft heart, and firm opinions on many subjects. She had no patience with wimps, and fortunately Cassidy wasn't one. "How about working until past midnight?" Okay, it wasn't exactly the truth, considering the nap she'd taken in Dave's office, but close enough. "What time is it?"

"After ten. You have yesterday's make-up around your eyes. Wash up and put on some clothes. Breakfast's in ten minutes."

"If that's an invitation, I'd be delighted to accept."

Humor danced in Ms. H's sky-blue eyes, but all she said was, "Don't be late."

Under the warm spray of the shower, Cassidy mused about last night. Hopefully, Dave wasn't too pissed off. She could live without having sex with him—though, man, dancing with him and kissing him had sure been a turn-on—but she'd hate to lose his friendship and her job. Maybe she should call and apologize, but she'd only said things he needed to hear. Surely he'd realize that. Best thing to do was show up for work tomorrow as if nothing had happened.

Resolved not to let worry spoil her day off, she dressed in shorts and a purple tank top worn over a pink bra. No make-up. With her coloring, she didn't need it, so she wore it only on special occasions. With a couple minutes to spare, she put last night's clothes in the laundry hamper, folded up the hide-a-bed sofa, and moved the coffee table back in place in front of it.

Her studio apartment had been created from the house's

original dining room and spare bathroom. The furniture wasn't fancy, but it was clean and functional. The sofa and a reading chair were grouped with a coffee table, an end table, and an old TV. A small table with two upright chairs served either for eating or as a desk. The mini kitchen had a sink, fridge, microwave, and toaster oven. Her landlady had told her that, if she wanted to do any real cooking or baking, she was welcome to use her kitchen.

The place was perfect for a nomad like Cassidy, and she loved having her own space rather than sharing an apartment.

She gave a quick double-knock on Ms. H's door, then entered the main part of the house. The welcome aroma of coffee and frying bacon met her. It had become a habit for the two women to have breakfast on Sundays if Cassidy wasn't working at the Wild Rose.

"Mmm, smells good," she called as she walked down the hall toward the kitchen. Most mornings, Cassidy had yogurt and some kind of Wild Rose leftover. Chef Mitch let staff take unsold goodies at the end of the day: cranberry bran muffins, peach Danish, gooey cinnamon buns, chocolate croissants. Delicious, but not the kind of real meal Ms. Haldenby believed in.

The woman, now wearing a navy bibbed apron over her blouse and skirt, turned from the stove. "I had some stale bread that needed to be used, so I made French toast."

"That's one of my faves."

The woman's lips curved momentarily, but then she straightened them and said briskly, "The word is 'favorites'. If you'd been my student, young lady, you'd speak like a civilized human being."

"Civilization's highly overrated." Cassidy noted that the table was already set. Glasses of freshly squeezed orange juice and a milk jug, sugar pot, pitcher of maple syrup.

Bone china plates, cream colored with gold rims, and matching cups and saucers. Empty cups. She went to the old-fashioned drip-through coffeemaker on the counter, removed the cone and filter, then poured from the full carafe into the two cups. By the time she'd put the carafe back on the stove element with the heat set to low, Ms. H had dished out French toast and bacon and taken her apron off.

The two women took their usual spots at the table. Ms. H said a quick grace. She'd told Cassidy that it wasn't because she was religious—she only went to church at Christmas and Easter—but because it reminded her of her mother.

And this ritual of turning Sunday breakfast into something special reminded Cassidy of how things had been when she and JJ were little kids and their parents were getting along.

"Tell me all about the wedding reception," her landlady said.

Cassidy took her time swallowing a delicious bite of maple syrup–slathered French toast and crispy bacon. Then, as the two of them savored breakfast, she described Karen's dress, everyone else's clothes, the food, the toasts.

Over second cups of coffee, Ms. H asked questions and shared snippets of information, including fourth-grade stories about some of the wedding guests. She was an astute observer, had the memory of an elephant, and was often wryly humorous but never cruel.

Cassidy rose to clear the table and refill their coffee cups. When she sat down, Ms. H said, "Well, I do hope Karen and Jamal will have a long and happy life together." There was an unaccustomed note in her voice. Envy? Yearning?

For a moment, Cassidy felt something similar. "Me too," she said quietly. Maybe the newlyweds would beat the odds and turn out like Dave's parents rather than her own multidivorced ones. Then, because she and her landlady had hit it off from day one, Cassidy dared to say, "You never married, Ms. H. I can't believe it's from lack of opportunity."

"A nice compliment." The woman, who wasn't normally a fidget, toyed with her coffee cup. "Lack of opportunity. In a way, I suppose that's true."

Cassidy let her eyes ask the question.

"There was someone. A special someone. When I was studying to be a teacher."

And she'd carried a torch for almost sixty years? Had she not had sex in that long? The woman was worse than Dave Cousins. Cassidy kept that opinion to herself. "It didn't work out?"

Those sky-blue eyes gazed levelly at her. "Her name was Irene. It was the nineteen fifties. We both loved children and wanted to teach them."

And the world would have censured them. "I'm so sorry. That's not fair. Wasn't there any way?"

"If we wanted to lie. Pretend we were just roommates and friends. Live a life of deceit."

Cassidy had learned how principled Ms. H was, so she knew that would have been impossible. "I can't believe how ignorant and prejudiced people were. I wish you'd been born in a different time." Today, she and Irene could get married and have children of their own.

"Wishes like that are a waste of time," she said briskly.

"True. Did you keep in touch with Irene?"

She shook her head. "It was too painful for both of us. When we graduated from the University of British Columbia, I got a job here and she went to teach in Nanaimo. We never contacted each other again."

"Things are different now. Did you ever think of trying to track her down?"

Her brows rose in a schoolmarmish look. "I never took you for a romantic, Cassidy."

"A romantic? Give me a break. I know the statistics about marriages breaking up. My parents *live* those statistics. I just thought, if you've never forgotten Irene, never fallen for anyone else, then who knows, maybe it's the same for her."

"Would you like to calculate the odds of that?"

"You know perfectly well they're incalculable." And yet there was a spark of interest in those blue eyes. So Cassidy pushed a little. There was nothing Ms. H liked more than a challenge. "You probably couldn't even find her. She could have moved a dozen times, she might have married and changed her name, anything's possible."

"She might be dead," she said softly.

"If so, wouldn't you like to know where she's buried or her ashes are scattered?"

Her landlady rose, took her cup and saucer to the counter, and began to rinse dishes and load the dishwasher.

Cassidy got up to help.

Ms. H glanced at her. "Do you know what I like about you?"

"Not a clue," she said cheerfully.

"You were never my student."

Cassidy processed that, then grinned. "They're too intimidated by you to act like adults around you."

"Precisely." She shot Cassidy a sideways glance. "However, they are better schooled in logical analysis."

"Ouch. How much logical analysis can you teach a fourth grader? And what's so wrong with mine?"

"The fact that your parents epitomize the statistics

on divorce does not mean that you're doomed to follow their example."

"You can bet I won't, because I never intend to get married in the first place."

"Then you'll turn out like me. Eighty-one, living alone, with only a handful of friends in my life to share an occasional meal."

A sense of bleakness, loneliness, stole Cassidy's breath for a moment. She forced it away and said brightly, "Eighty-one? I'm not thinking about being eighty-one, or fifty, or even thirty-five. One day at a time, that's my way."

Chapter Nine

Sunday morning, Dave finally got to sleep around five o'clock and woke a few hours later to find Merlin beside the bed, staring at him with a "take me out" plea in his eyes.

Dave groaned and threw on gym shorts and a tee, then took the dog downstairs for a run around the block. Often, on mornings when Robin wasn't there, he and Merlin would go several miles, but today he felt drained, physically and emotionally. It was just as well that his daughter was at Jessie and Evan's, yet he missed her and was glad she'd be back with him tonight.

As his shoes slapped the pavement and the poodle kept pace beside him, he wondered whether he was a good dad. Cassidy had suggested that he'd put his own needs ahead of his daughter's.

He could ask Jessie. Confess to even more failings as a father. She thought he was overprotective and they sometimes argued over what Robin could and couldn't do. But hell, he'd lost Anita, and then two summers ago, Robin had been hit by a car and could have died. That night had been sheer horror. No way could he bear the thought of losing his daughter.

And yet, while he'd been so busy protecting her body,

had he put enough thought to her emotions? Her grief over Anita's death?

Going in the back door of the inn, he said to the dog, "Too short a run for you, pal. Sorry. Later, we'll go out with Malibu and meet up with Robin." He got a brief bark in response.

Upstairs, Dave fed Merlin, showered, and dressed in his work clothes, and then the two of them went down to his office. His gaze went straight to the couch. No white-clad figure, just . . . He walked over and picked up a wilted, peach-colored blossom. As he lifted it to his nose, a hint of sweetness rose from it. Some crazy instinct kept him from tossing it out. Instead, he laid it on his desk beside the photo of Robin on Concha that he'd taken last summer. She was beaming.

He glanced at his office walls, where two of her horse drawings hung among various awards he and the Wild Rose had won. "She's happy, right?" he asked the dog.

Merlin, who'd gone to lie in his usual out-of-the-traffic-flow spot, glanced up, then put his head down to rest on his paws.

Cassidy was a free-spirited drifter. What did she know about raising kids, about commitment, about anything serious? And yet—

A knock on his door interrupted his thoughts. Brooke came in, cradling baby Nicki in a pouch-style sling. "Morning, Dave."

"Hi." He gave her a one-armed hug and dropped a kiss on the top of Nicki's dark curls. There was another thing he'd lost when Anita died. They'd planned to have a child or two. Rather than give in to the ache, he focused on Brooke. "You're here to pick up the presents?"

She nodded. "Jake got sidetracked by Mr. Bateman, who's telling him that the pedestrian-crossing light on the corner isn't long enough."

"Yeah, like that's RCMP business."

"Caribou Crossing is definitely an adjustment for Jake after years of undercover work." She gazed up at him. "The Wild Rose did a great job of the reception."

"Thanks to Madisun."

"And you." A pause, then, "Are you all right?"

"Sure. Why?"

"Sally left early."

He stifled a groan. "How many times do I have to say that we're not dating?"

"You really aren't? I'm glad to hear that."

"What?" Would he ever figure women out? "Didn't you say last month—the last time I said I wasn't dating Sally—that you were glad I was seeing someone?"

"Yes, but now I've met her."

"You don't like her?" He felt offended on Sally's behalf.

"Oh, she seems nice enough, but she's not right for you."

No, he wouldn't ask why.

That didn't stop Brooke. "She's too somber. You need someone sunnier."

"I don't need anyone." Only his daughter.

Was he being too needy when it came to Robin? He bit his lip. "Does Robin, uh . . ." Damn, it was hard to talk about this. "Does she ever say anything about Anita?"

Brooke's blue-green eyes widened. "Yes. She tells me about things the two of them did together, or the three of you did, or advice Anita gave her. She misses her. Uh, why do you ask?"

"I don't talk about her."

"I know." Her brow creased and she hugged Nicki closer to her chest. "I almost never talk about my ex-husband. That's because so many of the memories are bad. I wasn't a good person when I was with him. He wasn't a good person either. We both hurt Evan, and we hurt each other too. But with you and Anita, it's different. Your love for each other was so strong."

"It's too painful," he said quietly.

"If you don't talk about it, does the pain go away?"

It was the same question Cassidy had asked last night. He figured that Brooke, like Cassidy, knew the answer.

"Dave, we're friends. You've been there for me when I needed someone to talk to. I'd be happy to return the favor if you ever—" She broke off as Jake strode through the door.

With Brooke supervising, the men got the wrapped boxes and gift bags loaded into Jake and Brooke's SUV. Once Nicki was stowed in her car seat, Jake climbed in the driver's side.

Brooke rested a hand on Dave's arm, stretched up to kiss his cheek, and murmured, "The offer's open. Any time."

"Thanks."

Right now, the person he really needed to talk to was his daughter. It would be tough. Really tough, for him. But if it made things easier for Robin, he had to do it.

And maybe he could use a little moral support. Or maybe he just wanted to see Cassidy.

Back in his office, he texted Robin to call him when she got a chance.

She phoned promptly. "Hey, Dad. I'm just mucking out stalls."

"That's why they pay you the big bucks." He took a breath. "It's still good if I ride over to meet you later, and you stay here for a few days?"

"Sure."

"I wondered if you'd like me to invite Cassidy along for the ride. And after, the three of us could maybe make pizza and watch a DVD. If she's free." Cassidy had never been to his and Robin's suite, and inviting her felt like a big step. Toward what, he had no clue.

"Cool!"

Wishing his own feelings were as uncomplicated, Dave dialed Cassidy next.

Midafternoon, Dave walked to Westward Ho! with Merlin striding eagerly beside him. Sometimes Dave thought the poodle's feet were spring-loaded, he had such a bounce, as if moving through the world was pure pleasure. Dave's own feet dragged, not just from lack of sleep. Cassidy was meeting him at the stable. What the hell was he going to say to her?

When he saw her walking toward him, she was a sight for sleep-deprived eyes. Her trim body was clothed in her usual riding garb of jeans, boots, and straw cowboy hat, together with a well-worn Western-style shirt he hadn't seen before. He'd learned that she got most of her wardrobe from Days of Your. No brand-new shirt could have suited her better than this trimly fitted one, its faded denim making her blue-gray eyes even brighter in her olive-skinned face. His gaze skimmed down the snap-button front. Oh yeah, Western shirts were the best. If you hooked your hands in both sides at the top and tugged gently, the buttons popped, one by one.

Should he be having that thought about Cassidy?

There would never be another Anita, but did that mean he'd never have sex again? The prospect of decades of celibacy wasn't appealing. Maybe the women in his life were right; it was time for casual dating. With Cassidy? She didn't want a serious relationship, didn't plan to stay in Caribou Crossing for long, so she was safe. She wouldn't have unrealistic expectations.

And that was all very logical, but the truth was, she was the one woman who attracted him, on so many levels.

"Hey, Dave."

"Hey," he said warily. With her, he never knew what to expect. He just hoped she wouldn't poke at him. He'd had way too little sleep to cope.

She gave him a smile as sunny as the sky. "What a beautiful afternoon for a ride. I'm glad you and Robin invited me." Bending, she gave the dog's coat an enthusiastic scrub with both hands. "Hey there, Merlin. How's my beautiful boy?"

Happy to see her, from the way he squirmed and tried to lick her. Dave tried not to envy his dog. If he wanted, he could have Cassidy's hands on his body. She'd made that clear last night. Damn, he was confused. "Let's get our horses ready," he said gruffly.

On their first ride, Cassidy had bonded with Cherry Blossom and since then she booked the mare whenever possible. Cassidy had quickly learned how to care for her horse and put on the saddle and bridle. She related well to horses and had proved to be a natural on horseback.

Ten minutes later, he and Malibu, Cassidy and Cherry, and an ecstatic Merlin were on the road. Cassidy was unusually quiet. It occurred to him that she might be worried that she'd pissed him off enough last night that it would cost her her job. But surely she knew he wouldn't have invited her to go riding if he planned to fire her. Or might she think he intended to tell her today, rather than have her report to work on Monday only to be fired?

Here was a prime reason he shouldn't get involved with her. Staffing issues were complicated enough when they didn't involve personal relationships.

"Dave?" Her voice broke into his thoughts. "That scowl may chase the sun away."

He forced himself to relax his face. "If you're worried I'm going to fire you, I'm not."

She nodded. "I didn't think so, but it's good to know for sure."

Curious, he tilted his head. "Why didn't you think so?"

"You're too smart for that."

Her cheeky grin won a reluctant one from him. "Yeah, I guess. Anyhow, I heard you last night, what you said about Robin. Can we leave it at that?"

"Yes."

He gave a relieved sigh. But he should have known better because she added, "For now."

"Good Lord, what *is* it with you women? See, this is something I like about Sally. When we talk, it's about Ryland Riding or the Wild Rose. Not about . . ."

"Feelings?" she teased. "Well, that proves it. Sally is just plain unnatural. Every woman talks about feelings."

"Then talk to each other," he grumbled, "and leave me out of it." Yet a smile twitched at the corners of his mouth. Speaking of *feelings*, Cassidy Esperanza sure did mess with his. She could make him mad one moment, then have him grinning the next.

For the rest of the ride, they spoke little, and it was an easy, companionable silence.

When they arrived at Riders Boot Camp, Jessie was in the stable yard doing orientation with a new batch of students. She waved hello and he and Cassidy waved back as Robin untied Concha from a hitching rail and mounted.

As the three horses and riders, along with Merlin, moved out of the yard, Robin said, "Let's ride to Colcannon Lake."

As they rode, the tiredness and tension eased from Dave's bones. A good horse, beautiful country, and, most of all, his daughter well and happy. Yes, he'd lost Anita, but he still had a lot to be thankful for. With a start, he realized that he actually *felt* thankful, even happy. Since Anita's death he had often reminded himself of his blessings, yet his emotions had felt disengaged as if he was seeing the good stuff in his life through a gray fog. But today the sun shone through that fog. And damn, it felt good.

When they reached Colcannon Lake, Cassidy exclaimed with pleasure. The spot was indeed scenic: deep blue water sparkling in the sun, surrounded by scattered trees and rock formations. On one side, a narrow road fed into a gravel parking lot, but Robin and Concha led the way to the side that was accessible only on horseback or by foot. On this Sunday afternoon, they had it to themselves. Across the lake, families and groups of teens splashed and picnicked, their happy sounds carrying across the still water.

While the riders dismounted, Merlin made for a strip of coarse-sand beach and plunged into the water. The dog loved to swim. Dave wished Robin had revealed her plans earlier, so they could have brought bathing suits and joined him.

Cassidy bent to remove her boots and he stared at her shapely rear. Cassidy in a bikini . . . Now that was dangerous territory. He forced his gaze away from her assets and concentrated on pulling off his own boots and socks, then rolling his pant legs. He joined Robin and Cassidy on a tumble of large rocks where they could sit and dangle their feet in the cool water.

Cassidy pulled off her hat and peeled off her shirt, revealing a yellow tank top. She braced herself on her arms and tilted back, lifting her face to the sun. "What a perfect place."

"What's your favorite place, of everywhere you've been?" Robin asked.

"I don't play favorites. I go somewhere, enjoy what's to be enjoyed, and then move on. But right now, if you made me pick, I'd have to say Caribou Crossing ranks high on the list."

"It's the best," his daughter asserted. "I've been to the Big Apple, and it's really cool, but this is better."

Cassidy straightened and gazed at her with surprise. "You've been to New York City?"

"Evan lived there for ten years. He took Mom and me for a visit. We rode in Central Park, went up the Empire State Building, and saw 'The Lion King' on Broadway."

"Nice," she said.

"We had brunch with my Facebook pal Caitlin and her family at the Waldorf Astoria. And we had dinner with the Vitales, who're board members at Boots."

"Sounds like a great trip. Did you see the Museum of Natural History? I love it."

"Yeah, it was totally cool."

As he listened to the two of them compare notes, Dave watched the dog romp in the water. He and Merlin were perfectly happy here. He'd thought Robin was too. But Evan had broadened her horizons. Jessie's as well. Dave was confident that Caribou Crossing would always be home for his horse-addicted daughter and ex. Yet Evan had given the two females something that Dave hadn't even realized they might want.

Life had been so much easier before Evan came back to Caribou Crossing. Dave sure didn't begrudge Jessie reuniting with the boy who'd been her first love, her true love. Yet it was hard seeing Evan become a second dad to Robin. Her stepdad.

And her biological father.

Would they ever tell her? He, Jessie, and Evan had agreed that if they did it wouldn't be until she was older. If they did, would she feel betrayed or take it with her usual equanimity?

Now Robin was urging Cassidy to talk about some of her other travels. The colored fairy lights of Santorini at night. The freaky toilets she'd run into in different places. The weird foods people ate. It seemed she'd taken it all in stride, embracing every new adventure.

Dave felt stodgy. But hell, there was nothing wrong with living in one place all your life if that place resonated deep in your bones. If your family lived there. If you'd built, with your own blood, sweat, and tears, a business you loved. Robin had asked Cassidy how long she stayed in one place and she'd said usually a few months.

He and Cassidy were polar opposites. Anita, now she'd been like him. She believed in history, roots, in commitment to people and places.

He caught himself, waited for the thundercloud of negative emotion to descend, but somehow Robin and Cassidy's happy chatter kept it at bay. So he let himself muse further.

Anita had accepted him for who he was. She hadn't teased, pushed, challenged, provoked, the way Cassidy did. There'd been no reason to. They'd fit together from the beginning as if they'd been made for each other, everything so easy and compatible. That was why, even though he was married at the time and he and Anita had both known their attraction was wrong, it had been so difficult to resist.

Cassidy's musical burble of laughter broke smack-dab into the middle of his thoughts. He glanced at her, seeing the sparkle in her eyes, the white flash of her smile. Animated, genuine, totally engaged with his daughter. This woman, too, was hard to resist.

He would never love again, and he knew Cassidy was all about the moment, about having fun. She had brightened his life, at work and in his leisure time. His female friends urged him to date, have fun, get back in the game, and Cassidy had made it clear she was into that. With him.

Oh shit, was he actually contemplating sleeping with her?

Chapter Ten

Cassidy woke slowly. The rough grass under her back reminded her she was at Colcannon Lake. She'd found herself yawning and Dave and Robin had urged her to take a nap in the shade of a cluster of aspen trees. Without opening her eyes, she lazily inventoried sensations. The air was cooler. Much as she loved the sun, these days it tended to wipe her out. The fresh scent of lake water mingled with the dry, dusty aroma of sunshine on yellowed summer grass. Distant voices laughed, occasionally shrieked. Closer at hand, father and daughter talked in low voices about how Robin had again volunteered to babysit her little brother and her gramma Brooke's baby daughter if their parents wanted to go line dancing tonight.

That was one good kid. Responsible way beyond her years, but she also knew how to have fun. Although Robin had an unusual family—the girl was babysitting her own aunt!—Cassidy, with her own unusual family, envied them their closeness.

She opened her eyes, gazing up to watch leaves dance a slow waltz. How long had she napped? Stretching to ease out the aches from sleeping on rough ground, she discovered that Merlin was flaked out beside her. When she sat up, the dog woke, jumped to his feet, and shook.

The two of them went to join Robin and Dave on their rocks.

"Hey, sleepyheads," Robin said, hugging the dog.

"Hey." Cassidy put her hat on to block the late afternoon sun. "I can't believe I dozed off. It's not like I've had a tough day. I slept in, then had breakfast with Ms. Haldenby, then—"

Father and daughter both interrupted, in equally disbelieving tones, "You had breakfast with Ms. Haldenby?"

Cassidy stifled a grin. "Why wouldn't I?"

The pair exchanged glances. "She scares the bejeezus out of me," Dave admitted.

"Me too," Robin said.

"Gee, Robin, I wonder where you got that notion?" Cassidy cocked an eyebrow at Dave.

Sheepishly, he said, "Ms. Haldenby intimidates everyone. Even Sam, and he was a cop for twenty-five years."

Cassidy shook her head. "You all should grow up. She's a little brusque, but she's nice."

"She's smarter than anyone else in this town," Dave said, not making it sound like a compliment.

"Which is a blessing, not a curse. Good Lord, Dave, people say you're nicer than anyone else in this town, but it doesn't stop them from liking you."

Robin giggled. "They don't know him as well as I do. Dad's not always nice. Like when he makes me text him anytime I go anywhere, to let him know I got there safely. And when he wouldn't let me take Concha overnight camping alone. Or go down and stay with—"

Dave cut in. "I'm only trying to make sure you're safe. But to get back to Ms. Haldenby, I've often wondered why she taught elementary school, and why she stayed in

Caribou Crossing. She could've taught—oh, I don't know, physics or English literature at some big university."

"You should ask her," Cassidy said.

Ms. H taught children because she loved them, and it was the closest she could get to having kids of her own, Cassidy figured. The woman had been demanding of them because that was her way of caring, of helping them succeed in the world. And she'd been brusque because she couldn't let herself care too much, because they'd never be her own children. It didn't take a genius to figure all of that out, not if you spent a little time actually getting to know her.

But then that wasn't just the fault of townspeople like Dave. As with Sally Ryland, Ms. Haldenby didn't go out of her way to be all warm and friendly. Cassidy had to wonder what she'd have been like if she'd grown up in a time when being a lesbian was accepted. When she could have lived a full, genuine life with the person she loved, rather than hiding a big part of herself. Hmm. Was that why Sally was so reserved? Might she, too, be hiding a secret?

Dave rose. "Time to head home and get dinner on the go." He paused, then said, "What would you say to chicken fajitas?" For some reason, his voice sounded strained.

"Chicken fajitas?" Robin stopped in the act of drying one foot against the opposite leg of her jeans. She cocked her head toward Dave and said tentatively, "Those were Anita's favorite."

Cassidy stared at Dave as he said, "I know."

"Because they rhymed with her name."

"Yeah." He glanced at Cassidy. "You like fajitas?"

Oh yes, he had heard what she'd said last night. And he'd taken a step forward. She beamed at him. "Love them."

"Um," Robin started, "Anita always marinated the chicken first."

"I put some in marinade before I left."

They rode to town mostly in silence, and when they

talked the subject of Anita wasn't raised again. But later, when they were in the grocery store shopping for dinner ingredients, Dave asked Robin, "Do you remember which kind of tortillas Anita liked to use?"

Cassidy guessed he hadn't forgotten, but was making an opportunity to slip Anita's name into conversation, to test how he felt about it and to let Robin know it was okay to mention her.

"The corn ones," she said. "Flour ones for wraps, corn for fajitas."

"Right. Now I remember." His gaze lingered on his daughter, so tender it made Cassidy's heart give a big, mushy throb.

They purchased everything they needed, then carried on to the Wild Rose.

Inside the top-floor suite, boots and socks went by the door. This was Cassidy's first visit and she glanced around curiously. Most of the furniture was the same as in the inn's guest rooms, but this was obviously a home. The horse drawings on the wall—quite skilled ones—were clearly Robin's, like the couple in Dave's office downstairs. A copy of *Hotelier* magazine, a crocheted afghan tossed across a chair, a light clutter of books and DVDs all hinted at the father and daughter's life here.

She followed them into the kitchen. Robin fed Merlin and Dave went to light the barbecue on the rooftop patio. Cassidy took the groceries out of the bags.

When Dave came back, she asked tentatively, "Can I help with dinner?" She hoped he wouldn't think she was trying to take Anita's place.

The pain in his eyes made her touch his arm in a gesture of support.

"Do you know how to make guacamole?" he asked slowly.

Excuse me? She *was* half Mexican. Still, she said, "In a

general way, but if you or Robin tell me how Anita did it, then it'll be perfect."

Robin giggled. "Remember the time you got store-bought and Anita—" She quickly clamped her mouth shut.

Dave touched her shoulder. "Yeah, she believed in making it from scratch."

"Because we deserve the best," Robin said, obviously parroting Anita. "Even if we have to do the hard work to make it happen."

Dave gave Cassidy a chopping board, knife, and bowl. "Right. And speaking of hard work, did you have a busy morning at Boots, Rob?"

Cassidy figured that was a deliberate change of subject, but she gave him major points for the little exchange about Anita.

Dave set avocados, a lime, a garlic clove, and a chili pepper in front of her. That was it? That was all Anita put in guacamole? Oh well. She started peeling avocados.

Robin, busily grating cheddar, said, "It was turnover day, so I gave the horses an extra-special grooming, cleaned the tack, and spic-and-spanned the barn."

"You pull your weight around there," Cassidy commented.

The girl grinned. "I can't believe they pay me to do this stuff. I'd do it for free, just for the fun of it."

Dave, chopping tomatoes and cilantro, smiled. "No one says you can't have a job that you love doing, that still pays decently. Like your mom running Boots, Evan helping his clients do financial planning, Gramma Brooke cutting people's hair and making them feel good about themselves. And of course me running the Wild Rose." He tossed some of the chopped tomatoes and some of the cilantro into a bowl.

"I know. Cassidy, this is such a cool story. Dad fell in love with the inn when he was a kid and Grandma Sheila and Grandpa Ken took him and his brothers and sister there for ice cream sundaes."

"From ice cream sundaes to owning it?" Cassidy said as she mashed the peeled avocado and other ingredients together. "Impressive, Dave."

He shrugged. "The owner had trouble making a go of it and the Wild Rose got quite run-down. People started saying maybe the old girl should be torn down and a new hotel put up."

Cassidy winced. "That wouldn't have been right. Not for Caribou Crossing." She smiled at Dave as he added some of the tomatoes and cilantro to her guacamole.

"That's exactly what Dad thought," Robin said. "So he saved her. You tell her, Dad."

He was slicing purple onions and green peppers now, deft with the knife. "I was a teenager and the history of Caribou Crossing fascinated me. I even made that the theme of my valedictory speech at high school grad. I said that moving into the future should also mean respecting and preserving the past. I'm not sure that's what the other kids wanted to hear."

"It's a good theme," Robin defended him.

"It is," Cassidy agreed.

Dave diced a few of the onion slices and added them to the guacamole. "Anyhow, I wanted to preserve and restore the Wild Rose. I made that my mission." He gave Robin a quick smile. "Along with marrying Robin's mom and raising our little girl, of course. So I went to work at the poor old inn, doing whatever jobs needed to be done. Kind of like you, Cassidy, though I also fixed plumbing, mended leaks in the roof, flipped burgers. I fit in night school and correspondence courses on business administration and on running hotels. Read a ton of books. Jessie was great, never begrudging the time I spent." He gave a fond smile. "Bless her heart, she never once said I was chasing a foolish dream."

"It wasn't foolish, Dad!"

"Thanks, sweetheart. Anyhow, fortunately, the old owner didn't want to see the place torn down. And the bank knew my family and trusted us. My father cosigned a loan." He raised an arm and used the back of his wrist to push back the sandy hair that flopped over his forehead. "Cassidy, you know how, when I was talking about Jessie getting Boots off the ground, I said that it took a village?"

She nodded.

"Same with me and the Wild Rose. I had Jessie and Rob, my parents and hers, a friendly bank manager, an obliging inn owner, former classmates, and other townspeople who tossed in labor and supplies. City officials and a chamber of commerce who helped out with the heritage designation and the required permits. Turned out, the old Wild Rose had a lot of friends."

More likely, Dave Cousins did. The same as his ex-wife. Again Cassidy felt a twinge of envy. What would that be like? She had a ton of acquaintances all over the world, whom she kept up with via Facebook and e-mail, but her lifestyle precluded the kind of deep friendships where people pitched in to help you out.

"Okay," Dave said. "I'm going to grill the chicken. Cassidy, how about you sauté the onions and peppers? Rob, you put the salsa, guacamole, and cheese in bowls and set the table."

When he'd gone up to the roof and Cassidy was sautéing vegetables, she thought about him and his ex. He and Jess were both confident, resourceful people, yet they didn't mind accepting help. Unlike Cassidy, who felt the need to make her way in the world with complete independence. Oh, she'd happily eat Ms. H's pancakes and let Dave pay her first couple of weeks of salary in advance, but she always paid back in full measure. She mowed Ms. H's lawn and read to her when her eyes were too tired for her e-reader or the large-print books she borrowed from the library. She worked her butt off at the Wild Rose. In her head, there was a running tally so she could make sure not to be beholden to anyone. Not to rely on anyone.

In her life, Gramps had been the only person she could rely on—until he'd up and died.

A few minutes later, Dave came in with the cooked chicken, and sliced it up.

The competent way he wielded a knife was sexy. The way he moved, whether on horseback, strolling the streets, or fixing dinner, was sexy. They'd both avoided talking about last night, when she'd offered sex and he'd . . . Had he really turned her down, or just got upset when she started talking about Anita?

Today, she'd caught his gaze on her from time to time, and best as she could tell he was ambivalent. Attracted, but still worrying rather than going with the flow.

As Cassidy tipped the cooked onions and peppers into a serving bowl, Dave said, "Anita loved the Wild Rose too. We shared a love of history and historic buildings."

And there was the thing that worried him, that held him back. His memory of, loyalty to, love for a woman who died three years ago.

He handed the dish of sliced chicken to his daughter to put on the table. "Rob, remember how you came along a couple of times when we shopped for things to restore for the inn?"

The girl nodded. "And I was bored, and I wished I'd been riding instead, and I let you both know it. I wish I hadn't been whiny to Anita."

"Sweetheart, you were a little kid then. We should have known that browsing through old stuff would bore you." He paused. "Anita loved you. Even when you were whiny. She so looked forward to being your stepmom."

"Me too." Robin's eyes were damp. "I miss her."

"Yeah." He gathered her in for a rough hug, and his own eyes were squeezed shut.

Cassidy felt like an intruder, yet she was happy to have helped these two reach this point.

Dave opened his eyes, released his daughter, and said briskly, "Okay, let's eat."

Once they were seated, each stuffing tortillas with whatever combination of fillings appealed to them, the conversation turned to safer topics. Robin asked questions about Karen and Jamal's wedding, and she told stories about her mom's last group of students at Boots.

When they'd eaten all they could and started to clear up, Dave's cell rang. He checked the display, then answered. "Hey, Jessie."

He listened, then said, "Hang on a minute. I'll talk to Rob." He went over to his daughter, who was putting leftovers into containers. "Your mom and Gramma Brooke are checking about that babysitting offer you made."

"You don't mind if I have the babies here, do you, Dad?"

"Not at all." A note of sadness in his voice made Cassidy think that he and Anita had planned to have kids. Another thing he'd lost. "Cassidy, we invited you for the evening, maybe for a movie. How do you feel about having a couple of infants along for the ride?"

"I love babies." In fact, she loved people of all ages, as long as they were good-hearted.

"Or you and Cassidy could go line dancing," Robin suggested.

Cassidy immediately thought of their slow dance last night.

Dave glanced at Cassidy and heat sparked in his eyes.

"Maybe we will." His gaze locked with hers. And this time, for once, he didn't look away.

"I'd like that."

Back on the phone, he said, "Bring the babies along. We'll see you in a bit."

He studied Cassidy again. "Other Sunday nights, you've been working. Haven't had a chance to try out line dancing. You think you'd be up for it?" His tone was teasing, but a note of something else, something sexy and purely male, lurked below the surface. Was he talking only about line dancing, or asking whether she was still interested in hooking up?

She struck a pose, one hip cocked. "I'll have you know, I've line danced in Austin, Texas. Jimmy B and Bets can't toss me anything I can't handle." Nor could Dave, sexually, and the prospect of "handling" him made her breath quicken.

He gave an appreciative grin, which faded to a look of concern. "How about your leg?"

"It feels fine." She'd be furious with her stupid leg if it ruined another special moment.

"You really should see a doctor."

"It's just a pinched nerve or something. I strained it and it's never quite healed."

"If it's a pinched nerve, it might do some permanent damage."

A few minutes ago, he'd looked at her as if he thought she was sexy. Now he was lecturing her. Bummer. "Dave, I'm not your daughter." She tried to keep her voice even, but a touch of snippiness crept in. "I'm a grown-up and I can look after myself."

"Well, pardon me for—"

He broke off, but she knew he'd been about to say "caring." She also knew that he didn't mean anything more by it than if he'd been nagging Madisun or Sam about something.

"Doctors are okay," Robin said. "They fix you up, and then you're on the go again."

"I'll think about it." They had valid points. If it was a pinched nerve, maybe the doctor could send her for physio or whatever.

But what if it wasn't? she wondered as she rinsed dishes and handed them to Robin to put in the dishwasher. Gramps's mother-in-law had had multiple sclerosis. GG had deteriorated until she couldn't talk properly, couldn't walk, and was incontinent. Cassidy, a little kid at the time, had almost been glad when she died and there were no more visits to the care home. When Cassidy was a teen, Gramps had told her to watch out for symptoms because it was one of those diseases where there could be a genetic predisposition.

She'd argued that no one else in the family had it, and he'd said it was possible his wife did, and that she'd died before being diagnosed. She had been only twenty-eight— a year older than Cassidy was now—when she'd fallen down the basement steps and broken her neck. What had caused her to fall? Had her leg tingled, gone numb, and given out on her?

No. Cassidy refused to consider that possibility. No way was she going to lose her mobility, her freedom, her independence.

Chapter Eleven

Cassidy's expressive face told Dave that she was troubled. But she'd made it clear she wanted him to butt out. He couldn't help but worry about that leg thing, but he wouldn't push anymore tonight. He only hoped his and Robin's words sank into Cassidy's brain the way her advice last night had with him, about letting his daughter talk about Anita.

The kitchen tidy now, Robin turned the dishwasher on. She said to Cassidy, "Want to watch an episode of *Heartland*?"

"What's *Heartland*?"

"You'll love it! It's a TV show set in Alberta, about this family who have a ranch and lots of horses, and they've also got guest cabins."

"Sounds cool." Cassidy's interest seemed genuine.

"Totally," Robin said eagerly. "And they take in kids who are, you know, in trouble. But the coolest part is the star, Amy, who's, like, a horse whisperer."

"Wow."

"Did you know that Mom knows a horse whisperer? He heals rescue horses and Mom uses some of them at Boots. He and his wife live down near Vancouver and they said I could come stay with them and learn from him. But"—she frowned at Dave—"Dad said I can't until I'm eighteen. Which is, like, forever."

"Hmm." Cassidy tilted her head consideringly. "But if you stayed with them, you couldn't help out at Boots. What would your mom do without you?"

Huh. Dave would've expected her, with her "new day, new adventure" attitude, to support his daughter. He mouthed a silent "Thanks" over the top of Robin's head, which Cassidy acknowledged with a slight dip of her head.

"Well yeah, that's true," Robin said thoughtfully.

"C'mon, let's go watch *Heartland*," Cassidy said. "It's on TV tonight?"

"No, I have DVDs. Dad gives me each season's for my birthday, because I want to watch them over and over."

"Seems like you have a pretty good dad," Cassidy said. "Even if he does have some pesky notions like not wanting you to get hurt or to grow up too fast. You should be glad he's paying attention." There was an edge to her voice when she made the last comment.

He gathered that her parents had been so caught up in their marital dramas that they hadn't paid enough attention to Cassidy and her brother. She spoke very fondly of her grandfather, but she'd lost him when she was fifteen. She always seemed so self-sufficient and poised. Happy to sample bits of life here and there and then move on. Was it her lack of stable, loving roots that had turned her into an independent gypsy?

When he'd first met her, he'd thought she might be superficial, but no, she was responsible and perceptive. She'd helped him recognize that it wasn't healthy for him or Robin to not talk about Anita. Yes, his throat hurt when he spoke Anita's name, and dredging up memories brought an ache to his heart. But hugging Robin while they shared their grief had felt good.

Cassidy paid attention to others. But who was paying

attention to her? Did she settle in one place long enough to give anyone that chance?

She and Robin had headed into the living room, with Merlin on their heels. Dave followed, finding Cassidy seated on the couch, her bare feet resting on a magazine on the coffee table. Robin sorted through DVDs and Merlin was settling in his usual spot on the rug.

Dave took the recliner chair. When he glanced at Cassidy, her clear gaze met his. She cocked an eyebrow in a silent question.

He wasn't sure what she was asking, nor was he sure what he intended to say when he smiled at her, except that he was glad she was there.

She smiled back, and neither of them looked away. It was weird how natural this felt. Having dinner together, cleaning up, settling in to watch a show with Robin.

"Okay," Robin said. "Cassidy, this is from season one, and it's the episode where Amy gets this race horse that needs healing. It's a really good one." She clicked the remote, then hunkered down by Merlin.

As she watched the show, Robin combed grass seeds and burrs from the dog's coat and silky ears. Cassidy seemed to quickly be caught up in the adventures at *Heartland*.

Dave did enjoy the show, for the scenery, the horses, and the family drama—which made his own rather unusual family seem almost normal—but tonight he had trouble concentrating. It wasn't because he'd already seen this episode. It was Cassidy's presence.

What was this woman to him? A friend, yes. Did he want more? A sexual relationship?

In three years, she was the only woman he'd felt this way about. She wasn't like some of the women who'd come on to him. Her sexiness wasn't about abundant breasts and hips in a tight shirt and painted-on jeans. It wasn't about made-up eyes and red lips. No, it was in her animated face and pixie haircut, the gentle sway of slim hips in nondesigner jeans, the row of snap buttons down the front of her thrift store shirt. And there was more to her appeal than sexiness: her musical burble of laughter, her easy way with Robin, her persistence in trying to drag him out of the past.

Her itchy feet made her safe. She didn't want things he couldn't offer: commitment, love, a future. For her, those things were undesirable.

For him, they'd once been the most important things in the world. He'd lost them, and that agony was something he never wanted to—never would—face again.

As he'd told Cassidy, he'd never been into casual dating and sex. But he was feeling pretty darned motivated to try it out.

Oh yeah, Dave thought a couple of hours later, Cassidy sure did know how to line dance. She followed even the most complicated movements, and looked as if she wasn't even trying.

Watching her, Dave, who'd been line dancing since he was a kid, found himself stumbling in his cowboy boots. He didn't know whether to be glad or sorry when Jimmy B and Bets called a break.

A couple of women headed for the jukebox to cue up some tunes. Keith Morton, a young cowboy who was popular with the ladies, came toward Cassidy, his intent clear on his face.

An unfamiliar sensation stabbed Dave. He moved fast, touched Cassidy's shoulder, and identified that burning in his gut as jealousy. His grip tightened and Keith veered off toward one of the other women. "Dance with me," Dave said to Cassidy.

She glanced at his hand. "Only if your dance hold won't bruise my shoulder."

"Sorry. Let me try that again." He let go and held out his arms in an invitation.

"Much better." She slid one hand into his and rested the other lightly against his shoulder.

"Know the two-step?" he asked.

"You bet."

He wrapped his arm around her back and, as Shania Twain sang "Any Man of Mine," he led her into the quick-quick, slow-slow motion of the dance. She did know the moves, following him easily. Though she felt delicious, all warm and vital, he couldn't relax. He spun her out and brought her back. "Keith is interested in you."

A knowing smile flickered. "Uh-huh."

"Are you interested in him?"

"Not in the dating sense. I've hung out with Keith. A few other guys too."

Last night, when she'd said she was trying to seduce him, he'd figured she must not be dating anyone else, but he needed to make sure. "Just hung out with?"

"Drank some beer, shot some pool. No, I'm not dating anyone."

"Why not?"

"You're the only man I'm interested in. In that way." Her hips shifted forward, brushing his, leaving no doubt what "that way" meant.

His body reacted immediately. Though he wanted to grab her and pull her tighter, he forced himself to ease away. Two-step wasn't a clutch-and-sway dance. "Jeez, Cassidy, let's not give Caribou Crossing something to gossip about."

"Then you shouldn't have raised the subject here."

He gave a rueful huff. "I can't argue with that. But I had to know. The way Keith was eyeing you . . ." He spun her out.

When she returned, she said, "You grabbed my shoulder like you were staking a claim."

"Life was straightforward before you came to town," he complained.

"But not half as much fun."

She said it so confidently that he had to grin.

"Okay," she said, "one of the things that worries you is that I work for you. You don't want anyone thinking you're being unprofessional. Right?"

He nodded, leading her into a promenade.

Gazing sideways at him, she said, "So, while it's been nice of you to dance with one of your staff, we should both now dance with someone else."

He didn't want to. "You're right."

"The next time we both have some free time—personal time, not on the job—we'll get together and"—she winked—"*talk* about where we want to go with this. Or better still, not talk at all. Because, you know, actions speak louder." And with that, she whirled herself out of his arms, leaving him gaping after her.

Wednesday night, pacing his suite while Merlin watched curiously, Dave was nervous as hell. After three nights with him, Robin had gone back to her mom and Evan's house. And Cassidy was coming over.

She'd turned down his offer to take her out for dinner—in a neighboring town, so the gossips wouldn't go nuts. Instead, she said she'd drop over after dinner and bring a movie.

It sounded low key, no pressure, except that he'd be alone with her in his apartment, with the bedroom just down the hall. Casual dating didn't necessarily mean casual sex. But it might. She'd made it clear she was open to it. He'd even taken a drive to the next town down the highway and bought condoms. Just in case.

He shoved his hands in the pockets of his tan shorts. He

had no idea how he ranked as a lover. Since high school, he'd slept with only two women. Cassidy, though . . . How many men had she slept with? A dozen? More?

When her light knock finally sounded, he flung open the door with a mix of pleasure and trepidation. Merlin bounded over to join him.

"Hey there, beautiful boy." She was talking to the dog, bending to greet him.

This wasn't some femme fatale in a revealing dress, just Cassidy in a purple tank top and shorts. But that was plenty sexy. Toned arms and legs, the wild goose tattoo, slim curves, pink straps along with the purple ones. Lots of women layered their tops. If she'd gone braless and he'd seen her nipples, that would be blatantly sexy. Why was it a turn-on to see those pink straps and wonder whether they belonged to another tank top, a sports bra, or something lacy?

Straightening, she said, "And hello to you, too, handsome man." She stretched up to press a kiss to his cheek. It was a quick, light one, but tingly heat radiated out from the spot, all the way to his groin.

She held up a cloth tote. "I brought wine, popcorn, and a movie."

"What movie?" Her movie choice might give him a clue as to her expectations.

"Dirty Dancing." She pulled a DVD case from the bag and handed it to him. "Tell me you don't hate it."

The name rang a vague bell. "I don't think I've ever seen it."

"Seriously?" She cocked her head. "I know you were a baby when it came out, but it's a classic. I can't believe no woman got you to watch it."

"Jessie doesn't like movies unless they have horses in them. Anita was into foreign films." It was getting easier to say her name, to share memories. Some of the memories even made him smile, like now when he added, "She needed glasses to read the subtitles, and that bugged her."

Cassidy smiled back. "I hope you like it. I'm going to make the popcorn." She headed for the kitchen with the poodle trailing after her.

"Be right there." Dave slipped the disc into the DVD player and strolled into the kitchen.

Cassidy had already opened the wine—a pinot gris from Grey Monk—and poured two glasses. She handed him one. "To getting to know each other better."

He touched his glass to hers, then took a sip. The chilled wine was crisp and fruity. "Thanks for bringing this. You didn't have to. I mean, I have wine, and popcorn as well, and—"

Cassidy pressed her index finger firmly against his lips, silencing him. "You've taken me riding, fed me dinner, let me freeload off your parents. I wanted to do this."

She lifted her finger and he missed its warm, gentle pressure.

"You didn't have—"

The finger silenced him again. "Just say thank you."

Actually, he'd rather suck that finger into his mouth and nibble on it. And maybe, later tonight, he would. For now, he didn't stop her from easing her finger away. "Thank you, Cassidy. I appreciate it."

"You're welcome. Now give me a microwave lesson."

He did, then found a bowl for the popcorn and filled a ceramic wine cooler with ice.

As popping sounds filled the room, she said, "I bought plain popcorn because I wasn't sure how you felt about butter and salt."

"I like them, but I'm good with plain too."

"God no. If butter and salt are an option, I'm so there."

Her enthusiasm made him smile again.

The microwave pinged. Cassidy took the popcorn container out and poured the contents into a bowl, while he melted butter in the microwave. He scooped a few kernels of plain popped corn into the dog's dish and let Cassidy doctor the humans' treat.

On the way out of the kitchen, he told Merlin, "Stay in the kitchen, pal." The poodle was well behaved, used to being banished occasionally when Dave had company. He curled up in the basket by the kitchen window, rested his head on his front paws, and sent Dave a soulful look.

Dave closed the door gently and joined Cassidy on the couch. He sat close, but not too close, and took a sip of wine as she clicked PLAY.

Dancing couples filled the screen—in black and white, and slow-mo. The sexy, suggestive dancing matched the title of the movie. Oh man, if Cassidy's movie choice was a clue to her expectations for the evening, he was in for a steamy one.

Chapter Twelve

Cassidy sighed with pleasure. Wine and popcorn. One of her all-time favorite movies. A handsome man beside her—one with sexy bare legs below his shorts, a man she might very well have sex with tonight. What a perfect way to spend an evening.

It was her mom who'd introduced her to this movie, when Cassidy was thirteen and her parents were married for the second time. Justine loved to dance. Gramps had given her all sorts of dance lessons. He said that if she'd applied herself, she might have been able to dance professionally. But discipline had never been Justine's forte, and her doting dad hadn't pushed her. He'd known dance was a hard life and had wanted only for her to be happy.

He'd felt the same about Cassidy and her brother. But as much as he'd tried, by giving them gifts and taking them on outings, a grandfather's attention couldn't make up for their parents' frequent inattention. That was why things like movie night with Justine had been so special. When dance scenes came on in any movie and Luis wasn't home, she'd get Cassidy and JJ up to dance with her. Of course when Luis was home, it was the two of them. Sexy, teasing, smoking hot. Her parents knew all there was to know about dirty dancing.

She glanced at Dave. The movie seemed to have caught his attention. She hoped he enjoyed it, and yeah, she also hoped the sexy parts gave him some ideas. But really, what she wanted tonight was for the two of them to relax alone together—away from work, his family, and the good-hearted but nosy residents of Caribou Crossing. Just a quiet time to be two adults enjoying some R&R. If that R&R didn't turn X-rated tonight, there'd be other chances. He couldn't keep resisting the attraction between them.

For her, the simple fact of his presence beside her was enough to put her body on alert, each cell aware and craving his touch. She sure hoped it was the same for him.

She plunked the popcorn bowl on the couch between them, where their fingers would brush if they dipped in at the same time. Then she raised her bare feet to the coffee table and settled back.

When the movie's heroine, Baby, first saw the staff dancing, some of the moves like sex with clothes on, Cassidy asked, "Do you like the dirty dancing?"

"Very hot."

Other than making an occasional comment, she and Dave watched quietly, sipping wine, nibbling popcorn, and yes, brushing fingers occasionally. The popcorn was finished by the time Johnny Castle was teaching Baby how to dance so she could fill in for his usual partner. Cassidy moved the empty bowl to the coffee table. When she settled back into the couch, she shifted closer to Dave so their shoulders bumped.

After a few minutes, Dave's arm came around her shoulders. She nestled closer, enjoying the firm, warm feel of him, and slid her foot against his on the coffee table, let her bare knee brush his. Ramping up the level of awareness in her body and, she hoped, in his.

"This is nice," he murmured, his fingers gently caressing her shoulder, where her wild goose flew with the moon on her wing.

Keeping it low key, Cassidy didn't do much more than occasionally shift position so her hand, knee, or foot brushed against his bare skin. The movie seemed to engage him, which for her meant a lot of points to Dave. A chick flick with substance, and he could relate to it. Being a father probably helped, since part of the story involved a father and daughter.

When the movie ended, she shifted inside the curve of his arm so she could look at him. "What did you think?"

"Good movie. Interesting characters and story, and a good message."

"If Robin was Baby, what would you think?"

"She'd be grounded for life. For disobeying me, for having sex before the age of thirty. But I'd be proud as hell of her."

"I figured you'd say that."

"She's a lot like Baby. She'll help any kid or animal that's in trouble. She gets that from her mom."

"And her dad."

A startled expression flicked across his face. Didn't he realize what a role model he was for his daughter? After a moment, he said, "Uh, thanks."

Wanting to create a more intimate, sensual mood, she trailed her fingers up his arm. "You liked the dancing?"

"Uh, yeah. I've sure never danced like that."

Excellent! She could give him a first. Rising, she held out her hands. "Let's give it a try."

"You want to launch yourself into the air and hope I catch you?" he asked, referring to the famous lift scene. His hazel eyes twinkled.

"Ha ha." She took his hands and tugged.

He cooperated and rose, maneuvering around the coffee

table to stand in front of her. "I don't have any sixties music like in the movie."

Wishing that she'd thought to look for music at the library when she'd picked up the movie, she did a quick check of his collection. Country music tended to be sad, about lost love, so she avoided it. Rock didn't suit the mood. Hoping she wasn't picking one of Anita's favorite albums, she chose a Diana Krall collection of light jazz.

When the song "'S Wonderful" came on, Dave's eyebrows rose but he didn't protest.

She stepped from the large blue and tan area rug onto the hardwood. "Let's not start out too ambitious. How about a clutch-and-shuffle to warm up?" She slung her arms around his neck and leaned in, resting her hips lightly against his. Oh yes, that felt good.

His arms came around to circle her back, and that felt good too. Slowly, he began to move. His athletic body had a natural rhythm. His feet caught the beat and she let him lead, keeping the contact between them minimal. Letting their bodies get used to each other; letting anticipation build. Hers certainly was, as she moved gently against the graceful strength of his muscular body.

Her fingers brushed the skin of his neck above the collar of his short-sleeved shirt, toyed with the ends of his sandy hair. Mmm, everything about Dave felt good.

His hands slid down her back until they rested at her waist, above the curve of her butt.

She rested her cheek against his shoulder. Through cotton, she savored his heat, the firmness of his muscles. Arousal quivered through her and she felt the press of his growing erection.

"You feel good," he murmured. "I like this."

"Me too." Figuring they were both ready to kick things up a notch, she said, "You know the secret to dirty dancing?"

"Haven't a clue."

"It's in the hips. You have to feel the music, the pulse, the heat, all of it in your hips." She slid her hips forward to press more firmly against him, swiveling them back and forth slowly, relentlessly.

He pumped his hips gently. He was hard now, behind his fly. As she continued to tease her pelvis back and forth, each brush against his erection fueled her own arousal. He was holding back, though, clearly not entirely into the vibe of dirty dancing.

She leaned back in the circle of his arms and gazed up at him, noting the flush of color on his cheekbones. "Relax and let go," she urged softly. "Feel the rhythm, our rhythm."

"Do you know how hot you are?" His voice rasped.

"Show me."

He lowered his hands to cup her butt, then thrust harder into her. His movements weren't fast and demanding; they were slow and sultry, like the music.

She kissed him through his shirt, then unbuttoned three buttons and pressed her lips against his bare skin. He smelled fresh, a little woodsy, a touch like soap. He'd showered before she came over, as she had. Delicately, she trailed her tongue across his skin to the hollow at the base of his neck, where his pulse throbbed quickly.

His hands caressed her butt cheeks and their hips gyrated in a sexy rhythm.

She hooked her hands behind his neck again, went up on her toes, and found that he was gazing into her eyes, his own hazel ones burning golden. "Cassidy," he murmured.

"Yes?" she whispered. "What?"

"This." And then he kissed her. Saturday night, his kiss had been hard and needy. This time, he went slower, as if he knew they had plenty of time. As if he wanted to explore her mouth, to learn every detail, to make this kiss last forever. His firm lips, teasing tongue, sweet breath, the slightest hint of salt from the popcorn were bliss.

She ran a hand up the side of his neck and into his hair, twining the springy strands around her fingers, messing it up. With a final lick across his lips, she broke the kiss, let go of his head, and leaned back.

Automatically, one of his arms came around her waist, helping her balance as she arched farther back, thrusting her breasts out, gyrating her hips against him.

"Oh, man," he groaned.

She wanted to groan too, from the sweet pressure that, even through their shorts and underwear, had her pussy damp and pulsing with need. Lifting her upper body slightly, she undid the rest of his shirt buttons. His shirt hung open, baring a swathe of muscled torso, a scattering of hair on his chest, a trail of darker hair arrowing down to his waistband. Delicious. She wanted to touch, to taste every inch of him. Wanted to feel him do the same to her.

Everything she'd seen Dave do, from riding to cooking to managing the inn, he'd been super competent at. He was also a perceptive, considerate man. She'd bet that lovemaking was one of his special talents.

Still relying on his support, keeping the hip motion going, she worked the tank top over her head, leaving her bra on. When she tossed the tank aside, his gaze was glued to her breasts, clad in pink trimmed with lace. Her nipples were hard, poking at the satiny fabric.

She trailed her fingers down his torso. When she traced the waistband of his shorts, grazing his flesh, he groaned. Taking that as permission, she undid the button, unzipped the fly, then took a step backward, separating their bodies so she could pull his shorts down. As she did, he impatiently shrugged off his shirt and it hit the floor too. Leaving him naked but for seriously tented blue cotton boxers. And wasn't he a sight for sore eyes, and a needy pussy.

Quickly, she slipped out of her own shorts, which left her in a lust-dampened thong that matched her bra. It was one of the few times she wished she had long hair, because she'd have given it a sultry toss over her shoulder. The gesture would probably have been lost on him anyhow, since his gaze was focused well below her neck.

"So pretty," he muttered.

"You too." She moved close again and straddled his naked thigh, letting him know how wet he made her.

He pumped, his boxer-draped erection brushing her thigh.

She shifted back to stand between his legs, pressing her pelvis close against his while she ran her hands up his chest. Vaguely, she was aware of Diana Krall singing "All or Nothing at All." The singer was referring to wanting love, but what Cassidy wanted was all of this sexy man's body. She twined one leg around him, as high on his hip as she could reach, trying to bring their most intimate parts into contact.

Dave surprised her then, reaching under her thighs and lifting her off the ground.

Automatically, her other leg wrapped around him too as he held her exactly where she wanted to be, with his thick, rigid shaft rubbing the crotch of her panties. She gripped his upper arms, steadying herself.

His head was thrown back, his eyelids at half mast as he concentrated. His hips thrust in raunchy, sex-mimicking motions, each stroke sliding firmly back and forth, pressing damp silk against her swollen labia and clit.

She whimpered, the sweet tense ache of arousal building, climbing with each thrust. There was absolutely no reason to hold back, so she didn't. She ground against him, rode him, let him take her exactly where she wanted to go— and climaxed with a cry of pleasure.

Lost in sensation, she had squeezed her eyes shut. When she dragged them open, breathing hard, she gazed up into his face.

His expression was pleased, but almost disbelieving. "You can come like that?"

She gave a satisfied purr. "You give great dirty dancing."

It was time to move the action off the dance floor. She was afraid that if they went into the bedroom memories would surface for him and spoil things. Instead, she tapped his chest to get him to release her, and then she let her feet drop to the floor. Quickly, she shed her bra and thong and, while he was gaping, she dragged off his boxers as well.

His dick sprang free, thick and bold and beautiful, the tip damp with pre-come.

Her greedy fingers reached for it.

When she touched him, he jerked, thrust convulsively, then pulled away. "I'm too close."

"You're nowhere near close enough." She bent to reach in her shorts pocket and pull out the condom she'd stashed there. After opening the package, she asked, "May I?"

Humor twitched the corners of his mouth. "Extremely carefully."

She obeyed, not wanting him to come until he was inside her. And, from the looks of him, that had better happen sooner rather than later. Fortunately, she was as primed as he.

The area rug was made of braided cotton, soft underfoot. It would be soft under their bodies too. She knelt on it and pulled him down to kneel in front of her. Then she reached up to tangle both hands in his hair again, and she kissed him.

He responded hungrily, and in a moment he'd taken charge, urging her down on her back.

Still kissing, she bent her legs, opening them in clear invitation.

"Oh God," he muttered against her lips, his cheeks flaming with hectic color. "I want to touch you, kiss your breasts, but I want you so bad, Cassidy."

"I want you too. Inside me," she said. And then, in case she'd left any doubt in his mind, she said, "Now."

He made a growly sound of relief and desperate need, and then he stroked between her legs. One finger slid into her and she gave a welcoming moan; then another finger joined the first.

"Now, Dave."

Then he was between her legs, his erection probing hungrily, and in a quick surge he entered her.

She gasped with pleasure as her body adjusted to his size. He felt so amazingly good, rubbing against her sensitized flesh. She wrapped her legs around his waist, opening herself wider, urging him on as he thrust deep, fast, almost desperately, over and over.

Arousal peaked inside her, crested. She gripped his taut butt, dug her fingers in, and he gave a wrenching groan. He jerked into her deep and hard, and she surrendered, letting his orgasm ignite hers.

They gripped each other fiercely as tremors wracked their bodies, then finally stilled to ripples. Eventually, she unhooked her rubbery legs and let them drop to the rug.

Dave, chest heaving and arms trembling, levered himself off of her and collapsed on the rug beside her. "Man," he gasped. "Wow."

She rolled onto her side so she could look at him. Should she ask? But it was crazy to pretend that there wasn't a ghost in the room. After he'd dealt with the condom, she said, "Are you okay?"

"Jesus. Wow." He turned his head to gaze at her. "It's been a while. And yeah, I'm . . . good." His voice was tentative, like he was checking in with his body, mind, heart to verify the truth of his words. He pressed his lips together, and then, to her surprise, he rose.

Damn. Was he going to call it a night? Send her away?

But again he surprised her. Pleasantly. "Let's lie down where it's more comfortable." He held out his hand.

After he pulled her gently to her feet, he rested his hands on her shoulders and touched his forehead to hers. "Thank you, Cassidy. Now let's go to bed. We need to talk."

Wasn't it the woman who usually insisted on talking? Still, if issues over his deceased fiancée were a problem, she wanted to know. So she gazed into his eyes and said, "Sure."

The album had ended at some point and Dave didn't bother turning off the player. But, as they passed the closed kitchen door, he said, "Damn, I need to let Merlin out."

"The responsibilities of pet ownerhood," she teased. "Go ahead. I'll tidy up."

"Way to spoil the mood," he grumbled.

"If it helps, I didn't plan to put on my clothes. If you hurry with Merlin, you can watch me wash dishes naked."

"Incentive indeed." His smile was affectionate, yet a shadow lurked in his hazel eyes.

Chapter Thirteen

Dave shoved his hands in his shorts pockets as he stood at the hotel's back door, waiting for Merlin to water a telephone pole. How prosaic, almost ridiculous, when fifteen minutes ago Dave had been deep inside Cassidy. Yet maybe he needed these few minutes to reflect. If he could make his brain function.

He'd had sex for the first time in well over three years, and it had been amazing. Not just for the spectacular orgasm, but because he'd been with Cassidy. Lighthearted, generous, sexy Cassidy. This was good, great, and yet—what was he doing? No, what were *they* doing? Was this really going to work out okay?

Merlin came running back, and Dave took him upstairs. They'd obviously lingered too long, because the kitchen was empty and the lights were off. He got the poodle settled again and walked out of the kitchen to hear water running from the hallway bathroom. It stopped, the door opened, and Cassidy stepped out, stark naked.

Earlier, he'd been too aroused and hurried to truly take her in. Now he stared, admiring her as his body tightened. She was slim, yet her curves were purely female. So was the delicate vee of pubic hair, the same shiny black as the pixie cap of hair on her head. Her natural skin color was olive-brown, her nipples a dusky brownish pink. That tattoo of the wild goose and the moon was subtle and sexy. She was sleek, fine, slightly exotic. Beautiful.

"Come lie down with me," he said, taking her hand and leading her into the bedroom.

Three years ago, he had refurnished this room, removing all signs of Anita. Cassidy was the first woman, aside from the housekeeper, to cross the threshold, and he felt surprisingly fine with having her here.

When he flicked the switch that turned on a bedside lamp, she said, "You have a four-poster bed. Cool."

"It came from one of the guest rooms. A party got a little wild and one of the columns and the top canopy cracked. We took the canopy off and glued the column back together." He liked it this way, with the simple dark wood columns and light tan bedding, rather than the fancier, flouncier version they had in the guest rooms.

"No chamber pot?" she teased.

"En suite through that door." He gestured. "All the modern conveniences."

Cassidy seemed completely at ease with her nakedness, but it disconcerted Dave—rather, it aroused him. He'd told her they needed to talk, and they did. Before they had sex again. Which meant he had to get her covered up. He tugged the duvet down. "Climb in."

When she did, he tugged off his shorts and shirt and slid in the other side of the bed.

"You sure you want to *talk*?" Her teasing tone let him know that she'd seen his erection. She slid over to curl against him, her hand resting on his chest, one warm leg draping over his thigh. High on his thigh, only inches from where he craved her touch.

He forced himself to say, "I'm sure." He put his arm

around her shoulders. How good this felt, to have Cassidy's slight body nestling close. It was a different kind of intimacy from sex; in fact, it was almost more intimate.

Dave swallowed a lump in his throat. "This is nice." He wanted to be honest with her, but would she be hurt if he mentioned Anita? Still, she was the one who'd told him that not talking about Anita was unhealthy. So he swallowed and admitted, "I never thought I'd do this again. Cuddle up with a woman. But it's confusing."

"Because of Anita." Her tone was gentle and accepting, thank God.

"Yes."

"Do you feel like you're being disloyal to her?"

Trust Cassidy to cut to the chase. He examined his heart. "No, not disloyal. Mostly I just feel . . . strange. Since high school, I've been with only two women. Being with someone else is different." Quickly he added, "Nice, really nice. I mean, it was great."

"It's okay, I know that. I was there too."

No one had ever teased him the way Cassidy did. "Believe me, I noticed."

"And I noticed that you have a pretty good recollection of how to fit tab A into slot B." The leg that lay across his body moved upward to brush the base of his shaft.

"You're wicked." He shifted away, afraid of getting so turned on he'd lose his train of thought.

"Is that a problem?"

"Not hardly. I've just never known a woman who, you know, kept things so light."

She lifted her head from his chest, propped herself up on one elbow, and gazed into his eyes. "D'you think I'm superficial?"

He shook his head and caressed her tattooed shoulder, trying to ignore the sweet press of her breast against his side. "No. You're responsible, and you're generous and perceptive."

She ran her finger down the straight line of his nose. "You're pretty perceptive yourself, Mr. Cousins. At least about other people."

"A backhanded compliment if I ever heard one."

"I think it hurts you to look too deeply inside yourself, so you avoid doing it. And while it's great that you're so concerned about others, maybe fixing their problems helps you avoid facing your own issues."

He might have been offended if he hadn't seen the warmth and concern in her eyes. "That's an interesting notion," he admitted. "Like, maybe with you, all the gypsy stuff might be a way of avoiding facing your issues." Such as how her parents had never given her a stable home, or made her feel like she came first.

"Ouch." Her eyes widened and she sat up, the covers sliding free of her torso.

Gaping at her beautiful nakedness, he tried to be articulate. "I'm sorry. I didn't say that to criticize. I thought it was okay to talk about this kind of stuff. I mean, you started it."

"I did," she said slowly. "But really, I don't have issues." Absentmindedly she tugged the duvet up and secured it under her arms so it covered her chest, which was a pity but at least it helped his concentration.

"I admit," she went on, "that my parents set a crappy example. My brother tried out marriage and it lasted for all of, oh, a nanosecond. But my family's not unusual. Divorce stats are high and I bet there are more unhappy marriages than there are divorces."

"But look at—"

"Your parents," she finished. "I know."

Lying on his side, propped up on one elbow, he watched her face. "Jessie's parents too. Miriam told me that she and Wade went through some tough times in their twenties, but their relationship is rock solid. And look at Jimmy B and Bets—they've been happily married for sixty years." The spry octogenarians led the Sunday night line dancing.

"You're quoting individual cases. Of course some marriages work. But the odds are against it." She pressed her lips together. "Maybe I shouldn't mention this, but you're divorced."

He sighed. "Yeah. Okay, I give you that." But he and Anita would have made it, if they'd had the chance. They had truly belonged together.

Cassidy read his mind. Gently she said, "I'm not saying you and Anita wouldn't have made it. But, Dave, it didn't happen. Not because one of you fell out of love or found someone else, but it ended all the same. And it broke your heart."

He frowned, puzzling over the truth of that. "Am I crazy or are you actually starting to make sense?"

"Gee, thanks for that." She lay down again, on her side so that they faced each other. "But you see what I mean? If you were like me and never got involved, you wouldn't have had your heart broken. And that's how you feel now, right? That you'll never fall in love again."

"I won't." He said it with certainty. Then he shook his head. "This is a really strange conversation to be having like this. Naked together in bed." He was still semierect, but the seriousness of the conversation had taken the edge off his lust.

"No, it's not. Nakedness, sex, they help people open up and share."

"I guess that's true." He wondered how many guys she'd been with like this, naked after sex talking about personal issues. The thought gave him a twinge of jealousy, which was stupid.

"So," she said, "are we good?"

He reached for her hand and their fingers wove together,

resting on the bed between their bodies. "I need to know what we're doing. And I guess it's, uh, casual dating? Friendship and sex for as long as it works for both of us?" Never before had he thought in terms like that.

She nodded firmly. "Friends with benefits."

"This is what you do. Wherever you go." There was that silly twinge again.

She frowned. "I don't find a lover every place I go, if that's what you mean. Sometimes I make male friends, and occasionally one of them becomes a lover because there's just, I don't know, something special about him. Something special between us."

That didn't make him feel any less jealous. "So why me?"

"You intrigue me, Dave. You're sexy, smart, and you're a good guy."

His ego—and his erection—swelled.

She went on. "A good boss, a good dad, a good friend. You respect women, you have women friends. And you were kind of going to waste."

"Going to waste?"

"You seemed so sad and lonely."

He winced. That definitely wasn't sexy. "That's how I come across?"

"You try to bury it. You figure by keeping busy and smiling, people will think you're happy. But you're not the best actor in the world. I heard about it from lots of people. How when Anita died, you lost your vitality, your spark."

"So you made it your mission to save me?" His voice had an edge to it. She'd started out saying she found him sexy and now it was more like she thought he was pathetic.

She squeezed his hand. "You are the most attractive, intriguing guy in Caribou Crossing. I want you, and I want to give you something that no one else has been able to."

That was a little better. "And what, exactly, is that? Sex?"

"Yeah, and a bit of freedom from the past. Just because

you loved one woman all to pieces, that doesn't mean you have to be miserable for the rest of your life. Maybe you'll fall in love again, and if you do, then I hope it works out like it did for your parents."

He shook his head. "Even if I could fall in love again, I don't want to." And how weird this felt, to be lying naked in bed with a woman he'd had sex with talking about not falling in love. Any other woman probably would've been hurt or insulted. Cassidy really was amazing.

Her clear blue-gray eyes showed only concern for him. "I'm not saying you should. You could be like me and enjoy life one day, one person at a time. Have fun. Get back your spark."

"Have fun," he echoed.

She released his hand and tapped his chest with two fingers. "Don't sound so skeptical. It's not a sin to have fun. Give yourself permission to be happy. Let that dimple out to play."

Before Anita's diagnosis, she'd told him she loved his dimple. After, she'd said that she missed it. No matter how hard he'd tried, no matter how many smiles he'd managed to give her, he could never get that dimple to show.

He studied Cassidy, who was completely unlike any other woman he'd ever known. "This is feeling one-sided, like it's all about what you can give me. That's not how a relationship should work. I like you, Cassidy. I care about you. What do you need, that I can give you?"

Her eyes widened. He saw surprise, maybe a hint of vulnerability. It was almost as if no one had asked her that before. Her dark lashes swept down, paused, then swept back up. That vulnerable expression was still there. "Just be you, Dave," she said softly. "That's what I want."

She cleared her throat, and when she spoke again her voice held a teasing edge and the sparkle had returned to her eyes. "Talk is good, but there's a time to stop talking. How about you stop worrying about things and relax and enjoy the moment?"

That seemed to be her philosophy of life. Maybe it was a way of avoiding her own issues and maybe not.

Her hand slid down his chest, her fingers tweaking his nipple on the way, trailing over his rib cage.

Issues? Who cared about issues? His groin tightened in awareness and anticipation. By the time her fingers dipped below his waist, an erection was rising to meet them. When those fingers curled around him, he sighed with pleasure. "You've convinced me."

The first time they'd had sex, his body had been on overload. This time he was determined to slow down, to appreciate her lovely body, and to give her pleasure. The deft strokes of her fingers up and down his shaft tempted him to forget his plan. And when her lips closed around him, he groaned and surrendered to sensation. Enjoy the moment, she'd said, and damn it, he was going to. God, she was talented. In seconds, she had him ready to explode. And that wouldn't be fair.

He caught her head in both hands and tried to tug, but all the strength in his body was focused in one swollen organ. "Stop," he gasped. "I'm going to come."

She mumbled something, her lips and teeth brushing his sensitive flesh. Rather than release him, she slipped her hand around his balls, which had tightened and drawn up. She caressed, squeezed gently, and—

"Holy shit!" His orgasm burst through him, all the way from the base of his spine. He was vaguely aware of the gentle suction of her lips holding him, of her throat muscles working as she swallowed, but mostly he was lost in physical ecstasy.

Eventually, he came back to earth, to find Cassidy releasing him. She sat up, breasts bare and nipples hard, legs curled to one side, grinning smugly.

"That was amazing," he got out between gasps. "But you shouldn't let me be so selfish."

Mischief tipped her grin higher. "You think that didn't give me pleasure?"

She was so sexy, such a generous lover.

"Not as much as . . ." Strength was returning to his muscles, at least enough so he could sit up. He intended to flip her back on the bed and lavish her with kisses and caresses until she climaxed. But that smiling mouth drew him. He captured her smile with his own lips and slid his tongue into her mouth to do a little dirty dancing with hers.

She leaned into the kiss eagerly, but this time he was going to take things slow if it killed him. He pulled back and said, "Thank you."

Her eyes twinkled. "For the blow job?"

"Well, yeah, for sure. But mostly, for dragging me out of my cave." He studied her face, exotic yet familiar, lovely yet genuine and approachable. "Actually, no. For being you."

"That's a very nice compliment, Mr. Cousins."

"You're a very nice woman, Ms. Esperanza."

"Having established that, are you now going to be very nice to me, Mr. Cousins?"

"You bet your sweet ass I am, Ms. Esperanza." He'd never in his life said the word "ass" to a woman. His parents had trained him to always respect women, and he did. They'd also trained him to be a gentleman. But Cassidy often teased him about being an old-fashioned guy, which, to be honest, made him feel stodgy. She brought out a different side of him. A side that could maybe get a little . . . raunchy. With dancing, and perhaps in bed as well.

Hmm. That opened up all sorts of possibilities . . .

Dave woke just before five-thirty. That was normal. What wasn't normal was the warm body entwined with his and the feeling of satiation that filled him. Man, that had been some night. It hadn't been just about the orgasms; it had been an ongoing thing—touching and tasting each other whenever they weren't sleeping.

He usually looked forward to starting his day by checking in with Sam—or, on Sam's nights off, with Randy, the alternate night manager. This morning, though, he'd rather have stayed in bed and found a creative way of waking Cassidy. If he hurried, he could be back while she was still asleep.

He turned off the alarm clock and slid cautiously away from her and out of bed. Collecting boxers, shorts, and a tee, he went to the hall bathroom to take a quick shower.

In the living room, he glanced at the area rug, all askew. He grinned and left it that way. To his surprise, he had no regrets. A sense of well-being put a spring in his step.

Merlin, asleep in his basket in the kitchen, woke when Dave entered the room, and jumped to his feet.

"Yes, let's go for a run." Dave collected his leash. "But a short one." In the time it would take to run around a couple of blocks, he'd have decided how to wake Cassidy.

He and the dog went down the stairs to the main floor and greeted Sam. While the wannabe writer patted Merlin, Dave asked, "How was your night?"

"Quiet on the hotel side, productive on the writing side. How was yours?"

"Uh, good. It was good." Dave fought to hold back a self-satisfied grin.

"You don't say." Narrow-eyed, Sam studied him, reminding Dave that some folks said his face was an open book. He'd never believed it, but Cassidy had suggested that it was true.

"We're going out for a run."

"I kinda figured."

"When Deepta comes in, tell her to call my cell if she needs me." Typically, Dave greeted her in person when she came to work at six-thirty. "I have some things to do upstairs."

"Uh-huh."

Dave hurried for the back door, Merlin trotting at his heels. When they were outside, his steps were as springy as the poodle's. He could have run for miles, but a sexy naked woman awaited him at home. A friend with bene-fits. He'd never realized what a great concept that was.

His feet were still spring-loaded as he raced Merlin up the four flights of stairs. They both arrived at the top panting and grinning. "Shh," Dave told the dog. "I'll give you break-fast, then you're on your own." But when he opened the door to his suite, something unexpected greeted him: the scent of coffee. A delicious scent, but one he'd rather not have smelled; it meant Cassidy was awake. Merlin, on the other hand, was delighted. He rushed into the kitchen.

Dave followed, to see Cassidy dressed in last night's clothes. Bummer. All the same, she looked so pretty and her smile was so wide that he had to smile back. "Good morn-ing, beautiful."

"You only say that because I'm cooking breakfast."

"I hadn't even noticed." He glanced past her to the counter, to see a bowl and a cutting board with a bunch of chopped veggies. "You don't have to do that."

She rolled her eyes. "Jeez, Dave, it's no big deal." She wiped her hands on a dish towel and came over to loop her arms around his neck. "Good morning."

He put his arms around her. "It sure is. Almost as good as if you'd still been in bed."

She tilted her head. "What would you have done?"

"You'll never know."

"It wouldn't have gone like this?" She pressed a feather-light kiss on his mouth.

"Maybe to start with. But it would have turned into this." He caught her head in one hand, feeling the dampness of freshly washed hair. Then he kissed her thoroughly, trying to put "thank you," "good morning," and "let's go back to bed" all into one kiss. When he finally broke the kiss, he was fully aroused, reinforcing the last message he'd been trying to get across.

"Hold that thought." Her eyes laughed at him, but the flush on her cheeks testified to her own arousal. "I have to work this morning, and the boss is a tough taskmaster."

"Damn, I forgot you were on day shift."

"I need to eat, go home and change, and be back by eight."

Quickie sex would take no longer than cooking and eating breakfast. He was about to say that when she yawned. One of those big yawns that seemed to sneak up on her.

He'd kept her up for most of the night. He knew that she got fatigued easily and that her leg sometimes bothered her. And now she had a full day's work ahead. The woman needed breakfast more than she needed sex. "Okay, what's for breakfast? Let me help." He moved to the counter and saw she'd chopped onion, mushrooms, and green pepper, and beaten some eggs. "Omelet?"

"Not quite. Frittata. Want to grate some cheddar and mozzarella while I get this going?"

"Sure. But I can make breakfast. You're my guest. Why don't you—"

"Dave, stop. Are we going to argue over everything?"

"Only if we can have make-up sex after."

That laugh he loved burbled out. "I've created a monster. Now, can he grate cheese?"

Resigned to letting her have her way, he took cheese from the fridge and got to work.

She melted butter in a cast-iron frying pan, lightly sautéed all the vegetables together, tossed in the egg mixture, and sprinkled the cheese on top. Then she put the frying pan cover on. "That'll be done in two or three minutes."

"Nice. I'll remember that." He had fed Merlin and now poured coffee for both of them.

"I like quick, easy food. And one-dish meals. Sometimes all I've had is a hot plate or a microwave. It's easy to nuke meals or buy fast food, but that's not healthy." She turned off the heat and plated the frittata.

"That looks great." Putting the cover on the frying pan had made the mixture puff up, kind of like a low soufflé, and the cheese had melted. It smelled mouthwatering. "Juice?"

At her nod, he poured orange juice, and then they sat down at the kitchen table to eat. "Tastes as good as it looks," he said. Struck by a wicked thought, he added, "Just like you."

"Now there's an interesting compliment."

"How about tonight? Are you free? Can you come here again?"

"*Come* here? That's up to you, isn't it? But I suspect you're *up* to the task."

"Joking aside, does tonight work?"

"Because you want me to cook breakfast again tomorrow morning?"

"If you do something that well, of course I'm going to want more of it." He winked. "And you know I'm not talking about cooking, right?"

Chapter Fourteen

Cassidy's workday on Thursday was a tough one. Though last night had been wonderful and she'd actually seen Dave's dimple flash at breakfast, her fatigue was back and her leg was acting up. After her shift, she wasn't too proud to accept a four-block ride home from Madisun. A cool shower and a nap helped reinvigorate her, but she was still dragging when she snuck in the back door of the Wild Rose at seven o'clock and took the elevator to the top floor.

When she stepped into Dave's suite, he greeted her with a heart-stopping kiss, then settled her on the couch with her feet up. "What would you like to drink? I have beef and veggie skewers marinating to put on the barbecue. How about I open a bottle of Syrah?"

"Perfect. Can I do something to help?"

"You can sit right here and enjoy your wine."

How rare and lovely to be waited on. Especially when her server was a hot guy in a white tee and khaki shorts that nicely displayed his physical assets. A few minutes later, he was back with two glasses and a bottle of Road 13 wine. "What kind of music would you like?"

"Country and western." She sipped, finding the wine rich and fruity.

He slipped a CD into the machine, handed her the case, then took his own wineglass back to the kitchen.

A woman began to sing about silver linings. Kacey Musgraves. Good pick. Cassidy yawned, sipped wine, mused on silver linings. If her teen years hadn't been so messed up, she likely wouldn't have discovered the joy of exploring the world. If she hadn't heard the woman at the hair salon talk about Caribou Crossing, if she hadn't been so exhausted that she face-planted in the lobby of the Wild Rose, she wouldn't be here right now.

Sheer, blissful laziness slid through her body. This was nice, being looked after. Pampered. By her sexy, considerate lover. Last night, Dave had asked what she needed that he could give her. No man had ever asked her that. It made her think of Gramps. He'd treated her and JJ like they were the most important things in his life, and it had felt wonderful.

A few songs later, Dave came back with two plates of food.

The meal was simple but tasty and the conversation drifted easily. Dave told stories about Robin, Cassidy mentioned Ms. H, and then they both shared some reminiscences about school days. Dave told her that he'd been captain of the high school basketball team and now served as volunteer coach, with occasional help from Jamal Estevez. Cassidy speculated as to whether Karen and Jamal were checking out the beach in Hawaii or spending all their time in bed. They talked about Riders Boot Camp, and she found out that Dave was on the board of directors.

When they finished their dinner, Dave insisted on cleaning up. Mellow and sleepy, she didn't argue. Shortly after, he came back with the dog on his leash. "Taking Merlin out for a minute." She waved a hand in acknowledgment. This was so nice, vegging on the couch, sipping her third glass of wine as she fought back yawns. When man and dog returned, she didn't move an inch.

A minute or two later, Dave stood beside her. "How are you feeling?"

"Blissed out. I'm not sure I'll ever move again."

"Come to bed."

She smiled up at him, so handsome and sexy. "Okay, those words might get me moving."

He helped her to her feet. Then he caught her off guard, swooping her up in his arms. Mmm, she liked strong and masterful.

In the bedroom, he placed her on the bed and removed her clothing. She stretched out, naked, waiting for him to undress. But he didn't. He rolled her onto her stomach, sat on the side of the bed, and began to massage her. A real massage, with firm, warm hands working the muscles of her shoulders, back, butt, legs, even her feet, paying special attention to her troublesome left leg.

Her muscles softened and released at the same time that arousal coiled between her legs. "You're really good at this."

"I like touching you. And I feel guilty."

"Guilty?"

"For keeping you awake most of last night, when you had to work a full shift today."

How totally sweet. "I thought it was the other way around," she teased. "That it was me keeping you *up* all night."

"Tonight you're getting a sound night's sleep."

Arousal was winning over the therapeutic effects of his touch. "That's a pretty thorough massage you've given me, but there's an important set of muscles you've missed." She rolled onto her back, to see him sitting beside her, gazing quizzically down at her, the usual few unruly locks of hair tumbling over his forehead.

She reached under the hem of his tee, brushing his flesh

with her fingers and feeling his muscles ripple in response. "And believe me, they're definitely achy and in need of your firm touch." And firm he was as she undid his shorts and reached inside.

Smart man, he had the sense not to suggest she might be too tired for sex. Likely he'd noted her wriggles of pleasure and the moisture on her inner thighs.

He rose, peeled off his clothes, and took a condom from the bedside table. When he was sheathed, he slipped a pillow under her butt. "Lie back and let me do all the work."

"You consider this work?" She spread her legs so he could kneel between them.

"I consider this"—he paused as the tip of his erection brushed her inner thigh—"the nicest thing that's happened to me in one hell of a long time." His fingers slicked moisture across her skin, two of them entered her gently, readying her, and then, on an exhale of pleasure, he slipped into her. He leaned forward and they kissed, slow and easy like the movements of their bodies. Sweet and intense.

The nicest thing that had happened to him. Sex. Such a simple physical act. She'd done it loads of times, with her fair share of guys. Handsome guys and plain ones, rich men and poor ones, talented ones and guys who were struggling to find their way. Straightforward guys and complicated ones. Some had been terrific lovers.

Dave was complicated. Intriguing. Sweet. But, bottom line, just another guy. So why, with him, did this simple physical act feel so utterly wonderful? Pleasure rippled through her with every slow, controlled stroke, until it crested and shattered in waves that pulsed through her entire body. A moment later, Dave groaned, gripped her tighter, and found his own release.

She clasped him in her arms, as satisfied as a woman could be.

A few minutes later, he lifted off her and dealt with the

condom. Lying back beside her, he put his arm around her shoulders. She turned on her side, nestling close with her head resting on his chest. Earlier, he'd said he wanted her to get a good night's sleep, and she was well on her way. Drowsily, she murmured, "All those people are right. You really are the perfect man."

"Who are 'all those people,' and are you talking about my skill in the sack or what?"

She gave a lazy chuckle. "Well, yes, but no. I mean . . . never mind." She yawned. "I'm too tired to make sense."

"Go to sleep, Cassidy."

She smiled against his firm chest. Yes, perfect.

Sneaking out of Dave's apartment early Friday morning, for the second morning in a row, made Cassidy uncomfortable. Like she was doing something clandestine. But she knew Dave hated being gossiped about.

Her leg felt fine after that wonderful massage and a good sleep, so rather than take the elevator and risk being seen by Sam, she went down the back stairs. She slipped out the inn's back door and hurried across the parking lot. An impulse made her glance back, and yes, Dave was watching from his bedroom window. When he waved, she blew him a kiss.

Then she glimpsed another face at a window: Mitch, the chef, gazing curiously from the kitchen. Damn. Pretending she didn't see him couldn't undo the fact that he'd seen her. So she gave him a smile and a wave. He'd have no way of knowing it was Dave she'd been with. It could have been a hotel guest. And didn't that make her look so professional . . .

After a quick trip to her apartment, she hurried back to work and found that, as luck would have it, she was assigned to wait tables in the restaurant. Mitch took her aside and cautioned her against getting involved with the guests. She bit her lip, then told him he was right.

Even though Cassidy had vowed not to let her personal relationship with Dave impinge on their work one, she decided he needed to know about this. At coffee break, she found him in the lobby. While he arranged a trail ride for a family of five, she chatted with Deepta at reception. When Dave was free, she said, "Could I have a minute to discuss my work shifts?"

His brows rose. "Sure. Come on into my office."

As they headed down the hall, Merlin, who'd been sleeping in a patch of sun near the front door, picked himself up and came with them. Inside the office, Dave closed the door, gestured her to a chair, and took the chair beside it. "Your schedule?"

She shook her head. "Mitch saw me leave the hotel this morning. He assumed I'd spent the night with a guest. He gave me a lecture."

"Oh man." He raised a hand and shoved back his unruly hair. "I'm sorry, Cassidy."

"It's okay." Though really, it wasn't. While she liked being a fun, free-spirited person, she prided herself on doing a good job. "But it's going to make it hard, me visiting you at night."

He nodded thoughtfully. "I was thinking."

"About?"

"There's a party Saturday night at Miriam and Wade's. They own Bly Ranch, just down the road from Boots?"

"Right. Jess's parents." Another of the "sprinkled with magic dust" couples.

"Yes. Anyhow, it's Jessie and Evan's second anniversary. Robin will be there, of course, and I'm invited. I thought maybe you'd like to go."

What did this have to do with Mitch? "That sounds nice."

Except . . . Ah, she was beginning to see the connection. "You mean, go as friends like we've done in the past? Or . . . ?"

"It's hard keeping secrets in Caribou Crossing. And there's no reason to. Is there?"

She shook her head. "Not for me. You're the one who's had all the women in town speculating about your dating life."

"And now I'm actually seeing someone. So why not be open about it? I don't like deceiving people."

"Me neither. But will your family be okay with you dating some drifter who's working at the Wild Rose?"

He frowned. "They've met you and like you. As for working here, they'll assume that I'll be professional."

He was right. His staff and the townspeople would likely think the same, because they knew him well. "Then great, let's do it."

"Good. But what do we do? Do we have to make some big announcement?"

Humor twitched her lips. She reached over to clasp his hand, threading her fingers through his. "This'll do it. No one in your family's slow on the uptake."

He squeezed her hand. "Good point."

Her hand felt like it belonged in his. Her lips yearned to touch his. But her coffee break was almost over, not to mention that anyone might knock on the door and pop in. She freed her hand gently and stood. "I need to get back to work."

"I'll have a word with Mitch."

"Thanks. I appreciate that."

"You know folks will have questions."

She winked. "No one says we have to answer them."

Chapter Fifteen

For Friday dinner, Dave had been happy to go along with Cassidy's request for what she called "the elegant simplicity" of barbecued hamburgers. They ate on his private rooftop patio, sprawled on lounge chairs, each with a chilled bottle of Caribou Crossing ale.

Both hungry, they wolfed down the food without saying much. She put down her empty plate and patted her stomach. "Mmm, there's nothing like a classic burger."

He wiped his fingers on a paper towel and reached over to take her hand. "Beer, a burger, and a pretty woman. Can't beat that on a Friday night."

She toasted him with her beer bottle. "A man of simple tastes."

"Classic," he corrected her. "So how was your day?"

Her brow wrinkled. "My brother JJ called. He's getting married again."

"Oh yeah? You mentioned he'd been married once, and it didn't last."

"No longer than a nanosecond."

Remembering that her parents had married each other three times, he asked, "He's not marrying the same woman, is he?"

She snorted. "God no. He's not that dumb. But still, I asked him what he's thinking."

"And?"

"JJ says it was so nice when we were a real family, he wants that again. That's why he rushed into marriage before. But this time he says he's really sure this is the right woman."

"Have you met her?"

"Yeah. They're in Victoria, and I went over for a couple days when I was working in Vancouver. Mags seems nice, but . . ."

"You don't think she's right for JJ?"

She sipped some beer. "It's not that. It's the marriage thing. Why can't people be satisfied with a happy here and now?"

"You haven't been in love."

"Nope. Thank heavens."

"When you're in love, you get . . ." He drank some beer as he searched for the right word. "Greedy, I guess. It's not that you want to own the other person, but you want everything."

She eyed him curiously. "What d'you mean?"

"Everything you can have together. All the sharing, trust, love. You don't just want a wonderful 'here and now,' you want a future." His mouth had run ahead of his brain and a painful stab in his heart shut him up. A future. That was what he and Anita had been denied.

Cassidy squeezed his hand and said quietly, a little sadly, "But there are no guarantees of that future actually coming true."

"No, there aren't."

"So it's better not to fall in love and make plans, or you risk getting your heart broken."

Was she right? He freed his hand, stood, and headed down to the kitchen with his empty plate and beer bottle, reflecting. He had never felt so gloriously alive as he had with Anita before she'd been diagnosed. Had that been worth the pain that followed? Was anything worth that kind of pain? Yet, to never have experienced that kind of love . . . He was almost sorry for Cassidy. Her parents had really done a number on her, to make her shun the notion of love.

"Want to take a couple more beers back to the roof?" Her words broke into his thoughts and he realized she'd followed him into the kitchen.

"Sure." He took the bottles from the fridge and they went back up the stairs. Curious to learn more about the family that had influenced her philosophy of life, he said, "When your parents first got married, were things good?"

"Yeah. Really good." She plunked into her chair. "Until they weren't anymore."

He sat sideways on his lounge chair, feet on the patio deck, so he could see her face. "You said they first split up when you were seven? What went wrong?"

"All I saw at the time was lots more fighting. Later, I heard the story from both sides. She thought he was too charming with his female clients. He said she got bitchy when she wasn't always the center of his world. She said he hated it when she didn't fawn over him the way his female clients did."

"Your parents were young. Immature?"

"I guess. Finally they had this horrible blowup." She swallowed some beer. "Luis had this wealthy female client who was moving to the south of France. He went with her."

"Rough on you and your brother. You stayed with your mom?"

"Yeah. She dated a lot. JJ and I missed Luis. He sent postcards with pretty scenes, cute animals, little notes. But his lady friend and his life in France meant more to him than we did."

Dave winced. If you had kids, they should be the most important thing in your life.

"The person who gave us a sense of security, who put us first, was Gramps."

"He sounds like a good guy."

She nodded fervently. "The best. He babysat us, and we stayed with him whenever Justine went off with a boyfriend. He was a successful businessman, but he always had time for us. He let us know how much he loved us." She paused. "Dave, you need to talk to Robin."

"Huh?" Where had that come from?

"About us dating. She can't just find out when we turn up tomorrow night."

He hadn't thought of that, but she was right. "I'll have a private chat with her before then. I think she'll be happy. She likes you."

"I like her. That's a good kid you've got, Dave Cousins." Her lips curved. "As if you don't know it."

"I do. Go on with your story."

"Okay, well, Justine finally got semiserious about one of her guys. He was offered a good job in Toronto and we moved there with him. I really missed Gramps. Then she split with the guy, and Luis and his south-of-France lover broke up. There was all this drama about how Justine and Luis had never really loved anyone else. We ended up back in Victoria, with them getting married again. I was ten, JJ was eight."

He leaned forward to rest his hand on her bare leg. "How did you feel about it?"

She worried her bottom lip. "Tentatively happy. At times it seemed great, but I wasn't sure I could trust in it. I was older, I knew my parents better. And I could see Gramps was skeptical. He took Luis back into the realty business, but things between them were strained. I think Gramps was afraid Luis was going to take off with another female client."

"And?" He finished his beer and put the bottle down.

She shook her head. "This time it was Justine. Eventually she got restless. She was in her thirties, the mom of a teenage daughter and son. I think she felt kind of, uh, drudgy. Not the exciting, passionate woman she liked to think of herself as. And then Gramps died." She rubbed her hands across her face, then left them there.

He stroked her leg gently. "I'm sorry."

"Yeah." She lowered her hands, but didn't look at him when she went on. "It was a stupid accident. He hit black ice on the Malahat, driving up to show a property in January. We were shattered. We all loved him so much. Luis was scrambling to hold the business together, not paying much attention to Justine." She shook her head and said sarcastically, "So of course, she did the mature thing."

"That was when she went to Europe with a man?"

"Yup."

"Leaving you and JJ with your father."

"Yeah. Luis worked hard, played hard. I tried to keep the house together and make sure JJ did his homework and didn't get in trouble. I loved Luis and JJ, but they were both a bit of a pain. And I missed Justine and Gramps. I envied my mother, off in Europe having fun. I was sixteen and I'd have dropped out of school except Gramps would have hated that. So I hung in. The moment I graduated, I went to Greece, where Justine and her guy were living."

She glanced down, rotating her beer bottle in her hands. "JJ was going into eleventh grade. I figured he was old enough to look after himself, with some help from Luis."

He heard a touch of guilt. "He was your parents' responsibility, not yours."

Finally, she looked at Dave, and he saw that guilt, along with pain, in her eyes. "That's what I told myself. But he'd had his gramps die and his mom run off. His dad was there but not exactly there. Then I took off." She worried her bottom lip again. "*You* never run out on people."

No, he didn't. At pretty much the same age, he'd taken on responsibility for a pregnant girl and an unborn child who wasn't his. Still, he'd had a far different upbringing from Cassidy's. He'd had parents who taught him about commitment and stability. He squeezed her leg. "You were what, eighteen?"

"Not quite."

"Cut yourself a break."

She shot him a grateful look. "Thanks."

They went downstairs and tidied up the kitchen, then drifted into the living room and sat on the couch. "What do you feel like?" he asked. "If your leg's okay, we could take Merlin for a walk and get an ice cream cone at The Soda Jerk." The soda fountain sold a bunch of flavors of ice cream, gelato, and sorbetto.

"Ice cream's good, but how about sharing this instead?" She reached into her bag and pulled out a hand-rolled cylinder.

The sick lurch in his stomach told him what it was. All the same, he found himself asking, "Is that a joint?" Near the end, Anita had used medical marijuana. He was glad it had helped her, but the pungent earthy scent would always, for him, be associated with her dying.

"Well, duh. And I'm told it's primo stuff."

"Where did you get that? No, don't tell me." If it was from one of his staff, he didn't want to know. No doubt some of them used marijuana, but it was still an illegal drug.

"Got a match?"

"No! Damn it, no, Cassidy. We're not smoking that."

Cassidy rolled her expressive eyes. "Oh, come on. It's legal in a lot of places and soon will be here too."

"I don't care."

"People use it for medical reasons, like to cope with pain and nausea."

How well he knew. "Are you in pain?" He knew his harsh tone was an overreaction, but he couldn't temper it. "Are you nauseous?" His own stomach roiled with memories.

"I can't believe you're such a Puritan. But fine, whatever." She tucked it back into her purse. "I don't smoke weed often myself. I just thought it'd be fun to share."

His lurching pulse steadied and he took a deep breath, then another. And now he found the right words. "Anita used it when she was sick."

Her eyes widened with comprehension. "Oh jeez, I'm sorry."

"It's okay." He managed a ragged attempt at a smile. "The truth is, I was never big on recreational drugs anyhow. So, yeah, I'm a bit of a Puritan."

"You're so responsible. Were you ever just footloose and fancy free?"

He thought back. "My folks taught us to be responsible. I cut loose a few times. Broke curfew and snuck in late; hung out at the lake drinking too much beer. I wasn't exactly a rabble-rouser but . . ." He shrugged.

"You weren't always Mr. Straightlaced? That's reassuring. Was it parenthood that changed you?"

"When you're responsible for another human being, you grow up fast and take things pretty seriously."

"Unless you're my parents."

He grimaced. "Sorry about that."

She curled into her corner of the couch, feet tucked under her, facing him. "You and Jess were young when you had Robin."

"Fresh out of high school." He put his feet up on the coffee table, angling his body so he could look at her.

"I'd have thought you were the kind of guy who'd have headed off to college and waited a while to get married."

That was what he'd intended, and what his parents had wanted for him. "Pregnancy has a way of changing the best-laid plans." He remembered the day Jessie had come to him, distraught, and told him that Evan had knocked her up before leaving town to attend Cornell. She said she planned to have the baby but she didn't want to tell Evan about it. Evan had always, since he was a kid, wanted to get out of Caribou Crossing. She was pretty sure that if he knew she was pregnant he'd feel obligated to marry her and it would ruin both their lives. Dave had never seen spunky Jessie Bly look so whipped.

When he had reflected on her dilemma, the solution was obvious. He and Jessie liked each other a lot and could build a happy family. So he'd proposed, and persuaded her to accept.

"You had unprotected sex?" Cassidy asked. "You don't strike me as that kind of guy, even back when you were cutting loose."

He wasn't stupid. Nor were Jessie and Evan. "The condom broke."

"Ah. That'll do it. Did you guys consider abortion?"

"Never. The very thought that Robin might not exist . . ."

She nodded. "The world would be worse off, that's for sure."

And his world would be unthinkable.

"Is it hard, now that Jess has remarried and you have to share Robin with Evan?"

Dave swallowed. Cassidy did have a knack of nailing the tough issues, at least in other people's lives. "Yeah, it's hard." Harder than she could imagine, because Evan now knew the truth. He'd been a good guy about it, agreeing to maintain the pretense that Dave was Robin's biological father. Yet in some indefinable way it changed things.

Dave had loved Jessie. Even if it wasn't that earth-shaking, once-in-a-lifetime feeling he'd had for Anita, he'd loved her as his best friend, his wife, the mother of their daughter. Now, she was Evan's life mate. Dave had loved Anita with every fiber of his being, and she was gone. Robin was the most important person in his life, and now he shared fatherhood with Evan.

Too many losses. This was what happened when you let yourself love people. Maybe Cassidy was right. It was safest to avoid love.

"Ice cream." Her decisive voice broke into his thoughts. "Let's walk the dog, see the sights of Caribou Crossing, and stop at The Soda Jerk on the way back. But not cones. A carton of . . . hmm, I think Sinful Chocolate." She uncurled her body and rose.

"A carton? You're that hungry?"

She held out her hands to him and he let her tug him to his feet. "No, but licking ice cream out of a cone is boring." She planted a teasing kiss on his lips. "I'd rather lick it off you."

Late Saturday afternoon, Dave drove his Jeep out of the Wild Rose parking lot with Cassidy in the passenger seat. They'd discussed riding horses over to Bly Ranch, but she didn't want to wear jeans to an anniversary party. And considering how she looked now, Dave sure wasn't complaining.

When Robin was little, money had been tight. He and Jessie had made more than one purchase at the predecessor to Days of Your. But he'd never before met a woman who treated a thrift store as her regular clothes-shopping spot. On Cassidy, the results always looked good, but especially today. It was the first time he'd seen her in a dress. It had an abstract pattern in shades of blue, little straps that left her shoulders mostly bare and showed off her wild goose tattoo, and a top that hugged her breasts and waist.

He had CXNG, the local country radio station playing, as usual. Cassidy hummed along to Stompin' Tom Connors's "Sudbury Saturday Night," one leg crossed over the other and her foot swinging in time with the beat. Her bare legs looked hot and so did her feet, in sandals woven of multi-colored strips of leather. Her toenails were painted turquoise.

"You told Robin that we're dating?" she asked.

He chuckled. "Her reaction went pretty much like this. 'Well, duh.' Followed by 'I like Cassidy. She's cool.'"

"Good. I hope everyone else is as happy about it."

"Well," he teased, "you *are* cool." He sure enjoyed her company. In bed and out. Thinking how much he'd miss Cassidy when she left, he asked, "You given any thought to how long you're planning to stay in Caribou Crossing?"

"Planning? Like that word's in my vocabulary?"

"I couldn't live like that."

"Don't know unless you give it a try." On the radio, Taylor Swift lamented that she knew some guy was trouble when he walked in. After a moment, Cassidy said, "But yeah, when you have a kid, that has to change things. Or at least it should."

Realizing she was thinking of her parents, he said firmly, "Yeah, it should."

"Well, anyhow . . . No, I haven't really thought about how long I'll stay. The only thing I know for sure is that I'll be in Victoria just before Christmas for JJ's wedding." She wrinkled her nose. "Winter's the worst season to be in Victoria. Unless you happen to like gray skies and drizzle."

"No thanks. I like winter here. Crisp weather, snow. It's fun to ride in the snow or go cross-country skiing. You'd love it."

She shot him a sideways glance. "Trying to talk me into staying?"

Kind of. "I think you're a woman who makes up her own mind and no one's going to talk you into anything."

"Smart man."

They'd arrived at Miriam and Wade Bly's ranch house, a rambling old log building that to him had the familiarity of home. When Dave had married Jessie, her parents had taken him in wholeheartedly. There'd been a bumpy patch during the divorce, but they'd come around and again accepted him as part of the family. His former in-laws were pretty damned terrific.

He parked the Jeep among several other vehicles. At the front door, the Blys were talking to Brooke and Jake. Cassidy hopped out and Dave walked around. He took her hand, its warm suppleness feeling right in his. They walked to the house and went up the steps.

While Dave hugged Miriam and shook Wade's hand, Cassidy exchanged greetings with Brooke and Jake. Dave then introduced her to their hosts.

After they all said hello, Cassidy said, "This is a lovely home. It has a real sense of history."

"Wade's grandfather started Bly Ranch," Miriam said. "He built the house and Wade's parents added onto it." She linked her arm through her husband's. "We've done some modernizing, but other than that we left it alone. It suits us."

"That it does," Wade said.

Cassidy studied the two of them, then glanced at Brooke.

"I can't believe you two ladies are Robin's grandmas. You both—and Sheila too—look way too young."

Miriam's sandy hair was threaded with silver, but it suited her warm, attractive face. Blond Brooke glowed with health. Both women, Miriam in a pink blouse and denim skirt and Brooke in a sleeveless green dress, were trim and toned. They were both a fair bit younger than Dave's own mom; they'd given birth to Jessie and Evan in their teens.

"You are so sweet," Miriam said. With a wink to Dave, she added, "I like this girl." And then, to Cassidy again, "Would you like a tour of the house?"

"Love it." A squeeze of Dave's hand and she was off.

Wade said, "Most folks are in the back garden. Come along and I'll get drinks for you."

"I could use a beer," Jake said. "It's been a rough day."

"Rough?" Wade asked. "Not compared to undercover policing, surely."

"Hah," Jake said. "You don't know 'rough' until you have to get Mr. Morton back into his pajamas before he flashes the whole town."

Mr. Morton, who was ninety if he was a day, lived in a care home. He was a nice, harmless guy with dementia, but he kept escaping and wandering downtown.

Jake and Wade headed off, and Dave made to follow.

Brooke stopped him with a hand on his arm. "You're dating Cassidy?"

So the hand-holding had been noted. "Casually."

"What does that mean?"

Oh, great. Cassidy had said they didn't need to answer questions, but he had no idea how to avoid a direct one from a good friend. "Just fun. Not serious. Don't tell me you disapprove. You're the one who told me I needed someone sunny."

"And she is. I like her. I just want to make sure you're okay, Dave. You haven't dated casually since high school, have you?"

"This is the new me."

"Hmm." A slight frown tugged at the corners of her eyes. "When Jake and I got together, we told ourselves it was casual."

"We're not Jake and you. Cassidy's a gypsy. She never stays anywhere more than a few months, and she has no interest in a long-term relationship. She's . . . safe."

"Safe?"

"I can enjoy being with her and not worry about where it's going."

"Not worry about getting your heart broken again."

"Exactly." He studied her face. "What are you trying to say, Brooke?"

She opened her mouth, seemed to hunt for words, then gave her head a shake, setting her blond curls tossing gently. "I honestly don't know. Just, I guess, be happy. You deserve it."

Happy. There was a time he wouldn't have believed he'd ever feel happy again. But somehow, in the past days, happiness had snuck up on him. "Thanks. I will."

Chapter Sixteen

"My father and grandfather both sold high-end real estate," Cassidy told Miriam Bly, "and I've traveled to tons of different places. I've seen loads of houses, but honestly, this is one of the nicest." The two women were walking along the upstairs hallway, which was decorated with framed family photos.

"Thanks, but it's nothing special. It's just"—Miriam gazed around affectionately—"you know, home."

Yes, that was the element that made it special. Realistically, Cassidy knew that the families who'd lived here must have had their fights, but a sense of peace and happiness permeated the place. What would it have been like to grow up here, in a real home, with parents like Miriam and Wade? She envied Jess, just like she envied Dave for his stable home life. No wonder the two of them had grown up to be so home-and-family oriented.

But that was them. Whatever went into shaping an adult, she was different and her way was great too. She'd learned as a teen that it was pointless to long for things you could never have. You had to make your own way, take charge of your own happiness.

One of the photos drew her eye: a pretty sandy-haired

girl in a lacy wedding dress and a handsome chestnut-haired guy in a tux, arms around each other. Their smiles were so loving, you could almost see the stars in their eyes. "Your wedding picture. You and Wade were so young."

Miriam gazed at the picture with a fond, reminiscent smile. "Fresh out of high school."

"Like your daughter and Dave. High school sweethearts."

"Not exactly." She turned to Cassidy. "I mean, yes, Wade and I were. We knew for years that we'd get married. But Jessica . . ." She shook her head. "She'd never been a secretive girl, and as far as we knew, she wasn't dating. She had lots of friends, though Evan was always her best friend. Wade and I kept expecting the two of them to start dating, but they never did. Anyhow, it was a total surprise when she told us she was pregnant and she and Dave were getting married." Miriam moved down a couple of photos and gestured to the wall.

This picture had been taken at Jess and Dave's wedding. The bride's Empire-waisted dress hid any baby bulge she might have had, and Dave was in a tux. They, too, were smiling at each other. But they didn't look starry-eyed. Their smiles held what looked like genuine affection, but also a touch of . . . what? Uncertainty? Well, no doubt. That had to be scary, a wedding initiated by an unplanned pregnancy rather than by years of love and commitment.

Gently, Miriam touched the frame of her daughter's wedding photo. "It sure wasn't what her dad and I wished for her at the time. We told her that she didn't have to get married, that we'd help her with the baby. But Dave was a responsible boy and the two of them swore they wanted to get married and be there for each other and for the baby."

"They were happy? Until, uh, Anita?"

"Very happy. In a different way from Wade and me. Wade and I started out romantic and naïve. We had to learn how to hang in there through the tough times. With Jessica and Dave, it was more like they started out committed to the long haul, and grew into loving each other."

She sighed. "When Dave met Anita, I was angry. I thought he should have honored his marriage vows. But Jessica told me that he and Anita had a special kind of love. She said that it was the kind Wade and I had. And that she and Dave weren't like that." She gave a rueful smile. "I thought she was talking about the fact that they'd married because she was pregnant. At the time I didn't realize she still had feelings for Evan."

Still had feelings? Cassidy had to wonder why Jess and Evan had never dated as teens.

"But then Evan came back to town," Miriam went on, "and now they have that special kind of love. And Dave"— she turned assessing eyes on Cassidy—"has you."

"It's not the same. It's just casual."

"That's too bad."

Cassidy shook her head. "No, really. Dave and I don't want the kind of relationship you and Wade have. And Jess and Evan."

"And Dave's parents, and Brooke and Jake. Huh. I didn't think Dave was the type for a casual relationship."

"Right now it's what he needs."

"And you're so sure of what he needs?" Her tone was neutral.

"Sorry, I don't mean to sound . . . whatever. Arrogant, pushy. I'm not a know-it-all, believe me. Dave and I have talked. About Anita and—"

Her head jerked; her eyes widened. "He's talked to you about her?"

Cassidy nodded. "A little."

"He wouldn't even speak her name for years."

"I know. And that wasn't healthy. Not for him, and not for Robin. He realizes that now."

The older woman's eyes lit with a knowing gleam. "He'd do anything for Robin. That was a clever approach. Maybe you do know what's good for Dave."

"I hope so. He's had some pretty heavy stuff happen in his life. Unplanned pregnancy, early marriage, raising a baby. Building the Wild Rose into what it is today. Anita coming along and shaking up his life. Dave's a moral guy, as I'm sure you know. He's not someone who'd just go and cheat on his wife."

"I do know that."

"And then Anita getting sick, him being with her while she died."

Miriam nodded slowly. "Robin's accident two years ago. Evan coming into Jessica and Robin's lives. Yes, you're right, a lot of heavy stuff. I can see that something light, fun may be just what he needs at the moment."

"Robin's accident?"

"She's always been a tomboy, just like her mom was." Miriam ran her fingers through her shoulder-length bob. "These gray hairs Wade and I have? Blame our daughter and granddaughter. We'd almost reconciled ourselves to Robin's bruises and bashes, a few stitches now and then, even a broken bone." She amended, "Well, Wade, Jessica, and I had. Dave's more of a worrier, especially since Anita died."

"I've seen him be a little overprotective, and seen Robin chafe at it. What happened two years ago?"

"It was late afternoon, dark, pouring rain. She walked from her friend Kimiko's to the Wild Rose. A car came around a corner, going too fast, and skidded. Hit her. Her spleen was lacerated and they had to operate and remove it."

Cassidy winced. "Poor Robin. But she's perfectly healthy now, isn't she?"

"Oh, yes. She bounces back, our Robin. It was Dave who got hit—sorry, unintentional pun—the hardest. He blamed himself for not picking her up. He was terrified that he might lose her. And then, while Robin was still in the hospital, Evan and Jessica got engaged. It's been tough for Dave sharing his daughter with a stepdad."

"He loves her to pieces."

"She loves him that way too. The girl has a huge heart; there's room for everyone."

Gramps had been that way. Unlike Cassidy's parents, whose love for each other was so fiery that it eclipsed their feelings for their kids. Even now, she missed her grandfather. Brushing away the momentary sadness, she said, "It's great that Dave and Evan get along. Were they friends back in high school?"

"Evan didn't really have friends other than Jessica. He was an odd boy. Polite and helpful, intimidatingly smart, not the least bit outdoorsy or athletic. He made no bones about the fact that he hated 'Hicksville,' as he called it, and couldn't wait to leave."

"How could he hate Caribou Crossing? It's a wonderful place."

A warm, knowing smile spread over Miriam's face. "Indeed it is. As Evan realized when he returned ten years later. And as Jake realized, when his undercover work brought him here. And Karen MacLean, when the RCMP transferred her here a few years ago, and Jamal, when he came here on the same case that brought Jake."

"I suspect the men's fondness for Caribou Crossing has something to do with the women they met here," Cassidy joked.

"And isn't that a large part of what makes a place special? The people you care about?"

Gramps's house had felt like home not because it was particularly warm and cozy, but because he was there. Since then, even though Cassidy had met some great people in her travels, none had made her want to stay in one place and set down roots. Or maybe, to be fair to her hundred or so Facebook "friends," she'd never stayed long enough to get really close to anyone. The very notion of roots, of basing your happiness on a relationship, made her antsy. Maybe it worked for some people, but she didn't see that happening for her.

As they rode home in the Jeep, Robin asked from the backseat, "Did you meet Grandpa Wade's parents, Cassidy?"

"Yes, we had a nice chat. They said if my travels ever take me to Phoenix, I have a place to stay." The senior Blys had moved to Arizona more than twenty years ago because of her health, and that was when Miriam and Wade took over the ranch. Robin's great-grandparents were now healthy, happy retirees who enjoyed an occasional visit to Caribou Crossing.

"You gonna take them up on it?" Dave asked. And then, "Sorry, wrong question. You don't plan ahead."

"Hey, you're getting to know me." She shifted position, trying in vain to ease the tingling in her left leg.

On the heels of a yawn, Robin said, "I hope Madisun remembered to take Merlin out."

"Have you ever known Madisun to forget anything?" Dave asked.

"Yeah, she is kind of anal," the girl said. "In a good way, I mean."

Given Madisun's upbringing with an alcoholic dad and a mom with nine kids to look after, it wasn't surprising that she'd turned into a control freak.

"Want me to drop you at the Wild Rose before I drive Cassidy home?" Dave asked his daughter. "So you can check."

"Thanks. Besides, I'm kind of tired."

"Me too." Cassidy yawned. She would miss spending the night with Dave, but she could use a long, uninterrupted sleep.

After he dropped his daughter off and watched her go in the inn's front door, he unhooked his seat belt and leaned over to give Cassidy a long, thorough kiss. She responded eagerly, then teased, "If you want to go parking, this probably isn't the best place."

He buckled up and pulled onto the road. "I've been wanting to do that all evening."

"Me too." At the party, they'd clasped hands, put their arms around each other, made no secret of being together, and every touch had made her long for more.

"Did you have a good time?" he asked as he drove toward Ms. Haldenby's.

"Yes, though it was a bit stressful. You have a lot of people who care about you."

He frowned. "Did anyone give you a hard time?"

"No. There was just, you know, small-town stuff. Sideways looks, people whispering to each other. Comments. Your sister said that I was good for you, that it's nice hearing you laugh."

For three years he'd gone through the motions of life, trying to hide the melancholy, the anger, the guilt. He felt bad that he hadn't done a better job of concealing his feelings. "It is nice to laugh again." It was so amazingly nice to genuinely enjoy the things he knew he should enjoy, and to share his enjoyment with his family and friends. He owed that to the woman beside him.

"One of Jess's old friends from high school said that every single female in town had gone after you and failed, so obviously I was a better woman than any of them."

"You're a special woman."

"Thanks. Oh, and Jess said that if I hurt you, I'd have her to answer to."

He groaned. "What did you tell her?"

"That I'm not exactly heartbreaker material. So how about you? What did people say?"

"Lots of guys told me I didn't deserve you." Of course, Cassidy would be heartbreaker material if a man had a heart that was capable of loving again.

"Astute judges of character," she joked.

"A few people commented about Sally. I think I finally got them to believe that we never had been dating."

She studied his handsome profile as he turned onto Ms. H's street. "You're sure she sees it the same way? It'd be awful if she has feelings for you, and gossip got back to her about us."

"I'm sure. But I'll mention it to her. I'm heading out to Ryland Riding tomorrow to help her out." He glanced over. "You have the day off. Want to come?"

"I'd love to, if you think it'd be okay with her."

"I'll check with her first."

Wincing, she shifted position again.

"On the other hand," he said, "maybe you should keep your feet up and rest."

"God, I'm not an old lady."

He stopped the Jeep in front of Ms. H's and turned off the engine. "Then see a doctor, find out what's wrong with your leg, and get it fixed." He touched her shoulder. "Go see Dr. Carlene Young. You'll like her. She's our family doctor."

"I'll think about it."

"Are you scared of doctors?"

No. Only of the possible diagnosis. But damn it, she wasn't her great-grandmother. She was healthy and active, and she just had a pinched nerve or something else that was easily treatable. "Of course I'm not, and you're right. I'll call on Monday for an appointment."

Chapter Seventeen

Dave felt like a fourth grader as he climbed out of the Jeep and tucked his Western shirt more neatly into his clean, belted jeans. He'd even polished his old Ropers, the boots he wore for grubby ranch work, such as he'd be doing at Sally's this afternoon.

Clasping a bouquet of mixed summer blooms, he started up the walk toward Ms. Haldenby's forest green rancher with its white trim. Of course he saw his former teacher around town. She even dined at the Wild Rose occasionally, on her own or in the company of one or two other retired schoolteachers. But he'd never set foot inside her house and would have been happy to leave things that way.

The garden, with its lawn, shrubs, and flower borders, was neat as a pin, but nowhere near as fancy as it had once been. It seemed age was catching up with Ms. Haldenby. He hoped it had mellowed her.

This morning, not wanting to wake Cassidy if she was sleeping in, Dave had texted to say that he'd called Sally and she'd be happy to have Cassidy come along this afternoon. An hour or two later, Cassidy had phoned to accept the invitation. And to issue one: "Ms. H says why don't you have brunch with us before we go to Sally's."

Dave had never been a coward. He'd faced down the mayor to win funds for the Heritage Committee, and he'd ejected drunken brawlers from the bar at the inn. There was no reason that the thought of brunching with an octogenarian should make him quake in his Ropers.

He rang the doorbell, and a few moments later Ms. Haldenby opened it.

Automatically, he straightened his spine. "Good morning, ma'am. Thank you for the invitation. These are for you." He thrust the bouquet toward her.

She took it from his hand. Some women, as they aged, got fragile and delicate looking; some got round and sort of fluffy. This woman had done neither. Her hair was a white version of the short, neat hairstyle she'd always had. Her tailored shirt, skirt, and low-heeled pumps might be the very ones she used to wear. Only her glasses were different: thicker lenses on the ones she wore, and another pair on a gold chain around her neck. Behind the lenses, her sky-blue eyes lit with something that might have been a twinkle. "Relax, Dave."

"Uh, sorry."

"Thank you for the flowers. I do love flowers and my arthritis keeps me from gardening the way I used to."

"I'm sorry about that."

"Certain aspects of aging are hell. Don't let anyone tell you otherwise." She said the words dryly, and now the twinkle was distinct.

Surprised to find himself warming to her, he said, "All right, I won't."

"Cassidy's in the kitchen. But wait a moment, I want a private word with you."

Uh-oh. Nervous again, he waited as she stepped onto the porch and eased the door closed.

Her words surprised him. "She tells me you persuaded

her to make a doctor's appointment to see about that leg of hers."

"I hope I have."

"Good. I've been nagging her too. I'm glad you got her to listen to reason."

"Cassidy has a mind of her own."

"She does. A rather intriguing one."

He grinned. "She's unique." Then, realizing the stupidity of that comment, he said, "Well, of course everyone is, but she's, uh . . ."

"More so than some? I quite agree." She studied his face. At five feet seven or so, Ms. Haldenby wasn't a short woman; the heels gave her an added inch or two; and her spine hadn't curved with age. When he was a boy, she'd loomed imposingly over him. Now it felt odd to have her tilt her head slightly to look up at him. "She says the two of you are dating."

"Yes, ma'am." He'd learned last night to respond as simply as possible.

He expected a probing follow-up question. Instead, she said, "Don't underestimate her."

"I try not to underestimate people." A memory flickered in his mind. "You told us that in fourth grade. To respect people and not to underestimate them." He'd internalized those principles so deeply, he'd forgotten where they origi-nated until he heard her brisk voice speak the word "underestimate."

"I also told my students not to underestimate themselves. I gave all sorts of advice to my students. Sadly, that had the result of intimidating most of them."

Sadly? Hadn't she intended to intimidate them? Not knowing what to say, he was relieved when the front door opened and Cassidy said, "There you are. I thought I'd lost both of you. Ms. H, the timer went off but I'm not sure the scones are done." She looked pretty and fresh in well-worn jeans, a sage-green tank top, and a plaid Western shirt worn open over it.

"I'll take a look. You bring Dave along"—the twinkle was back—"when you've had a chance to say good morning." She strode away with her bouquet, as sure-footed in those pumps as she'd always been. The woman might have arthritis, but clearly she wasn't surrendering to it any more than she absolutely had to.

Cassidy grinned at Dave. "So the two of you had a private chat. Did she tell you not to corrupt my virtue? Or not to let me corrupt yours?"

"She told me not to underestimate you."

Her brows rose. "Huh. That's one of the things I like about Ms. H. She's not predictable." She rested her hands on his shoulders. "I believe I was instructed to say good morning." She was wearing yesterday's multicolored sandals, and rose up on her toes as he bent down to kiss her.

With Ms. Haldenby down the hall, and neighbors possibly watching, he kept the kiss light. Then he put his arm around her shoulders and they went inside. Off the entrance hall, he glimpsed a rather formal living room with shelves full of books.

Cassidy said, "Come and see my room. It used to be the dining room and guest bathroom." She gestured him toward an open doorway off the hall.

He stepped in, to see a sunny, efficiently organized studio apartment. "This is nice."

"It has everything I need." She winked. "The sofa pulls out into a bed."

Even though he and Cassidy were officially dating, he wouldn't want to spend the night here. He'd be too aware of every moan, every creak of the bedsprings.

They went to the kitchen, another neat, efficient, attractive room. The table was laid for three. The flowers he'd brought, now in a blue ceramic vase, occupied the fourth spot. The scents in the air made his stomach growl: maple-cured bacon, onions, coffee, and something sweet and fruity. Ah, Ms. Haldenby was sliding blueberry scones off a cookie sheet onto a cooling rack.

"Sit down and stay out of the way," Cassidy told him, and went to help her landlady.

As the two women moved around the kitchen, it was clear that they'd prepared meals together before. Soon the food was assembled and they were all seated.

"This looks great." The dishes were classic: crisp bacon, fluffy scrambled eggs with slivers of chive, hash browns cooked with onions. Orange juice, coffee, and those golden scones studded with blueberries.

When he'd tasted everything, he said, "A delicious meal. Thank you, Ms. Haldenby."

"I'm no fancy cook and I realize it's rather presumptuous preparing a meal for the man who owns the best restaurant in town."

"I'll pass that compliment along to Mitch, our chef. And believe me, it's a treat to have someone cook brunch for me." He dug in, letting his appetite prove his words.

After a few moments, his hostess said, "I hadn't realized, when I first started teaching, how fascinating it would be to watch my students grow up and see what kind of lives they created for themselves."

"Did Dave surprise you, Ms. H?" Cassidy asked.

"No, he didn't." The white-haired woman gave him a smile. "You had an interest in history, you were smart, you were a considerate child. It made perfect sense that you would rescue a historic building and turn it into a lovely inn that provides hospitality for locals and tourists alike."

"Even in fourth grade, your future was set," Cassidy teased. "How predictable is that?"

Ms. Haldenby then asked him some questions about the inn's history and its restoration, and to his surprise he found himself enjoying the conversation. Before he could hold it back, a chuckle escaped him.

Both women stared at him.

To his former teacher he said, "I'm sorry. It just occurred to me, you're treating me like a grown-up."

"You're acting like one," she responded. Then she said, "Actually, I think part of my problem as a teacher was that I tended to treat children like grown-ups, and they weren't ready for it. Unfortunately, I had little experience with children myself. I was an only child and I attended a strict private girls' school. Perhaps I expected too much from my students."

"Seems to me, most of us turned out pretty well," Dave said. "Many of your lessons stuck with me, and I'm sure that's true for others as well."

"Thank you for that."

"I don't think it's a teacher's job, or a parent's, to be best friends with kids," he mused. "Some of Robin's teachers have been too lax. It's hard to keep her motivated when the teachers seem more concerned about the kids liking them and having fun than about them learning their lessons and some discipline. Anita said the same thing about a few of her colleagues at the high school." Each time he spoke or thought about Anita, it got easier. Sometimes, like now, it was even pleasant, as if her memory was a warm presence keeping him company.

"I met her, you know," Ms. Haldenby said.

"No, I didn't know that."

"It was in the bookstore. We had a nice chat. A lovely woman, and I'm quite sure she was an excellent teacher. I'm very sorry about what happened to her."

"Thank you." He used to hate it every time someone said that, because it sparked all those roiling dark emotions. This morning, in this sunny kitchen, all he felt was a poignant but rather mellow sense of sadness.

By the time Dave pulled up in the barnyard at Sally's, Cassidy's leg was giving her trouble again. He was glad she'd finally agreed to see a doctor.

He helped her down from the Jeep and kept an arm around her to steady her as they crossed to the barn, Merlin at his heels. Not many dogs were allowed to visit Ryland Riding, but Merlin had won acceptance with his impeccable behavior.

"Sally? You around?" Dave called.

"Hey, Dave," her voice responded. A moment later she emerged from the barn wearing her usual jeans, boots, and T-shirt under a Western shirt. After removing a pair of work gloves, she held out her hand. "Hello again, Cassidy."

"Hi, Sally. Thanks for inviting me."

After they shook, Sally stroked Merlin's back, then returned her attention to Cassidy. "What would you like to see and do? Want to take a horse out for a scenic ride?"

"I'd love to, but my leg's a little sore."

Sally glanced at Cassidy's jean-clad, now booted leg, then at Dave's arm around her waist. Her jaw tightened. "What happened to your leg?"

"A pinched nerve, maybe. It gets tingly sometimes. And yes, I'm going to see a doctor. Dave persuaded me to."

"Did he?" Sally's greenish gray eyes fixed on his face for a long moment, and then her expression lightened. "Yeah, he'd do that. He likes to look after people."

"You don't say." Cassidy's teasing tone brought a flicker of a smile to Sally's mouth. "Now, how can I make myself useful? Is there some work I can do sitting down?"

Sally ran a hand through her short, reddish blond curls

and pressed chapped lips together. "You shouldn't work. You're a guest."

That was Sally's pride speaking. Dave found the quality admirable but also frustrating.

"A guest who likes to keep busy," Cassidy said cheerfully.

That earned her an actual half smile. Sally had an attractive smile, but it rarely appeared. Her husband's death had hit her hard. Dave wished she could lighten up and find some joy in life. He squeezed Cassidy's waist. He owed her a lot.

"You ever cleaned tack?" Sally asked her.

"No, but I'm a quick learner."

"That's true," Dave confirmed.

He helped Cassidy into the tack room, and Sally got her set up. Then he said, "What can I do, Sally?"

"Campion panicked during that lightning storm we had a few nights ago. Kicked a big old hole in a box stall, and I haven't had a chance to get it fixed." As she spoke, they walked to the back of the barn, trailed by Merlin.

He surveyed the damage. "No sweat. I'll deal with this."

She gazed down at her boots. "I can never pay you back for everything you do for me."

"Don't talk that way. We're friends." He reached out to cup her chin, intending to tilt her face up.

Before he could touch her, she took a quick step backward. Now her head was up, her eyes wide as she stared at him.

"Sorry," he said. He'd noticed before that she didn't like people invading her personal space. The only ones who seemed welcome were her young riding students.

"No, it's okay. I'm just, uh, a little on edge." She sighed. "You're a good man, Dave."

He shrugged. So were lots of folks in Caribou Crossing,

as she'd find out if she gave them a chance rather than insisting on being self-sufficient.

Softly she said, "I didn't think you were looking for, you know, a relationship."

"I wasn't." An awkward thought struck him. "You, uh, weren't, were you?"

"God no." Then, as if she realized how that sounded, she went on. "Not because of you. Like I said, you're great. A wonderful guy and a terrific friend. But I will never get into a relationship again."

Now he realized where she was coming from. She'd thought the two of them were the same, both having lost the one person in the world for them. "Cassidy and I, it's just casual. Neither of us want anything serious."

He studied Sally's face, attractive but, as so often, looking tired and strained. "You don't think I'm being disloyal to Anita, do you? Cassidy's terrific, but I'm not going to fall in love with her or anyone else. Anita's it for me, just like Pete was for you. But I'm fed up with being so lonely all the time."

"Sometimes lonely is better." The words were barely a whisper.

Better than what? But he and Sally had always avoided this kind of topic and he wasn't about to probe, so he changed the subject. "I'm glad you came into town for Karen and Jamal's wedding, but you sure didn't stay long at the reception."

"No, I . . ." She brushed a blond curl off her face. "People were nice to me."

"You sound surprised. I told you Caribou Crossing is full of friendly people. If you didn't isolate yourself out here, you'd know that."

"It's hard. I'm not used to . . . socializing."

"Sally, you used to be a barrel racer. Before you got married, you were on the rodeo circuit. That's pretty social, isn't it?"

"It was." The hint of a smile teased her lips, but then her face went solemn again. "I was a different person then. I can't find my way back to that carefree girl."

"No, at our age, with our responsibilities, carefree's pretty much out of the question," he agreed ruefully. "But we can still take a break every now and then."

"Maybe." Her tone said she doubted it. Her shoulders—too bony under her well-worn shirt—squared. "But this sure isn't the time for a break. I have eight little kids coming for a lesson and I need to get the horses ready." Her expression lightened.

He'd seen her with her students and knew how much she loved children. What a pity she and Pete hadn't had any. Kids created more work, but they also forced you to play, gave you joy. Loved you. Without Robin, how would he have survived Anita's death?

If anything ever happened to Robin—

No, he wasn't going there. She was healthy and strong, and though she was too much the daredevil for his peace of mind, she wasn't a huge risk taker. Besides, he kept a close eye on her.

Never again would he lose someone he loved so deeply.

Chapter Eighteen

Cassidy whistled as she strode toward Dr. Carlene Young's office. Four weeks ago, on the way to her first appointment, her feet had dragged. Things sure could change in a month.

On this Monday after Labor Day, the weather was still warm, tourists still explored the town, but there was a different feel to the late afternoon air. A hint of autumn. She loved that season: leaves turning color, a crispness to the air, the scent of wood smoke on the breeze. She'd bet autumn in Caribou Crossing was terrific. She had been here two and a half months and her feet weren't the least bit itchy yet. Perhaps she'd stay until December, when she'd go to Victoria for her brother's wedding.

Her job at the Wild Rose was the best ever. When Madisun had returned to university in Vancouver, Dave had promoted Cassidy to assistant manager. He gave her lots of autonomy, listened to her ideas, and supported her when she needed it.

Their personal relationship was wonderful too. The sex just kept getting better, and so did everything else. She loved his company, whether they were riding, fixing meals, hanging out with Robin, visiting his family, or sprawling on the couch watching a movie.

It wasn't just Dave and his daughter who'd drawn her into their lives. Cassidy had become good friends with Ms. H, and often had coffee, lunch, or drinks with Jess, Brooke, the newly wed Karen, and Dave's sister, Lizzie. She and Maribeth from the thrift shop went to dinner and a movie together every couple of weeks. When she left, she'd miss them all. More people to keep in touch with via Facebook and e-mail. Though it wouldn't be the same . . .

She brushed away that thought. Sometimes she couldn't wait to leave one place and head to the next, and sometimes there were people, scenery, activities she'd miss. Always, when she reached the next destination, she dove into life there. She'd perfected the concept of moving on.

Besides, why was she thinking about the future? That wasn't her way. Today, right now, was perfect. Especially perfect was the fact that her leg hadn't given her the slightest bit of trouble in more than a week. Dr. Young had referred her to a neurologist in Williams Lake who'd sent her for all sorts of tests, and now Cassidy didn't have to worry about the results. Whatever the mysterious problem had been, it had finally healed, perhaps due to the yoga Dr. Young had recommended.

How crazy she'd been to worry that she might be turning into her great-grandmother.

Rather than forcing herself to step through the door of the doctor's office, today she went in blithely, a smile on her face as she greeted the very pregnant redheaded receptionist, Sonya.

"I'll take you in right away," Sonya said, starting to heft her bulk out of her chair.

"No, you sit. I can find my way. Aren't you almost due to go on mat leave?"

"I'm working right up to the end. What better place to be when the labor pains start?"

"Good point."

"Go on down to the doctor's office, Cassidy. She'll be with you in a couple of minutes."

Cassidy followed instructions and took a seat in one of the two chairs placed across from Dr. Young's desk. The walls had the usual framed certificates. More interesting were the dozen or so drawings and paintings done by patients, ranging from vivid finger paintings to quite nice works of art. One of the better ones, as Cassidy had noted on a previous visit, was Robin's painting of a couple of horses drinking from the stream that ran through Bly Ranch.

"Hello, Cassidy." Dr. Young came into the office and closed the door. The petite doctor had her long black hair in a braid, as usual, and wore a yellow shirt over tailored blue capris. She carried a file folder.

No longer worried about the contents of that folder, Cassidy greeted her cheerily.

Carlene Young put the file on the desk and sat in the chair beside Cassidy, turning it to face her. "How are you feeling?"

"Terrific! My leg hasn't bothered me in at least ten days. Whatever it was, I'm cured. And I'm addicted to yoga. So all those tests weren't necessary after all."

Solemn brown eyes studied her. "I'm glad you feel better. But, Cassidy, the tests were necessary. I'm afraid—"

"No." Any sentence that started with those two words, she didn't want to hear. "I'm fine." She stood, ready to leave.

The doctor rose too and rested her hands on Cassidy's shoulders. "Sit down." Gently but firmly she pushed Cassidy back into the chair, then sat beside her again. "You may *feel* fine, but the tests show that you do have a problem. You have multiple sclerosis."

"No!" She shook her head vigorously, trying to eject those horrible words from her brain. "I don't! I'm healthy. My leg is fine now."

"That period of days back in Vancouver when your leg was numb? That was what's called an attack, an exacerbation, or a relapse. And remember how you told me about the vision problems you experienced for two or three days last year?"

"It was eyestrain!"

"No. It was another attack. A clear diagnosis of MS can't be made until there are two attacks, separated in time."

Scowling, Cassidy leaned forward. This doctor was clearly incompetent. "Blurry vision, then a tingly leg a year later, and you say it's MS? That's nuts. They're not anything alike."

"The diagnosis was based on a number of tests, including the MRI and the Visual Evoked Potential. As for the vision and leg problems being different, that's typical of how MS works. It attacks the myelin sheath around the nerves of the central nervous system. The symptoms are based on where the attack happens and how extensive it is. A frustrating aspect of this disease is that it's unpredictable."

"I don't care! I don't have it." She sprang to her feet again.

Dr. Young reached for her hand and tugged gently. "Please sit down, Cassidy. I know this is hard to take."

Realizing that her legs were trembling, Cassidy sank back into the chair.

The doctor went on. "There are different kinds of MS. You have the most common one, relapsing-remitting MS, or RRMS. That means you may suffer relapses, but you'll also have remissions when you'll have full recovery. It's not a path of progressive deterioration with no remission, although people with RRMS may over time transition to . . .”

As Carlene Young went on, Cassidy knew the doctor was speaking, but her words were a garbled mess that didn't register. Until one caught her attention: great-grandmother.

“You may well not end up like her,” Dr. Young said. “It's possible her MS was progressive. Also bear in mind that she'd have been diagnosed forty or more years ago. Treatments are much better now. Some people with RRMS do suffer a lot of deterioration, but others have some symptoms and attacks and still lead relatively normal lives. There are even some who go into a lengthy remission for decades, possibly even for the rest of their lives.”

Was Dr. Young deliberately trying to be confusing? Honestly, she was the most incompetent doctor.

“We've diagnosed it early,” she went on, “and that's a good thing. Even if you aren't currently suffering any problems, it's still best to start treatment early.”

“Treatment? There's a cure?” GG had died a long time ago. Of course medical science would have found a cure by now!

For the disease that Cassidy definitely did *not* have.

“No, sadly there's no cure. Not yet, but there may well be in the future. However, several treatments have proven quite effective. The earlier treatment is started, the better the results.”

No cure. Well, who cared, because she didn't have MS. “I need to go.”

“I know this is a lot.” Those brown eyes were so sympathetic, as if Dr. Young truly believed that Cassidy had this awful disease. “I have some literature.” She opened the file folder and took out several pamphlets. “These give the basics about the disease and the treatment options. I'd like you to read through them, take some time to get your head around this, and then come back and we'll discuss it more thoroughly. When you can concentrate and take it in."

Cassidy shook her head.

Undeterred, Dr. Young went on. "I advise bringing a friend with you. Two pairs of ears, two people to ask questions, it leads to better understanding. And having practical and emotional support is critical to the treatment plan."

Treatment plan? Didn't Dr. Young realize Cassidy didn't *plan*?

"Perhaps Dave Cousins could come with you," the doctor suggested.

Dave? Here, listening to words like "attack" and "no cure"? Dave, who'd been there when the love of his life was diagnosed with a terminal illness? Who'd been at Anita's side as, day by day, she got sicker and sicker and finally died? Dave, who'd been so shattered by that experience that he'd become a shadow of the man he used to be?

Until Cassidy came along and helped him move on, to again find joy in life.

That was her role in Dave's life. To brighten it. Not to bring him a fresh tragedy.

And why was she even thinking this way? She didn't have this stupid disease!

This time when she sprang to her feet, her legs were strong with the need to get out of this place. Though she tried always to be honest, right now she was willing to lie her head off to win her freedom. "Fine, yes, I'll talk to Dave." She grabbed the pamphlets, which felt shiny and slimy in her hands. "I'll read these. Make an appointment. We'll come talk to you."

"Good. And, Cassidy, try not to worry. We'll build you an effective treatment plan and a strong support team. You'll still live a full, active life."

Of course she would. Because she didn't have fucking MS!

"Your last name, Esperanza," the doctor said. "It means hope, doesn't it? There's every reason to be hopeful."

Cassidy did not slam the door behind her and she did say good-bye to Sonya, but her racing heart urged her to slam, run, scream, cry—mostly to run.

So much for Caribou Crossing. This town sucked and she couldn't wait to see the end of it. As she hurried down the street away from the doctor's office, there was only one thought in her panicked brain: she had to leave.

A new place, new opportunities, new people. That was what she needed. Somewhere else, she would be a new person. No, she'd be her old self. The healthy, strong, vital, free-spirited Cassidy. The person she'd been before she came to this godforsaken place.

Her racing feet took her past the Wild Rose and she almost stumbled. Dave. How could she leave town without seeing Dave again?

No, she couldn't. She needed one last night with him. A night to . . . finish things off.

Closure, people called it. Okay, that was what she needed. Maybe it was selfish, but she needed closure. Then, tomorrow, she'd be on her way. Somewhere, anywhere. Anywhere but here. In the meantime, she needed to keep busy. She would get organized to move on, rather than replay that crazy visit to the doctor.

Resolved, she hurried back to her apartment to pack. When she started to open her door, she realized she still grasped the pamphlets. She whipped around to the back of the house and buried them deep in the trash can, where they belonged.

Feeling lighter, cleaner, she entered her little home and pulled her old backpack out of the closet. She'd accumu-lated more things than would fit in it, but that was often the case. A few comfy faves would go with her, and she'd give the rest to Maribeth. After all, wherever she went next, there'd be a thrift store where she could pick up whatever she needed.

She held up the blue sundress Dave loved. No, she wouldn't take it. But she'd wear it tonight, along with her pink bra and thong. Dave had a Heritage Committee dinner meeting in one of the conference rooms at the Wild Rose. He should be finished by nine-thirty, and they'd agreed that she'd go to his place then.

Oh God, she would miss Dave so much. It was hard to imagine a day without him. And Robin, that precocious, sunny girl.

No, she couldn't think that way. She couldn't *think*, period. She needed to keep moving.

Backpack almost full, she opened the coffee tin where she stored her passport and money. For once she'd saved way too much cash to put in her wallet. Dave had paid her well and she hadn't had much to spend money on. She piled the bills into a sock and stowed the sock deep in her pack. She hugged her old Winnie-the-Pooh, then tucked him in too, leaving his head free so he could look out. Then she pulled on her rattiest shorts and tee and stuck in earbuds. Rejecting twangy country and western—Caribou Crossing music—she chose hard-driving classic rock and set to work cleaning the apartment.

When the place was spic and span, she showered and put on the blue dress. She added the gifts Dave and Robin had given her for her twenty-eighth birthday in August: a silver necklace with a Canada goose pendant and a woven friendship bracelet.

With an hour to kill, she had no appetite and definitely didn't want to chat with Ms. H. She pulled on a Western shirt to keep her shoulders warm, and headed out into the dark evening with two garbage bags. One went into the trash can, the other in the donation box at Days of Your.

Next, she went to Westward Ho! to feed carrots to

Cherry Blossom, who she had to admit she'd miss, and to Dave's palomino, Malibu. Too bad Facebook didn't allow you to keep in touch with animals.

Horses and riding had sunk into her blood. Maybe she'd go to Alberta, or south of the border to Arizona or Montana. She'd learned a lot from Robin; perhaps she could work as a dude ranch wrangler for a while. Her savings would let her take a bus, rent an apartment, and provide for herself while she job hunted.

She'd be leaving Dave without giving notice. He didn't deserve that.

But in the long run, it'd be for the best. No way could she stay here a couple more weeks. Perhaps run into Dr. Young on the street. Her parents, even Gramps's death, had taught her that you had to put yourself first because you couldn't count on anyone else doing it. And what she needed now— or at least tomorrow—was a clean break and a fresh start.

Cassidy jogged up the four flights of stairs to Dave's suite. Perfectly healthy, not the slightest problem with her leg—so there, Dr. Young! She snapped the buttons of her Western shirt closed, because Dave got a kick out of ripping them open. And tonight, she wanted physical sex, fiery passion, driving need, not gentle, tender intimacy.

Something inside her warned that too much tenderness might break her.

And she didn't break. Not since Gramps had died.

She tapped lightly on the door, then opened it and went in. "Howdy, cowboy," she drawled as he came to meet her, tall and handsome in jeans and a white Western shirt that showed off his tan.

"Hey, you." When she reached up to clasp his face between her hands, he said, "You smell of horse."

"I visited Cherry and Malibu. Want me to wash my hands?"

"Nah. I like it, country girl." He leaned down to kiss her. A light hello kiss. "Guess what? I snagged a few of Mitch's gold rush trail cookies before the committee ate all of them."

The cookies, studded with dried fruit, nuts, and coconut, were a favorite of hers.

"Cookies, a cup of tea or a glass of wine, a little TV?" he suggested.

How cozy and domestic. They'd spent a number of evenings that way, ending up with lazy lovemaking either on the couch or in his bed. Perfect evenings.

No, she couldn't do that. Not tonight. She shook her head. "I'm hungry. But not for cookies." She hooked her hands in the top of his shirt, one on each side, and pulled downward, hard. The snap buttons popped and the sides of his shirt parted to reveal his rangy, muscled torso.

She'd learned his erogenous zones and now went for the spot at the base of his neck, sucking and tonguing it until he moaned. His distinctive masculine scent was an aphrodisiac.

Breathing hard, he pulled his shirt off.

Next she went for his nipple, the pebbled bud hard under her tongue. When she closed her teeth gently around it, his hips thrust toward her.

Running her hand over the growing bulge behind his fly, she said, "That's what I'm hungry for." She dropped to her knees, and by the time she'd freed him from his jeans and boxers, he was fully erect. Mmm, that was her favorite aphrodisiac. Her pussy throbbed in needy response to the sight of him.

When she closed her lips around him, inhaling his sexy musk, he groaned again. "Jesus, Cassidy. I don't know what's gotten into you, but I like it." His fingers wove through her short hair, cupping her head, steadying her as he thrust slowly in and out of her mouth.

As he did, she sucked him, licked him, used her fingers to slick moisture down his shaft, caressed his balls, using all the tricks that she'd learned heightened his pleasure. Each one sharpened the ache between her legs—and, thank heavens, shut down her ability to think about anything other than sex.

His voice husky, he said, "Oh man, that's good." He tugged her hair. "Come here. I want to kiss you, be inside you."

She wanted him deep inside her, driving hard and fast. So she released his erection and let him pull her to her feet. When he kissed her hungrily, she knew he was tasting himself—and she was tasting his need, giving him hers. Their tongues darted fiercely and they nipped and sucked each other's lips, inflicting tiny barbs of pain that only heightened arousal.

She whimpered against his mouth and went up on her toes, trying to grind her needy sex against his hard-on.

He thrust her away and ripped her shirt open. As she shrugged it off her shoulders, he reached for the zipper at the back of her sundress. The dress joined her shirt on the floor.

Dave freed himself from the jeans and boxers that had tangled around his lower legs, then fumbled in his jeans pocket to find a condom. She'd taught him to always be prepared.

Cassidy pulled her bra over her head, not bothering to undo it. While Dave sheathed himself, she yanked her thong down her legs. "Now. Now, Dave." She hooked her hands behind his neck and jumped up, into him.

Though she took him by surprise, he caught her, gripping her as she wound her legs around him. "You are so hot tonight," he gasped.

"You make me hot." She reached down to grasp him and guide him to her entrance.

He pumped his hips, thrusting deep and strong. Another thrust, and he filled her completely, stroking every needy cell to tingly sensation.

"God yes," she gasped. "More. Give me more."

And he did. She clung, riding him as he pistoned back and forth, slick with the moisture of her arousal.

She whimpered. "Everything, give me everything." Shifting slightly, she maneuvered so that her clit ground against him with each stroke. Oh yes, that was it, exactly right, the pleasure was so intense she couldn't take it any longer, she had to—"Oh God!" She cried out as her orgasm hit like a flash of lightning, sharp and bright and fierce.

A moment later, Dave broke too, jerking hard into her, the force of his climax prolonging the rhythmic pulses of her own.

Then, his legs finally giving out, he staggered toward the couch and managed to tip their still joined bodies down onto it. Breathing hard, they clung together in a messy tangle of arms and legs. Eventually, they sorted themselves out and he dealt with the condom.

He spooned her as she curved her butt into his belly. "How was your day?" he asked.

Her heart jumped. "Fine. Good. Nothing exciting. How was the Heritage Committee meeting?" She didn't want to talk. And now she realized she didn't want a night with Dave. No way could she handle that. She had to get moving. Should she tell him she was leaving town? If she did, he'd ask why. She'd say she'd been struck with itchy feet; they'd fight; it would be bad. A horrible way to end an amazing relationship.

"Good." He yawned. "Sorry. Long day and you drained me, totally. Anyhow, the oral history project is making great progress, and we worked on a strategy"—yawn—"to try to persuade old Mrs. Peabody's beneficiaries not to tear down her house."

Good. With some encouragement, he would fall asleep. "That's the one that used to be a gold rush bordello?"

Another yawn. "A fact that the dear old lady always denied." Her pulse raced and she had to force herself to hold still. He yawned again. "But our records provide evidence that's hard to refute." His words were coming slowly. "We should go to bed."

She couldn't. "In a minute. Tell me about your strategy."

"You wouldn't believe some of the . . ." Yawn, stretch. ". . . famous people who . . . frequented that . . . bordello . . . So we thought . . ." She waited, holding her breath, forcing herself to lie absolutely still. No more words came. His breathing was slow, his arm heavy.

She gave him five minutes. Another five, her heart hammering like she was running a marathon. Then she eased away, lifting his arm, sliding out, laying his arm gently on a pillow.

Quickly she pulled on her clothes.

Before clicking off the light, she took one final look at him. The nicest guy in town. He would be hurt and annoyed, and she hated that. But at least they'd kept things light.

She liked to think she'd been good for him. He wasn't stuck in the past any longer. While he clearly still loved and grieved for Anita, he'd figured out how to move on and enjoy life.

And he'd continue to do it, once she was gone. As would she. There was absolutely no reason that she should feel a pang in her heart, a hint of moisture in her eyes.

"Good-bye, Dave Cousins," she whispered.

Outside his apartment, she sprinted down the stairs. Her legs couldn't move fast enough. It was time to go. Waiting until morning was going to kill her. Was there a bus leaving tonight? She used her phone to check. Aha! One for Vancouver left just before midnight.

What would she say when she texted folks to explain her sudden disappearance? Something bright and breezy about moving on. Itchy-footed Cassidy: easy come, easy go. And if her heart secretly yearned for more—well, she'd learned long ago not to chase unrealistic dreams.

Chapter Nineteen

Dave drifted from sleep to hear a distant jangling. Wincing as pain stabbed into his neck, he straightened his body and opened his eyes—to find that he was on the living room couch. The persistent jangle was the alarm clock in his bedroom.

Had Cassidy slipped off to bed and left him on the couch? But no, as he forced his kinked-up body to walk to the bedroom, he saw that the bed hadn't been slept in. He jammed a hand down on the alarm to silence it, then scratched his head.

They'd had crazy-wild sex, then curled up on the couch. She'd asked him about the Heritage Committee meeting and he must have fallen asleep in the middle of telling her. But why had she gone back to her place rather than wake him and go to bed here?

Women. No doubt she had some reason that made perfect sense to her. It was her day off, so maybe she wanted to sleep in without him waking her.

All the same, he wished she had stayed.

He took Merlin for a run, the exercise easing out most of Dave's aches, then fed the dog and went to stand under the pounding warm spray of the shower. When he was dressed, he went downstairs again, the poodle at his side, to check in with Sam.

The night manager stared at him with a befuddled expression.

"Something wrong?" Dave asked.

"I finished. Typed 'The End.'"

"Wow." Dave held out his hand. "Congratulations. That's big."

Sam shook absentmindedly, without his usual firm grip. "I guess. But what happens next?" His bewildered tone indicated that the question was serious.

"I'm no expert, but when I do reports or funding proposals, I revise them until they're as good as I can make them."

Sam nodded slowly. "Yeah, that makes sense." He barked out a laugh. "You're saying 'The End' means I have to start all over?"

"That's your decision. But take a moment to feel good about finishing, okay?"

"Yeah. Yeah, good idea." Finally, he leaned down to pat Merlin, who'd been waiting patiently for the usual attention.

Sam gave Dave a summary of the night's events, finishing up with, "I noted a couple things need doing, things Cassidy can attend to. Sent her an e-mail. They can wait until tomorrow, since she has today off."

"Sure."

"She's worked out well, hasn't she?" Sam winked. "In more ways than one. Never would have guessed that first night when she flaked out on the lobby floor."

"I suppose not." He remembered his own first sight of her, and the way long-dormant feelings had sparked to life. Attraction. Curiosity. He'd felt an odd desire to know her better, to help her find work, but little had he guessed that she'd be the one to make him laugh again. To become his good friend, his sexy lover, an integral part of his life.

No, wait, he couldn't think that way. Couldn't let her

get too deeply under his skin. Come December, or perhaps earlier, she'd be off on her gypsy way. Man, he'd miss her.

Feeling a little depressed, Dave headed to the kitchen to grab coffee and a muffin. With Merlin at his side, he took his breakfast into his office and focused on work.

An hour later, his office phone rang. Robin said, "Where's your cell phone?"

He slapped a hand against his jeans pocket. "Must have left it upstairs. What's up?"

"What happened to Cassidy? Why did she go?"

"Huh? Go where? What do you mean?"

A pause, then, "You don't know? She didn't tell you?"

"Rob," he said patiently, "I have no idea what you're talking about."

"Cassidy left town! She texted me to say good-bye."

He shook his head, feeling residual stiffness from his night on the couch. "She hasn't left town. Whatever she texted you, you're misinterpreting."

"I am not! Listen, Dad. She says, 'Robin, it's time for me to leave Caribou Crossing. I don't have time to say good-bye in person, but I wanted to tell you how much I enjoyed getting to know you. You're a fabulous person. And we're Facebook buddies, right? We'll stay in touch. Give your dad a hug from me. xo, Cassidy.'"

"No." He realized he was still shaking his head, and it still hurt. He stopped and rubbed his neck. "It must be some bizarre joke."

"She didn't say anything to you? She didn't text you?"

"Oh, hell."

"Dad, you swore."

"Sorry. I'll run upstairs and check my cell, then call you back."

With the dog at his heels, Dave raced up the four flights, burst into his suite, and located his cell on the kitchen

counter behind the wrapped plate of cookies he'd brought
back from the meeting. And yes, there was a text.

> Dave, the time's come 2 move on. Wherever the
> wind blows, right? Hope I'm not lvg U in the lurch
> at the WR. It's bn gr8 knowing U. U R a truly terrific
> guy. Give Robin a hug from me. xo, Cassidy.

What the fuck? This made absolutely no sense. As he'd
told Robin, it had to be a bizarre joke. But it wasn't funny.

Frowning, he phoned his daughter. "I got a text too, but
I don't believe it."

"I tried calling her, but it went to voice mail. And I
checked Facebook. She posted yesterday morning, saying
how great she felt and how she was looking forward to
autumn. That's the last thing."

"I'll try calling. If she doesn't answer, I'll go to her place
and find out what's going on."

"Let me know, okay? Even if I'm in school. Text me and
I'll check when I can."

Dave rang Cassidy's number and he, too, got voice mail.
Annoyed, a little worried, he said, "It's Dave. Got your message. Give me a call." Then he headed for the door.

Merlin almost tripped him up. Dave gave his head a
quick pat. "Sorry, pal, not this time." He traded his boots for
running shoes and headed out at a sprint.

When he reached the rancher, he went around the side to
knock on Cassidy's door. A couple of taps brought no response, so he knocked louder. Still nothing. It wasn't eight
o'clock yet. Would Ms. Haldenby be up? He took a few tentative steps into the backyard.

The kitchen door opened and Ms. Haldenby, clad in a tailored navy dressing gown, peered out through her thick-
lensed glasses. "Dave Cousins. Are you coming or going?"

"Coming." He was too worried about Cassidy to be embarrassed that his former schoolteacher might think he'd spent the night. "Do you know if Cassidy's home? I knocked but she didn't answer."

"Come in, come in." She waved him into the kitchen. "I don't know. I just got up myself and was making coffee. Let's see if she answers if we knock from this side."

Dave followed her. On the floor outside Cassidy's door lay a piece of paper.

"It's a note," he said, bending to pick it up.

When he held it out to Ms. Haldenby, she waved it away. "I left my reading glasses by the bed. Read it to me."

Cassidy's familiar handwriting was larger and a little less messy than he was used to seeing, no doubt designed to be read by a woman with vision problems.

Dear Ms. H,
*   I'm off on another adventure. I*
cleaned the apartment so it's all ready
for a new tenant. I'll miss our chats.
You're the best landlady ever! Take
care of yourself.

*   Hugs,*
*   Cassidy*

P.S. Track down Irene!!

"She's gone?" Ms. Haldenby looked as stunned as he felt.

Without asking her permission, Dave knocked once on the door to the studio apartment and then opened it. The room was neat and clean, empty of any trace of Cassidy. "I don't believe this." Annoyance now trumped concern. "She just took off?"

"I need to sit down." The elderly woman turned on her heel, made for the kitchen, and sank into a chair.

Dave followed, and she asked, "When did you last see her?"

"Last night." Too upset to sit, he paced aimlessly.

"She didn't say anything? Did you have a quarrel?"

"No quarrel and she didn't say a word," he said grimly, remembering the wild sex and falling asleep with his arm around Cassidy. "How about you?"

"We had a cup of tea and a chat two or three days ago. I had no idea she was thinking of leaving."

"Nor did I."

"She didn't give notice at the Wild Rose?" She shook her head impatiently. "No, of course she didn't. I apologize; I'm being stupid. It's a shock."

"It is. Damn it, she always talked about her gypsy lifestyle, how she never planned, she treated each day as a fresh start. But I never thought that one day she'd just take it into her head to leave." When he hired her, she'd promised to give fair notice. She sure as hell hadn't done that for her job, much less give her friends any warning.

Ms. Haldenby rose and went to the coffeemaker. "How did she leave? And when?"

"I have no idea." He checked his cell as she poured two cups of coffee. "Her text to me was around one in the morning. God, I hope she wasn't hitchhiking in the middle of the night."

"Where might she be going?" She gave him a cup and took hers back to the table.

He shook his head and took a swallow, almost burning his tongue. "Her brother's getting married in Victoria in December. Maybe she went there. But why now? I wonder if she got an emergency phone call? But why wouldn't she say so?" He took a more cautious sip, hoping caffeine might stimulate his brain. "Wait, what's that thing about Irene? Does she mean she's gone to stay with some friend named Irene?"

"No, it's—" Was Ms. Haldenby blushing? "That's something else entirely."

"Oh? Well, damn, how could Cassidy be so irresponsible? She's not the woman I thought she was." And that hurt him to the core. Even more so when he realized that when she was with him last night she must have known she was leaving. She'd already cleaned her apartment.

Ms. Haldenby frowned. "Apparently I misjudged her character too. That's rare for me."

"She had us all fooled," he said bitterly. "She didn't even say good-bye to Robin, just sent her a text."

"It can be hard to say good-bye, especially when you care about people," she said thoughtfully, her hands wrapped around her coffee cup.

"Care? Hah. If she cared about us she wouldn't have left." He thought of the trail of people Cassidy kept up with, using her phone in spare moments to access Facebook and e-mail. By leaving this way, she'd made it pretty damned clear that her friends in Caribou Crossing meant no more to her than any of the others she'd met during her travels.

Why would he have thought differently? And why should he care? He'd known all along that she didn't intend to stay here. Hadn't he just been thinking that he couldn't let her get any further under his skin? And yet she *was* under his skin . . . Damn her.

"Sometimes there are reasons for leaving, even when you do care about someone." Ms. Haldenby sighed. "I'll miss her."

"Don't waste time missing her," he said bitterly. "She chose to move on, and so should we." Realizing he still gripped the note, he put the piece of paper, crumpled now, down on the kitchen table. "Speaking of which, I need to go post an ad for a new assistant manager."

Even as he said it, he knew no one could replace Cassidy—not at work, and definitely not in his personal life.

* * *

A couple of hours later, Dave, still in a foul mood, answered the phone in his office.

"Dave, it's Daphne Haldenby."

Daphne? He'd never even thought of her as having a first name. "Hello, Ms. Haldenby." Heart racing, he leaned forward in his desk chair. "Have you heard from Cassidy?"

"No, I haven't. But . . ."

"Yes?" he prompted when she didn't continue.

"You know those tests the doctor was doing? Cassidy never said if she got the results."

"Her leg problem cleared up, so she figured it was just some strange thing that healed itself, or that yoga cured."

"Hmm. But Dr. Young never actually told her the test results?"

"Not as far as I know. Why do you ask?"

"The garbage pickup was today. They're not the most meticulous young men, and after they'd gone I found a few items lying on the ground. One was a pamphlet on multiple sclerosis."

"There was a pamphlet on multiple sclerosis in your garbage can?" What did that mean?

"Anyone could have walked down the back alley and put it in the can. Or . . ."

Or Cassidy might have. Had Carlene Young told her the test results, and Cassidy had kept them a secret? Did she have a serious illness? Heart pumping so fast he had trouble thinking, he said, "Do you know anything about MS?" Wasn't it some kind of nerve disease?

"read the pamphlet."

"Right. Of course."

"The disease attacks the myelin sheath protecting the nerves of the central nervous system." She went on in her precise, schoolmistressy tone. "The damage affects the flow of nerve impulses, and that results in symptoms, depending on where the attack occurs and how bad the damage is. Cassidy's leg, and the fatigue that she said was unusual for her, could both be symptoms. Or, as I said, anyone could have put the pamphlet in the trash can. After all, if Dr. Young had diagnosed Cassidy, surely the last thing she'd do would be to leave town. I'd understand it if she was close to her parents and wanted to be with them while she started treatment, but from what I've gathered, they're quite self-centered."

"True." He pressed his free hand to his forehead, as if that would somehow help him think logically. If Cassidy had this disease that caused nerve damage, would she have gone to her parents? To her brother? Why wouldn't she have told him?

He swallowed. "You mentioned treatment. So the disease is curable, right?"

"As of now, there is no cure."

His hand fell with a thunk to the desk, but the pain barely registered. Oh God, he'd heard those words before. When Anita was diagnosed. "It's . . ." He forced the word out. "Terminal?"

"No. Most people with MS live a normal life span."

He let out a long, relieved sigh. That was something, at least. "Wait a minute, isn't that what Mrs. Roland has?" The woman had been a successful Realtor, but then a debilitating disease had struck her down. She'd had to go into a care facility. She was only in her early fifties.

"I believe so. But the pamphlet says there are different forms of the disease, it varies greatly from individual to individual, and its course is unpredictable. It also says that early diagnosis and treatment can have a significant impact."

He tried to corral his tumbling thoughts and still his pounding heart. "The pamphlet could have come from anywhere. It could have blown out of the garbage truck."

"True. I only hope that if Cassidy does have this disease or any other medical condition she has the sense to commit to the proper treatment."

"You think she wouldn't?"

"If it was something like a broken bone being set, I believe she would. A quick, straightforward fix. But according to the pamphlet, MS treatment is an ongoing thing and it needs to be carefully monitored. Having a stable life helps a great deal, as does having a support team of family and friends as well as medical professionals." She sighed. "None of that fits with Cassidy's gypsy lifestyle. Nor with her determination to be independent."

"I hear you."

They were both quiet for a few moments. Then she said, "No doubt I'm a foolish old woman who is making a mountain out of a molehill that never existed in the first place."

Yes. Please. Slowly, he said, "I doubt that anyone who's met you would ever call you foolish. Let's just hope you're mistaken."

"Indeed." The word lacked her usual conviction.

Thursday afternoon, Dave listened impatiently as an inn guest, a petite sixty-something-year-old with obviously dyed brassy blond hair, explained her precise needs when it came to pillows. Normally, he enjoyed providing guests with the best possible experience, but for the past two days he'd been in a rotten mood. Besides, dealing with linen requests was the job of his assistant manager—and he didn't have one.

No assistant manager, no lover, no friend. Maybe it was stupid, but he felt betrayed. He'd known his sexual relationship with Cassidy was casual, and that's exactly what he'd wanted. But he cared about her. A friend didn't run off without a word of warning or explanation.

She'd hurt his daughter's feelings, too, which was even less excusable. Oh, Robin said they'd had a couple of conversations through Facebook, but he knew Robin had wanted—and deserved—a more personal good-bye. She, like Dave, Ms. Haldenby, and everyone else who'd cared about Cassidy deserved an explanation.

He refused to phone Cassidy again. She hadn't returned his call.

As for Facebook, he'd always thought it was a waste of time—face-to-face or phone communication was so much more effective—and he was damned if he was now going to sign himself up and send a "friend" request to Cassidy. So it was through Robin that he'd learned that Cassidy was now in Cannon Beach, Oregon. She'd posted on Facebook that she'd found a discarded newspaper with an article on the beach town and was enticed to go there.

It seemed there was no good explanation for her departure; it was just her perennial itchy feet. She hadn't gone to see her parents or brother, which at least reassured him that she wasn't sick and allowed him to be mad rather than concerned.

He had completely tuned out his guest, who had finally shut up and was gazing at him expectantly. He forced a smile. "You know what? Because I want to make sure you get exactly what you want, I'm going to take you on a behind-the-scenes expedition. How'd you like to see our linen room and choose your own pillow?"

The blonde's overly made-up eyes lit. "Behind the scenes? How exciting. Mr. Cousins, when my friend Abby recommended the Wild Rose, she said you folks treat every guest as if they're special, and I see that she's right."

This time his smile was genuine. "Of course you're special. We want to make your time here at the Wild Rose, and in Caribou Crossing, something you'll always remember."

His smile soured. At this moment, was Cassidy regaling someone in Cannon Beach with stories of her travel adventures, with a passing mention of riding horses in Caribou Crossing?

After he dealt with the guest, he went to his office, intending to check e-mail to see if there were any new applications for the assistant manager position. He'd interviewed a couple of locals: an empty-nest mom who wanted to return to the workforce but knew nothing about the workings of a hotel, and a young man who was clearly more interested in chatting up waitresses and chambermaids than applying himself. With effort, the mom might be trained, but he'd rather have someone who could more readily step in and do the job. As Cassidy had.

He really needed to stop thinking about her. She'd left town on a whim and chosen Cannon Beach on a whim. Ms. Haldenby had indeed created an imaginary mountain out of one pamphlet that had escaped the garbage truck. And yet . . . The retired teacher had made excellent points about Cassidy's personality.

Cassidy had the discipline to do a job well, yet she never stuck with one job for any length of time. She never stuck with one place. Or one friend, except in a superficial Facebook way—and more fool him for having thought he and she shared something special.

She prided herself on her strength and independence. He'd seen how it irked her when her leg gave her trouble. If she was diagnosed with a life-altering disease that affected her physical mobility and strength, one that might cramp her gypsy lifestyle, how would she react?

Might she simply pack up and run away?

"Damn it," he muttered. "I can't stand not knowing."

Dr. Young's office number was in his cell phone. Even as

he dialed it, he knew the effort was probably futile. Doctor-patient confidentiality would prevail.

Her receptionist, Sonya, answered.

"Hi, Sonya, it's Dave Cousins. Hey, you must be due any day now. How are you doing?"

"I'm fat and fed up and can't wait for junior to make an appearance," she said cheerfully. "How are you? Want to make an appointment? Yourself or Robin?"

"Actually, I wondered if I could talk to Dr. Young on the phone."

"Sure. I'll get her to call as soon as she has a spare moment."

He thanked her, then opened his e-mail and scanned a couple of applications. Neither person was ideal, but both were possibilities. He'd conduct phone interviews; then, if the applicants looked worthwhile, he'd invite them to come for in-person interviews.

His cell rang, showing Dr. Young's name. "Hi, Carlene."

"Hi, Dave. What can I do for you?"

"It's actually, uh, about Cassidy."

"Ah. I'm glad she talked to you. I wasn't sure she would."

He swallowed. So there'd been something to talk about? "She's pretty independent."

"She is. What do you think? Are you willing to come in with her?"

She hadn't heard that Cassidy had left town. Maybe that worked to his benefit. "Well . . ." He hoped the doctor would go on, and she did.

"She needs a support person, but I know it's a lot to ask when you haven't known each other very long. And for you, having gone through what you did with Anita . . ."

Crap. Shit. Ms. Haldenby was right. "It really is true? The diagnosis doesn't allow for any other possibilities?"

"No, I'm sorry. As soon as I heard that her great-grandmother had MS, I knew it was something to test for. While it's not an inherited disease, research indicates that genetic factors can increase the risk of developing it. It's possible her grandmother had it too, though it hadn't been diagnosed. The fall that killed her might have resulted from an attack rather than from her simply tripping."

He hadn't known about her great-grandmother and all she'd said about her grandmother was that she'd died at a young age. "I guess I'd like to know what's involved in being a support person."

"Of course you would, before you commit to it. Did she share the pamphlets I gave her?"

Only with the garbage can. "No."

"I'll stay late this afternoon if you can come in. I'll fill you in on what your role would be, and on the time demands and emotional demands. I'll give you more pamphlets, and then you can go away and think about it. And talk to Cassidy, if you feel comfortable doing that. If you decide you can't deal with it, I'm sure she'll understand."

He swallowed against a lump in his throat. Was that why Cassidy hadn't told him? She knew what he'd gone through with Anita. She wouldn't ask him to be a support person to someone with a serious illness. Or maybe she didn't think he was capable of doing it.

Was he? He believed in helping others, but he'd barely held it together to be strong for Anita. He couldn't do it again. Whatever Cassidy's reasons, it was a good thing she'd left town.

"Dave? I know this is difficult, but decisions need to be made. It's important to develop a treatment plan and start treatment early."

If Cassidy had gone to her parents or brother, he could believe she was going to start treatment. But not in Cannon Beach. No way could she afford medical treatment in the States.

He thought about Cassidy's personality: her itchy feet, her self-sufficiency, her need to be in control of her life. She would hate the idea of a debilitating disease. Maybe she'd been trying to spare him, but she'd also been running away. "A diagnosis like this is a big shock," he said. "She didn't take it well."

"No, especially since she's been feeling fine recently. She said that I was wrong, that she didn't have MS. I asked her to read the literature, try to get her head around it, then find a support person and come back to talk to me. To be honest, I was afraid she wouldn't tell you about it."

"Yeah, I hear you," he said grimly.

"It's a big thing for you to get your head around too. You need information and you'll have questions before you make a decision. Will you come in to see me?"

Chapter Twenty

Sitting on the couch in her new apartment late Friday afternoon with Pooh Bear on her lap, Cassidy picked up the smartphone that both connected her with the world and provided entertainment. Who needed a computer or tablet when this little device gave her the Internet, Facebook, e-mail, a camera, books to read on the miniature screen, videos, games, and—oh, yeah—even the ability to make or receive a phone call?

On her Facebook page, she posted a photo she'd snapped with her phone. It showed Cannon Beach's dramatic sea stack rocks looming out of a misty morning fog. She typed:

Fab news! Got a chambermaid job at a hotel on the ocean, and an apartment share with another girl who works there. Walked on the beach this morning. How gorgeous is this?

The scenic beauty lived up to what she'd read in that newspaper on the bus. The discarded paper with the travel article had been a clear sign leading her to her next destination.

The Seaside Hotel didn't have the character of the smaller Wild Rose, but its beachfront location was terrific and it was clean, nicely decorated, and seemed to be well run. Chambermaid work wasn't as cool as being assistant manager, but there was satisfaction in cleaning rooms.

Joe Donnelly, the HR person who'd hired her, mentioned that the chambermaid who'd left had shared an apartment with one of the waitresses. He'd introduced Cassidy to Kristie, a chirpy blonde who was engaged to a soldier stationed in Afghanistan, and the deal was done.

Of course, Kristie wasn't Ms. H. . . .

That was negative thinking. Cassidy loved having happy memories of places she'd been, but she never let those get in the way of enjoying her latest adventure. As long as she didn't think about Dave, she felt fabulous. "A new day, a new place, a fresh start," she told Pooh.

She and the bear had the apartment to themselves, since Kristie was working tonight. The place was homey, with her roommate's magazines, posters and photos, plants, and knitting project—a scarf for her fiancé. The only things of Cassidy's in the living room were Pooh and her phone. But then, aside from her backpack and its contents, neatly stowed in the smaller bedroom, she didn't own anything else. In the past, that fact had always made her proud. Why now, faced with a smiling photo of Kristie with her guy, a stack of wedding magazines, and the striped scarf suspended from knitting needles, did she feel a little . . . deficient?

Maybe Caribou Crossing hadn't been so good for her. While she made friends and found interesting activities wherever she went, she'd never been drawn into a community in the same way as she had there over the past few months. Dave's family had come to feel . . . well, more like family than her own did, to be honest. Robin was like—she fingered the woven friendship bracelet—the cool little sister she might have wished for. And then there was Dave. To be totally objective, she'd never dated a man as wonderful as Dave.

She really hoped that whatever he was looking for in life he found it. If he wanted to remain heart-true to Anita, she hoped he still found lots of great women to have fun with. If he did fall in love again, she truly hoped he'd beat the odds this time and the two of them would grow old and gray together. And if the thought of either option gave her a twinge or two in her own heart, it certainly wasn't envy, or jealousy, only . . .

Oh, who knew? She'd never been one to obsess over emotions.

Why was she hanging around this apartment anyhow? This town had a pub or two. She'd get herself a beer and a burger, and see if she could make some friends.

Cassidy's first day of work ended at four o'clock on Saturday. "Whew," she said to Rosita, one of the other chambermaids, as she pressed her tired hands into her aching lower back. "I'd forgotten what tough work it is, doing this full-time."

"You get used to it." The older woman fished a light jacket out of her locker and flashed Cassidy a smile. "It makes you strong." She pulled the coat on over her uniform.

"True. See you tomorrow." Cassidy planned to browse into a few art galleries and shops on the way home, so she wanted to change into street clothes.

She sponged her armpits, chest, and face with damp paper towels before putting on her jeans and T-shirt. Her time was her own. No one to account to. Just the way she liked it.

No cooking dinner with Dave, no friendly bickering with Robin over which movie to watch. No lawn mowing for Ms. H, or early evening rides with Dave. No barbecues at his parents' house, or—

She grabbed her bag and headed out. Outside, the

September sun was still high in the sky. On second thought, the beach was more appealing than shops and galleries. Fresh ocean air would feel good after a day of vacuuming, stripping and making beds, and cleaning bathrooms. Her stride already springier, she headed for the beach.

"Cassidy?" A male voice stopped her. Dave's voice.

No, that was impossible. Squinting against the sun's glare, she saw the shape of a man approaching. When he arrived in front of her, it was indeed Dave, dressed in his typical jeans and Western shirt, but barefoot, sandals dangling from one hand.

A leap of joy caught her breath, made her stumble. Then worry flooded in. "Is something wrong? Is Robin okay?"

"Everything back home is fine." His words were measured, his expression noncommittal. No smile, no hug. No doubt he was pissed off that she'd left town without telling him.

"Then what are you doing here?" God, it was good to see him, yet he had her nerves jangling. He wouldn't have come all this way just to say he was angry; he could have texted. "How did you find me?"

"An oceanfront hotel in Cannon Beach? There aren't that many."

"The hotel shouldn't have told you." Hotels weren't supposed to hand out employee information.

He held out a piece of paper.

Automatically, she reached for it and saw that it was a check made out to her.

"I told the manager I had your final paycheck and needed you to sign some forms. She verified my credentials; then as a courtesy from one hotelier to another she confirmed your employment and told me when your shift ended."

"What forms?"

"I made that up." His jaw was tight; she knew he hated to lie.

"You didn't come all this way to bring me a paycheck."

"*I* believe in honoring my responsibilities." A muscle twitched at one side of his jaw.

She bit her lip. "I'm sorry I skipped without giving notice."

"Why did you do that, Cassidy?"

She shrugged. "Oh, you know." Not wanting to keep standing there staring at each other, she slipped off her sandals and walked down onto the beach. He fell in step beside her.

"I had the impulse to pick up and go somewhere new," she said.

"When I hired you, you said you'd give fair notice."

"All I can say is I'm sorry."

"You'd already cleaned Ms. Haldenby's apartment when you came to my place Monday night," he said grimly. "You knew you were leaving and you didn't say a word."

She wouldn't say "sorry" a third time. "What can I say? I suck at good-byes."

"Robin deserved one in person. So did Ms. Haldenby."

And so did he. It went without saying. Maybe she *would* say it a third time. "Okay, I'm sorry. My bad."

"Why?"

As they crossed the sand, heading toward the ocean's edge, she kept her gaze straight ahead. "Why do I suck at good-byes?" Would he accept the sidetrack?

"Why did you leave?"

"It's what I do. You know that. I was there, now I'm here. Isn't it beautiful?" She waved a hand at the beach, with its scattering of people, the calm ocean lapping the shore, and craggy Haystack Rock and the pointy Needles standing guard.

"It is. I walked down here while I waited for you."

"I've moved on, Dave." Despite the fact that she'd really love to wrap her arms around him. "You need to do the same."

He scrubbed a hand over his jaw. "Yeah, wouldn't that be nice?"

She frowned. "So do it. What's holding you back?" He sure showed no signs of wanting to wrap *his* arms around *her*.

His only answer was a long sigh as they strolled past three kids decorating a sand castle.

"Why did you come?" she asked.

He gave another sigh. "You have multiple sclerosis."

Her heart stopped and she stumbled. "What? No, I don't! What are you thinking?"

His voice was level. "Dr. Young says you do."

"You . . ." She grabbed his arm, stopping him, and glared at him. "You talked to my doctor? You had no right! She had no right!" An incorrect diagnosis *and* a breach of patient confidentiality? Dr. Young should be reported. Or sued.

He freed his arm from her grip and kept walking. "She thought I was calling because you'd talked to me. Like she'd recommended that you do. I didn't enlighten her. For which she reamed me out in a major way when I eventually confessed."

"I don't get it." She kept pace, though she was tempted to leave him and run back to her apartment. "Why would you call Dr. Young?"

"Ms. Haldenby figured it out, about the MS."

"I do *not* have MS. There's nothing to figure out." Blood pounding in her temples, she stared at the sea stack rocks, hoping their majesty would calm her, but the tactic didn't work.

"Yeah, I thought you might be in denial."

"Stop treating me like a child!"

"A child? Robin's more mature than the way you're

acting. Did you even read those brochures before you threw them out?"

Light dawned. "Ms. H found them in the trash? Damn, I shoved them way down."

"When the garbage guys dumped the can, one of the brochures fluttered out. Ms. Haldenby found it, read it, and phoned me."

"You two have no right to interfere in my life!" Her bare feet thumped the wet sand. "Damn it, Dave, I look after myself."

"Are you seeing a doctor here? Getting treatment?"

"How many times do I have to say it? I'm not sick!"

They'd walked some distance down the beach, away from most of the people. Dave stopped and caught her arm, not gently, making her stop too. "Cassidy, you can say it a million times but that won't make it true. And as for looking after yourself, you're doing a piss-poor job of it." She'd rarely heard him swear before, and he'd never glared at her with such a thunderous expression: anger, disappointment, and something else. Fear?

She choked out words. "I'm doing fine."

"I know the diagnosis was a shocker. It was for me when I heard, so I can only imagine how scary it must be for you. But denial isn't going to fix the problem."

"I'm not in denial and there isn't a problem. What is it with you? You're so into fixing people's problems, you have to imagine ones that don't exist?" She scowled at him.

He scowled back.

"Well, guess what?" she said. "If this problem you've imagined really did exist, you wouldn't be able to fix it!"

His scowl faded. Pain replaced it. "I couldn't fix Anita's either," he said quietly.

"Oh God, I'm sorry. I didn't mean to remind you."

"It's been on my mind since I found out about your diagnosis."

Of course. Which was one reason she'd never wanted him to know about her *mis*diagnosis. She sighed. "Dave, I'm sorry that Dr. Young made you think I have MS. But I don't. And whatever problems I might have, they're mine, not yours. I'm not Anita. You two loved each other; you were engaged. Of course you stood by her. Me, I'm just, you know, someone passing through your life." Saying those words sent a twinge of melancholy through her. She forced it away. She'd chosen her lifestyle and it suited her. She pressed the fingers of both hands to her temples, where a tension headache had begun to throb.

His mouth twisted ruefully. "If you were, then this would be easy."

What did that mean? That he didn't want her to just pass through? But she wasn't the kind of woman who people loved deeply, the kind they built a life around. "What are you saying?"

"Dr. Young says you need a treatment plan and a support team."

She shook her head, wincing at the pain. Of course. Dave was playing the fixer again. He'd do the same thing if any of his friends had a problem. It wasn't that he thought she, Cassidy, was special.

"I don't have MS." Even to her own ears, her words sounded a little . . . pathetic. Was it possible the doctor was right? That Dave was right, and she was in denial? Terror stabbed into her. She could end up like GG? Defiantly, she said, "I feel fine now, perfectly healthy."

"Which doesn't mean you don't need treatment. The earlier you start treatment, the more effective it's likely to be. You may well not end up like your great-grandmother."

She sucked in a surprised breath. "How do you know about . . . Oh. Dr. Young again."

"She thinks it's possible your grandmother had it too. An attack could have caused the fall that killed her. If she'd lived longer, she might have been diagnosed."

She bit her lip and admitted reluctantly, "Gramps wondered about that. He warned me to be on the lookout for symptoms, but I didn't even want to think about it." And she still didn't.

"Your grandfather would want you to do everything possible to take care of yourself so you can live a full life."

The thought of Gramps brought moisture to her eyes. "I do live a full life. I take care of myself." Tears swam in her eyes, blurring her vision. "I don't have MS." But the last words came out as a plea, rather than a statement.

The tears spilled over and she wailed, "Oh, fuck. I do, don't I?"

Hating her weakness, her disease, hating Dave for making her acknowledge it, she dropped her bag and thumped her fists against his chest. "Damn you, D-Dave, you shouldn't have come. I was f-fine!" The words came out between hiccupy sobs. "I d-didn't want to know. It's not fair!"

He wrapped his arms around her shoulders, pulling her tight, capturing her arms between their bodies and stilling her flailing fists. "I know. It sucks, Cassidy."

She raised her head and gazed at him through tear-soaked eyes, furious at him and the world in general. "My l-life will never be the same again!"

Maybe she hoped he'd deny it, but instead he shook his head. "No, it won't."

She struggled to free her hands to thump him again, but he held her too tightly. "I d-don't want to be sick."

"I know."

"I don't want to be stuck in a wheelchair, l-lose my ability to talk coherently. Be in-incontinent." Visiting GG as a little kid had been scary, not just because of her great-grandmother's physical symptoms but because Cassidy could see that her brain was active and she was frustrated with her body's inadequacies.

"That may well not happen. This is why you need to get all the information and start on treatment. Early diagnosis and treatment can make a huge difference."

"Suddenly you're some k-kind of expert," she scoffed.

"Right now I know more than you do. But you can change that."

Cassidy hardly ever cried. It never solved anything. Now, crying all over Dave, she felt like a powerless child. Fighting back the tears, she said, "Let me go. I need a tissue."

Cautiously, he released her and she bent to retrieve her bag and hunt inside. She wiped her face, blew her nose, then said shakily, "That wasn't fair. Playing the Gramps card."

"I'm right, though, about what he'd have wanted."

She nodded, keeping her head down, feeling vulnerable. "Gramps was the one person who always looked out for me."

"Now you're going to need others. You'll have them back in Caribou Crossing."

"What do you mean?"

"Come back with me. You need to discuss treatment options and develop a plan."

"Plan," she echoed ruefully. "Not my favorite thing."

"You'll learn. Dr. Young says you also need a support team. You may not have your gramps, but you won't be alone. You'll have me, Ms. Haldenby, Robin, my parents—"

"What? Stop, wait!" The ache in her temples pulsed harder. "You *told* all of them? How dare you discuss my health with—"

"I didn't. Stop jumping to conclusions. But I know that, when you do tell them, they'll be there for you."

She frowned, again not understanding. "Why?" she queried softly.

He touched her cheek gently. "Because we care about you, Cassidy Esperanza. No one will want you to go through this alone."

Alone. It was the only way that she knew how to be. The only person she could count on was herself. How could she believe in what Dave seemed to be offering? And even if she did, how could she let herself rely on others?

"You need to think about your options," he said quietly. "You could go down to Acapulco and—"

"To my parents? You must be kidding." When had they ever been there for her?

"Your brother in Victoria?"

She shook her head. "We love each other, but we're not all that close. Besides, he's starting his new life with Mags. I can't dump my issues on them."

"He and his fiancée might want you to."

Whether that was true or not, she couldn't ask. She'd walked out on JJ when she was seventeen, leaving her fifteen-year-old brother alone with Luis while she ran off to Europe. She'd always felt guilty about that, but at the time she'd been desperate. Because of that guilt, she'd let the distance between them grow until they were little more than casual acquaintances.

Nor could she impose on her friends in Caribou Crossing. Especially Dave, after what he'd gone through with Anita. She gazed at his handsome face, so strained now. She'd taught this man to smile again, and now she'd reduced him to this. She tried to think. Dave had made the offer because of his compulsion to fix things, not because he truly wanted to support another woman with a serious illness. He'd be relieved if she decided to go to Victoria.

Really, Victoria was her only reasonable option. How depressing. Since she'd taken off on her own in Europe after her eighteenth birthday, her life had been all about freedom of choice. Now life had narrowed, a funnel directing her to one outcome: living with MS, in Victoria. "Okay," she said resignedly. "I'll go to Victoria, find a doctor, talk about treatment, and, and . . ."

"Tell your brother about your diagnosis and start building that support team?"

If she could bring herself to tell JJ, he'd try to be there for her. Her brother was a good guy. Mags seemed like a nice person. She'd probably be supportive. Victoria didn't have a lot of good memories for Cassidy, but she could learn to like it. It'd be easy to find work. And yet . . .

She'd felt comfortable in Caribou Crossing. She loved the spectacular countryside and the picturesque town, loved riding and even mowing Ms. H's lawn. And yes, the people there were nice. Ms. H, the staff at the Wild Rose, Maribeth, not to mention Dave's whole network of family and friends. And Dave himself . . .

"Is that what you want to do?" he asked.

If she was absolutely honest with herself, what she wanted was to go back to Caribou Crossing. But she couldn't do that to Dave. She gazed up at him through damp lashes. "You ask what I want. I want not to be sick. It's hard to see past that. To envision a future that's . . . well, I don't even know what it would be."

"You hate planning ahead, so don't worry about the distant future. I know you likely won't want to stay in one place forever, and you won't have to. But Dr. Young says that for a year at least, you should work with one medical team and one support team until you get a better handle on your disease. You can do that in Victoria or in Caribou Crossing."

A year. That was scary, but nowhere near as scary as thinking about the rest of her life—whatever that life might turn out to be, now that she had this stupid disease.

She could handle Victoria for a year. "Dave, your offer is amazing, but I couldn't do that to you. To you, or Robin or

Ms. H or anyone else in Caribou Crossing, but especially to you. I'm the one who's sick, and I'm stuck with the consequences." Whatever the hell they'd turn out to be. "You shouldn't be stuck with them too."

His hazel eyes were dark and shadowed on this sunny day. "You're saying that where you want to be is Caribou Crossing."

She should have phrased it differently. "No, I'm not."

He swallowed. "The easy thing would be to say that I believe you, and let you go to Victoria." Another swallow. "The easy thing would have been to not have come here. To have let myself believe you'd seek treatment on your own. The easy thing would have been to never have phoned Dr. Young." He studied her face for a long time, and she didn't know what to say.

Finally, his expression lightened and he smoothed teardampened hair back from her cheek. "Guess I've never been a big one for easy. Especially not when a friend's in trouble."

"Friends don't want their friends to feel obligated."

"I don't feel obligated. And I agree with you. If anyone offers to help because they feel obligated, we don't need them on your team. We only want the folks who truly want to be there."

"We?" Damn it, the tears were starting again.

Chapter Twenty-One

One thing Dave had learned from the women he loved was that even though instinct told him to do anything to stop a woman from crying, sometimes they needed to do it. So, standing on Cannon Beach and gazing at the stunning scenery, he hugged Cassidy to him and stroked her back. "Yeah. We. We're in this together now."

The immensity of that prospect almost brought tears to his own eyes.

"I h-hate crying," she muttered against his chest.

"I'm not so crazy about it myself."

"It makes everything hurt," she complained. "My eyes, my throat. I even have a headache. To add to my aching hands and back."

Shit, was she having another attack already? "What's wrong with your hands and back? Is it that tingly thing?"

She pulled back in the circle of his arms and stared up, tears on her cheeks but no longer overflowing. "What? Oh jeez, no, it's not MS. It's a hard day of chambermaiding when I'm out of practice." She frowned. "You can't keep seeing symptoms where they don't exist."

"You can't ignore them when they do."

She brushed at her wet cheeks and the tiniest hint of a

smile softened her lips. "Neither of us is going to be great at this, are we?"

He studied her blotchy face and bloodshot eyes. "Probably not. But I guess we'll learn." He sensed that that part would be harder than with Anita. His fiancée had welcomed his help and had shared the decision making—and almost always their minds were on the same track. He and Cassidy were going to butt heads. He stifled a sigh. "So you'll fly home with me tomorrow—"

She cut him off. "I just started a new job. I can't skip out on another boss."

He snorted, irked yet amused. "You pick now to develop a conscience? How about we tell her that your old boss stole you back? I'll pay the manager whatever she needs to hire someone on a temp basis until she can fill the position."

"You can't spend your money on me." She grimaced. "Speaking of which, it's not fair that you should pay to fly down here."

The head butting had begun.

Before he could say anything, she raced on. "I have enough saved for the trip back, and if you really do give me my job back, then I can pay you back in a—"

"Shut up," he said calmly. "We already established that none of this is fair, and that we're in it together. If I ever feel that you're taking advantage of me, I'll let you know. And yes, you can have your job back, with the proviso that we may need to adjust your duties and hours if—"

"Now you shut up." She held up her hand. "Don't assume I won't be able to do the work."

He considered that and admitted, "You're right. But if there's ever a problem, let me know and we'll work things out. Like with Roy and his migraines." His main bartender, Roy, the serious boyfriend of chef Mitch, occasionally got debilitating migraines and someone else had to fill in for him. "We all have issues, Cassidy. You've had to cover for me when something unexpected came up with Robin."

"I guess."

An almost concession. He should count himself lucky. "Okay. Let's go talk to your new boss, and I'll book a room at the hotel. Unless . . ." Should he stay with her? Make sure she was okay? Make sure she didn't run again? Honestly, he'd rather be alone because he felt pretty raw.

"It's best if you stay at the hotel. It'd be awkward with my roommate. I feel bad enough about telling her I'm bailing on her after I just moved in."

He nodded, hoping he could trust her not to vanish again. "After we book flights home, why don't we have a nice dinner at a restaurant on the beach and make it an early night?"

"If we have dinner, can we . . . not talk about it?"

"Sure." Until Cassidy had all the information from Dr. Young, more talking wouldn't serve much purpose. "I'll tell you about Sam." The night manager had started revising his book and was tearing his hair out—and the nearly bald man sure didn't have any to spare.

"Sam?"

"That's dinner conversation."

"I need to shower first and try to do something with my face. Why don't I do that, and you go to the hotel, then I'll meet you in an hour?"

He gazed deep into her red-rimmed eyes, trying to read her intention.

"I promise," she said softly. She blinked, and again her eyes were damp. "I won't run, Dave. I . . . surrender. To the truth. To a year in one place, getting my treatment organized."

She looked so defeated, this woman who'd always been so perky, fun, tough-minded. It almost broke his heart. He gripped her chin in his fingers. "Accept the truth, Cassidy, but never surrender to the disease. Promise me."

A chill shuddered through him as he remembered saying virtually identical words to Anita. No, she had never surrendered to her brain cancer. It was inoperable, but, with him at her side she'd undergone radiation, chemo, and laser treatment in hopes of beating the tiny odds, or at least surviving longer, maybe until a cure was discovered. In the end she lost, but she went down fighting. Fighting for her life and their lives together.

"I promise," Cassidy said.

The echo of Anita's words filled him with determination. This time, they would succeed.

Sunday afternoon, at the end of the hour and a half drive from Williams Lake airport, Dave heaved a tired, grateful sigh at the sight of the familiar WELCOME TO CARIBOU CROSSING sign. He glanced over. Cassidy had dozed for most of the trip, but now she was awake, staring out the window, her profile expressionless as she toyed with the Canada goose pendant around her neck. "Where to?" he asked.

"Ms. H's. I hope she hasn't rented out my room."

"You could stay at the Wild Rose. We could make a guest room into an apartment."

"I appreciate the offer, but I think Ms. H can keep a close enough eye on me," she said dryly.

Okay, maybe he did want to keep her under his own eagle eye. But if he had to pick someone else to trust, it would be Ms. Haldenby. He turned the Jeep toward the green rancher.

Once there, he insisted on carrying Cassidy's backpack as they walked to the front door.

When Ms. Haldenby answered the doorbell, she smiled.

"Good. You're back. Come on in, you two. Let's have a cup of tea." She led the way not to the kitchen, but to the living room. "Sit and relax," she commanded.

Dave sat on the blue-and-white-striped sofa, wondering if he would ever truly relax again.

Cassidy strolled to the window and looked out, wandered over to a painting and studied it, then finally settled in an armchair that was upholstered in the same fabric as the couch. Her fingers drummed on the arm.

It wasn't long before Ms. Haldenby returned with a tray, which Dave quickly took from her and lowered to the dark-wood coffee table. Tea and a plate of oatmeal cookies.

While their hostess poured with a steady hand, Cassidy said, "I came to see if you'd rented out your suite."

"It's yours." She handed a cup and saucer to Cassidy. "Spic and span, just the way you left it. Now, tell me why you're back."

The cup rattled in the saucer as Cassidy took it, her hand trembling. "You know why. You figured it out."

"I need you to tell me."

She put the cup and saucer down on the coffee table and stared at the older woman. Finally, she said, slowly and painfully, "I have MS."

Dave felt for her, and knew this was only the first of many times she'd have to say those words. It was good that Ms. Haldenby had forced her to do it here, in friendly company.

The elderly woman nodded. "I'm very sorry, Cassidy. I'll do anything I can to help you."

"I hate to ask for help."

"Refusing to ask for help has become a habit for you," she said. "Some habits are unproductive, even a hindrance, and one should break them." Peering intently at Cassidy through her thick lenses, she said, "I found Irene and contacted her."

Irene? Dave remembered the "P.S." to Cassidy's note.

Cassidy's face brightened and she looked like her old self, not the pale, downcast version he'd seen for the past day. "You did? What did she say?"

"We'll discuss it later. But I thought you should know." She busied herself pouring two more cups of tea, handed one to Dave, then sat beside him on the couch. To him, she said, "Irene was very close to me when I was much younger. For reasons that made sense at the time, we lost touch. Because of one of my own bad habits—cowardice— I never tracked her down."

Until Cassidy had prompted her to. "Ms. Haldenby," he said, "I think you and Cassidy are going to be very good for each other."

"Dave, I am no longer your teacher. Please call me Daphne."

Daphne. He tasted it on his tongue. A nice name, but . . . "I don't think I can," he confessed. "Maybe we could settle on Ms. H? It has a nice ring."

"I can live with that." She sipped her tea. "Now, what's the plan?"

"We'll call Dr. Young and make an appointment as soon as possible," he said. "And then—"

"Actually," she broke in, "I was asking Cassidy."

"Sorry. Of course."

Cassidy sighed, the animation gone from her face. "Yes, we'll see the doctor. Before that, I have pamphlets to read. Dave brought them for me, but I haven't . . . well, I'll read them tonight."

"I found two or three websites that appear useful, too," Ms. H said. "The more informed you are before you see the doctor, the more you'll be able to take in what she says."

"I suppose that makes sense." Cassidy's tone was reluctant.

"Avoidance won't make the problem go away," the older woman said.

Cassidy shot her a glance of wry humor. "You're not going to let me curl up in a fetal ball and just feel sorry for myself, are you?"

Dave smiled, encouraged by that flash of humor and spirit.

"No, I certainly am not," Ms. H retorted.

He drained the rest of his tea. "I think this is my cue to bow out. I need to get back to the Wild Rose and find out what's been happening in my absence." He'd left Sam in charge. "And I know you two are dying to talk about Irene." He rose and held out his hand to Ms. Haldenby. "Thank you for everything."

"And you, Dave." Her grip was firm.

Then he walked over to Cassidy and rested his hand on her shoulder. "Do you want to come to work tomorrow, or take the day off?"

"Come to work. It'll keep my mind off . . . things. Though I don't know what I'm going to say to people about why I left and why I came back. I don't want to spread the news about . . . you know. Not until . . ."

Until what? Until she felt ready, or until physical symptoms forced her to do it? He wondered how long she would—or could—cling to her secret.

"Keep it simple," Ms. H advised. "You missed Caribou Crossing so you came back."

"Simple is good." She gave the other woman a forced smile, then turned back to Dave. "We can call Dr. Young in the morning and arrange a time that works for you."

"Any time works."

She put her hand on top of his and squeezed. "Thank you. For being you."

Being someone else might be easier, but it wasn't like he got to choose. And the warmth of her hand, the appreciation in her voice, were a very nice reward.

* * *

Late Monday afternoon, Dave held Cassidy's hand as they walked from Dr. Young's office in silence. She had been quiet for most of the appointment, not asking many questions as the doctor went through a lot of the same information he'd heard a few days ago.

A police car slowed and Karen waved. Dave waved back, trying to smile. Cassidy didn't even notice. Her gaze was on the sidewalk in front of her. When she was feeling good, she had a bounce to her step, rather like Merlin, but today the tooled cinnamon-colored cowboy boots she wore for work barely lifted from the ground.

"How do you feel?" he asked.

"Fine."

He bumped his shoulder against hers, which was clad in a Western shirt, black with turquoise embroidery. "No, you don't. This won't work if you lie to me."

She heaved a sigh. "Okay. I feel overwhelmed, exhausted, and depressed."

"Yeah, I bet." What was the best way to help her? "Let's take it one step at a time." Organization was his forté. "How about we buy that notebook, and start with a list of things to do?" Carlene Young had advised Cassidy to start a notebook where she could record information, questions, and her thoughts and feelings. The doctor recommended daily journaling.

"I suppose," Cassidy said listlessly.

He murmured greetings to a couple of passing townspeople, then told her, "The bookstore has some nice ones." For years, he'd been giving Robin an annual diary for Christmas, always with horses on the cover.

"Fine. But I don't want to buy those books there, the ones Dr. Young recommended." Books on MS and on dealing with chronic illness, she meant.

"No, we'll order them online. As the doctor said, it's up to you to decide when to tell people." Obviously, the store salesclerk shouldn't be the first to know.

They went into the bookstore and he led her to the stationery section, where she stared at the couple dozen journals, everything from mellow Zen-type designs to vivid cartoony covers. She chose one with brightly colored hot-air balloons against a blue sky. Symbolic of what? he wondered. Freedom, the ability to fly away? If there'd been one with a wild goose, he'd bet she'd have chosen that.

As they walked through the store, he said, "Have you been hot-air ballooning?"

"Yes, in Sonoma. It was so much fun, and we had the craziest pilot." A smile flickered. "He reminded me of Indiana Jones. He had the hat and the attitude—kind of daredevil, though I'm pretty sure that was calculated. You know, to give us a thrill."

She stopped and looked him in the eyes for the first time since they'd left the doctor. "Imagine this. He takes us up into a cloud. It's misty, cooler, kind of magical. I mean, we're standing in the middle of a freaking cloud. It's touching our skin with cloud breath."

He saw the wonder in her eyes as she remembered.

"It's scary, though," she said. "We're flying totally blind. Trusting that this crazy pilot knows what he's doing. And then we burst out of the cloud, and the sky is this brilliant, blazing blue. The sun's shining and it's amazingly beautiful. We have distant views of the ocean and of San Francisco. He takes us low again and we drift over hills and vineyards, with deer and rabbits scattering below us, scared by our shadow. We even scoot down to dip our toes—well, the basket's toes—in a lake, and then we float up again."

"Sounds incredible."

She smiled. "It's one of my favorite memories."

Something happy to think about, he figured. To cheer her

up when she wrote in the notebook. Maybe to give her hope that after the year she'd committed to she could slip her tether and find new adventures.

He had missed her when she left. Yes, he'd been pissed, worried, overworked. But he'd missed her smile, her sassy comments, the warm tingle when she touched him. A year from now . . . Well, who knew? Maybe he'd miss her like crazy, or maybe by then they'd barely tolerate each other. No point worrying about it; he'd already committed.

As they approached the cashier, he pulled out his wallet.

Cassidy said, "Thanks, but no. My book, my thoughts. My money."

"Okay." He stepped back while she paid.

They left the store and walked across the town square toward the Wild Rose. The roses on the gazebo had faded and the bandstand was deserted. A few people hurried past the wire-framed caribou, on their way toward whatever evening plans awaited.

"How about coming back to my place?" he said. "You can call Ms. H and let her know where you are, so she doesn't worry. I'll cook you dinner and—"

"You don't have Robin tonight?"

"No. It'd just be us. We could start that list, then have an early night." He could make sure she started the list, and he could look after her.

She hesitated.

Trying not to be too controlling, he said, "But if you'd rather be alone or spend the evening with Ms. H, that's fine too."

"It's not that. It's, uh, the idea of me spending the night with you." Again, she wasn't looking at him.

Guessing where her thoughts had gone, he said quickly, "Look, just because I'm being a support person for you, that doesn't mean you should feel obligated to sleep with me." Oh man, how could he handle being close to her but not being able to touch her like a lover, to hold her naked in his arms at night?

She cocked her head to stare at him. "And you shouldn't feel obligated to sleep with me because you feel sorry for me."

His jaw dropped and he stopped walking. "Jesus, Cassidy, I don't feel sorry for you." He stopped, reconsidered. "Well, I guess I do, actually. And for me, and everyone else who's going to be affected. It's sure not what anyone would want."

"Yeah, well . . ." Her mouth twisted. "Like the Stones said, you can't always get what you want."

The next line was something about getting what you need, which sure wasn't true in this case either. "I'm just saying, the fact that I'm sorry you have this disease has nothing to do with me wanting to be your lover."

Her forehead pinched. "Before, everything was different. I was sexy and fun, and even if I had a bum leg every now and then, I was healthy, active, strong."

"Cassidy." He leaned down to rest his forehead against her frowning one. "You're all of those things now, and you don't even have a bum leg right now." Though God knew what might happen to her with future attacks. He straightened and managed a wink. "Though I'd still be happy to massage you."

"On the outside, I look healthy. But inside, I'm flawed."

"Is this the time to tell you that I never thought you were perfect?" He tossed it out, hoping to lighten the mood.

She didn't take the bait. "You know what I mean. Now I'm sick. There's this invisible thing inside me, like some kind of time bomb, and there's no telling when it's going to strike or what it's going to do."

A time bomb didn't strike; it exploded. But he understood her point. All too well. If he mentioned Anita, would it upset her? For three years he'd avoided even speaking

Anita's name, but now, increasingly, he found himself wanting to talk about her.

Tentatively, he said, "That's kind of how Anita felt about her cancer." He shook his head, remembering. "Her cancer," he repeated. "At first she called it 'the cancer,' like she was trying to disown it"—her form of denial, less dramatic than Cassidy's attempt to run away from her diagnosis—"but then she had to accept that it was part of her. So she claimed it, but she hated it. She waged war with it every waking minute."

Cassidy's frown had disappeared as she tilted her head, listening to him.

"Sorry," he said. "I got sidetracked. What I was going to say was that she felt like her cancer contaminated her."

Her eyes widened and he wondered if he'd offended her, but then she nodded. That encouraged him to continue. "She said she felt invaded, contaminated. She knew some people were wary of her. Most of the time it was just because they were uncomfortable and sad and didn't know what to say, but it meant that they avoided her. She felt like a leper. She said people looked at her and didn't see Anita, but this diseased creature. Having the disease inside her, and having people avoid her, she said it made her feel"— crap, this was probably a really bad idea, but he finished anyway—"ugly."

The word, such an ugly sound in itself, dropped into the air between them.

Cassidy's face was still, her eyes huge. Then she breathed, "Yes."

He reached for her hands and clasped them. "But she wasn't. She was still Anita, still beautiful. And so are you, Cassidy. I'm still attracted to you, I still want to have sex with you." He added on a note of discovery, "Actually, you're maybe even more attractive, because now I've seen how gutsy you are."

Chapter Twenty-Two

"I don't feel gutsy," Cassidy said. She tried for a smile but it wobbled. What Dave had said about Anita rang so true, and it sure didn't make her feel brave.

"Of course you're gutsy." His voice was full of conviction, as were his hazel eyes, staring intently into hers. "You're not running. You're facing this thing head-on."

Hah. She had done her best to run, but he wouldn't let her. "This *thing*." She swallowed. Tried out the words. "My MS." A part of her and her life, from now until the day she died or a cure was found.

His fiancée had faced a terminal illness and remained strong, a fighter. Which was worse: to be told you were dying and had a limited time to live, or to be told you'd have a normal life span but you were diseased and your future was completely unpredictable? And what did it matter? Anita had been given her diagnosis and she'd dealt with it. Now it was Cassidy's turn.

Anita'd had the man she loved at her side every step of the way. Dave didn't love Cassidy, but he'd been generous enough to offer her his support, at least until she pulled herself together and had a treatment plan in place. "I'm used to feeling like an equal in relationships," she said quietly. "Not the weak partner."

He frowned. "Of course you're an equal."

"But I'm doing all the taking and you're doing the giving."

"Tonight, you're tired and in shock. I want to look after you. Just like you've cooked dinner and rubbed my shoulders when I've had a rough day."

He was such a good guy and he was trying so hard. She imagined what it would have been like if she'd gone to the doctor on her own today, and come home alone afterward. "Tonight," she admitted, "I would love to be looked after. But remember, Dave, I'm perfectly healthy right now. So after tonight I'll do my share of looking after, and I'll work, ride, and do all that normal stuff too."

"Deal. Now let's go home. I could use some food."

And later, they'd have sex. She hoped that he'd told the truth when he said that he still found her attractive. She felt like such a mess. How could any man, much less a handsome, smart, almost perfect one like Dave, find her desirable? Well, he wouldn't if she acted like a mess. He thought she was gutsy, so that's what she'd try to be. "Food sounds great," she lied. "Let's go."

When they walked into Dave's suite, Merlin greeted them.

Dave said, "I'll take him out, then start dinner."

"I'll call Ms. H." She sat on the couch and dialed her landlady's number.

"I just wanted to tell you," Cassidy said to her, "that I'm staying at Dave's tonight."

"Thank you for letting me know. Are you all right? How did the doctor appointment go?"

"It was, uh, informative, I guess." If she could ever make sense of all that she'd heard.

"I'd like to hear about it."

"Hang on a minute, Ms. H." Dave, with Merlin on his leash, was about to leave and she stopped him. "Do you have Robin tomorrow night?"

"In theory. I was supposed to have her for the weekend and tonight, but, well, you know. We'll all be flexible. She can stay at her mom's a while longer."

"No, that's not fair on her or on you. I want to talk to Ms. H anyhow. Why don't you take Robin for the next few days? I'll have dinner with both of you one night. Just not tomorrow." His daughter was too bright, too inquisitive. Cassidy needed to build a tougher façade if she was going to keep her secret, and that would take a little time.

"Are you sure?"

"Absolutely." She couldn't cling to Dave. That wouldn't be healthy for either of them. Besides, she didn't want to shut out Ms. H, and she valued the older woman's opinion. She waved Dave and the dog away, then said into the phone, "I'll be home tomorrow after work. Perhaps we could get together in the evening?"

"Let's have dinner. I hate cooking for one."

Cassidy's lips twitched. "That might not be a problem much longer. Maybe you'll have a houseguest." Yesterday, her landlady had told her that she'd tracked down Irene via the Internet and they'd exchanged a couple of e-mails.

"Don't count your chickens, Cassidy. Or, rather, my chickens."

"We'll talk about that over dinner. And I'm helping cook." She closed the phone. And speaking of helping cook . . . She went into the kitchen, opened the fridge, and stared inside. What did Dave have in mind? Nothing appealed to her, yet she had to eat. Dr. Young had stressed the importance of a proper diet, regular exercise, and lots of sleep.

"Hey." Dave came up behind her. "I'm doing the cooking."

How long had she been staring into the fridge? "Thanks. I guess I should start that list."

He opened a bottle of red wine. "Or sit and relax. We could work on the list after dinner."

Like she could relax, with all the things jumbled around in her mind? "I'd rather get the list out of the way so we can take the rest of the evening off."

He handed her a glass of wine. "Now there's a plan."

A plan. How about that? She sort of had a plan.

She sat at the kitchen table and Merlin came to lie at her feet. She scratched behind his ears, had a swallow of wine, then took the notebook and a pen out of her purse. Gazing at the hot-air balloons, she wished she could fly up into the sky and escape her problems. Yet the picture did remind her that she'd had great adventures in the past, and would have many more.

She opened the book and stared at the lined page. She should write something there. Some kind of title. Maybe "Me And My MS." But she couldn't bring herself to do it, so she turned to the next page and wrote, "Things To Do," then drew a line under it.

"Number one," she said. "Buy notebook. Yay, I can cross it off."

He chuckled. "Great start."

"Two. Uh . . ."

"Order the books?" he suggested.

"Right. Three is to talk to Ms. H." She wrote it down. "That smells great, by the way." To her surprise, the aroma was giving her an appetite. "What are you cooking?"

"Stir-fried beef and veggies with ginger and soy sauce, to serve over rice."

"Mmm." She gazed down at the lined page. "What's four? I suppose, to read the information Dr. Young gave me on treatment options. And try to digest it." She gazed at the brown envelope Dave had dropped on the table. Wading through the medical stuff would be tough, not to mention frightening. The doctor had said there was no one best treatment. Several had proven to be effective, but each had potential nasty side effects, and none offered a cure.

"A suggestion?" he said.

"Sure." She tore her gaze away from the envelope.

"Dr. Young gave us two copies of the information. Tomorrow, let's make another copy and you can share it with Ms. H."

"The print's really small. She'd have trouble reading it."

"Too bad. That must be a pain for someone like her who's such an intellectual."

"It is. She loves her e-reader with the ability to pump up the font size. Even then, her eyes get tired. If she wants, I'll read the material to her. It might help me digest it better."

"Good idea. I'll read it too. Maybe the three of us can get together in a few days and discuss it?"

"Decision by committee?" she asked warily. Ever since she was eighteen, she'd controlled her own life.

He turned from the stove, shaking his head. "The decisions are yours. We, along with Dr. Young and the neurologist, can help you make informed ones."

Dr. Young had arranged for the neurologist in Williams Lake to Skype in for the next appointment. She'd said that Cassidy's health care team needed a neurologist.

A team. Cassidy had worked with teams, like the staff at the Wild Rose, but now she'd have a health care team and a personal support team. So much for independence and spontaneity. Not to mention, the doctor wanted her to join a counseling group with other people who had chronic illnesses or disabilities. But that would mean admitting publicly that she had MS.

"Want to eat here or in the living room?" Dave asked, plating the food.

"Living room." She closed the notebook, eased Merlin's chin off her foot, and stood. "Dave, you'll keep that medical stuff out of sight when Robin's around, right?"

He handed her a plate. "You don't want to tell her?"

She headed for the living room, where she took her usual seat on the couch. She didn't want to tell anyone. She didn't want the diagnosis to be true. The more people who knew, the more she'd be looked on with pity, treated like a leper, as Anita had said. "Not yet. It's a lot for a kid to deal with. I know how much you want to protect her, so let's hold off until . . ." Until when? She had no idea.

Dave sat down beside her. "Yeah, I'm protective, but this is different. It's like her Grandpa Wade's stroke and Anita's cancer. A fact of life. My daughter's a strong kid. Of course, I'd check with Jessie and Evan first."

And two more people would be in the loop. "I know, but . . ."

"It's a lot for you to deal with. I get it. For now, it'll be just you, me, and Ms. H."

"Thanks." She slumped into the couch, closed her eyes, and sighed. "This feels good. Can we watch a movie? I'll order those books tomorrow morning, and tomorrow night I'll start reading the medical stuff to Ms. H. But now, I'd like to goof off for the evening."

"You've earned it." He handed her the remote. "Pick something."

"Hmm . . ." What would be purely entertaining, a distraction from real life? She checked the menu and chose *The Big Easy*, with Dennis Quaid and Ellen Barkin. "This is set in New Orleans and it's about . . . well, you'll see." It was fast-paced, intriguing, and sexy.

"I should've cooked Cajun," he joked.

"This will do just fine." She picked up her plate and dug in.

Because she moved so often, Cassidy had often found

herself alone in a new place. Some nights she went out to explore, maybe look for company. Other nights, she stayed home and watched movies. This film, she'd seen a couple of times before. Glancing over, she saw that Dave seemed absorbed by her choice.

They ate and watched in companionable silence until he paused the movie to take their empty plates to the kitchen. Merlin trailed him.

Damn. Restless now, Cassidy rose. Without Dave by her side, without the distraction of the movie, it was hard not to think. She wandered around the room, checking out a horse drawing Robin had been working on, folding the crumpled afghan. The kitchen door closed and, relieved, she turned as Dave returned minus the dog but with the wine bottle. He refilled their glasses and she reclaimed her seat and restarted the movie.

When a shirtless Remy hiked Anne's skirt up and caressed her leg, Cassidy snuggled into the curve of Dave's arm and rested her hand on his thigh. She had missed this—missed him—so much when she'd been away. "Steamy, isn't it?" she murmured.

"The movie, or you?" He moved her hand higher to cup his fly, where he was growing beneath the denim of his jeans.

"For now, the movie. But later . . ." Cassidy pressed firmly and he pulsed in response.

The couple on screen, caught up in foreplay, were interrupted by Remy's pager. The cop had to go to a murder scene. Anne murmured that she'd never had much luck with sex anyway, and he said her luck was about to change. Later, when he got back from the investigation.

Remy and Anne might have to wait until later, but Cassidy was palming one very fine erection. And, unlike Anne, she *was* good at sex. While sex was a basic physical act, each time was unique. It was definitely a participatory sport, and the outcome depended on how well the partners played together. Dave Cousins brought great equipment to the table, and his skill, thoroughness, and attention to his partner made him something special.

Let's face it, Dave *was* something special. In bed, out of bed. And he made her feel special. He cared enough to chase her to Cannon Beach and persuade her to come back. He found her sexy, despite—no, she wasn't going to think about that. Not now.

With her free hand, she fumbled for the remote and pressed the PAUSE button. "You, Mr. Cousins," she purred, "are about to get very lucky." She swung over to straddle his lap.

"I'm liking this."

She shimmied her crotch against his erection. "I can tell." There were so many possibilities. Inspired by the movie, she chose sultry. Rather than rip open the row of snap buttons on Dave's shirt, she undid them one at a time, caressing his chest as she went. His body was so strong and lean, so perfectly male, just touching it made her body hum with arousal.

She undid his belt buckle and the button at the waist of his jeans and tugged his shirttails free. Then she sat upright on his lap and raised her arms above her head, stretching and undulating. She undid the snaps at the cuffs of her own shirt and slid each sleeve up her arm in slow, sensual touches that caressed her bare skin, making her whole body tingle.

"Need any help?" he asked huskily.

She shook her head. "Leave it to me."

Another thing she liked about Dave: unlike some guys, he didn't need to always control the sex. If he sensed she wanted to take charge, he went with the flow.

With those same slow movements, she unsnapped the front of her own black shirt. Under it, she wore a turquoise bra. A couple of shrugs sent the shirt sliding off her shoulders but, anchored by the sleeves shoved up her arms, it didn't fall. Sometimes, like in the movie, it was sexier to have disheveled clothing than to be naked.

She brushed her fingers across her own chest, then the tops of her breasts, knowing that Dave was imagining his hands there. She undid the front clasp of her bra and eased the cups aside, freeing her breasts, the nipples puckered with her arousal. Clasping her hands at the back of her neck, she arched her back so her breasts thrust toward Dave.

"Definitely steamy," he said. His cheeks were flushed; his eyes glittered.

There might be a horrible, incurable illness inside her, but there was no pity or sadness in his hazel eyes, only appreciation. And lust. Tonight she needed this. To be in control; to be the seductress; to be utterly desired as a woman.

And to stop thinking about MS, for God's sake.

She rose and, with movements constricted by her shirt, managed to free herself from her jeans. Her panties stayed on, along with the loosely hanging shirt and bra. Kneeling in front of Dave, she unzipped his jeans and tugged them off, but left his tented boxers on.

Then she sat back down astride his lap. Shimmying her crotch against the bulge in his underwear, she enjoyed the sweet build of pressure between her thighs. Her hands at his waist, she arched back, increasing the pressure where their bodies joined.

He groaned and finally moved, his hands coming up under her shirt to firmly stroke her back and urge her toward him so he could suck her nipple into his mouth. He teased it with his tongue, lips, and the edge of his teeth until this time it was she who moaned.

She wanted to hold his head, weave her fingers through his hair, but her shirt trapped her arms. Instead, she pressed kisses to the top of his head. Undulating her hips, she pressed against his erection, keeping her movements slow and sultry to suit that New Orleans mood.

Dave did the same. The perfect partner in this sensual dance.

Easing back, she reached into the slit in his boxers, freed his thick erection, and slid her fingers up and down the shaft, pausing to circle the damp head with her thumb.

He moaned. Muttered, "Shit, you're hot" against her breast. Then he raised his head, sitting back again, as she lifted up a little and reached her other hand between their bodies.

Her fingers trembling with need, she slid the moist crotch of her panties aside and opened her slick folds. Rising higher, she guided him to her center until he slid in, a tiny bit at a time as she slowly sank down to encompass him.

So sweet, feeling him fill her, skin to skin for the first time. She was on birth control, he'd had no other lover since Anita, and Cassidy's blood work had included HIV tests. Today Dr. Young had confirmed—in the one bit of good news—that there was no need for a condom. This nakedness was new for Cassidy, and she loved the flesh-to-flesh intimacy, the heightening of sensation.

Gripping his waist for balance, she lifted up and down, setting a slow but intense pace.

"You feel so good, Cassidy."

"I feel very good," she purred throatily.

He caressed her bare shoulders. Ran his fingers up her neck, into her hair. And all the time he gazed into her eyes, maintaining the connection, not letting her drift away into a private world of pure sensation. Yes, she was having great sex, but he wasn't for one moment letting her forget that she was having it with him. Not that she wanted to. The fact that this was Dave was what made the whole thing so perfect.

Pressure, pleasure, need. They built inexorably until, with a soft cry, she surrendered and climaxed in throbbing waves around him.

Now he took over, gripping her hips and holding her firmly as he thrust harder, faster, and she whimpered helplessly as a second orgasm echoed the first. Less intense, but perhaps even sweeter. He drove high and deep, his hoarse gasp and pumping hips signaling his own climax.

This moment. This man. Utter perfection. Pure happiness. If she could only stay in this moment forever.

Late Friday afternoon, Cassidy, at her desk in the lobby, saw Robin come down from Dave's suite, her backpack on her back. The girl hung around while Cassidy, speaking Spanish, finished listing the town's highlights to tourists from Mexico.

"Hey, Robin," Cassidy said after the family had headed out. "I hear you're having dinner and a sleepover with Kimiko."

"Yup. Her grannie's going to make doughnuts. She makes the best ones ever!"

"Have fun, and say hi to everyone from me."

"You bet. See you tomorrow when we go riding."

"You bet," she echoed, trying to sound cheerful.

Tonight, she and Dave were going over to Ms. H's for what Dave, the basketball coach, called a team meeting. They would discuss the various treatment options, so that the Monday appointment with Dr. Young and, by Skype, the neurologist, would be productive.

Shortly after Robin left, Dave came over. His hair was still damp from the shower he'd taken after basketball practice, and he carried two Wild Rose tote bags. "Three of Mitch's chicken pot pies, three salads, and three servings of blueberry pie."

"Sounds like a party," she muttered, standing and stretching. "Okay, let's go do this." And get it over with. Then she could try to enjoy the weekend. Although the word "enjoy" wasn't really in her vocabulary these days.

They walked the four blocks, stopping to buy homemade vanilla ice cream from The Soda Jerk.

Ms. H had the kitchen table set and, teetotaler that she was, glasses of iced tea poured. While Cassidy forced herself to eat Mitch's delicious food, Dave and Ms. H talked about some of the people who'd been in his fourth-grade class. A number of them had left Caribou Crossing to pursue careers and relationships, but many still lived there—or, like Evan Kincaid, had returned after an absence. It seemed that people either loved or hated small-town Western life.

Personally, she couldn't see a single thing to hate—but then big-city lights, exotic beaches, and all sorts of other locations had their advantages too. A year from now, she'd be exploring that world again. And why did that exciting prospect seem, for once, a little lonely?

After the kitchen was tidy, the three of them went to the living room. Cassidy upended the envelope containing treatment information so that the brochures and articles slid onto the coffee table. Although she'd rather be anywhere other than there, she forced herself to sit beside Dave on the couch. Ms. H had taken the reading chair.

"So," Cassidy said, "we've all been through this information."

"The good news," Ms. H said, "is that since you haven't suffered any symptoms lately, the only thing you need to worry about for the moment is deciding on a DMT." DMT was short for disease-modifying therapy, a treatment that attempted to alter the course of the disease itself, not deal with specific symptoms.

Yeah, that was really great news. "None of those drugs sound like fun."

"They can slow the course of the disease, reduce the number of lesions, and reduce attacks." The older woman sounded exactly like a teacher lecturing, which was hardly a surprise.

"I know," Cassidy said.

"You have to try one," Dave said.

"I know! Of course I'm going to fight this. Just allow me a minute to whine, okay?" Was she sounding like a frustrated child? That had to be better than sounding like a furious adult, which was the truth. Her mind kept repeating, *Why? Why me? What did I do to deserve this?*

"All we're doing tonight," Dave said, "is talking about the options so you're prepared on Monday."

"I know." One step at a time. She took a deep breath. "Okay. So basically there are the drugs that have been around for a while, and they're either injected into a muscle or injected subcutaneously." She shuddered. "I've never liked needles. Or there's the newer drug, and it just means taking a capsule every day, which sounds much better."

"But it seems to be more of a second-line choice if the other ones don't work for the individual," Dave said.

"You also need to consider the possible side effects of the various drugs," Ms. H said. "Flulike symptoms, injection site reactions, fatigue, depression."

Depression. Hah. Was it possible to have MS and *not* be depressed? "Bad side effects can happen with any of the drugs," she said gloomily. "There's no obvious right answer, is there?"

"If there was, Dr. Young would have told you," Dave said.

They discussed the various drugs in more detail, then Cassidy said, "With the injection therapies, sticking a pre-filled syringe through my skin seems a little more doable than injecting one into my thigh muscle or upper arm."

"If it turns out the best choice is the intramuscular one, I could do it for you," Dave said. He swallowed. "I think I could. I mean, I'm sure I could learn."

"I could do it," Ms. H said briskly. "You two are too squeamish."

Oh yeah. This whole thing made her nauseous: having to stick needles into her body to inject drugs that might make her feel worse, that wouldn't even cure her disease anyhow because there was no freaking cure. Damn it, she hated this. She grabbed the scattered material and shoved it all back in the envelope. "Okay, I'm prepared to talk to Dr. Young and the neurologist. Now can we please, please talk about something else? Something normal?"

Dave glanced at her, then at Ms. H. Trying to read his mind, Cassidy figured he was thinking that MS was her new normal. Thank God Ms. H spoke before he said it. "I have an old friend coming to visit next week."

Those words certainly distracted Cassidy. "Irene? Seriously?"

Something soft and vulnerable touched Ms. H's face. "Irene. Seriously."

"You're recapturing your old friendship?" Dave asked. "That'll be nice for both of you."

"I hope so," Ms. H said. "I truly do." She turned to Cassidy. "This is because of you."

"That nudge I gave you, at the bottom of my note?"

"Partly. And partly because after you left and I guessed you had MS I hoped you'd have the courage to face the truth. It made me realize how long I'd been avoiding an important truth of my own. I thought perhaps if I had the spunk to find Irene and contact her, then maybe you . . ." She gave a small, embarrassed laugh. "I'm not generally known for superstitious thinking."

"Well," Cassidy said, "I'm glad you found her and she's

coming to visit." How much more should she say, when Dave didn't know the story?

The retired teacher gazed at her former student. "Irene and I were in the same program at university, studying to become elementary school teachers." Her chin lifted. "We fell in love."

Cassidy smiled at her. How well she knew that saying something like that took courage. Knowing you'd likely say those words many more times, and sometimes get a negative reaction, was scary.

Dave's mouth opened, then slowly closed again. After a moment's reflection, he said, "That would have been a tough thing, back then."

"It was. In fact, we decided it was more than tough; it was impossible. We went our separate ways."

"I don't mean to pry," he said, "but why didn't you keep in touch?"

"It would have made things harder. Looking back, I wonder if we should have fought for what mattered. But in our early twenties neither of us realized how rare our feelings were. We thought we'd get over them, perhaps fall in love with someone more suitable."

"But you didn't." He nodded. "There's no getting over that really special kind of love." Cassidy knew he was thinking of Anita.

"There wasn't for me. Nor, as it turns out, for her. Even though she married."

Ms. H had already shared much of the story with Cassidy, so she sat quietly, but Dave said, sounding surprised, "She's married?" Then, "Sorry, I don't mean to be, uh, intrusive."

The older woman shook her head. "I think you, Cassidy, and I will get to know each other rather well. Besides, I'm tired of secrets. Irene did marry, a man she liked very much, and they had two children. But she and her husband were never truly happy. When the children were in their teens, he fell for another woman. He and Irene divorced. They shared custody."

"And ever since the children grew up, she's lived alone," Cassidy said.

"Yes," Ms. H said. Again, that gentle, vulnerable expression touched her face. "She says she learned her lesson. If she couldn't be with her true love, it was better to be alone."

Cassidy did a mental eye roll. No, it was better to stop moping and enjoy life. Would any "true love" want their loved one to be miserable? "Getting back to where this all started—you say Irene's coming to visit?"

"We spoke on the phone last night. For hours." A tender smile lit her face. "She lives in Nelson. Her son's in the Okanagan and her daughter's in Vancouver, both of them married with children. Irene says she's used to climbing on the bus to make visits, and she'd like to come here and see the Cariboo."

Cassidy smiled. "And to see you."

"Perhaps we're old fools, thinking that a fire that burned hot almost sixty years ago may still have glowing embers that will reignite." Again her chin went up. "But better to know than to always wonder."

Dave leaned forward. "I hope it works out. And if it does, then I hope Irene likes Caribou Crossing. We'd hate to lose you, Ms. H."

"Why, Dave Cousins, what a charming thing to say."

Cassidy tossed him a teasing look. "He's such a romantic."

"Hah," Ms. H said. "This, coming from the woman who urged me to contact Irene."

"Okay, maybe I have a soft spot in my heart," she admitted. "I don't believe that most relationships will succeed long term, but . . ." Hmm, how to phrase this?

"If we start out as octogenarians, how long is long term anyway?" Ms. H said.

"Uh, yes, I guess. Sorry, is that horribly rude?"

"No, it's practical." She winked. "Despite which, I will persist in believing there's a closet romantic lurking under your jaded, blasé façade."

"Persist away," she said. "That won't make it true." And thank heavens she wasn't a romantic who was looking for a happily ever after of her own. What man in his right mind would want to commit his life to a woman with an unpredictable, incurable disease?

Chapter Twenty-Three

I hate, hate, hate this! I'm sick of being sick! I hate not knowing what's going to happen to me!

Cassidy stared at the notebook she'd bought four weeks ago. Her scrawled words dug deeply into the paper. She curled her yoga-pant-clad legs and sock-clad feet closer to her body as she hunched into one end of Dave's couch, the afghan over her lap. Feeling shivery, she tugged the sleeves of her cotton hoodie over her wrists. A minute from now, she might be feverish.

She attacked the page again:

I hate having to remember to take meds and I hate sticking needles in myself. I'm sick of feeling nauseous and tired and achy. I hate waking up each morning not knowing if today I'll suffer another attack. I hate it that any time I have some physical problem, I don't know if it's a side effect of the meds, a new attack, a pseudoexacerbation—

Her hand slowed as she wrote the complicated word, the term used for symptoms that were caused by things like heat, fatigue, or stress, not by a fresh attack. She went on:

—or just some perfectly normal thing like everyone gets all the time. I hate that I sometimes miss work—and when I am at work, sometimes I feel like I'm barely functional. It's not fair to Dave or to the other staff.

She pressed her fingers to her temples, took a deep breath, then began writing again, more slowly this time:

Fair? Hah! I learned as a kid that life isn't fair, but I figured that if I moved lightly through the world, if I was nice to people and the environment, then the world would be nice to me too. That's so not true!!
There's no justice. There just isn't. I've been good, I've done these stupid injections religiously, and I feel worse than I did when I was first diagnosed. Way worse. I feel like crap!

"Cassidy?" Dave said. "Are you all right?"

She glared up at him, where he stood over her looking all big and strong and healthy in jeans and a blue and green flannel shirt. "Of course I'm not freaking *all right*! I have MS and it's not going away."

"I know that," he said patiently. "It's just that you're crying." He put out a hand as if he intended to brush her cheek.

She jerked away and swiped at her own cheeks, surprised to find that they were wet.

"I know you're sad," he said, "but—"

"I'm not sad, I'm mad!"

"And that's perfectly normal for someone—"

She snapped her notebook shut and leaped off the couch. "Do you always have to be so damned understanding and patient? So freaking *nice*?" Oh great, now she was being mean to one of the two friends who knew about her disease and were standing by her, yet she couldn't seem to stop herself.

His expression wary, he asked, "What's wrong with being understanding and patient?"

"You make me feel . . . Oh, I don't know." Sweat broke out on her skin. She peeled off her socks, then yanked off the hoodie that she wore over a skimpy tank top, and tossed it on the floor. "Like I'm some spoiled child throwing a temper tantrum. Like I ought to suck it up and be all rational about it, but I don't feel rational."

"I know," he said cautiously. "That's why I said it's normal to be mad."

"You *said* it, but you don't do it." She glared at him. "How come you never get mad? Don't you care enough about anything to get mad?"

The stricken look in his hazel eyes made her recant immediately. "I'm sorry! I didn't mean that you didn't care about Anita."

He swallowed. "Yes, I got mad about Anita's cancer. And I'm mad about your MS too."

She tilted her head. "Are you? Tell me about it."

"How will that make you feel better?"

"I don't know. Maybe it won't. Maybe neither of us will

feel better. But I want to hear it. These days, it's all about me. *My* stupid MS, *my* symptoms, *my* meds, *my* feelings. I want to hear about you for a change."

"I, uh, I'm fine, Cassidy. I mean, yeah, this is hard, but I'm fine."

She shook her head. "Cop-out."

"Leave it alone. Leave me alone."

Maybe she should, but some instinct told her to keep poking. "Tell me. What are you mad about, Dave?"

He walked across the room, absentmindedly picked up the hoodie she'd discarded, then turned to face her. "What am I mad about?"

She nodded.

"Like you, I'm mad that you got this disease."

When he didn't go on, she said, "That's it?"

"The rest sounds too awful."

She barked a humorless laugh. "Believe me, what I've been writing in this notebook for the past month is awful. Come on, Dave, stop being so nice. Tell me the awful stuff."

He ran the hoodie through his hands, from one to the other, then said slowly, in a controlled voice, "Don't get me wrong, I want to be here for you, but if you didn't have MS, our lives would be the way they used to be."

She nodded. "Go on."

"I'm mad that our lives have to be juggled around injections and how you're feeling. I'm mad that we have to make excuses when you need to pull out of going riding or going to my folks' for dinner." His voice rose; his words came faster. "I'm mad that we're lying to Robin and my family, to my employees. I hate keeping secrets."

His hands clenched into fists as he gripped the hoodie. "This disease has changed us. I'm lying to my daughter. And you're not the fun, happy, free-spirited Cassidy I used to know. You're moody and depressed, quick-tempered and—"

He shook his head and flung the hoodie back on the floor. "Shit! That sounds awful. And that's what makes me the maddest. What kind of person am I to be angry that my fucking life isn't so neat and tidy and fun because you got this horrible disease? It's . . . twisted. I'm twisted to think that way." His body taut with tension, his expression agonized, he stared at her.

"Wow," she breathed. This was a new side of Dave. Definitely a less perfect one. And yet . . . "I don't think it's twisted. Everything you said makes sense. In fact"— surprised, she found a slight grin curving her lips—"it sounds completely *normal*."

"Seems to me it's selfish and petty," he said gruffly.

Her grin widened and she went to stand in front of him. "Yeah, kind of. But that's normal. Hey, I finally get what you've been saying. You've been trying to tell me not to get so down on myself over my feelings, because those feelings are normal."

"Pretty much."

"And so are yours."

"Huh. I guess maybe they are." He sighed. "This is new for us. Over time, as we get your treatment and the side effects under control, we'll both adjust and start to feel better."

She thought about the things he'd said, and the pain he was going through because he'd chosen to support her. Slowly, she said, "There's something we could do now that would help with one of the problems."

He cocked his head. "What's that?"

Now she felt chilled, either from the meds or from what she knew she had to do. She bent slowly to retrieve the hoodie, pulled it over her head, and stretched the sleeves down so she could grip them with her fingers. "Tell people," she muttered.

"Really? Are you ready for that?"

Of course not! Rather than let the words snap out, she

used a relaxation technique she'd learned. A deep breath in, a long breath out, seek a sense of internal calm. "Honestly? I'm not sure I'd ever be ready. But you're right, it's terrible to lie to people. I only hope . . . Well, you told me how Anita felt when people found out she had cancer. I don't want people to treat me like I'm damaged, diseased. I don't want pity; I don't want avoidance. I just want to be *me*."

He took her shoulders, holding her gently. "You *are* you. But the truth is, you're a different you. People change all the time, right?"

She leaned her forehead against his flannel-clad chest. "This isn't a good change."

"Cassidy, if you tell people about your MS, will you also consider joining the counseling group Dr. Young recommended, with people suffering from chronic illnesses and disabilities? She said it would help to talk to others who are going through the same kind of things as you."

A bunch of depressed sick or disabled people sharing their woes? Yeah, that sure sounded like fun. "I'll think about it. One step at a time, okay?"

Chapter Twenty-Four

Three nights later, a Friday, Dave glanced over at Cassidy in the passenger seat of the Jeep. She hadn't said a word since she'd greeted him when he picked her up at Ms. H's.

When she'd decided to tell people about her MS, he had thought they should start with the adults in his family: Jessie and Evan, and Robin's three sets of grandparents. He wanted to make sure it was okay with Jessie to tell their daughter, and also to have a sense of how his family was going to deal with this. Although he was sure they'd offer support.

He was sorry Cassidy had to go through this, but he'd be so glad to have the truth out in the open.

The living room of his suite at the Wild Rose was too small to comfortably host the group, so he'd prevailed on his parents. Earlier, he'd had dinner with Robin, then delivered her to Kimiko's house for a sleepover.

It was mid-October now, the night outside dark and chilly. He had the Jeep heater working, and on CXNG Willie Nelson crooned "Always on My Mind." It should have been cozy, but the stiffness of Cassidy's posture told him she was anything but relaxed. Stress wasn't good for her. It could trigger a pseudoexacerbation. "Why don't I tell them?" he offered.

Her head turned toward him, but it was too dark out here on the country road to see her features clearly. "Because you don't think I'll do it right?" she asked, an edge to her voice.

Seemed he'd said the wrong thing. That was happening a lot these days. "No. I figured it might be easier for you."

"Easier? Crap, Dave, nothing about this is easy!"

Man, she could be a pain. As soon as he had the thought, he forced it away, feeling guilty. "I know. I said *easier*, not easy. You're supposed to be keeping your stress level down and I'm sure it's hard for you to say the words, so—"

"But I'm going to have to sometime, aren't I?"

He kept his mouth shut and his gaze on the road, feeling the force of her glare.

She went on. "I'm a grown-up. I can suck it up and do this. You don't have to protect me all the time, like I'm, I'm, Robin or something. Not that she's a baby who needs an overprotective father hovering over her all the time either."

Anger surged, quick and hot. "What the hell do you know about parenting?"

"Enough to know that kids, like adults, need some independence and room to do things their own way."

He clenched his jaw to prevent more of his anger from spewing out. Breathing fast, he told himself she was striking out because she was hurting. Striving to sound calm, he said, "I'm sorry, I shouldn't have—"

"Oh crap, I'm being a bitch." Her words cut across his.

"You're anxious about tonight."

"Well, duh." Then she clapped a hand over her mouth. "We should both just keep quiet."

Maybe she was right. He was smarting from her criticism of his parenting, and she was in a mood to take everything the wrong way. Which didn't augur well for the family meeting. "I hear you," he said evenly. "Maybe we should postpone the announcement until, uh . . ."

"Until what? Until I'm more reasonable?"

"Until you calm down a little and don't misinterpret everything someone says."

"How freaking condescending," she huffed.

On CXNG, Elvis began to sing "Love Me Tender," the song Dave and Cassidy had first danced to. He remembered how she'd felt in his arms that first time. His reaction had been physical: such shock and such pleasure, holding a sexy woman. Now that sexy woman was his lover and his friend. He needed to get over his injured ego and be there for her.

The song was so gentle, filling the dark night and the tense space between him and Cassidy. Slowly, the stress eased from him. He hoped the same was happening with her, because he was now driving the benchland road that led to his parents' place. Below them, the lights of Caribou Crossing were sparkly decorations scattered across a dark landscape. At another time, he'd have pointed out how pretty they looked, but tonight Cassidy would likely find some way to fault that comment.

Instead, he said, "I'm sorry if I'm saying things wrong. I'm here to support you. Just let me know what you need." Guessing that she'd immediately think that what she needed was a cure, which no one could provide, he quickly clarified, "What you need from me tonight."

Her head, pressed back against the headrest, turned slowly toward him. "Any way you can stop me from being a bitch?" She sounded tired, but the note of wry humor in her voice encouraged him.

"You're not a bitch. I guess we both need to think a little harder before we speak, and before we react. Can you try to remember that my intentions are good? That's going to be true of my family as well, even if they inadvertently say things that seem uninformed or inconsiderate."

"You're right." She reached over to rest her hand lightly on his thigh. "This is all so foreign to me. Not being in total control of my life. I don't like what it's turning me into."

He took his right hand off the steering wheel and put it on top of hers. "This is probably another wrong thing to say, but that sounds defeatist. Yeah, you have a disease. You're taking the meds that can modify its effect on you, and that gives you some control over the physical side. As for what it 'turns you into' in terms of your feelings and personality, that's up to you. Not up to it. You don't have to give it that kind of control." He swallowed. "Like I'm anyone to speak. I'm not doing so great at dealing with my own feelings."

"It's hard, isn't it? But you do make an interesting point."

Grateful that she'd tried to understand what he had so clumsily said, he made the turn into his parents' driveway. "Ready for this?"

"No, but I want to get it over with."

As he parked, he said, "They're all here." Jess and Evan's Riders Boot Camp SUV, Miriam and Wade's Bly Ranch truck, and Brooke and Jake's Toyota.

Cassidy was quiet as they started up the front walk. When he reached for her hand, she twined her fingers in his and held on tight.

Pops answered the door and ushered them into the spacious living room, where Dave's mother was getting drinks. There were quick greetings, curious glances, and a sense of expectancy in the air. All he'd told his parents was that he and Cassidy wanted to get together with the group.

A quick scan of the room showed that no babies were present. "Are Alex and Nicki in the nursery?" he asked his mom.

"Sound asleep." She held up crossed fingers. "Hopefully, they won't disturb us. Now, what would you two like to drink? Wine, beer, coffee, tea?"

Dave accepted a glass of red wine, but Cassidy chose herbal tea.

On any normal social occasion, everyone would have mingled, drinks in hand, chatting, but tonight people quickly took seats, each couple together. Dave and Cassidy sat side by side on a loveseat. She put her mug of tea on the coffee table, untasted. When he reached for her hand, she again clasped his. Hers was cold, a tremor running through it.

Everyone gazed expectantly at the two of them. Cassidy cleared her throat, then glanced at Dave. When she didn't speak, he got the ball rolling. "You're wondering why we wanted to get together with all of you."

"Some kind of announcement, we figure," his mother said, a twinkle in her eye.

"I wonder what it could be?" Humor teased at Miriam's eyes and the corners of her mouth.

Oh shit. It suddenly hit him that they might think this was an engagement announcement. Cassidy must have realized the same thing, because she jerked and said, "No! God, no, we're not . . . I mean, our relationship is just . . . you know, casual."

Dave felt an odd twinge of something he couldn't define. Of course she was right—neither of them wanted anything serious—but did she have to be so adamant? The two of them had a special bond that was more than casual.

"Oh," his mother said flatly, the sparkle in her eyes dying.

"So what's going on?" Jessie asked.

Cassidy opened her mouth, but didn't speak. He could imagine her wanting to hold on to her secret. As soon as she told his family, her world would, yet again, change irrevocably.

He could do this for her. But she'd made it clear she didn't want him to, so he kept quiet.

Her grip tightened on his hand and she said, in a rush, "I've been diagnosed with multiple sclerosis."

She gazed around the room and so did Dave, reading the reactions. Shock, mostly. Sadness and, yes, pity. He knew she hated being pitied, as Anita had, but how could you not pity someone who'd been hit with that kind of diagnosis? He also saw a lot of uncertainty. He'd told Cassidy that no one in his family had ever had MS, so they likely didn't have a clear understanding of the disease.

"I didn't know much about MS," Cassidy said, "but believe me, I've learned a lot." Her voice relaxed slightly as she went on to give a basic explanation of the disease.

Dave squeezed her hand as the others exchanged glances. His mom said, "Your leg?"

"Yes. When I was in Vancouver, it was completely numb for two or three days. That's what's called an attack. A year before that, I had double vision for a while, and that was another attack. The things that have happened here in Caribou Crossing, the occasional tingling and numbness, the fatigue, those aren't actual attacks, they're what are called pseudo-exacerbations. That's when symptoms act up for reasons other than actual disease activity. Heat, stress, and tiredness can cause pseudoexacerbations."

"That sounds hard to diagnose," Pops said. "Your doctor's absolutely sure?"

Dave remembered how Cassidy had at first tried to deny the truth. Now she said, "Yes, she is. My great-grandmother had it, so Dr. Young knew it was a possibility. She sent me to a neurologist, I had an MRI, and yes, there are MS lesions."

His mother rose, came over, and kneeled on the carpet in front of Cassidy. She took her free hand. "I'm so sorry, Cassidy. I think we're all a little in shock."

Bless his mom for saying the right thing.

Cassidy gave a forced smile. "Yeah. Tell me about it."

She squeezed Sheila's hand, then released it. "Okay, what else do people want to know?"

Another exchange of glances, then Brooke said, "All right, there's an elephant in the living room, so I'll tackle it. What's the treatment and the prognosis?"

Cassidy filled them in, telling them about her relapsing-remitting MS, answering questions as they arose, taking an occasional sip of tea. Then she said, "I'd really like to be the old me, but I can't. I don't know how MS will affect me and I just . . . I don't want people to pity me or act weird around me."

"It's a part of who you are now," Brooke said. "You can't change it, so you need to own it. Like me and my diseases."

"Diseases? I know you're a recovering alcoholic," Cassidy said cautiously.

"You didn't know that I have bipolar disorder?"

Cassidy gaped at her. "I didn't. No one mentioned it."

"It's no secret," Brooke said, "but I guess it's old news, not something people gossip about anymore. Anyhow, it's a significant part of my life because I need to take medication and have my lithium level monitored. But on a day-to-day basis, it's just this thing in the background as I live my normal life. I hope that's how MS will come to be for you."

"I could maybe live with that," Cassidy said slowly. "But one of the toughest things about MS is that you wake up each morning not having a clue what's going to happen. You could be fine. You could even go into remission for decades. Or you could"—she gulped—"*I* could wake up planning a day of work, riding, line dancing, then try to get out of bed and find that my leg's gone numb. Or that I can't see properly. Or that my words come out garbled."

Dave swallowed hard, thinking how strong she had to be to live with that reality.

So softly that she was almost speaking to herself, Cassidy went on. "One of my mottos used to be 'A new day, a fresh start.' I always envisioned that fresh start being something fun and exciting. Now each new day is fresh all right, because I don't know whether, or h-how, my b-body's going to fail me." Her voice faltered as she finished.

"That sounds really tough," Brooke said sympathetically. "One thing I've found with a serious chronic illness, it teaches you patience and flexibility."

From the way Cassidy's grip tightened on Dave's fingers, he guessed she was holding back one of her sarcastic retorts. Still, Brooke's words encouraged him. Cassidy might not be ready to see a silver lining to her MS, but maybe one day she would. Maybe he would too.

Cassidy took a deep breath, let it out, and her fingers loosened. "I'm sorry we didn't tell you earlier. I was having trouble dealing with it. But it was unfair to ask Dave to deceive you guys, and Robin. So now we want you to know and—"

"You know that we'll do anything we can to help." Pops, a normally quiet man, broke in.

"Of course we will," everyone else echoed.

Dave studied their faces and saw genuineness. Concern, sorrow, pity, but not disgust. No one was shunning her. He hoped Cassidy could see that too.

Maybe so, because her "Thank you" sounded just as genuine. "That's really nice of you, considering you've only known me a few months. I don't know that there's all that much you can do, but knowing you're behind me means a l-lot." Her voice choked up again and she took another sip of the now cold tea.

Then she said, "We'd like to tell Robin. Do you think that's okay? We don't want to stress her out too much. I know that losing Anita was really rough on her. Not that this is anything like that, but we've become friends and . . ." She trailed off.

"Rob's a strong girl," Jessie said. "She's bighearted, as you know, and strong-minded."

"I've seen all of that," Cassidy said with a smile.

"She's also smart about figuring things out," Evan put in.

"And she'll be hurt if she realizes she's been shut out," Miriam said.

Dave nodded. Of course he wanted to protect his daughter, but it was inevitable that she'd find out.

Cassidy looked pale and strained. Sensing that she'd reached the end of her fragile rope, Dave stood and drew her to her feet. "It's time for us to go. We'll talk to Robin and—"

"Tomorrow night," Cassidy said. "If you can keep the secret until then, that would be great. I want to tell her myself." Her shoulders slumped, but she straightened them. "Next week, I'll tell everyone at the Wild Rose, and my other friends in town."

Word would be out. The thing she feared would happen, and everyone would see her differently. As a damaged person. And—shit, this had only just occurred to him— they'd look at him that way too. Ever since Anita got sick, then died, he'd seen the pitying looks. He was the guy whose fiancée had died so tragically. Now here he was, by the side of another woman with a serious illness.

In the beginning, Cassidy had offered him something new and special: fun, lightheartedness, an escape from responsibility and from being that damaged guy. And now, through no fault of her own, she'd taken it all away.

His mom squeezed his arm. "Are you all right, dear?"

Startled, he gazed around to see that the others were getting organized to leave. Across the room, his father held Cassidy's jacket so she could slip her arms into it. "Yeah. This is hard, though."

Her knowing eyes studied his face. "I bet it is. I'm proud of you for being there for your friend."

The way she and Pops had raised him, he didn't have any other choice.

He gave her a hug, then joined Cassidy and they walked out to the Jeep.

She slumped back in the seat and closed her eyes.

"Are you okay?" he asked. "I mean, as okay as you can be right now?"

"Tired." She sighed. "Very tired. But not nauseous, thank God. I think maybe, just maybe, the side effects of the drug are fading."

Awkwardly, he said, "I don't know how to say this without pissing you off, but you handled that really well tonight."

"Thanks. Maybe it'll get easier."

"I hope so." As he drove down toward the lights of town, they were both silent.

On the radio, Blake Shelton was singing "Mine Would Be You." About that one special person. About how he'd rather die than lose her. Dave had felt that way about Anita, and he'd lost her all the same. But while she'd been alive, while they'd been together, she'd meant everything to him. Now maybe he was coming around to realizing, despite the lingering pain, that in a way he'd been blessed to have those feelings. Cassidy, with her will-o'-the-wisp lifestyle and refusal to let herself care too deeply, would miss out on something mighty fine.

As he drove through the outskirts of town, he said, "Where to? Want to come home with me?" He'd had Robin with him for the past couple of nights, so Cassidy had stayed at her place.

"Yes. No." She huffed out a sigh. "I'm tired and I don't feel one bit sexy. And isn't that the story of my life these days? I'm sorry, Dave, I'm not much fun in bed."

"We have our moments." Sometimes they just curled up and slept together, occasionally she turned into a voracious temptress, and every now and then she seemed like the same old Cassidy. The latter were the times he liked the best. Though he had to admit, the temptress had taught him a trick or two.

Tonight, sex or no sex, he wanted to be with her. Though they'd squabbled on the drive to his parents', he admired the guts she'd demonstrated in talking to his family and her patience in answering questions and fielding comments that, though well intentioned, could easily have triggered her temper. He didn't want her to be alone tonight. What's more, he didn't want to be alone either. "Come home with me. No sex required. I'd just like to hold you."

"I guess I wouldn't mind being held," she said softly. Then she put her hand on his thigh and left it there until he parked at the Wild Rose.

Saturday evening, Dave held up the pizza server. "Who wants the last slice?" He glanced questioningly at his daughter, seated in her usual place across from him at the kitchen table, then at Cassidy, who sat between them.

"Too full, Dad," his daughter said.

"Me too," Cassidy said.

He knew she was lying. She'd eaten one slice but only picked at the second one he gave her. She was worrying about telling Robin her news.

Robin would be sad, concerned for Cassidy. No, none of this was fair. He rose to clear the table, Robin loaded the dishwasher, and Cassidy made a quick trip to the bathroom.

When she came back, Robin said, "Now we get to watch the movie?"

Cassidy had dropped by the library that afternoon and picked up *The Sound of Music*.

"Not quite yet," she said, the high pitch of her voice

betraying her nerves. "There's something I want to tell you. Sit down, Robin. You too, Dave."

When they were all back around the table, Cassidy took Robin's hand. "I don't want you to get upset about this. It's not a big deal."

"O-kay," his daughter said dubiously, casting a quick glance at him.

"It's okay, Rob," he assured her.

Cassidy went on. "You know how there's a girl in your class, Candy, who has diabetes?" Dave had told her this, suggesting it as a starting point for the discussion. At Robin's nod, she continued. "I have a disease too. It's nothing like what Anita had. It's more like diabetes. It's a nuisance, and I have to take meds, and that's the reason I've had some problems, like with my leg, and being tired. Some of it's the disease and some of it's side effects from the treatment."

"But you're going to be okay?" his daughter asked anxiously.

"More or less." Cassidy glanced at Dave, then said bluntly, "It's not going to kill me." They had figured Robin would worry that Cassidy would end up like Anita. "I may have some more problems over time, or I may not. That's one of the weird things about this disease."

"You're taking medicine," Robin said slowly. "That's going to help, right?"

Dave said, "That's the plan, sweetheart. Like Cassidy said, this is really different from Anita's cancer. That was very serious and there was only a tiny chance that she could beat it. With Cassidy's disease, there's no actual cure right now, but even if they don't find one, she'll likely live as long as you or me. She's got a great health care team, including Dr. Young, and the treatment should slow the disease down so she has fewer problems."

Robin had listened solemnly. "Does the treatment make you sick, Cassidy?"

"Not anything like chemotherapy did with Anita," she assured her. "You know when I said I felt like I had the flu? That was from the treatment. But the side effects are easing off. I'm adjusting to the meds, and maybe soon there'll be no side effects at all."

"That's good." His daughter's face had lightened.

"It's not the least bit contagious," Cassidy said. "I can't possibly pass it to anyone else."

"What's it called, this disease you have?"

"Multiple sclerosis. People usually refer to it as MS."

"How long have you had it?"

"Not for very long. I'm still learning about it. Anyhow, like I said, this isn't a big deal. But I wanted you to know. If I say I'm too tired to go riding, that's because of the MS. It's not that I don't want to."

"Okay," she said thoughtfully. "I'm sorry you got it."

"Me too."

His sharp-minded daughter asked a few more questions, which Cassidy answered honestly and calmly. She was so good with Robin, so patient and considerate. With wry humor, he thought that she saved her ire for him.

His daughter turned to him. "Does Mom know?"

He nodded. "We told Mom and Evan and all your grand-parents last night."

"I'm going to tell more people on Monday," Cassidy said.

"So it's okay if I tell Kimiko and my other friends?"

Cassidy swallowed. "Sure. But let them know it's not a big deal."

Robin nodded. "Like with Candy and her diabetes." She rose and went to throw her arms around Cassidy in a tight hug. "I'm really, really sorry this happened to you."

Cassidy hugged her back. "Me too, sweetie."

"And I'm really, really glad you and Dad are dating."

A pang of worry hit Dave. The adults in his family understood the concept of casual dating. Did Robin? She'd seen him married to her mom, then seen him with his fiancée.

The same concern must have occurred to Cassidy because she eased out of the hug, took Robin's face gently between her hands, and gazed into her eyes. "I'm glad we're dating too. Your dad is a wonderful friend." She pressed her lips together, sent a questioning glance at Dave.

He shrugged helplessly. How did you explain "friends with benefits" to an eleven-year-old? He was way out of his depth.

Cassidy released Robin and started again. "You know how much your dad loved Anita?"

Robin cocked her head. "Course I do. I loved her too."

"I know. Well, he loved her so much, he might never have another girlfriend like her. He'll have different kinds of friends, like me and Sally and Karen, and of course he'll always love your mom, but maybe his heart only has room for one special girlfriend like Anita."

He nodded. There was—could only ever be—one Anita.

"You mean," Robin said slowly, "like Kimiko's my best friend and if something happened to her, no one could take her place."

On safer ground now, Dave said, "That's right, sweetheart, but it's not quite the same. A friend, even a really special one like Kimiko, is different from finding the one person who's your, uh"—he felt stupid using girly, romantic words, but all the same forced them out—"soul mate. I love your mom a great deal and always will. But with Anita it was like we were two halves of a whole. Totally compatible. Everything just clicked . . ." It had been irresistible; magic; the most amazing feeling in the world. "When you're older, you'll understand better."

"Or not," Cassidy mumbled under her breath, tilting a

cynical eyebrow in his direction. Then, to Robin, she said, "Besides, as much as I like and respect your dad, I don't want a serious boyfriend."

Robin frowned. "You don't believe in what Dad said? You don't think he and Anita were soul mates, or mom and Evan? Or Gramma Brooke and Jake, or—"

"Stop, stop," Cassidy protested, holding up a hand, laughing a little. "I admit, Caribou Crossing breeds more than its fair share of soul mates. But not everyone finds that kind of relationship or is even looking for it. Like me."

"But you live in Caribou Crossing too."

Dave had to grin at his daughter's logic. His grin faded, though, when Cassidy said, "That's temporary. Once I get my treatment sorted out and have a handle on this disease, I'll be on the road again."

"Why?" Robin turned a narrow-eyed gaze on Cassidy.

Dave always got nervous when his daughter turned that look on him.

"Why what?" Cassidy said warily.

"Why would you go? Where could you go that's any-where near as nice as here?"

"Caribou Crossing is wonderful," Cassidy said, "but you've heard me talk about some of the other places I've been. Watching baby loggerhead sea turtles hatching on a Carolina sea island. Whitewater rafting in the Grand Canyon. The world is full of so many wonders."

"But *we're* here," Robin protested.

That was what hurt. He and his daughter cared about Cassidy; she was special to them. Yet for her, they were no different from the dozens, maybe hundreds, of people she'd left behind as she wandered around the world. He knew the deficiency wasn't with him and Robin. Cassidy's parents had done such a number on her that she chose self-sufficiency and adventure over close personal relation-ships. Knowing didn't make the pain any less.

For a moment, Cassidy didn't respond. Then she tweaked Robin's nose. "And that's the very best part of Caribou Crossing. On the sea island, it was the baby turtles. Here, it's you guys." Her gaze flicked to Dave's face, including him, then focused back on Robin. "People are different, Robin. We want different things out of life."

"I guess." She didn't sound convinced.

Cassidy said brightly, "Okay, I'm ready for popcorn and a movie. How about you two?"

Feeling depressed, Dave rose. "I'll get the popcorn. Rob, you go set up the DVD."

When his daughter had gone, he put the popcorn in the microwave. Cassidy sat at the table, her shoulders rounded. When he first met her, her spine had always been straight, her head up, her eyes sparkling. She'd been an optimist. He hated the way MS had dampened her spark.

He came up behind her and rested a hand on one bowed shoulder. "You okay?"

Her shoulders lifted, then fell again. "Yeah. Robin was great."

"You were pretty great yourself." With the MS part of the conversation. And, truthfully, with the other part as well. She'd been honest with Robin. It was Dave's problem that he wished Cassidy had a different philosophy of life.

She twisted her head to look up at him. "You're not so bad yourself, Dave Cousins. I'm sorry I'm such a bitch sometimes. Honestly, I don't know how I'd do this without you. And now I've dragged your whole family into it."

"You didn't drag anyone into it." He shook his head, impatient with her. "Jesus, woman, don't you understand that people like you? They want to help. You just need to let them in."

"Maybe." The word held no conviction.

He thought again of her parents. Would she tell them

about her diagnosis? Or tell her brother, whom she seemed closer to? Now definitely wasn't the right time to ask.

The microwave dinged and Robin ran in, Merlin at her heels. The dog knew that, whenever he smelled popcorn, he'd get a few kernels before the butter and salt went on.

A few minutes later, they were all in the living room. Cassidy curled into one corner of the couch, Dave sat on the other side, Robin was between them with the popcorn bowl, and Merlin lay on the floor at Robin's feet. Cassidy clicked PLAY.

Immediately, Dave had a sense of déjà vu. He remembered seeing this movie when he was a little younger than Robin. His mom had played it for him and his siblings. All he remembered now was that a nun became governess to a bunch of kids and taught them to sing.

When the nuns queried, musically, how to solve a problem called Maria, Robin giggled. "I like Maria already."

"Me too," Cassidy said. "I'm—I was—like her. A wave on the sand . . ." Her voice faded in sadness.

Robin leaned forward to stroke Merlin, and when the nuns next asked how to solve their problem, Cassidy muttered, so quietly Dave could barely hear, "You give her MS."

"What?" His daughter straightened.

"Nothing," Cassidy said quickly.

Listening to the words of the song, he realized that the woman sharing the couch did make him feel much the way the nuns did about Maria. Cassidy frustrated and confused him, yet she brought joy into his world. Especially before she was diagnosed. Of course she was going through a tough time now. But once she came to terms with her disease, she wouldn't let it hold her back. She'd regain her optimistic, sparkly, will-o'-the-wisp personality. And she'd be gone.

His life would be easier. His life would be . . . less.

When it was time for her to go, he couldn't try to hold

her back. As the nuns said, you couldn't hold a moonbeam in your hand. And so, over the next months, he had to be careful not to let himself get too attached. He took a handful of popcorn and moved back farther into his own corner of the couch.

As the movie progressed, he watched the two females beside him as much as he watched the screen. As Cassidy was drawn into the story, she became her old self, totally engaged and animated.

During a lightning storm, Maria distracted her charges by singing about her favorite things. A couple of verses in, Robin cried, "The wild geese! That's your tattoo!"

Cassidy smiled at her. "A wild goose flying with the moon on her wing. She's me."

He'd always thought her tattoo was beautiful and haunting, a symbol of her desire to fly free and solo. Now he was curious to hear the full story behind it. Later, when they were alone.

When the children started to repeat the verses, Cassidy said to Robin, "How about you? What are your favorite things? Galloping Concha across a meadow filled with wildflowers?"

She nodded enthusiastically. "Watching a foal take its first steps." She glanced at Cassidy. "What are yours? Those baby sea turtles? Rafting in the Grand Canyon?"

"For sure."

"Picking wild strawberries."

"The scent of a wild rose. Is anything more perfect than that?"

"Making my baby brother smile."

"Oh, that's a good one," Cassidy said.

And Dave thought: *This. This* was a good one. Having the two of them beside him, lighthearted and having fun.

Chapter Twenty-Five

Cassidy knew her singing voice was pretty awful, but who cared when she and Robin were having such fun, singing along to "Do-Re-Mi," then trying to yodel to "The Lonely Goatherd"?

The first time she saw *The Sound of Music*, she was a year or two younger than Dave's daughter, and she and her brother had sung along too. They'd been staying with Gramps. Luis was living in France with his girlfriend and Justine had gone on a skiing trip with the guy she was dating.

Parents sure came in different flavors. She and JJ had got the self-absorbed kind. Robin's parents had divorced too, and no doubt there'd been some difficult times, but Dave and Jess obviously still cared for each other and supported each other. More importantly, they'd always ensured that their daughter knew they loved her and put her first.

Gramps had done that. With his daughter, Justine, and with Cassidy and JJ. If he hadn't died when she was fifteen, Cassidy probably wouldn't have rushed off to Europe as soon as she graduated. What would she have done? She'd been so driven to get away from her shitty life at home, she'd never considered an alternative other than escape.

A rich voice drew her from her musings. The abbess was singing "Climb Every Mountain." It sent shivers up and down Cassidy's spine. Wasn't that what everyone wanted? To find a dream that would last all your life, and to follow it?

But it had to be a realistic one. Her own dream had been to explore the world and enjoy life to the fullest, and that was exactly what she'd done for ten years. Now, she hadn't the faintest idea what restrictions MS might put on that dream.

And somehow, as she lounged here with Dave and Robin, a life of moving from place to place, from one set of strangers to another, no longer seemed so full. In fact, it seemed a little . . . hollow.

On screen, the abbess was chastising Maria for having run away from her feelings for Captain von Trapp. She told Maria she must face her problems and live the life she was born to live. Everyone had a different dream, a different life. Cassidy realized that what the abbess was really saying was that the most powerful dreams were about a deep, loving commitment—whether to a god or to another human being.

Love. What did Cassidy know about love?

Gramps had loved her absolutely. For her and JJ, he'd have moved mountains. She didn't doubt that her parents loved her and her brother, but it was always secondary to their passion for each other.

Gramps had died; her parents were almost strangers. The only other person she'd ever loved, her brother, was a near-stranger too. Justine and Luis always put themselves first, and, it dawned on Cassidy, that was what she'd done with JJ. Once, they'd been best friends, but she'd run out on him in their teens. Ever since then, she'd kept to the fringes of his life.

Now, that felt wrong. She needed to see if the bond between them could be restored.

With that resolved, she focused again on the movie in

time to see the Captain and Maria confess their love for each other. She kept her attention on the screen until the von Trapp family hiked to freedom and the movie ended.

Robin said, "Yay! They all lived happily ever after."

Cassidy stood and stretched. "They did. And I know that they eventually made it back to their home in Austria."

"Oh yeah?" Dave teased, sprawling at his end of the couch. "You mean they didn't travel through Switzerland, then on to, oh, maybe the south of France, then perhaps Greece, because there were so many exciting places to see?"

She rolled her eyes. "Ha ha."

Gazing up at her he said, "It strikes me as odd that one of your favorite movies is about a family and the home that means so much to them."

"Different people have different dreams." Sensible people chose dreams they could realistically achieve.

Robin bounced to her feet and hugged Cassidy. "It was a cool movie. Thanks for bringing it."

Cassidy hugged her back. "I'm glad you liked it. And now I need to get home."

"I'll give you a ride," Dave said, rising with the hugely appealing athletic grace that characterized all his movements.

This time she wouldn't snap about him being overprotective, but appreciate the thought behind it. "Thanks, but I feel good. Honestly. I'll enjoy the fresh air and the stretch."

"Oh my gosh," Robin said. "I forgot you were sick, Cassidy. How do you feel?"

"Just fine," she assured the girl gently. "You don't have to treat me with kid gloves." She glanced at Dave. "Neither of you do."

"How about this?" he said. "We'll try not to do that if you'll tell us when you're tired or not feeling well rather than tough it out and pretend to be okay."

She wrinkled her nose.

He said, "Yeah, that'll be hard, right? Well, it's hard for Rob and me not to fuss over you. But we'll try." He gave her a pointed look.

Compromise. The two of them were learning. "Okay, I'll try too."

When Robin had taken the popcorn bowl to the kitchen, Cassidy said quietly to Dave, "The movie reminded me of my brother. I'm going to call him."

A slow smile lit his face. "I'm glad."

Whenever she was near Dave, something about him tugged at her, making her want to move close and touch him. It wasn't only sexual. A brush of hands, a caress of sock-clad foot against sock-clad foot on the coffee table, things like that could be enough.

His daughter came back, dangling Merlin's leash, which brought the dog to his feet. "Merlin needs to go out. We can all walk you home, Cassidy."

"Rob, you need to go to bed," Dave said.

"Aw, Dad, it's Saturday."

"Okay, maybe this once. But we should ask Cassidy if that's okay with her. Maybe she'd like to be alone."

Happy that he was learning to respect her boundaries, she said, "I'd enjoy your company."

"Yay!"

Outside on the street, Robin and Merlin jogged ahead. Dave clasped Cassidy's hand and she squeezed his. She breathed deeply, enjoying the crisp autumn air, the starry night sky. The bar at the Wild Rose was still lively, as was another down the street, but other than that the town was quiet, the streets almost deserted. So different from a big-city Saturday night.

Dave said, "Tell me more about your wild goose tattoo."

Robin was probably out of earshot; still, Cassidy lowered her voice. "As a kid, I loved watching the wild geese. I thought how lucky they were to be able to pick up whenever they wanted and fly wherever they wanted to go. When things at home weren't great, I wished I was a Canada goose. That line from the song stuck with me. So beautiful, and symbolic of freedom."

"When did you get the tattoo done?"

"Just after I turned eighteen."

"When you were in Europe after high school?"

"Yeah. I went to Greece to visit Justine, but she was all wrapped up in her boyfriend, who I didn't get along with."

"Sounds rough."

She shrugged. "Whatever. Anyhow, I had my birthday and both my parents gave me money as their present. Right after, I took off on my own to travel around Europe. The first thing I did was hitchhike to Amsterdam and get this tattoo. It was my way of saying I was a grown-up, free to live my own life in my own way."

"Wild geese usually travel in flocks," he commented.

"Not this one. I like my independence."

For a few minutes, they followed the girl and dog in silence, then Dave said, "By the way, I have to go to the Okanagan next Wednesday and Thursday to meet with suppliers. It's a four-hour drive, so it'd be easiest to stay overnight."

"Do you need me to do anything? Robin will be at Jess and Evan's?"

"Yes. As for the inn . . ."

She bumped her shoulder against his. "This is why you have an assistant manager."

"Call me if you have any problems, and I can drive back. Sam could help out too, if needed. I wish I didn't have to go, but—"

"Dave, stop. Or I'll think you don't have confidence in me."

"It's not that. But who knows what could happen

with your MS, or side effects from the meds. And you're supposed to reduce your stress level. I feel bad about dumping this on you. Actually, on second thought, I should postpone—"

"Stop!" This time she punched his shoulder. Not lightly. "Stop now, or I'm going to get pissed off." Her job was one of the few things, these days, that made her feel like she was in control. If he chipped away at that, her self-esteem would crumble even further.

"How about this? If you're feeling okay on Tuesday, I'll go. If you're not, I'll postpone."

As if Tuesday was any indication of how she'd feel on Wednesday. He had read the same MS information she had, and should know that. She wasn't going to remind him.

When they reached Ms. Haldenby's house, it was dark except for a light upstairs in her bedroom. Ms. H loved to take a mug of hot chocolate to bed and finish the night with a chapter of a novel.

Cassidy gave Robin a good-night hug, Merlin a pat, and Dave a lingering kiss on the cheek.

As she stepped through her door, she thought about her brother. He'd always been a night owl. There was no excuse not to call right now, and if she put it off she might lose her courage.

She pulled out the sofa bed, propped herself on pillows, and scrolled her phone to the rarely used number. "Hey, JJ. Is this a bad time? If I'm interrupting—"

"Cass? Hey, it's nice to hear your voice. No, this is good. Mags and I were just vegging in front of the TV. Hang on."

She heard him say, "Honey, could you set it to record? It's my sister." Then she heard Mags say, "Tell her hi from me."

When he came back on the line, Cassidy said, "Say hi from me too."

"Sure. So, what's up?"

They never called each other to chat, only when there was important news to convey. It hit Cassidy that she missed the way they'd chattered to each other as kids. "I watched *The Sound of Music* tonight. D'you remember watching it with Gramps?"

"Uh, yeah, I guess." He chuckled. "That's the one where we tried to yodel, right?"

"That's it. We were pretty awful. I don't know how Gramps put up with us."

"He was a good guy." A pause. "I still miss him."

"Me too."

"When Mags and I have kids, that's the kind of dad I want to be."

"Gramps is the perfect role model." Just like Dave. "I hope things work out for you this time, little brother." JJ deserved to beat the odds and finally find—or create—a happy family.

"They will. Mags is smarter than me. When I screw up, she whips me into shape."

In the background, Cassidy heard his fiancée say, "JJ! She'll think I'm some kind of sergeant major. Or a dominatrix."

"Not that there's anything wrong with either of those things," Cassidy told her brother, tongue in cheek.

He laughed again. "Sis, it's good to hear your voice."

"You already said that."

"Yeah, but you're still on the line. Usually, we say about two sentences, then hang up."

"True." She took a breath. "I've been a crappy sister and I want to apologize."

"Huh? You mean for not being in touch more often?"

"Well, yeah, but more for walking out on you when you were fifteen. For going off to Europe and leaving you with Luis. And for never really being there since then. Which was mostly because I felt guilty for skipping out."

"Jeez, Cass, it's not like I was a little kid. I could look after myself and I had friends to hang with. Besides, Luis wasn't all that bad."

"When he was around, which wasn't often."

"True, but what teenage boy wants his dad around all the time? We did okay. And I knew you needed to get out. When Gramps died, you were kind of . . . well, I don't know what you were, but definitely not happy."

"No. Not happy. Thanks for understanding. But I didn't exactly do the responsible thing."

He snorted. "I was Justine and Luis's kid, not yours. *Their* responsibility, not that they seemed to notice. Cass, let it go. I never blamed you, so get over blaming yourself."

That easily, he'd absolved her of guilt. Why hadn't she apologized years ago? Feeling like a weight had lifted, she said, "*You* will be a wonderful, responsible, loving father." She really, really hoped that he and Mags turned out to be like so many of the couples in Caribou Crossing. "Hey, have you two ever thought of moving to the Cariboo?"

"What? You mean, where you are? You're not actually thinking of staying in one place?"

"No, of course not. Sorry, that's not what I meant. It's just, there seems to be some magic dust in the air here, and a lot of marriages actually work out."

"Huh. I've always had a secret yen to be a cowboy."

"You did! You had that cute little cowboy outfit and the toy six-shooter! I'd completely forgotten."

"We don't exactly dwell on childhood memories, do we? It's funny, but now that I'm older, more distanced from the bad stuff, it's kind of nice to remember yodeling in front of the TV, and pretending I was the Lone Ranger."

"You know what, Lone Ranger? You and Mags should come visit sometime. We'll get you up on a real live horse and see how you do."

"Who's *we*, and I thought you said you weren't staying. I'm confused."

She'd actually been thinking of Dave and Robin, but quickly said, "Oh, it's just the generic 'we.' I'm a pretty good rider. As for staying, well, I'm kind of committed to being here for a few more months."

"Yeah? Got a great job?"

"I have, as a matter of fact. And the scenery is amazing, the town is so cute and charming, and the people are terrific. But, uh . . ." Could she really do this? She didn't want him to think she'd called because she wanted something from him. "The thing is, I've got this little health issue and need to get settled into a treatment plan." *Plan*. No matter how many times she said it, the word still made her wince.

"A *little* health issue that requires a treatment *plan*?" he echoed slowly. "What's going on, Cass?"

She breathed in and on the exhale said, "I have MS. Multiple sclerosis. The same disease GG died of."

He let out a low whistle. "Well, shit."

"My sentiment exactly."

"Are you, um . . . Oh man, I have no idea what to say. How bad is it?"

For the next twenty minutes or so, she filled him in.

When she finished, he asked, "What can I do? How can Mags and I help?"

"Oh, JJ." Moisture filled her eyes and she had to wait a moment until her voice was steady enough to speak again. "It's so sweet of you to offer." And she didn't deserve it. "I'm doing all the right stuff and I've got friends here. Don't worry about me, okay? I want you and Mags to enjoy planning your wedding, and I'll look forward to seeing you then."

"Me too. But you have to let me know if you need anything before then."

"I will."

"You going to tell Justine and Luis?"

"Someday, I guess. I'm in no big hurry."

"I hear you. They may come for the wedding, but I'm not counting on it. In some ways, it'd be easier if they didn't."

"I know. It's your special day, yours and Mags's. When our parents are around, it always becomes about them."

They were both quiet for a moment; then Cassidy said, "Well, I'll let you go now."

"Okay. Look after yourself, Cass. And call me, okay? It's good to talk to you."

"It is. And you call me too. I love you, baby brother."

"I love you too, big sister."

When she ended the call, she felt a sense of peace. Despite her disease, something in her life was actually improving. She took Pooh Bear from the end table and hugged him to her chest. Maybe one day she and JJ would be best friends again.

Automatically, she picked up her phone again and scrolled to Dave's name. Then she paused. Would he still be awake?

Then she smiled. Even if he wasn't, he'd forgive her for waking him up once he heard about her conversation with her brother.

Chapter Twenty-Six

"I'm glad it went so well." Dave, who'd been reading in bed when Cassidy phoned, was proud of her for calling JJ. She'd grown a lot since he first met her. Or maybe he'd just come to know her better and discovered her internal strength. "You'll really enjoy seeing him in Victoria at the wedding."

"I will. It's okay if I take time off work? The wedding is December twentieth but I'd like to take a few extra days."

"Of course." Madisun would be working at the Wild Rose during her school holidays. "Would you stay for Christmas?" A sense of loss chilled him. He'd looked forward to showing her how wonderful a big Caribou Crossing Christmas could be. More than that, if he was honest. He'd looked forward to having her share and brighten his own Christmas.

"I . . . I'm not sure."

Maybe it would be better if she stayed in Victoria. If she shared Christmas with him and Robin, it would only build a closer emotional bond. It wasn't like Cassidy would be there the next Christmas, or the one after. "No rush in making up your mind. Madisun will be here."

"Right. She can do the job as well—better—than me. It's not like you need me around."

But he did. At work, but more importantly in his personal life. And that wasn't good.

"Well, good night, Dave." Her tone was subdued, not bouncy like when she'd first called.

"Night, Cassidy. I really am glad you and your brother are growing closer."

How could a person not grow closer to Cassidy once they got to know her?

Dave had a restless night, forcing himself to take a hard look at his feelings for Cassidy. He should build more distance into their relationship, yet he was one of her key support people. Not to mention her boss. And her lover. But sex was so intimate. At some point—quite a while ago, if he was honest with himself—sex had become lovemaking. Cassidy might be capable of keeping things casual, but it seemed he wasn't built that way. Or at least he wasn't when it came to the strong-minded, gypsy-spirited woman with the wild goose tattoo.

He couldn't let himself love her. When Anita died, he'd sworn he would never again let himself be vulnerable to that kind of loss. It was almost ironic that it wasn't Cassidy's illness that would take her away from him; it was her own free spirit.

Over a breakfast of French toast and bacon, Robin babbled happily about last night and how much fun she'd had.

"Sweetheart, you like Cassidy a lot, don't you?" he asked.

"Well, duh."

"You know she's not going to stay forever. Only until the doctor is confident she has a good treatment plan."

Robin shook her head. "She'll stay. People don't leave Caribou Crossing."

"Of course they do. She already did. She only came back because of her diagnosis."

"She would've come back anyhow. Like Evan."

"It took Evan ten years," he pointed out. "And he only came back because one of his clients asked him to check out an investment opportunity."

"Whatever," she said blithely. "Cassidy won't go. She didn't come back because of her diagnosis; it was because she belongs here."

It did feel as if Cassidy belonged here. "She doesn't seem to think she belongs anywhere. She doesn't want to belong. You've heard her talk about all those places she's been."

His daughter splashed more maple syrup onto her French toast. "She can live here and take holidays to other places. Like how Mom and Evan and I went to New York City."

"I know, but I don't think that's how she sees it. She doesn't like being tied down."

"Tied down?" Her childish brow wrinkled. "It's not being tied down when you belong somewhere and have people who love you. It's, you know, being home."

"That's exactly what it is."

But Cassidy didn't understand what "home" was. Her parents had taken that away from her at age seven.

He and his daughter finished breakfast and tidied the kitchen. Feeling the need for fresh air and exercise to clear his muddled brain, he took Merlin and joined Robin in the ride to Boots.

There, he spent a few quiet moments sitting atop Malibu, watching his daughter and ex-wife bustle about. Ever since he'd known Jessie, she'd dreamed of creating some horse-oriented business of her own, and he was so happy she'd finally managed to do it. He was proud of her, and glad that he, along with a number of relatives and friends, had helped her realize her dream.

She was so happy now. Her horses, her business, the fact that she was helping disadvantaged adults and children. Her love for Evan—a love that had never died despite her marriage to Dave, and ten years' separation. Her much-loved daughter, and her new baby. And, of course, her large and loving extended family. It hadn't all come easily for her. She'd worked, suffered, fallen down, and picked herself up. She deserved every moment of happiness.

He had worked and suffered too. He was picking himself back up, thanks to Cassidy. In his life, what would happiness look like?

Dave turned Malibu back onto the trail, trotting at first, then kicking up the pace until they raced along. Merlin loped happily along beside them. Dave took off his hat, hoping the wind in his hair would clear away the confusion in his brain. The confusion named Cassidy.

The first time he had talked to Anita, his heart had recognized her as his soul mate. She'd been a strong, self-sufficient professional, but she had happily let Dave look after her. They'd walked through life side by side, arms around each other, never butting heads.

With Cassidy, it was different. He and she weren't such similar people. They challenged each other, argued, and prodded each other's boundaries. They weren't a comfortable fit. But she was amazing. Fun, generous, competent. Passionate. Willing to experiment in bed and laugh when things didn't work out. Fantastic with Robin. Gutsy when it came to dealing with her disease. Tough-minded, self-sufficient, and damned frustrating sometimes.

What would Anita think of Cassidy?

As Dave slowed Malibu and turned toward Caribou Crossing, he knew the time had finally come. For more than three years, he had hidden two items in the back of his

closet and tried never to think of them. This afternoon he
was going to Sally's, but he had enough free time before
then to do what needed to be done.

Dave tied Malibu's reins to the hitching rail at the back
of the Wild Rose, then ran upstairs with Merlin. He collected the urn and the envelope with "Dave" on the front in
Anita's shaky handwriting, and placed them gently into a
bag that tied onto the back of the saddle.

When the dog, in the kitchen lapping water, glanced up
expectantly, Dave said, "Not this time, pal. This is something I need to do alone."

He ran back downstairs, not giving himself time for
second thoughts.

After strapping on the cantle bag, he headed Malibu in
the direction of Dragonfly Lake, one of the lakes that dotted
the countryside. This wasn't a large one like Colcannon,
where teens and families went to picnic and swim. It was no
more than an irregularly shaped blue dot in a remote grassy
field, accessible only by horseback. He and Anita used to
ride there for picnics. They would spread a blanket and
make love under the wide open sky.

The last time they'd come here, the last time she'd been
well enough to ride, she had asked him to scatter her ashes
here. He hadn't been back since.

Now he slowed Malibu as they approached the lake. It
looked exactly as he remembered, its blue waters reflecting
the crisp blue October sky and a few puffy clouds. Anita
always found shapes in the clouds, just as Robin did. He'd
never seen them himself, being more a practical guy than an
imaginative one.

That last time, it had been summer and Anita had lain
back on the blanket and named off a St. Bernard, a whale,
and a kitten. She'd taken off her clothes, her body ravaged

by illness and chemotherapy, and he'd made love to her as gently and slowly as he could. Because it would have to last forever. They'd both known it was the last time. They had both cried, and that was when she'd asked him to scatter her ashes here, and to ride out and visit now and then.

He dismounted, untied the cantle bag, and left Malibu to graze.

"I'm three years late," he said as he stood on the lakeshore. "I'm sorry, but it hurt too much. Every time I thought about you, my heart broke all over again. I don't know if I was wrong all those years, or if I did need time to heal a little, but now, the more often I think about you or talk about you, the easier it gets. There are so many memories, Anita. We had so much love. I'd shut it all out—the memories, the love—and I did both of us a disservice. Now I'm letting it back in. My heart hurts when I miss you, but it's kind of . . . warm, as well. Like you're in there, always with me."

He sat down in the dry grass and balanced the urn carefully beside him so it didn't tip. And then he opened the envelope. Inside were two pages from a simple lined pad. Her words were more printed than written because she'd had trouble writing by that time.

My dearest love,

Dave, darling, I wonder when you will open this. I imagine you'll take some time before you feel ready. I wish you never had to open it. I still hope and pray that one day a healthy me will rip this into tiny shreds and scatter them into the wind.

The reality is, that's . . . I don't want to say impossible, because that would be giving up, so I'll settle for unlikely. And so I must write while my fingers still have the ability to hold a pen.

*You taught me so many things. To love, that's the big
one. And you taught me that if you want something badly
enough, you fight for it.*

*You said I had to fight my cancer, and I did. I am. I
fought with everything I have in me, and then found more.
More strength than I ever knew I possessed. Because I feel
more love than I ever believed possible. I am fighting to beat
the odds so we can have a future together. And, if that won't
be granted to us, I am fighting for every single extra day,
or even hour with you.*

*If you are reading this, then I lost the battle. Please
forgive me for that, my love.*

Tears blurring his vision, Dave lifted his head. Forgive
her? Had she known, somehow, about the irrational anger
he fought so hard to repress? Anger against the cancer, of
course, and against the fate that had given it to her. But yes,
at Anita too. For making him fall in love with her and not
only dream of a future but plan one. And then for getting
sick, for betraying their future, for not winning against the
cancer. For leaving him.

Unfair, irrational, stupid anger. He'd had no place to vent
it, so he'd nursed it deep inside, his own private cancer
making him feel like a shitty person. It was only when
Cassidy had persuaded him to talk about Anita, to let himself remember all the good things, that the guilty ache had
begun to ease.

When his vision cleared, he went back to the letter.

*Forgive me for everything, and forgive yourself too. I
know how badly you want to make things right for people,
and this is one thing you can't fix. But you have given me
so much. So much help, so much love. You've been by my*

*side every minute and, wherever I may be now as you read
this, you are by my side still.*

*No guilt, Dave. No anger. Promise me to let them go.
Keep a little sorrow, a little melancholy, but hold on to the
joy as well. And the love. Always, the love.*

*But please, don't let that be the only love in your heart.
You have such an amazing heart—so big, so true. Don't
waste that heart by not loving again. I hope that one day
before long you will find someone else. She won't be like me
or like Jessica. She'll be special, and your love for her will
be unique. Allow yourself that love, my dearest Dave.*

> *Yours, always.*
> *Anita*

As tears slid down his cheeks, Dave carefully refolded
the letter and put it back in the envelope. This, he would
keep forever.

Then he curved his hand around the womanly shape of
the urn and rose to his feet. Holding the thought of Anita
in his mind and heart, he removed the top and flung the
ashes, letting the light breeze scatter them onto the grass
and into the lake. Tiny pieces of the woman he had loved.
Still loved. Yes, he would come visit her here.

Perhaps he should have done this long ago.

If Cassidy hadn't come to Caribou Crossing, he might
never have done this. His feelings for Anita might never
have evolved to this point, where he felt joy as well as
sorrow, and mostly a certainty that Anita would always be a
part of him.

He lay back in the grass, pillowed his arms behind his
head, and gazed up at the sky. "I still can't see anything
other than clouds."

He could almost hear her amused voice as she pointed.

"Over there, you dummy. Can't you see the sheep? Or the peacock spreading his tail?"

"No," he murmured. "I needed you to see those things. I needed you for so many things, Anita." He stared fixedly at a wispy cloud that looked like . . . a cloud, nothing more.

"I did meet someone. She doesn't know I'm here, but it's because of her that I am. At first, I thought we'd keep it light, you know? That's what we both wanted. Nothing more. She made me smile in a way I hadn't smiled in a very long time. It wasn't the same as when you and I met. It was so different that I didn't even feel disloyal for being with her. The thing was, I knew you were my soul mate, my 'once in a lifetime' love."

As the high clouds continued to drift across the cool blue sky, he thought about Cassidy.

"She's sick, Anita. Not like you, but it could end up being pretty bad. And she's stubborn and independent. She's so damned frustrating, but she's also so generous. She brought me back to life, but that's not why I love—"

Oh God.

Testing the words, he said, "Do I love Cassidy?"

If he did, it wasn't in the same way he had loved Anita, which wasn't the same way he had loved Jessie. Jessie was the spunky girl he'd known all through school, married, and grown to love, the woman who was now his good friend. Anita was the gentle, incredibly special woman who'd left him too early and would live forever in his heart.

And then there was Cassidy, who, without him realizing it, had captured his heart and become a huge part of his life. Life without her would be empty, flat, lonely. Of course, he'd have Robin, his family and friends, his work. Just as he'd had before she came into his life. And look how miserable he'd been then.

Her smile, her laugh, the sparkle in her eyes, those were highlights of his day. Holding her in bed, whether they were making love or just cuddling, made him feel warm and content, as if all was right with his world. When she accused him of being overprotective, it pissed him off, but only because he wanted to keep her safe from all the dangers that might hurt her. That might take her away from him.

Oh, shit. "Maybe I do love her."

And that sucked, because once she went through this tough time in her life, came to terms with her MS, recovered her equanimity and sense of adventure, she'd be gone.

Robin had said that people didn't leave Caribou Crossing. But that wasn't true. The ones who stayed were the ones who knew it was the home of their heart.

Anita said that Dave had taught her how to fight. Their love had motivated her and she'd battled terminal illness, she'd undergone horrific treatments, just to hang on to that love for even another hour. "But in the end you lost," he whispered.

If he fought to win Cassidy, to convince her that she could be happy living in Caribou Crossing for the rest of her life, would he lose? Or if he managed to win, would she indeed be happy or would she feel tied down, those winged feet of hers bound? Would the vibrancy that made her Cassidy fade, like that of a wild bird when it was caged?

And then there was another question. Was he strong enough to love a woman who would, on a daily basis, battle an illness that could strike without warning?

Chapter Twenty-Seven

At the crack of dawn Wednesday, in Dave's kitchen, Cassidy held back a yawn. "Dave, just go. I'll be fine."

He had to go to the Okanagan to meet with several suppliers today and tomorrow. It was a four-hour drive and it made sense for him to stay overnight, but he'd been waffling. In fact, he'd been just plain odd for the past couple of days: distracted and self-absorbed, yet she caught him watching her when he didn't think she was looking. It made her seriously antsy.

If he was thinking of demoting her to a less responsible job, she wouldn't go down without a damned good fight. She could handle the Wild Rose in his absence. Having MS didn't make her incompetent, but that's how he was treating her. Her self-esteem had suffered badly enough since her diagnosis; she didn't need him undermining it further.

Exasperated, she said, "You say you're worried about my stress levels? Arguing with me and not trusting me stresses me out way more than getting out of my hair so I can do my job."

Narrow-eyed, he snapped back, "Don't get mad at me for caring for you."

Caring? The word gave her momentary pause. Not because she didn't know he cared—as a friend. But because her heart gave a hopeful jump, almost as if she wanted more. The kind of caring that led to those happily ever afters that Caribou Crossing seemed known for. The kind she couldn't let herself believe in for herself.

"I'm sorry." She stepped closer and applied a lesson from the counseling group she'd joined. Though it was hard to talk about how her illness made her feel, people couldn't understand unless she did. "MS makes me feel less. Less strong, less attractive—"

"That's not—"

She silenced him with a finger against his lips. "Whether these things are true or not, they're how I feel." That was another lesson: her feelings were valid. She'd also learned that others suffering from chronic illness or disability had similar feelings. She removed her finger. "MS makes me doubt myself. When you get protective about me doing my job, it makes me feel as if you don't trust me and—"

"That's not—"

She applied the finger again. "*And* I was going to say that I know that's not what you intend, but even so it undermines my self-confidence." This time she kept the finger in place. "Dave, I know that in the future, if I have more attacks or have real problems with fatigue or meds, I may be restricted in what I can do. That'll be really hard for me. But I'm not there now. I'm feeling good, I'm capable, you hired me for a responsible job, and I want you to let me do that job." Now she moved her finger away.

He caught it, held it, and then, almost reluctantly, kissed it. "You're right. Thanks for explaining. I know I can take it too far when I want to protect the people I l—" He coughed, cleared his throat. "The people I like. I'll try to ease off if you don't try to be Superwoman."

"Deal. So we're good? You'll go on this trip and not

worry about me or the Wild Rose, and I'll promise to call if the inn burns down?"

He grimaced. "Don't even joke about it. But yeah, we're good. And we'll talk on the phone tonight."

"Make it latish, okay? You in your hotel room bed, me in my bed at home. I bet we'll rock phone sex."

A startled laugh burst out. "Oh man, that's a thought to keep me warm on the long drive."

Midafternoon, Cassidy finished giving directions in French to a couple from Quebec who wanted to visit Gold Rush Days Park. As the pair went out the door, she let out a long breath. Okay, the day could have been a little less busy. Nothing major had gone wrong, but there'd been a succession of problems, from plumbing issues to noise complaints to someone skipping on their lunch tab to a supplier's failure to deliver the fresh trout that were supposed to be the main course at the town council's dinner meeting.

She had dealt with everything, sometimes multitasking. In addition, she'd supervised the staff in decorating for Halloween on Saturday. Studying the lobby, she smiled at the carved pumpkins, black cats, and witches scattered among the displays of autumn flowers and foliage.

Now, though, she was more than ready for a break. Fatigue had set in and her leg was giving her the pins-and-needles warning sign that it needed a rest. She went to the kitchen for a tall glass of ice water and a couple of chocolate chip cookies, and then made her way to Dave's office, sank gratefully into his chair, and put her feet up.

She had just picked up a cookie when her cell rang. She pulled it from her pocket and saw that it was Jess. "Hi there."

"Cassidy, I'm so glad I got you." The other woman

sounded harried. "Dave's not answering his cell and I need to talk to him."

"He's in meetings. I'm sure he'll check as soon as he's free."

"I didn't leave voice mail. Can you tell him to call as soon as you see him?"

"Uh, Jess, he's in Penticton this afternoon."

"What? He's where?"

"He's meeting with suppliers in the Okanagan today and tomorrow."

"Oh, shit."

"What's wrong?"

A long, wavery breath came over the phone. "It's not really serious, but Rob and Evan were in an accident."

"Oh my God!" She jerked upright. "Are they okay?"

"Rob's fine. Bruised from her seat belt and a little shaky, but otherwise okay. Evan hit his head against the side window and blacked out for a couple of seconds. He's concussed and there's minor swelling, which they're pretty sure will subside, but they want to keep him in the hospital overnight and monitor him closely." She was talking at twice her normal speed. "I'd like to stay with him, so I was going to get Dave to pick up Rob, but if he's in Penticton—"

"Jess, stop. It's okay. Robin can stay with me. You're at the hospital now? Let me get a few things organized here; then I'll pick her up." Belatedly, it occurred to her that Jess might rather have Robin stay with a set of grandparents.

But no, Jess said, "Would you? That would be wonderful, Cassidy. Rob would love it. Listen, I know she likes to think she's so tough, but she can be fragile underneath. She's gone through a lot. A car ran a light and smashed into Evan's, and she got tossed around, and now he's in the hospital looking glassy-eyed."

"I understand. I'll keep an eye on her."

"Call me if there's a problem. I can always come get her."

"Okay. Are you going to call Dave?"

A pause. "If I do, he'll drive home. Four hours, after a long day's work, when he's upset. And she'll be asleep before he gets here. If she was seriously hurt, of course I'd call, but . . . What do you think?"

Cassidy's eyebrows rose. Dave's ex was asking her opinion? "Maybe we could hold off a while, then Robin and I can call him?"

"Good idea. She'll feel better by then, and when he hears her voice and she says she's okay—which she always says, even if she has a broken arm—he might halfway believe her."

They both chuckled. "Okay, I'll see you soon," Cassidy said.

It wasn't right to leave the receptionist in charge at the Wild Rose until Sam came on duty at ten-thirty. Cassidy dialed his number and explained the situation.

"Sure," he said. "I don't mind putting in a few extra hours if you throw in one of Mitch's dinners. I'll be there shortly."

"And be sure to call me if you run into any problems." As she hung up, she had to laugh. Now she was sounding like Dave.

She took the elevator to Dave's suite, munching a cookie and drinking water on the way. Into a recyclable bag went Robin's PJ's and a change of clothes for school tomorrow, horsy DVDs, and microwave popcorn. She added children's aspirin and Traumeel, an ointment that helped heal bruises. Active, outdoorsy Robin suffered her fair share of bruises and scrapes, and Dave's bathroom cabinet was well stocked. All packed, Cassidy gazed down at the poodle, who'd been following her around. "And what about you, Merlin?"

He cocked his head.

"Yeah, you're right," she said. Tonight, Robin needed her

dog. Cassidy knew Ms. H would be fine with it. Besides, her landlady was occupied with her houseguest, Irene.

Downstairs again, Cassidy found Sam ensconced behind Dave's desk. "Tryin' it on for size." He winked. "Don't tell the boss."

"My lips are sealed. Thanks again, Sam."

She called a cab and she and Merlin hopped in. When they arrived at the hospital, she asked the driver to wait five minutes. As she climbed out, she discovered that her left leg had gone numb. A stupid pseudoexacerbation—just what she needed right now.

Robin and Jess were in the waiting room, heads bent over the girl's homework. Doing her best to walk evenly despite her numb leg, Cassidy joined them. "Hey, you two. Robin, how are you feeling, sweetie?" Gently, she tugged the girl's messy ponytail.

"Oh, fine. The bruise'll be gone in a few days." Robin's smile lacked its usual voltage. "Thanks for inviting me for a sleepover."

"It's my pleasure."

Jess rose. "If you could wait with Rob for just a minute, I'll run to the hospital pharmacy and buy some aspirin and Traumeel."

"No need," Cassidy said. "I brought some."

The other woman smiled. "You've really gotten to know my daughter." Thankfully, she didn't seem upset about that. She bent to hug Robin. "You have fun. If you want to talk to me, give me a call. Anytime, sweetheart. Okay?" She glanced at Cassidy. "Thank you."

"You're welcome. You go look after Evan."

Walking slowly, her arm around Robin, Cassidy made it out to the taxi. When the girl's body tensed, Cassidy asked, "Are you nervous about getting into a car?"

"Not much," she said, chin high. "Though I'd rather be on Concha." Then she gazed into the backseat and cried, "Merlin!" Worries forgotten, she dove in to hug her dog.

Cassidy followed, giving the driver Ms. Haldenby's address. She wrapped an arm around the girl's shoulders and leaned back. The pressures of the day had caught up with her and knocked her out. She wanted to doze, but instead focused on Robin. "I thought we'd put on our jammies and climb into bed and watch movies. I brought *Flicka* and *National Velvet.*"

"My favorites!"

"Popcorn, of course. And for dinner, does pizza sound good?"

"Yay, we're going to make pizza."

Cassidy loved making pizza with Robin and Dave, assembling a bunch of toppings so each of them could craft her or his own portion of the pie. Her leg should be able to handle a trip to the grocery store. Or she could listen to Dave, and not try to be Superwoman.

"You know what? I've had kind of a tough day too. I'm tired and my leg's acting up. I know it won't taste as good, but how about we phone for delivery pizza tonight?"

"Sure. When your MS is acting up, you need to rest."

Cassidy gave an exaggerated eye roll. "You're channeling your dad, right?"

They both laughed, and then Cassidy said, "The most energetic thing either of us is doing tonight is nuking popcorn and letting Merlin out. And calling your dad."

"But we have to be careful what we say. We don't want him to worry."

Chapter Twenty-Eight

Following a long afternoon meeting at a winery, Dave returned to his hotel in Penticton and decided he'd rather have room service than eat alone in a restaurant. He called in the order, then thought about phoning Cassidy. He missed hearing her voice, but if he phoned now she'd think he was checking up. She'd specifically said she wanted to talk later—and try out phone sex. That was worth waiting for.

Instead, he dialed Jamal Estevez. Jamal, like Dave, was into basketball and occasionally helped him out coaching the high school team. Today, he'd filled in at the after-school practice.

Jamal answered. "Hey, man. Good practice. I'm heading home now."

"Thanks again for filling in."

"No sweat. Gave me a chance to pick up a couple servings of Mitch's lasagna. Karen says it's the best in the world. So I'm gonna be getting a nice thank-you from my wife tonight."

"Too much information," Dave said, chuckling. "Married life suits you."

"Sure does. I still wake up every day almost scared to open my eyes, in case I'll find out the past year and a half has been a crazy dream. Never imagined I could have this kind of life."

Dave knew a bit about his friend's past: a crappy child-hood, police work, a decade of undercover assignments, a battle against alcoholism. A happy marriage and home life was likely the last thing Jamal had believed possible for himself. "Good thing you met Karen."

"Can say that again. A woman sure can change a guy's perspective on life."

The conversation turned to the basketball practice, and they discussed the players until Dave's dinner arrived. He ate a decent steak and drank a beer, watching the news on TV. After, he pulled out his laptop, checked e-mail, and typed follow-up notes from his meetings.

Then he called Robin on her cell. After several rings, she answered.

"Hey, Dad. Had to find my phone and wipe butter off my fingers. Cassidy and I are watching *Flicka*."

"Cassidy and you?"

"We're having a sleepover at her place."

"Is your mom okay?" he asked anxiously.

"Mom's fine, but she's with Evan in the hospital."

"My gosh. What happened to Evan?"

"We had this car accident, but—"

"You had a *car accident*?!" he yelled into the phone, rushing toward the bathroom to grab his toiletry kit so he could toss everything in his duffel and drive home.

"This car, like, kind of crashed into us. But I'm fine. Just a little bruised from the seat belt, but Cassidy put Traumeel on it, and I've taken aspirin. I'm really fine, Dad."

Thank God. "How about Evan?"

"He has a concussion but he should be okay. We're going to phone Mom and check when the movie's over."

After relief came anger. "Did it occur to any of you to tell me about this accident?"

"We planned to call after the movie. Mom and Cassidy and I decided we'd wait, because we didn't want you worrying and driving home."

Robin was his daughter. He had a right to know the moment anything bad happened to her. Cassidy might not get that, but Jessie damned well should. He tossed his suit jacket helter-skelter into his duffel. "But I want to be there with you."

"You can't come *here*." She sounded horrified. "It's a *sleep*over. Girls only."

Cassidy's voice said, "Let me talk to him, Robin." And then, "Dave, she really is fine. We're having a nice relaxing evening, just the two of us. Oh, and Merlin as well."

A moment later, Robin was back on the phone. "Yeah, Dad. We're taking it easy because we both had a rough day and Cassidy's MS is acting up a little." And then, quickly, "But she's *fine* too. Honest. You don't have to worry about us."

He sank down in a chair. "Of course I have to worry about you. I love you, sweetheart. People worry about the people they love."

"I know. That's why we worry about you too. We don't want you driving all this long way back when there's no reason to."

"Rob, you're the child. You're not supposed to worry about me."

"But I do. Though not as much as I used to before Cassidy came. I wish she was your for real girlfriend."

"Robin!" he heard Cassidy say.

He refrained from saying that he wished so too. "Let me talk to Cassidy again."

A moment later, Cassidy said, "Tell me you're not going to drive back and wake us up in the middle of the night."

"And crash a girls' sleepover? I wouldn't dare."

She chuckled.

He said, "Robin said you had a rough day too. What happened?"

"A longer list than usual of odds and ends. Nothing I couldn't handle. And when Jess phoned—she called me when she couldn't get through on your cell—I asked Sam to come in early and mind the shop, and he was happy to."

"You're making me feel superfluous," he grumbled, half serious.

"Never." The warmth in her voice, even over the phone, cheered him up. "How did your meetings go? Oh, wait a sec." He heard her say to Robin, "I'm going to talk business with your dad for a few minutes. Want to let Merlin out, since we have the movie paused? Don't go outside yourself, not in your PJs."

He gave her a quick summary of his successful meetings, then asked about those "odds and ends" at the inn. She gave him a rundown and he let out a low whistle. "Man, you did have a busy day. You did great, Cassidy. But how do you feel? Honestly."

"Tired and my leg's acting up. A pseudoexacerbation. No biggie. Robin and I are taking it really easy, like Dr. Young said to do."

Thank God she was being sensible. Gradually, she was coming to terms with her disease.

"I'll give you back to Robin," she said. "Night, Dave."

He spoke a few more minutes to his daughter. After wishing her good night, he put his phone down and went to gaze out the hotel window at the darkness of Okanagan Lake.

Cassidy had run his inn with capable hands, and she was giving his daughter a fun, relaxing sleepover after a car accident. The woman was impressive.

And he loved her. What the hell, there was no denying it. Was there any possibility that she could feel the same way, and their relationship could have a future?

Jamal had said that a woman could change a guy's perspective on life. Karen's love had turned a tough-guy loner into a small-town happily married man.

Could Dave's love change a free-flying wild goose into . . . What did he want Cassidy to be? Could he imagine asking her to be his wife, Robin's stepmom, an intrinsic part of his family? When he lost Anita, he hadn't believed he could ever again open himself up to the risk of such pain and loss. He still wasn't sure he could.

Nor was he sure that Cassidy could ever be happy with a life that, to her, would no doubt feel limited and confined.

Friday morning, Dave couldn't wait for Cassidy to get to work. His meetings—all successful—had run late yesterday, so he hadn't called her when he finally got back to town. It was amazing how much he could miss her in two days. He only hoped she felt the same.

When she came into his office at ten to eight and closed the door, her smile was bright.

He strode purposefully toward her and, without even saying good morning, pulled her into his arms for a long, steamy kiss.

When they finally surfaced, she said, "Mmm. You should go away more often."

"I missed you." He studied her face, feature by feature. Cassidy Esperanza. The woman he'd like to spend the rest of his life with. Was there any hope she'd come to feel the same?

Her face softened. "Missed you too."

There was genuine affection in those blue-gray eyes. He was sure of it. But how deep did her feelings run? Was she willing to let herself love? Would she ever let herself believe in the kind of things Jamal had thought were so impossible for him, until he'd met Karen? Love, a home, a family . . .

"Dave? What are you thinking?"

Things he couldn't share with her. Not yet, anyhow. He forced a quick grin. "That I'd like to show you how much I missed you, but someone might walk in. So let's talk business."

They sat in comfortable chairs and he said, "The hotel looks great. All ready for Halloween. Thanks for doing that, as well as handling everything else that came along. I couldn't have done better myself."

She gave a pleased smile. "Thanks."

"You're sure you're feeling okay?" His intent gaze rested on her face. "That pseudoexacerbation went away?"

"An evening's rest with Robin, and a good night's sleep fixed me up fine. Yesterday was a pretty easy day too and I felt fine."

"Thanks for looking after Robin so Jessie could stay with Evan."

"No problem. I'm glad the swelling in his brain went down and he could go home."

"Me too. He's a good guy."

She cocked her head. "Do you genuinely like Evan, or are you just, you know, adapting, for the sake of Robin and Jess?"

"I genuinely like him. Always did." Remembering Evan back in school days, he shook his head. "Man, was he an odd kid. An egghead, didn't go out for sports, never fit in, and made no bones of the fact that he wanted to get out of Caribou Crossing."

"Huh. So, how come you liked him?"

"Because of how he was with Jessie. He'd have done anything for her."

"But they didn't date?"

He shook his head. "Evan didn't date, didn't even hang

out with the other kids except for Jessie. She didn't date either, though she socialized a lot."

"But she dated you, obviously. I mean, she did get pregnant."

"Uh . . ." Oops. Off balance, he rose and walked over to straighten one of Robin's drawings. As much as possible, he always avoided lying, even when he couldn't tell the whole truth. Best to keep his back to Cassidy, though, as she had that knack of reading his face. "Yeah, she did get pregnant."

"Miriam Bly once told me that she and Wade didn't even know their daughter was going out with you. They kind of expected her and Evan to start dating."

Jessie and Evan never dated; they just had sex one night, and the condom broke. "I've heard her say that before." Searching for more truth to share, he said, "Evan spent a lot of time at their house. He and Jessie were best friends ever since grade two." He strolled over to where Merlin had curled up on the floor and squatted to pet the dog.

"Hmm. So they were more like sister and brother? But then he came back ten years later and they fell madly, passionately in love? That sounds a little . . ." Her voice trailed off.

He wasn't going to offer a comment.

"No, wait—" she started, then broke off.

Dave glanced over his shoulder, to find her staring at him. No, he wouldn't ask.

Slowly, she said, "I hope this doesn't hurt your feelings, but Jess's mom seems to think she maybe did have feelings for Evan back then, and harbored them over the years."

He swallowed, then ducked his head again and stroked Merlin. "Maybe she did."

"But then why would she have sex with you?" Her words were soft, as if she was speaking to herself. "She's loyal, responsible. So are you. If you suspected that Jess was interested in another boy, you wouldn't have dated her. Would you?"

Dave's hand had fisted in Merlin's close-cropped curls. The dog raised his head and stared questioningly at him. Dave stared back, hunting for words. "We were teenagers. Teens do stupid things."

It was quiet in the room. He imagined he could hear the racing thud of his own heartbeat.

"Oh, my God," Cassidy breathed.

His body taut with tension, he turned his head and stared over his shoulder at her. "What?"

Her words came out slowly. "Who is Robin's father?"

He struggled to keep his face expressionless. "What are you talking about? I am."

"Her biological father. Is it Evan?"

Scowling, he said, "Shit, Cassidy. Why would you think that?"

"Dave?" She came over to him, where he squatted by the dog, and held out her hand. "I promise I won't tell anyone. Please don't shut me out."

Oh God. It wasn't his secret, or at least not his alone. And yet he loved Cassidy. He glanced down at Merlin, who was still gazing questioningly at him, and then back up at Cassidy. Her eyes held compassion, not judgment. He sighed wearily. "I don't want to shut you out."

He put his hand in hers and let her pull him to his feet.

"Is it Evan?" she asked again, softly.

Decision made, the tension eased from his shoulders. "Yes."

"Does he know?"

"Now. He didn't back then."

"She didn't tell him? Did you know, when you married her?"

"Yes, of course." Another sigh. "It's complicated." Hearing his own words, he curved his lips in a small, wry smile.

"Obviously." He led Cassidy back to the chairs and they both sat. "Jessie and I had gone to school together forever. She was a good friend. I asked her out once, but she said she wasn't into dating. I found out later that she had a crush on Evan, even though they never actually went out."

Cassidy's brows lifted in an unspoken question.

"They had sex once, that's it, and the condom ripped." He shook his head. "Jessie was always so perky, so spunky. Until the day she came to me crying because she was pregnant. Evan had no idea. He'd left town right after they'd had sex. He had a scholarship to Cornell University. Anyhow, she told me she wanted a guy's opinion, from a friend she could trust."

Cassidy nodded as if that made perfect sense.

"I thought she should tell him. Evan was a good kid. He cared about her and he'd have done the right thing. But she reminded me that he'd always hated Caribou Crossing and he had a bad home situation. His dad ran out, and Brooke was—well, it was before her bipolar disorder was diagnosed, and she was an alcoholic. She'd be the first to tell you she was a crappy mom. Evan was desperate to escape."

Cassidy let out a low whistle. "And I thought I had parent issues."

"For ten years," Dave went on, "Evan had worked hard to build a path out of 'Hicksville,' as he called it, to the Big Apple. He was the smartest kid in school, worked his butt off, got a scholarship. Jessie was sure that if he came back, married her, and stayed here he'd be miserable. Perhaps she was right. Who knows? We were kids. Anyhow, I guess I kind of knew at the time that she really loved him, but I figured it would fade with distance and time."

"You loved her, though? You proposed to her."

"I liked her a lot." He ran his free hand across his forehead, shoving back the hair that tumbled across it. "To be honest, I proposed because I couldn't stand seeing her look so whipped. I wanted her to be spunky again. I'd never had a serious girlfriend and I figured the two of us might really work out. She married me because, I think, she liked me a lot too and she figured it would be the best thing for her baby. And so did I."

"Taking on another guy's child . . ."

Remembering, smiling, he shook his head. "From the moment I first felt Robin move, she was mine. Jessie and I never had sex until months after she gave birth. Our feelings for each other grew into love over months, maybe years. But when Rob's little foot kicked against my palm through the wall of Jessie's belly, I was a goner."

Cassidy smiled softly; then her smile died and her eyes darkened with compassion. "You were her dad. You and Jess split up, but you were still Robin's dad. And then Evan came back."

He nodded. "Two years ago. He was kind of forced into it by an investment client, and he fully intended to return to New York. Long story; I'll tell you some other time. As it happened—thank God—he was here when Robin was hit by a car."

She frowned. "Why was it good that Evan was here?"

"Rob inherited a rare blood type from him. She needed a transfusion and the hospital didn't have enough blood banked. We were in the middle of a storm, and the chance of getting blood flown here in time was slim. We had no choice but to tell Evan. I hated doing it."

Her eyes had widened as he spoke. Now she said a heartfelt, "I bet."

"But then he and Jessie fell in love again, or realized they'd been in love all along, so probably we'd have had to tell him anyhow."

"That must have been so hard for you."

"In a lot of ways," he admitted. "But it's good to see Jessie so happy. Evan's been great. He's fine with having everyone including Robin believe that I'm her dad and he's her stepdad."

"In the ways that matter most, it's true. He contributed sperm, unintentionally. Then you took over and did everything else."

He reached over to touch her cheek, appreciating her loyalty. "Thanks, Cassidy."

Oh yes, he loved this woman. Now what the hell was he going to do about it?

Chapter Twenty-Nine

Halloween was definitely cool in Caribou Crossing, Cassidy thought as she strolled in her best imitation of a cat's lazy grace through the lobby of the Wild Rose. Costumed as a black tuxedo cat with one white stocking, she wore close-fitting black yoga pants and a black turtleneck sweater, a white bib, one thick white kneesock, cheap white sneakers with one dyed black, plus cat ears and theatrical make-up.

As a child, she'd loved dressing up for Halloween—a ladybug, a princess, Maria from *The Sound of Music*—and going trick-or-treating. Gramps had taken her and JJ.

When she'd been informed that many adults as well as children dressed up for Halloween in Caribou Crossing, she'd talked to Dave and the staff and they'd decided to make it a costume day at the Wild Rose. It added a great spirit of fun, especially when one of the waiters, who was involved in local theatre, helped them with costumes and make-up.

Now she watched with a grin as the vampire at the front desk—Nora—doled out treats to a rather wary bunny rabbit and a tough-guy superhero. School had let out early and the streets were filled with costumed children begging for treats from businesses and residents.

An hour ago, Robin had popped into the inn with her BFF, Kimiko. Dave's daughter was a hippie dressed in tie-dye, fringe, and ragged jeans embroidered with peace signs and flowers—items drawn, to Dave's horror and Cassidy's amusement, from his mom's old trunks of clothes in her attic. Kimiko was a charming Japanese woman in a kimono and exaggerated make-up, her long black hair in a complicated style decorated with a butterfly clip.

Dave came into the lobby, carrying his coat and Cassidy's. He'd been transformed into a mime: black pants with suspenders over a black-and-white-striped T-shirt, a black beret, and white face paint with black and red diamonds around his eyes. As much as possible, he had tried to communicate with gestures rather than speech all day, which had led to lots of laughs.

Still not speaking, he held her jacket out and she slipped into the three-quarter-length sheepskin, another treasure from Days of Your. Not that, on the salary Dave paid her, she couldn't afford to buy something new, but why would she when Maribeth's thrift store had everything she needed? That store supported several wonderful local charities.

"I'm a cat in sheep's clothing," Cassidy joked as Dave put on his own coat and they headed toward the front door.

It opened, letting in two princesses. The bunny and superhero went out, and Cassidy and Dave followed. The air was crisp but not cold, the sky clear, and laughter rang out.

She slipped her arm through Dave's as they crossed the street, heading toward the town square half a block away. Members of the chamber of commerce and the fire department had been setting up all day, and now the celebration was in full swing. It was almost dark and the old-fashioned lamps added a dramatic touch to the scene.

Cassidy and Dave snagged cups of hot apple cider but

turned down bright red candied apples. As they watched kids bob for apples, she realized, "I don't think I've seen a single cowboy hat. Am I really still in Caribou Crossing?"

With his free hand, he gestured toward a pair of wire caribou decorated for the holiday. One was an elephant, the other a giraffe.

"Okay, I'm in Caribou Crossing. Could you break the sacred law of miming and tell me why no one's costumed as a cowboy?"

He started to speak, cleared his throat, tried again. "It's an unofficial rule. You can borrow from town history and dress up as a gold miner, but it's cheating to be a cowboy because almost everyone owns boots and a cowboy hat. Even if you add a mask and say you're the Lone Ranger, you'll be branded a loser."

She chuckled. "JJ'd be in trouble. He liked to dress up as the Lone Ranger."

"You're looking forward to seeing him."

"I am. I'm so glad I phoned him and cleared the air."

Robin and Kimiko ran over. Cassidy straightened the circlet of artificial flowers that held Robin's chestnut brown hair in place. Normally, the girl pony-tailed it, but her grandmother had insisted that today she wear it loose, straight, and parted in the middle. She also had a pink and blue peace sign painted on one cheek.

"Have you been in the haunted house?" Robin asked. "You have to go!"

After the girls ran off to join friends, Dave said, "Feeling brave?"

They entered the haunted house and screeched merrily as ghosts, giant spiders, and other horrors popped out at them. When they reemerged into the crisp air, they followed the delicious scent of chicken stew and biscuits to a booth operated by The Gold Pan, one of the town's restaurants. For dessert, they indulged in slices of pumpkin bread and pumpkin-shaped cookies with orange icing baked by members of the Parent Advisory Council at Robin's school. Once they finished eating, they pulled on their gloves and Cassidy tucked her hand through Dave's arm.

"How are you feeling?" he asked. "Need to sit down?"

"No, my leg's great today. Let's keep strolling."

Since they had arrived, they'd exchanged greetings with dozens of people. By now, Cassidy knew many of the residents. Now they stopped to talk to Karen Estevez, in her RCMP uniform. "No Jamal tonight?" Cassidy asked.

"Sadly, no. He's on duty in Williams Lake. We're building good karma. When we have kids, we'll deserve to get Halloween off."

A woman in a firefighter uniform came over and said hello. Dave and Karen greeted her, and then Karen said, "Cassidy, have you met Lark Cantrell, our fire chief?"

Cassidy was about to say no, then realized the woman's strong, attractive features, appraising brown eyes, and hint of Native Canadian blood rang a bell. "You were Karen's maid of honor, weren't you?" The only person in the wedding party who hadn't brought a plus one.

"Yes, I was. You were helping out there. I remember."

"I'm surprised I haven't run into you around town," Cassidy said. "It's such a small place."

"My job and my son keep me busy."

"I think it's very cool that the fire chief is a woman."

Lark smiled. "I think it's pretty cool too. This is a good town. So, you folks looking forward to the fireworks?"

"The ones here," Karen joked, "or when Jamal and I finally both make it home tonight?"

Lark smiled, but it seemed forced to Cassidy. "Whatever rocks your boat, my friend. Well, I'd better go. We're going to light the bonfire. Come on over."

Cassidy and Dave followed her. Soon the blazing but carefully controlled fire was the center of attention, its orange flames providing not only beauty but heat. Cassidy cuddled into the curve of Dave's arm. "There's something magical about a bonfire."

"Wait until you see the fireworks."

"To echo Karen, which ones?"

He hugged her closer to him. "When we make love later, we should get back into our roles. I can't speak and you can only purr."

"Mmm, I bet you can make me purr very nicely indeed."

When it was time for the fireworks, Cassidy noted that Kimiko stood between her mom and dad, and Robin had joined Jess and Evan, who'd left little Alex with his gramma Brooke. Evan dropped a casual hand on Robin's shoulder. How odd it must be for him knowing he was the girl's biological father yet pretending to the world he was her stepdad.

It seemed all families were complicated. It was how they dealt with the complications that mattered. As she'd gotten to know the magic-dusted Caribou Crossing couples, Cassidy had found they all had their tales of tribulation. A happy marriage, she'd come to realize, took a lot of hard work. Miriam Bly had told her that it was surviving the tough times that made you appreciate your spouse. Too bad Cassidy's parents had never figured that out. Whenever they faced a tough time, they split up.

The first rocket soared into the sky, then exploded noisily in a starburst of white and red against the black canopy. The crowd cheered and Cassidy joined in.

Dave drew her back, apart from the others, to stand under a tree that had lost almost all of its leaves. He leaned against the trunk and put his arm around her.

She nestled into him, careful not to let her made-up cheek rub against his coat. "Autumn's a nice season here."

"All seasons are great."

"Not that you're biased or anything."

They watched a couple more dazzling fireworks, and then he said, "About your brother's wedding . . . Are you interested in taking a date?"

Startled, she glanced away from the pyrotechnic display. So odd to hear Dave's familiar voice but see the made-up face of a mime. "You'd go with me? Really?" It would be fun to introduce him to JJ—she knew they'd get along—and to share the whole experience. But then a thought occurred to her. "Wait a minute. Is this your way of making sure I don't overdo?"

"Huh. Now that you mention it . . ." His tone was light, but then sobered. "No, honestly, that didn't occur to me. I'd just like to be with you, meet your brother and his fiancée, see where you grew up."

She settled back against him and again turned her gaze to the sky. "I'd like that too. You'd be okay with leaving the Wild Rose for two or three days?"

"I need to learn to be. My sense of responsibility may be, uh, a little overdeveloped."

"Gee, you think?"

He shrugged. "Madisun will be here in December and she ought to be able to manage the inn for a few days, with Sam for backup. Besides, there's phone and e-mail."

"I'm impressed, Mr. Cousins. And yes, I'd love it if you came with me."

They watched some red spirally, fizzy fireworks. Then he cleared his throat and said, "As for Christmas, I was hoping you'd want to spend it here. With me."

"Oh, Dave, that would be wonderful." Christmas here would be warm, colorful, old-fashioned. "Are you sure? Christmas is for families." Happy ones. The kind she hadn't been part of in a very long time.

"I'm sure." He paused, and when he next spoke his voice sounded stilted. "But you know that there's something else about Christmas, right? It involves presents."

Did he think she wouldn't want to spend her money on gifts for his family? What better way to spend her savings? "I do recall presents. And I'd love to get presents for your family."

"Uh, that's great, but that's not what I meant. You'll be getting them too."

"Oh, no one has to buy presents for me." The most she'd done in past years was exchange cards with family, and participate in a "Secret Santa" thing wherever she worked.

"They'll want to." Another pause. "And you wouldn't be able to fit them all in your backpack. It'd be rude to leave them behind if you left Caribou Crossing, so, uh . . ."

"Even more reason that people shouldn't give me gifts. Tell you what, if they want to give me something, how about a donation to their favorite charity?"

Overhead, a dramatic display of glittery gold and white lights sparkled and crackled.

"Cassidy, what I'm saying is, I want you to stay."

The fireworks were loud. Maybe she wasn't hearing correctly. "Right, for Christmas. Isn't that what we were talking about?"

"It's not what we're talking about now." He sounded frustrated.

"Okay," she said, puzzled.

He stepped away from her, turned to face her, and took her gloved hands in his. "I want you to stay here, in Caribou Crossing. Not just until your treatment plan is established, but after. I want you to stay with me."

Her mouth opened. What was he saying?

"I love you, Cassidy, and I want you—"

"What?!" she yelped. For a moment, her heart leaped with joy—but no, this wasn't right. Panicky, she jerked her hands free. "You don't love me. You can't. That wasn't the deal. Dave, you love Anita."

"I do, and always will. And Jessie as well. And now I

love you. This isn't a *deal*, Cassidy, it's a relationship. I want you to stay, to open your heart to the possibility of a future together, to see if maybe you could love me too."

Didn't he know her at all? She didn't *do* permanent. "You want to change me. That's not fair. I thought you liked me the way I am."

"I do. But I love the idea of something more, of the kind of love we could build together."

Oh God. Could they? The idea was so tempting—but so impossible. It wasn't right for either of them. "Dave, I'm sick. Flawed." No man in his right mind would want to build a future with a woman like that.

And then it hit her. He was doing this out of pity. This was the guy who always tried to fix things for his friends. When Jess told him she was pregnant and alone, he'd proposed to her. Now here was Cassidy, dealing with an unexpected and chronic illness. He didn't trust her to look after herself; he had to do it for her. "Oh my God, Dave. Don't you get it? I do fine on my own. I don't need you."

Realizing how rude that sounded, she softened her tone. "I appreciate your support more than I can say. I hope we'll always be friends and stay in touch. But—"

"But you don't love me," he said bitterly. "You can't see yourself ever loving me. Shit."

As the fireworks display crescendoed over their heads, he strode away.

His final words hung in the air and sent a pang of sorrow through her heart. Love? What did she know about love? Even if she was capable of loving, no way could she and Dave build a future. There were too many obstacles. Weren't there? Her heart urged her to run after him, but she forced herself to stand still and catalogue all those obstacles.

Cassidy didn't need any man's pity. Dave might say he loved her, but he meant as a friend. She wasn't the kind of person whom people loved, not in the way he had loved Anita.

Building a relationship based on affection and Dave's do-gooder nature worked for a while with him and Jess, but look how it ended up. Even Jess couldn't compete with Anita.

With Cassidy's MS, her own future was so uncertain. Bad enough that she had to wake each morning never knowing what her body might do. That she had no idea whether in five, ten, or forty years she'd be in a wheelchair or unable to speak articulately. No way should Dave, who'd already gone through so much with Anita, have to take that on.

Besides—she touched her fingers to her shoulder—she was the wild goose, always flying solo. It had worked for her when she was eighteen, and worked ever since. She wasn't destined to nest in one place.

Even if Dave, and Caribou Crossing, made the thought undeniably appealing.

Sunday morning, Cassidy slept in, having spent much of the night tossing and turning. As she stood in the tepid shower—she'd given up her beloved hot showers because heat could exacerbate her symptoms—she pondered what to do.

Where did things stand with Dave? Had she hurt his feelings, rejecting his generous offer so brusquely? Could they still be friends? Could she keep working for him? Maybe it would be best to move on now. To go to Victoria, find another doctor and counseling group.

Whatever feelings Dave had for her, they'd pass once she was gone. Loads of women would volunteer to fill her place. Healthy women. He'd be fine.

That thought should make her happy, rather than depress her.

For heaven's sake, she'd be fine too. MS was her reality now, but within its constraints she'd be fine.

She checked the fridge for breakfast food, finding nothing that appealed to her. Most Sundays when she wasn't working, she had brunch with Ms. H. But Irene was here now. Cassidy was happy for the two women and hoped the reunion was going well, but missed her frequent chats with her landlady, not to mention the delicious meals they put together.

Dressed in yoga pants and a cotton hoodie, she unrolled her yoga mat and started her stretches. Not only was she doing yoga, but she'd added exercises recommended by the physical therapist on her health care team. On days when she was fatigued, it was a slog to exercise, but she was stronger and more flexible, and the routine gave her a sense of calm and control.

This morning, she'd almost found serenity when a firm knock sounded on the hallway door. Ms. H called, "Cassidy? Are you home?"

"Come on in."

She gazed up from the mat at her landlady, clad this morning in tailored navy pants and a lightweight turquoise sweater. If she left, she would miss this woman a lot.

This was a good reason not to stay in one place for too long: you could get too attached. Best to go now, before parting became even more difficult. And so much for serenity. Now she felt depressed again.

"Irene and I have a broccoli cheddar quiche in the oven. Would you like to have brunch with us?"

"Love to, thanks," she said promptly. She could use the distraction, the quiche sounded wonderful, and Cassidy was dying to know how things were going with the two old friends.

"Come along when you're ready."

Cassidy changed the hoodie for a pink and blue plaid

shirt, and headed for the kitchen, calling out "Good morning!" to announce her arrival. She found the two women moving companionably around, setting the table and pouring juice. Irene, whom Cassidy had met a few days earlier, was shorter and rounder than Ms. H and had a cheerful face framed by curly white hair. The coral sweater she wore over black pants matched the flush on her cheeks.

"It smells wonderful in here," Cassidy said. "Thanks for inviting me."

Irene poured a cup of coffee and handed it to her. "Sit down, dear."

Normally, Cassidy would have helped out but she could see the two older women had things under control and enjoyed sharing the kitchen. Feeling a little displaced, she took a chair. "Thanks, Ms. Peabody."

"Oh for heaven's sake, it's Irene."

"And it's time you stopped calling me Ms. H," her landlady said. "That's a ridiculous way to address a friend."

Until now, Cassidy would have had trouble calling her Daphne. Though her landlady had been the kindest, most supportive person imaginable, a slight edge or brusqueness had made her Ms. H. Today there was a softness to the older woman's features, even her movements, that let Cassidy say, "I'll give it a try, Daphne."

She sipped coffee as the two women finished their breakfast preparations. The natural way they interacted indicated that the reunion was going well.

When they had all served themselves, Irene said, "Did you have a good Halloween, Cassidy? We had so many children around trick-or-treating, in such wonderful costumes."

"We did," Daphne agreed.

Normally, her landlady spoke efficiently, avoiding repetition. It was cute the way she savored that "we" as she said it.

"It was amazing." Cassidy told them about the goings-on in town.

"How delightful," Irene said. "Perhaps we should go to the town square next year, Daphne, at least for the earlier part of the evening."

Cassidy smiled and sipped orange juice.

Daphne smiled too, and addressed her. "Yes, Cassidy, we do believe there will be a next year. Irene and I have both been fools for an excessively long time. We worried too much, we made mistakes, we lacked courage." She reached for the other woman's hand and their aged fingers wove together. "But better late than never."

"We owe you an immense debt, Cassidy," Irene said. "Daphne told me it was because of you that she tracked me down."

"I'm glad I could help."

"You're a true romantic," Irene said.

Cassidy gave a snort of laughter. "If you knew me better, you wouldn't say that."

"Our young friend," Daphne said, "is skeptical that true love exists. Despite considerable evidence to the contrary."

"I admit that Caribou Crossing has more than a normal share of happy long-term relationships," Cassidy said, "and I truly hope yours is one of them. But I'm not the kind of person who's into all that happily ever after stuff."

"You might be if you gave yourself a chance," Daphne said, "rather than picking up and moving every few months."

"I like my gypsy lifestyle." Even if the idea of leaving Caribou Crossing didn't excite her the way moving on used to. But being a gypsy was the only way she knew how to live, and once she was on the road, her old sense of adventure would reawaken.

"Someone who spends her time wandering is looking for something," Irene said.

"Sure. New places, experiences, people."

Thoughtfully, Irene said, "Really? I'd say the opposite. You're looking for a home."

"Home is where I hang my hat," she said flippantly.

The two older women exchanged glances; then Irene said, "I'll top your platitude with this one: home is where the heart is."

And, Cassidy knew, a piece of her own heart would forever be tied to Caribou Crossing. To Daphne Haldenby and Robin Cousins; to the other friends she'd made here.

To Dave.

Chapter Thirty

Inside Dave's suite, Cassidy hung her coat in the closet, pulled off her boots, and slid her sock-clad feet into the sheepskin slippers that sat by the door. Expecting the place to be empty—with Dave at Sally's, as was his custom on Sunday afternoons—she was surprised when Merlin greeted her.

"Hey there, beautiful boy. Why did Dave leave you at home? Oh, right, Sally's boarding that new horse that's paranoid about dogs."

When Dave had given Cassidy a key, he'd told her to make herself at home anytime she wanted. Now she wasn't sure exactly what she needed, but some instinct had led her here. Her journal was in her bag; maybe she'd curl up on the couch and try to process her thoughts by writing them down, as she'd done many times in the past months.

She picked up a sweater she'd left behind the last time she was over, and noted her travel magazine lying open beside Robin's sketch pad. She thought of her comfy yoga pants and tees folded in Dave's closet, her toothbrush and body lotion in his bathroom. In small ways, she'd started to become part of this home. And Dave had offered her a chance at the real deal.

Toying with the Canada goose pendant that hung around her neck, she gazed out the window. In the town square, chattering groups of people cleared away the Halloween trappings.

The Wild Rose was in the geographic center of Caribou Crossing. More than that, it was the heart of the quirky, vital, historic town. Because Dave was the heart, the person everyone turned to and relied on. Could she imagine herself beside him as his partner in life?

The first and only time Cassidy had truly believed she had a home, she'd been a little kid. In her innocent world, it had never occurred to her that parents might tear a family apart, but hers had done it. When Justine and Luis had reconciled and remarried, things had seemed good at first but she'd never fully trusted in it. And she'd been right; the happy family thing had been an illusion. And then the one person she'd counted on to always be there for her, Gramps, had died. Of course, that hadn't been his fault, but all the same it had been the final straw. Never, since then, had she allowed herself to count on anyone.

Even Dave and Ms. H—no, make that Daphne. Cassidy had, rather grudgingly, taken the support they offered, but she'd never let herself rely on it. Never let herself believe it would always be there. Because, of course, she didn't need it to be. When she had come back to Caribou Crossing, she'd imagined a year, max.

She was doing fine. Sticking needles in her body was routine; the side effects of her treatment were minimal now; the pseudoexacerbations were manageable. If she had another attack—well, she'd deal with that then. There was no reason not to move on.

Or was there every reason to stay?

"I'm so freaking mixed up!"

She had just pulled her journal out of her bag when her

phone rang. Her pulse jerked. Dave? What would he say? What would she say?

She didn't have to decide. The number was an unfamiliar one and when she answered, she couldn't believe it. "Justine?" When was the last time she'd spoken to her mother? They exchanged occasional notes on Facebook, but that was it. "Is everything okay?" She could just guess what was going on: her parents were divorcing again.

"I'm here too, *mija*." It was Luis, his voice slightly muffled.

"Hi, Luis."

"We're fine, baby," Justine said, "but how are you? JJ says you have MS? I can't believe you didn't tell us."

Oh, shit. "He wasn't supposed to tell you." She was going to kill her brother.

"He didn't mean to. We called him yesterday and it slipped out. But why didn't you tell us?"

"I didn't want to worry you. I'm doing fine. They have much better treatments than back in GG's day."

"I know. JJ researched it, and so did we."

Ah yes, the joys of the Internet. "Well, I'm on a DMT." Was she testing Justine?

If so, her mother passed. "A disease-modifying therapy? Good. Which one?"

"Seriously? Look, I have a good family doctor, a neurologist, and a treatment plan. You don't need to know the details."

"Don't shut us out," her father said rather sharply.

"Luis," her mom said, "calm down. Cassidy, you're coming to JJ's wedding so we'll have an opportunity to talk then."

If they really did show up, something she'd believe only when she saw it.

"In fact," Justine said, "we have news. We are moving

back to Victoria. We're selling the house here and will buy a new one there."

"Seriously?" she said again. "Look, I don't want to be rude, but are you sure Victoria's a good place for you? You've lived there twice, and each time, you got divorced."

"That won't happen this time," her father said with certainty.

Yeah, right.

"We've changed, baby," Justine said. "We've always loved each other but we weren't the most mature people . . ." She paused, then said, "I'm waiting for the snort or snide comment."

"I bit my lip," Cassidy said truthfully.

"People can learn," her mother went on. "We don't want to make the same mistakes, or new ones either. We've been seeing a marriage counselor. We're learning to talk about our needs, insecurities, doubts, and fears, rather than keep quiet or fight."

"That sounds good," Cassidy admitted. It was a lesson she was learning too, thanks to her counseling group. It was the kind of lesson that, along with a sprinkling of magic dust, kept so many Caribou Crossing marriages strong when problems arose.

Luis said, "We are learning to believe in the strength of the love that has kept us returning to each other for almost thirty years, rather than to doubt it."

"I'm glad for you. I really hope things work out." Of course she did. "But why are you going back to Victoria?"

"JJ's getting married," Justine said. "We want to be part of their lives. He and Mags will have children one day, our grandchildren. We don't want to be those people down in Mexico who send presents on birthdays. We want to be involved."

She really, really hoped that her parents didn't get JJ's hopes up, then disappoint him.

"We haven't been good parents, baby," Justine said. "We know that and we're going to do better."

"That's nice." It was another thing she'd believe when she saw it.

"We want you to move back to Victoria too," Luis said.

"What? Me? Why?" She'd been thinking about it herself, but their move wasn't necessarily an incentive.

"So you can be with people who love you," Justine said. "It's the closest thing you have to a home, and once we were all happy there."

"A very long time ago," she pointed out.

"We're all older and wiser," her mother said. "We want to look after you, baby. To be there for you. And so does JJ, and he says Mags feels the same."

With JJ and Mags, she might actually believe it. But still, she didn't need to be looked after. "I'm not sick, Justine. I'm working, doing just fine. I'm riding, doing yoga, I'm strong."

"I'm pleased to hear that," she said. "But in the treatment of MS, having the support of loved ones is important. You shouldn't be with strangers; you should be with family."

"We are not a perfect family, *mija,*" Luis said, "but we are yours, and we will do better. Your mother and I promise you that."

"I . . . I don't know what to say."

"I know this all comes as a surprise," Justine said. "You need time to think."

"I do."

"We love you, baby," she said.

"Te amamos," Luis affirmed.

"I love you too." And she did. But at a safe distance, where they couldn't hurt her.

Now they said they wanted to help her. Did she have any reason to trust them? She stared unseeingly out the window as they all said good-bye, and she slid the phone back into her pocket.

A sharp bark made her glance down. Merlin sat at her feet, his head cocked up toward her, a hopeful expression on his face. He wanted a walk; even better, a run. "Yeah, me too." In fact, she'd love a ride, and knew the poodle would like to come along.

Dave's dog. She'd have to call him. Did she want to?

Yes. She needed to hear his voice. Hear what he had to say. Was he mad at her? Even worse, hurt? Had she perhaps even misunderstood what he was saying last night? The fireworks had been loud. Had she been obsessing for no reason?

Before she could think twice, she pulled out her phone again and called him.

"Cassidy?" he answered.

"Hi."

"Look, I'm sorry about last night."

"You are?" So he hadn't meant the things he'd said. She should be glad. Now they could get back to normal. She didn't need to leave. So why did her heart ache?

"I shouldn't have pushed and I shouldn't have walked away." He sighed. "Hang on a sec." A moment later he said, "I'm mending fences at Sally's, just wanted to set down my tools."

Mending fences. She guessed that was what the two of them were doing too. "You didn't exactly push. But I thought we knew how things stood between us, and it seemed like you wanted to change that, though now—" Before she could finish, to say she realized she was wrong, he broke in.

"I do. I love you."

Her heart gave a startled, stupidly ecstatic leap. Oh God, he really meant it. The idea scared the shit out of her, mainly because of how good it sounded. But it couldn't be true, couldn't work. She wasn't the kind of woman who stuck around. Or the kind people stuck around for.

She shook her head, calmed her racing heart. Dave knew all of that. When he said "love," he meant friendship-love, like he and Jess had shared as teens. Not love-love.

"And I meant everything I said," he went on. "Cassidy, if you think there's hope that you could love me, I'll be patient. We can go on the way we have been, and see where that takes us."

Work with him, play with him, sleep with him, and see where things went? But where could they go? Wasn't it better for her to leave now, before . . . before her heart did any more hoping? And aching?

"But," his voice grated as he went on, "if there's no hope, I want you to tell me. You can still stay in Caribou Crossing as long as you want, I'll still be on your support team, but I have to know if . . . if I have to stop hoping."

Stop hoping? Hoping that she'd love him? That sounded almost as if . . . as if he really did love-love her. If that might possibly be true, how could he be so generous? If love meant putting someone else's needs ahead of your own, and if she truly cared for Dave, wouldn't the best thing be to leave and let him find a healthy, whole, less complicated and pigheaded woman? "I need to think," she whispered.

"Okay." A pause. "Did you call to tell me that?"

So much had gone through her mind, tugged at her heart, in the last few minutes, she had no idea why she'd called. A glance at Merlin reminded her and energized her. Now, more than ever, she needed to get out on horseback. "I'm going for a ride. Is it okay if I take Merlin?"

"Sure. You'll have your phone?"

"I will." Even before her diagnosis, Dave hadn't liked the idea of her riding alone. Finally, he'd come to terms with it as long as she took a charged-up phone.

"Do you want to get together tonight?" he asked. "After that, I'll have Robin for a few days."

Get together and talk? Was there any hope she'd have sorted through the mess in her brain so she had something sensible to say? "Can I let you know later? See how I'm feeling?" By which she referred more to her emotions than her physical state, which she figured he knew.

After they said good-bye, she leashed Merlin and they walked toward her place so she could change into riding clothes.

Maribeth, who was coming out of a gift shop, stopped her. "Cassidy, I was going to call you," the curvy redhead said. "This gorgeous red sweater came in. Can't have been worn more than a couple times. I almost snagged it myself, but I don't look so great in red. It'd be perfect with your coloring. Want me to hold it for you until you have a chance to pop in?"

If Cassidy left Caribou Crossing, she'd be donating clothes to Days of Your. If she stayed, a red sweater would be perfect for winter. For Christmas. "Can you hold it?"

Next, she came across Karen Estevez, in uniform, taking a report on a car with slashed tires. "It's probably Halloween vandalism," Karen told the well-dressed couple who owned it. Smiling ruefully at Cassidy, she added, "Caribou Crossing often seems idyllic, but there's a reason we have an RCMP detachment here."

The town did seem idyllic. It was almost reassuring to be reminded that it wasn't perfect. No place on earth was perfect—as Cassidy, the world traveler, well knew. And no person was perfect. When she'd first arrived here, more than one female had told her that Dave was the perfect man. No, he wasn't. He could be stubborn, high-handed, and over-protective. Maybe that, too, was reassuring.

When she was a little kid, she thought her family was

perfect. When her parents tore that family apart, she was shattered. A person shouldn't believe in perfection; it was a façade. Better to see the flaws as well as the strengths, to not expect more than was humanly possible.

Her parents seemed to be admitting to their flaws. They'd never sought marriage counseling before, and on the phone they'd both sounded committed to making things work. They'd apologized to her. They'd said they wanted to be there for her.

Earlier today, she'd pretty much decided it was time to move on, and was thinking of Victoria. It would be great to spend more time with JJ, to get to know Mags. As for Justine and Luis . . . She was wary, but maybe a little hopeful too.

Esperanza. Hope. Sometimes she thought it was a naïve emotion, yet how miserable life was when you assumed the worst.

Victoria might actually work out. If she decided to run away from Dave. Run away from her feelings for Dave.

Life without Dave, the same kind of life she'd enjoyed so much in the past, would be empty, lonely, sad. Yet she couldn't stay unless she agreed to the possibility of a future together. The prospect was appealing in so many ways, but how could she believe it was realistic? Might it be possible for her—a woman who had no experience with or faith in permanence—and Dave—a divorcé who'd lost the love of his life—to build a loving, supportive long-term relationship like the one his parents had?

As she went up the walk at Ms. Haldenby's house, she remembered her landlady's girlfriend, Irene, saying, "Home is where the heart is."

Did Cassidy dare let her heart take root with one person, in one place?

She was still musing over that question half an hour later, sitting easily in Cherry's saddle as they loped along with

Merlin running happily beside them. The brisk air warned of winter coming. She was glad of her sheepskin jacket.

Two weeks ago, the aspens and cottonwoods had blazed with golden leaves, but now their branches were mostly bare and the only gold was in the faded grass. Behind the rolling ranchland, hills rose dark green, clad in hemlocks and cedars. The sky was a cloudy bluish purple. The natural grandeur was such that you could turn in any direction and snap a calendar-worthy photo.

Every time she went out, the scenery had changed a little, and so had the activities on the ranches and farms she rode past. Did a search for new sights and experiences have to mean a gypsy lifestyle? She couldn't imagine losing her yen to explore the world, but could it be satisfied by a holiday or two each year? How would Dave feel about that?

But wasn't the real question, how did she feel about Dave?

As she slowed Cherry to a walk and turned back toward Caribou Crossing, she said tentatively—to the horse, the dog, the bluish purple sky—"I love him."

None of them responded. Nothing terrible happened. In fact, her heart didn't jerk in shock; instead, it pulsed warmth that spread through her body. A warmth that felt like . . . joy and rightness.

Could she trust in that feeling? Could she trust in Dave, the man who reminded her so much of the one man who'd never let her down, her grandfather? Yes, Dave might die as Gramps had, but while he drew breath he would be loyal to the people he loved. She knew that, with utter conviction.

Could she trust in herself, in her ability to be a person like Gramps rather than like her parents?

Could she let herself believe that Dave truly loved her and wasn't just trying to rescue her? Did he even know for sure himself?

Cherry whinnied, and another horse answered in the

distance. Cassidy saw a lone rider on a black horse, too far away to make out whether it was a man or woman, much less identify the person. All the same, they both gave friendly waves.

If Cassidy lived here, she could get her own horse, maybe even buy Cherry Blossom. That is, if she figured her MS would let her keep riding. Her health was a big unknown. That still pissed her off and scared her, but she wasn't going to live her life expecting the worst. One woman in Caribou Crossing had been in remission from MS for thirty years. Cassidy was going to take her treatment seriously, rest when she needed to, and hope for the best.

Though she couldn't control her MS, there were things she could control. She could be a loyal, reliable, loving person like Gramps. She couldn't promise Dave that she wouldn't get sick, but maybe she could be a woman who deserved his love.

They had time. It wasn't like he'd gone down on bended knee and proposed. He'd asked her to stay, to see if she could love him—well, it seemed that one was easy!—and to be open to the possibility of a future together.

But would it be selfish of her to take him up on that? Really, wouldn't he be better off with another woman?

She needed to decide whether to go or to stay, but it wasn't right to make that decision on her own.

Chapter Thirty-One

Driving home from Sally's, Dave was glad Cassidy had called to say she would cook dinner at his place. Well, he could've cared less about the food. And actually, "glad" wasn't the right word. He was pretty much scared shitless.

If Cassidy said she could never love him . . .

Crap, how had he let this happen? He'd been so convinced that Anita was the love of his life, he'd never even considered that a second, much different love might two-step her sassy way into his heart. He'd been defenseless against the magic that was Cassidy Esperanza. On the radio, Elvis was again singing "Love Me Tender." During that first dance with Cassidy, Dave's body had stirred to life. At some point, his heart had stirred too. Yes, he loved her tenderly; he also loved her passionately. He wanted to protect her and to lean on her. She was strong. Stronger than he was. She'd handled the trauma of her diagnosis better than he'd dealt with losing Anita.

He wanted Cassidy as his partner in life. But if that wasn't what she wanted, he had to have the guts to let her fly free. The solo wild goose, the moonbeam he couldn't hold in his hand.

He parked his Jeep at the back of the Wild Rose and,

stomach in a knot, went up the stairs. Inside the apartment, he hung up his work jacket and pulled off his dirty work boots. Man, was he sweaty and grubby. Merlin greeted him, tail wagging happily. "Hey, pal, where's—"

Cassidy answered his question by stepping through the kitchen door looking more tentative than eager. "Dinner's ready—" she started to say just as Dave said, "I need a shower." Then he said, "Sorry, what did you say?"

"I'm making baked chile rellenos. They're ready to go in the oven." She rubbed her hands on the faded jeans she wore below a blue Western shirt. Often when she came here she slipped into form-fitting yoga pants and a T-shirt in some interesting color. The fact that she hadn't done so wasn't a hopeful sign. "So you can go take a shower," she said, "and I'll—"

"Cassidy." He strode toward her. Yeah, he should shower, but he had a more urgent need. "I have to know. Tell me what you're thinking."

Her blue-gray eyes were soft, troubled. "I'm confused." She toyed with the pendant that hung around her neck. He thought of a wild goose, deciding whether to take flight or to stay.

He nodded, forcing himself not to touch her cheek or kiss her. "Go on."

"Dave, I do love you, but—"

"What?" Had she actually said that, or had wishful thinking made him imagine it?

Her lips curved, trembling. "I do. I didn't really know what love was, and I wasn't looking for it, but you made it pretty much impossible to not love you."

"You love me?" Maybe he sounded like a dummy, but he had to be sure.

"I do." She stated it firmly this time. "I love you, Dave Cousins."

"My God." He grabbed her in a big hug, hoisting her off the ground in his exuberant relief. "You love me!"

By now she was grinning, her eyes sparkling as he pressed his lips to her smiling mouth. She kissed him back; then her kiss turned urgent, almost desperate. Then she surprised him again by pulling back. "Let me down. That doesn't answer anything."

"Huh?" He lowered her. "I love you, you love me. That's what's important. We can work out the rest."

"Maybe." Her expression was solemn now. "Want to talk now, or take that shower?"

He glanced down, having momentarily forgotten how grubby he was. He'd rubbed off on her too; he flicked some dried dirt and grass from her shirt. "Shower with me."

Her expression lightened. "You think you can use sex to persuade me?"

"I'll give it a shot." His very best shot.

The grin came back. "Fire away."

He hoisted her into his arms—who cared if he got more dirt on her clothes?—and carried her toward the en suite bathroom. When she looped her arms around his neck, his heart clutched. Cassidy loved him. It was still sinking in, like the slow fire of good whisky burning through his veins. Combined with the euphoric fizz of champagne bubbles. Things had to work out.

After he lowered her onto the bath mat, he tugged open the snaps of her shirt and slid it off. Under it, she wore a skintight purple tank top, which he peeled over her head. No bra, just small, firm, beautiful breasts. She toed off her sheepskin slippers. He peeled her jeans and panties down her legs and she stepped out of them.

She was the prettiest thing he'd ever seen. Slim and sleek with unmistakably feminine curves. Long, elegant neck with the pendant resting in the hollow at the base. Oval face framed by that elfin cap of midnight hair; lovely light brown skin. And her dark-lashed eyes, their blue-gray so striking, so clear and honest and loving.

The best part was, her physical beauty was only a small part of what made her so special.

No, the best part was that she loved him.

Her fingers worked busily to free him from his own clothing, and he cooperated until he, too, stood naked. Fully erect. Mischief sparked in her eyes. "You've been mending fences? I think you need a very thorough shower." She turned on the water and adjusted the temperature, then stepped in behind the shower curtain. "And I'm going to make sure you get it."

When he followed her in, he knew the shower would be warm but not too hot, and knew also how much she missed being able to have steaming hot showers and baths. As for him, he didn't care about the temperature as long as Cassidy was there. She lathered oatmeal soap onto a turquoise bath sponge, both items she'd added to his bathroom.

When he reached for her, she said, "Uh-uh, you're not touching me again until you're clean from head to toe, and everywhere in between." Clearly, she intended to torture him.

Great plan!

"Turn around, facing into the spray," she ordered.

He obeyed. The warm needles of water were stimulating, but nowhere near as much as the firm circles she drew on his shoulders with the soapy sponge. Up his neck, down again, out to his shoulder cap, in to his spine. The fluffy sponge had a gentle abrasiveness that made his skin tingle. The fact that it was Cassidy wielding it added a sexy edge that kept him erect.

But he needed to apologize, to explain. "Last night? That wasn't how I planned to do it."

"Planned? You had a plan?"

"Hey, it's me. Of course I had a plan." Dinner and wine, words that he'd rehearsed. But then fireworks had exploded, overhead and in his heart, and he couldn't wait. "When I'm spontaneous, things don't always work out so well—as last night proved."

"Yet here we are." She'd worked the sponge down to his lower back and now circled it around one of his butt cheeks.

Damned happy they were there, he tensed, waiting to see if she'd trace the sponge down his butt crack and between his legs. Shifting weight, he slid his legs farther apart to allow her access. "I'm glad I didn't totally screw it up."

"Why did you deviate from your plan?"

He'd asked himself that question more than once, giving himself a mental kick for being such an idiot. "The whole evening. You, with me in the middle of Caribou Crossing on one of the most fun nights of the year. You belonging here, it seemed to me. Belonging *with* me. I always love fireworks and I guess I was feeling romantic or something, and I blurted it out."

The sponge paused in circling his other butt cheek. "It actually was pretty romantic. But you scared me. It was too much, too soon."

"And that's why I had a plan," he said ruefully.

"Tell me your plan." Her tone told him she was smiling, and the sponge now did drift down the groove between his butt cheeks.

"Over an excellent dinner and some very expensive wine, I intended to cover off some stuff first," he said absentmindedly. The rough caress moved between his legs, brushed his balls.

"Such as?"

He wanted to grip his cock. Better still, have her do it. The sponge gave more teasing flicks, then moved down his sensitive inner thigh, and finally to the less erotic back of his leg.

"Dave? Such as?"

"Such as what?" He had no clue what they'd been talking about.

"You planned to cover off 'some stuff.'"

"Oh, right." He breathed in and out more slowly. "Like, I know you love going to new places, seeing new things."

"I do. Caribou Crossing is terrific but I can't imagine never traveling anywhere else."

"I figured. And I'm good with that, Cassidy. I admit that I've barely gone anywhere, but it's not that I'm not interested. If there were places you'd like to go together, or with Robin, we could do that. You got her all excited about those baby turtles." The sponge rubbed his calf now. He gazed down over his shoulder to see Cassidy squatting on the floor of the shower, black hair plastered to her head. "Or if you want to travel on your own, you could do that."

She glanced up. "You wouldn't mind?"

"I don't want to tie you down. I know your independence is important to you."

"It is." She moved the sponge to his other calf. "But traveling together would be fun too. How would it work? Leaving the Wild Rose for two or three weeks, maybe even longer?"

"I could do that." Anxiety made him swallow. "We'd have to train someone to take over. Maybe Madisun would be interested in working here full-time when she graduates. She has a lot of potential and she's very responsible."

"She is. No wonder, growing up in a family like hers." Cassidy's sponge had reached his thigh now but the serious topic diluted the sexiness of the touch. "Thank God for Evan, and for you," she said.

"Much more him than me." Evan—a child of abuse— had figured out that Madisun's father abused her and his wife. Evan told the man that if he ever hit any of his family again, he'd call the cops. Then Evan funded Madisun to go to university. When she focused on the hospitality industry, Dave had hired her.

"Dave?" Cassidy was standing now, touching his back,

urging him to turn around. When he did, she rested her hands on his shoulders. "I need to know you aren't rescuing me."

"What?"

"You kind of rescued Madisun."

He shook his head. "I gave her a job. Turns out she's the best employee I've ever had, except for you."

"It seems to me you rescued Jess when she was pregnant."

He opened his mouth to deny it, then slowly said, "I guess I kind of did. It seemed like the right thing at the time."

"And maybe it was."

"Or maybe it wasn't," he admitted. "If I'd encouraged her to tell Evan, maybe they wouldn't have lost ten years. She and I both figured he wouldn't be happy in Caribou Crossing. But hell, if he loved her, maybe he would have."

"It's the past. You and Jess did what you thought was best at the time. But Dave, I'm not her." She gazed earnestly into his eyes. "I'm not seventeen, I'm not pregnant. I've looked after myself for ten years and I can keep doing it. I don't need to be rescued."

"I get that. Just because I can be a little overprotective and controlling—something I'm working on—doesn't mean I'm trying to rescue you." He sighed and admitted something. "I was the one who needed rescuing. I'd wallowed too long; then you came along and rescued me."

"Is that why you love me? Because I broke you out of, uh . . . ?"

"Depression. Hopelessness. I don't know exactly what it was, but it was a dark, dead place. Even with the wonderful stuff in life, like Robin, it was like I was distanced from it, seeing it all through a gray fog. Now the fog's gone. I see life in all its"—he broke off—"I was going to say beauty. But it's not always beautiful, is it? I see all its complexity."

"Your dimple's been getting exercise." She stroked his

face and, as he grinned, tucked the tip of her little finger into the pocket in his cheek. "I love that dimple."

"I love you, Cassidy. I guess it's partly because you rescued me, but you did that because of who you are. And I love you because of who you are. Feminine and strong, independent and generous, fun and responsible." He shook his head. "I'm listing off attributes, but it's so much more than that. It's how everything combines to make this amazing person. It's how I feel when I'm with you, or even think about you. Does that make any sense?"

Her eyes glowed. "Yes. It's the perfect description, and it's how I feel about you."

"So does that mean . . . we're good?"

"Oh, we're very good," she purred mischievously.

"Will you think seriously about it? About staying here and giving our love a chance?"

Slowly, she shook her head, but her eyes were dancing. "No. No more thinking. I've decided. Yes. Yes, Dave, I want to stay with you."

Yes. The most beautiful word in the world. He squeezed his eyes shut with relief, breathed in gut deep, then slowly let air out. A sense of peace seeped into his soul. Opening his eyes, he reached out to hug her, but she took a step back.

"Oh no"—she lifted the sponge—"I still have your front to wash."

Delicious, sensual torture. On the other hand, sometimes a guy needed to exert control. Firmly, he took the sponge from her. "I'm clean enough."

The sparkle in her eyes glinted brighter. "Clean enough for what?"

"This." He bent his head to take her lips, delving between them to possess the sweet depths of her mouth.

Cassidy was his. For laughter and joy, for arguments and worries, for life in all its full, amazing complexity.

Chapter Thirty-Two

Cassidy gazed around Jess and Evan's living room. It was everything that Christmas morning should be. A fire blazed in the river stone fireplace, carols played softly in the background, and a tall Douglas fir sported twinkling lights, tinsel, and a variety of ornaments, most of them homemade. Under the tree were dozens of brightly wrapped packages.

It brought back happy memories of family Christmases when she was small. Now here she was, having been more or less adopted into this family gathering: Jess and Evan, Miriam and Wade Bly, Brooke and Jake Brannon, the two babies, and of course, most importantly, Robin and Dave. This afternoon, the three of them would head over to Dave's parents' place for a second family gathering, and a turkey dinner. Robin had told her that her mom's family and her dad's traded each year who got Christmas morning with them and who got dinner.

Cassidy, wearing the red cashmere sweater Maribeth had saved for her, accepted a mug of hot chocolate from Evan and a slice of blueberry cinnamon coffee cake from Jess. Settling contentedly on a couch beside Dave, she watched Robin commandeer the doling out of gifts.

It was a slow process. One gift to her mom, and then everyone waited while Jess opened it and exclaimed with pleasure. Then a gift to Miriam, then Brooke.

Cassidy thought that, while there were bound to be gifts for her under that tree, she'd already received everything she could possibly want. What a weird trick of fate that only months after being diagnosed with a life-altering chronic illness her life was fuller and happier than she'd ever imagined it could be.

She still woke each morning wondering if her body would let her down, and she still suffered an occasional pseudoexacerbation, but there'd been no fresh attack of MS. One thing she'd learned: having an unpredictable disease made her feel grateful and lucky for each healthy day.

And she'd had some terrific days. Last week, she'd spent hours with her brother, sharing memories and catching up, and then she'd watched him wed lovely, warmhearted Mags. She'd also spent time with her parents, some of it awkward, but she could see the changes in them, including a willingness to put her and JJ first. At least sometimes.

And then there was Dave. Their relationship was real. Not perfect, but perfectly wonderful as they shared fears and doubts as well as tenderness and passion, every moment filled with love.

While Cassidy was busy counting her blessings, Robin had identified presents for the babies, which she helped them open, and moved on to presents for the men. With glee, she said, "And now it's my turn!" She chose one from Cassidy, a calendar with photos of wild horses for each month, and seemed thrilled to bits.

"Oh gosh, Cassidy, I forgot about you." Robin's eyes twinkled as she handed over an envelope. "This is from me."

Inside was a Christmas card with a drawing of several wire-mesh caribou pulling a sleigh holding Santa and a bag of gifts. An original work of art by Robin. "What a terrific card!" A slip of paper fell out and Cassidy bent to retrieve it. It was a check for twenty-five dollars drawn on the girl's bank account and made out to the Multiple Sclerosis Society of Canada. Cassidy gazed up in wonder.

"So they'll find a cure," Robin said.

"Oh my gosh. That's the best present ever." She reached out to hug her warmly, this girl who'd become as dear to her as a sister or a daughter.

Jess rose. "I'm glad you think so." She came over and handed Cassidy another envelope. "This is from Evan and me."

"From Jake and me," Brooke chimed in, flourishing another card.

"From Wade and me." Miriam had another.

"And me." Dave added one to the pile accumulating on her lap.

By now, tears were slipping down her cheeks. "You guys, this is amazing. Thank you so much."

Dave handed her two more. "These were entrusted to me. They're from JJ and Mags, and your mom and dad."

Miriam leaned forward to offer a tissue and Cassidy blew her nose, which must have been as red as her sweater. She had a chance to recover as, for the next half hour, Robin choreographed more rounds of gifts. Thank heavens Cassidy's presents had all come in one fell swoop, or she'd have been a teary mess all morning.

The pile was seriously reduced when Robin flourished another envelope. "This is for you too, Cassidy. Open it."

Another check? But she'd already received checks from everyone in the room. She slipped a finger under the sealed flap and drew out the card. This, too, was Robin's artwork. A wild horse stood on a hillside, gazing up at the moon,

where three wild geese flew in a V. "Wow, that's gorgeous."
She opened the card and read, in Robin's neat handwriting:

> *To Cassidy,*
>   *This card entitles the bearer to a tattoo of*
> *two wild geese to join the goose with the moon*
> *on her wing.*
>
> >   *Love,*
> >   *Robin and Dad*

"Two wild geese?" She gazed at the girl, touched. "What
a cool idea."

"They're me and Dad." Robin put her hand on Cassidy's
shoulder, where her sweater covered her tattoo. "So you
don't have to fly alone anymore. Do you like it?"

"I love it. It's fantastic! I love you, Robin." Again, she
hugged the girl; then she flung her arms around Dave. "And
I love you too. I would be so proud and happy to fly with
both of you."

"Did you see the goose in front?" Robin asked eagerly.

"The goose in front?" Cassidy held the card closer and
noticed that Robin had glued a bit of silver glitter on the
edge of the goose's wing. "It has a sparkle. Is that the moon
on its wing?"

"No," Dave answered. "It's Caribou Crossing magic
dust."

"What?" Cassidy turned to him and her mouth fell open
as he held out a little box covered in black velvet. Was that
what it looked like?

He snapped it open to reveal a gorgeous ring, a gold band
with Native American carving inset with several small,
sparkly diamonds.

"Yes!" The word burst out of her mouth.

Soft chuckles rose around her.

The man she loved with all her heart grinned at her, his dimple flashing. "That's my Cassidy. Always one step ahead of me. You're not going to wait for me to ask?"

Embarrassed, laughing and crying at the same time, she said, "No! I mean yes. I mean, oh God, Dave, yes! Yes, yes, yes!"

Author's Note

When I wrote *Home on the Range*, the second Caribou Crossing Romance, I knew that Jess's ex-husband, Dave Cousins, the nicest man in town, deserved his own romance. I also knew he wasn't yet ready for it. He needed a longer time to grieve the loss of the woman he believed to be the love of his life. Now, in the fifth Caribou Crossing title, it's Dave's turn to find romance.

If Dave and Cassidy's love story resonates with you, I hope you will consider making a donation to a multiple sclerosis society to assist in supporting and finding a cure for others like Cassidy.

Thank you to my editor, Martin Biro at Kensington, for letting me continue the Caribou Crossing series, and for being so amazing to work with. Thanks to my agent, Emily Sylvan Kim at Prospect Agency, for her unwavering support. And thank you also to my wonderful critiquers, beta readers, and research assistants: Nazima Ali, Michelle Hancock, Crystal Hunt, Celia Lewis, Linda Locke, Mary Ann Clarke Scott, and Brenda Worthington (all errors are mine, not theirs).

I love sharing my stories with my readers and I love hearing from you. I write under the pen names Susan Fox, Savanna Fox, and Susan Lyons. You can e-mail me at susan@susanlyons.ca or contact me through my website at www.susanfox.ca, where you'll also find excerpts, behind-the-scenes notes, recipes, a monthly contest, the sign-up for my newsletter, and other goodies. You can also find me on Facebook at facebook.com/SusanLyonsFox.

Corporal Karen MacLean and Sergeant Jamal Estevez
make for an unlikely couple,
but together they forge a future more hopeful
than they'd ever thought possible
in Susan Fox's

STAND BY YOUR MAN

A Caribou Crossing novella, printed here in its entirety.
Also available as a Zebra eBook.

Chapter One

Corporal Karen MacLean grabbed the bag holding two bottles of bubbly and jumped out of her truck. Yesterday, she had helped put away a drug-dealing murderer who also happened to be a chauvinistic pig and, worst of all, a dirty cop. Today's paperwork at the Caribou Crossing RCMP detachment had felt like hammering nails into Sergeant Miller's coffin. Her former boss was going to jail and he'd stay there a very long time.

Satisfaction and adrenaline gave a bounce to her step. As did, let's face it, anticipating some off-duty time with Sergeant Jamal Estevez. That man was seriously hot.

As Karen approached the gate in the white picket fence, Brooke Kincaid emerged through the open front door of the country cottage.

Karen's trained eye snapshotted the picture: well-maintained green and white bungalow, bright flower borders, comfy porch furniture, and the smiling blonde who'd turned this rental cottage into a home. Sudden wistfulness made Karen's hand fumble with the latch. The place was so different from her own functional half duplex in town. Brooke's place was the kind of home Karen had grown up in and dreamed of one day having herself. If she ever found that special man who wasn't put off by her corporal's uniform, and who shared her determination to make a difference in the world.

It wouldn't hurt one bit if that man loved Caribou Crossing as much as she'd grown to in the four years since she'd been assigned here. The town, which dated back to the 1860s gold rush, was picturesque, with its historic buildings and small businesses that catered to both locals and tourists. The countryside was a gentle feast for her eyes, with its rolling hills and ranch land. The townspeople were, for the most part, friendly and law-abiding. Karen had acquired a few friends, a horse, and a German shepherd, but her love life was pretty much nonexistent.

She shrugged off a momentary sense of yearning and focused on the here and now. Yesterday, she and Corporal Jake Brannon had collared a true scumbag with the help of Brooke Kincaid. The buzz of excitement returned. She answered the blonde's smile with one of her own and hurried to join her. Slender and fit in a denim skirt and a sleeveless shirt that matched her greenish-blue eyes, Brooke looked closer to Karen's thirty-two years than her own forty plus.

Karen bounded up the steps and wrapped her free arm around the shorter woman's shoulders. "We did it!"

Brooke made a sound of surprise, reminding Karen that they barely knew each other, then returned the embrace. "You and Jake did."

"Nope. Couldn't have done it without you." Karen was firmly against involving civilians in police operations. However, circumstances had dragged Brooke into the middle of this one a week before Karen found out what was going on. Brooke had provided Jake, an undercover cop, with his cover story as her visiting cousin. When Karen busted that cover two days ago, Jake had filled her in and they'd hatched the scheme that had resulted in Sergeant Miller's arrest.

Karen teased Brooke, "We should make you an honorary member of the force."

"No, thanks. I'm too risk-averse. A little bit of excitement every now and then is all I can handle."

The attractive woman was almost five years sober, taking meds for bipolar disorder, and, despite her young age, a grandma. Karen figured Brooke was stronger than she gave herself credit for. She'd done a great job building Jake's cover despite the fact that Brooke's true relationship with the rugged undercover cop was anything but cousinly. Karen winked at her hostess. "You can handle Brannon, and I'm guessing that's more than a *little* excitement."

A flush tinted Brooke's cheeks. "You haven't told anyone? I don't mind you knowing, but . . ." She shrugged.

Caribou Crossing had that small-town "thing" where everyone minded everyone else's business. Jake and Brooke wouldn't be able to keep their powerful mutual attraction a secret much longer. But Brooke's reaction almost suggested that they were breaking up. Surely that wasn't true.

"Your private life is your private life," Karen said slowly. "But do you mean you're not going to keep seeing each other? You're perfect for each other."

"Far from it. But it was fun while it lasted. No, we have no plans to see each other again."

Although the pair had met not much more than a week ago, it seemed to Karen that their connection went much deeper than casual sex. She was certainly no expert on relationships, but she wouldn't be at all surprised if the couple's "plans" changed and they kept dating. Keeping that opinion to herself, she said, "Something smells great." She hoisted the bag she'd carried in from the truck. "I brought champagne."

"Come on into the kitchen." Brooke led the way.

The room was homey, yellow walled, and neat as a pin, its counters bare of cooking mess. Brooke's cat, a marmalade named Sunny, leaped from the windowsill and strolled over. Karen, who'd met the cat two nights ago, stroked him, then took the two bottles of nonalcoholic bubbly from the bag.

Brooke's brows rose in apparent surprise. Had she thought Karen would bring alcohol? Brooke's sobriety wasn't exactly a secret in this town.

"You've got to drink the toasts too," Karen said.

"Thanks." A smile curved her mouth. It widened as, from outside, car tires crunched gravel. Jake had arrived. Brooke rushed toward the front door.

Karen's pulse jolted and her breath quickened. Jamal Estevez, the supremely hot Jamal, would be with Jake. She lingered in the kitchen to collect herself. Since the moment she'd first laid eyes on Jamal, he'd attracted her the way no man had in a long time—or, let's face it, ever.

The sergeant, who'd run the Royal Canadian Mounted Police investigation from Vancouver, had traveled up last night with a team of officers. The Caribou Crossing detachment was under investigation to determine whether any other members had been involved in Sergeant Miller's drug trade. Karen, thanks to her work with Jake, was the one member who'd been cleared.

Her fingers—rock steady yesterday when she'd aimed her service pistol at Miller and ordered him to drop his weapon—trembled as she smoothed back her dark brown hair. Tonight it hung loose to her shoulders rather than being confined in the bobby-pinned knot she wore on the job. Though she'd never been the "girly" type, she did have a feminine side and wished she was wearing something fancier than jeans and a gold tee. Unfortunately, her couple of dresses and skirts lay crumpled in the laundry hamper.

She straightened her spine, took a deep breath, and moved into the living room. Jake and Brooke were hugging inside the front door. The tall black-haired man and the curvy blonde looked so right together. Surely they wouldn't throw away something so special. Karen felt a momentary twinge of the same yearning she'd experienced earlier at the sight of Brooke's cozy home. But then her gaze moved past the embracing couple to the man standing on the threshold. She stopped a few yards away, in the shadows, where he wouldn't notice her, and enjoyed the view.

Jamal Estevez took her breath away. Probably in his midthirties, she guessed him to be half black and half Latino. His skin was a warm coffee-brown, his features boldly masculine, his eyes and wavy hair so deep a chocolate as to be almost black. He was tall—a couple of inches taller than Jake, she'd peg him at six feet three—and had the same kind of lean, well-muscled build, currently molded by a navy tee and faded jeans.

A distinctive man, yet she could imagine him with dreads or a shaved head, facial hair, fake tattoos, gang clothing—or with an expensive haircut, a designer suit, and a Rolex watch. Like any good undercover cop, the man could be anything from a CEO of a multinational corporation to an aspiring rapper to a drug-dealing biker.

The sergeant was watching Brooke and Jake and hadn't yet seen Karen.

She kept to her shadowy corner and tried not to fantasize about peeling that tee and jeans off his supremely ripped body. Oh my, but he put a zing in her blood.

A number of times today she'd felt his gaze and glanced up to see something in his eyes. Something charged, heated. Or was that her imagination? As a cop, she was good at reading people, but when it came to her dating life, she kind of sucked.

Jake had mentioned that Jamal wasn't married, but it hadn't seemed appropriate to ask if he had a girlfriend. Hard to believe that he wouldn't, but policing—and particularly the undercover work that Jamal sometimes still did—was hard on relationships.

Being a female cop was even tougher. Men were intimidated, or they thought she was butch, or they couldn't handle being with a woman who risked her life daily. Or—she shuddered, remembering one particularly icky first date—they wanted her to handcuff them and play weird sex games. After having used handcuffs on countless perps, sex was *not* what she associated with those tools of her trade.

Other sex games, though . . . the less kinky kind, with the right man. A man like the one standing in the doorway. Jamal was still staring at Jake and Brooke, an odd expression on his face, almost as if he too felt a twinge of envy.

Brooke finally tore her attention away from her lover and turned to Jamal. "Nice to see you again, Jamal."

He gave a quick grin, all traces of his previous expression vanishing. "You too, Brooke." He added teasingly, "Or babe, as some may call you." Karen had heard Jake use that term.

She moved out of her shaded corner and Jamal said, "Hey, Karen." Was there something different, something sexually charged, in his smile now, or was that wishful thinking?

"Jamal." The voice that had yelled at Sergeant Miller came out breathy and feminine. Her gaze locked with his. She couldn't look away and he didn't seem in any hurry to.

Brooke said, "Karen brought champagne. Nonalcoholic, so I can drink it."

Now Jamal did break the eye lock to glance at the blonde. "Sounds good. Karen, why don't you pop that cork, and let's start celebrating?" His deep voice didn't have a specific accent, but it flowed as thick and rich as molasses, heating her blood.

Karen led the way to the kitchen. Yes, she liked his looks, his voice. In fact, from what she'd seen throughout the day, there was nothing not to like. He was efficient, decisive, patient, and had a teasing sense of humor. Jamal had shown her absolute professional respect, which wasn't something she'd always had from male colleagues, including that pig Miller.

Whom she'd never have to work with again! Happily, she eased the cork out of the first bottle and poured the faux champagne into juice glasses Brooke provided.

Jamal hoisted his glass and glanced around at them. "To your good work. You took a major bad guy off the streets."

After everyone drank the toast, Brooke said, "Sit down, and I'll put dinner on the table."

They ended up with the men at opposite ends of the table and Karen between them. She glanced from striking, dark-skinned Jamal to equally strong, handsome Jake with his neatly cut black hair and smoky gray eyes. Truth to tell, she was a little blown away by the tough undercover guys, but she was determined not to let it show. She was a cop too. True, she spent a lot of time giving warnings to teens drinking beer at the lake, or returning ninety-year-old Mr. Morton—an escape artist with dementia—to the care home. But those tasks had value, and so did dealing with domestic abuse, bar fights, drunk drivers, petty theft, and vandalism. As did the law and justice workshops she gave free of charge at the community center, and her work on the board of the women's shelter. She did her part in making Caribou Crossing a safe, happy community.

Deftly, Brooke set food on the table: a bowl of salad with mixed greens and slices of yellow pepper, tomato, and cucumber; a steaming pan of lasagna; and slices of Italian bread in a woven basket.

"Man, that smells good," Jamal said.

Jake touched his lover's hand. "Brooke's a great cook." His tone was smug, almost possessive.

Yes, their relationship was new and there were definite

issues, like living in different places, Jake's dangerous job, and Brooke's risk-averseness. Still, it seemed to Karen that if you found something as special as their connection, you'd be a fool not to fight for it.

The four of them served themselves and dug in. The crusty bread was warm and soft on the inside, and chilled butter complemented the slightly yeasty taste. The salad was crisp and fresh, the dressing light and tangy. And the lasagna was rich, meaty, a little spicy. "If you ever want to leave Beauty Is You, you could open a restaurant," said Karen. Brooke was a beauty consultant at the salon.

"Thanks, but I love my job," she said. "And now I want to hear about yours." She glanced around at the three RCMP members. "How did things go today?"

Karen left it to Jake and Jamal to decide what information they could share. She listened, ate, and thought how nice this was, the four of them at the dinner table, almost as if they were two couples. Aside from the occasional crappy date, her usual social life consisted of hanging out with a couple of girlfriends, or married friends where she was the third wheel, or a platonic guy-pal like Dave Cousins, who owned the Wild Rose Inn. If she and Jamal dated . . .

No, she couldn't imagine that working: a Caribou Crossing woman who yearned for a home and family, and a tough Vancouver cop who headed off on undercover assignments. Sex, though, she could definitely imagine. But she shouldn't; she wasn't the kind of woman who was into cheap sex. No matter how great it might be—and instinct told her it would be pretty damned great.

She forced her attention back to the conversation in time to hear Brooke say, "He should be locked up for life. Dealing drugs to children, and killing that poor girl."

Karen nodded vigorously. "Especially when he was a cop whose job was to uphold the law. I *hate* dirty cops. They're the lowest of the low." Frowning, she put down her fork and confessed to something that gnawed at her, the only sour note in Miller's takedown. "Maybe I should have realized. I knew he was a sexist pig, a homophobe, a racist. He drank too much; he was a shitty role model. But you don't want to suspect a member of something dirty even if he is a major jerk."

She swallowed hard. "If I'd trusted my instincts, maybe I could have stopped him before he killed that poor girl." The victim, a teen runaway, had been an addict and a prostitute in Vancouver's Downtown Eastside.

Brooke touched her hand. "It's not your fault. Of course you wanted to trust your superior officer."

"Shit happens to all of us," Jake said. "Point is, you learn from it." He glanced at Jamal.

Their gazes locked for a moment, and then Jamal gave a curt nod. "That's the truth."

A weight lifted from Karen's conscience. Her colleagues hadn't excused her; if they'd tried, she wouldn't have bought it. What they had done was to normalize her experience. They'd been there themselves. She wondered what kind of shit had happened to Jamal and Jake. In undercover work, it could be virtually anything.

"I always liked my job," she said, "but the detachment will be so much nicer without that ass Miller."

"Who'll be taking over for him?" Jamal asked.

She shook her head. "Don't know yet. But I'm going to be the acting commander."

"Congratulations!" the others all said.

She shrugged, trying not to act too excited. "Well, I *am* the only one they're relatively sure is clean, who knows the community."

"It's still a compliment." Jamal gave her an approving nod before he dished out a second helping of lasagna. "It'll look great on your record. Though I suppose in the long run they'll want a sergeant."

His approval gave her warm tingles, but she tried not to let on as she answered matter-of-factly, "Yup. Replace a sergeant with a sergeant."

"How long've you been a corporal?" Jamal asked. "Enough to write your sergeant's exam?"

"Not yet. But I'm studying. I want that promotion." She wanted to run things her way rather than kowtow to idiots like Miller.

Jamal shot a pointed glance at Jake. "Unlike some folk."

"Hmm?" Brooke raised her eyebrows.

"I wrote the damned exam." Jake scowled at Jamal. "Got tired of you hounding me."

"And you passed with top marks, God knows how. But now you won't apply for a sergeant's job."

"I like what I'm doing. Not everyone wants to be a desk jockey." He gave his friend another scowl. "Old man."

The two men reminded her of her and her brother: affection and respect, a shared secret or two, and issues they had no qualms about poking at.

"You've lost me," Brooke said.

Karen explained. "Generally, as you rise through the ranks you do less active duty. You coordinate others rather than doing the street work yourself."

"And you're in less danger?" Brooke asked.

"That's usually true," Karen said. At least if the member didn't keep going out undercover the way Jamal still sometimes did.

"If a promotion means being tied to a desk," Brooke said, "I can see why Jake wouldn't want it." She sent a humorous glance in Jamal's direction. "Though I'd hardly call you an old man myself."

"Nor I," Karen agreed. There were a lot of adjectives she'd apply to Jamal Estevez. Smart, responsible, sexy, perceptive. "Old" was nowhere on the list.

He glanced at her, an eyebrow cocked, his dark eyes gleaming.

Her breath caught and she couldn't look away. She was so freaking naïve about male-female signals, but she'd swear—almost swear—this man was interested in her.

This man, who was so damned hot and fascinating that he made her want to strip off her tee and jeans, toss her undies after them, and jump his bones . . .

A corner of his mouth kinked up knowingly as if he'd read her mind.

"Dessert?" The question, spoken softly and almost seductively, came from Brooke.

Oh yeah. Bittersweet chocolate, all hers to nibble from head to toe. And in between.

"I made chocolate-mint layer cake."

Mmm-hmm, chocolate . . . No, wait, what was that? Layer cake? Grateful that she'd never been a blusher, Karen quickly said, "Sounds delicious."

"Delicious," Jamal echoed. With his gaze focused on Karen's mouth, he murmured in that rich molasses voice, "I confess I have a sweet tooth."

Karen blinked at the subtle undertone that seemed intended for her. Was he talking about cake? Did she want him to be talking about cake? Flustered, she pushed back her chair and jumped to her feet. "I'll clear the table while you get dessert, Brooke."

Jamal's chuckle was a low, knowing rumble.

Chapter Two

Watching Karen MacLean eat chocolate cake gave Jamal a hard-on.

Observing people closely had become automatic, even when he was off duty. And this observation was sensual torture.

The slicing off of a forkful, an act of grace and deliberation carried out by a tanned, nicely shaped hand with short, unpainted nails. The lift of fork to mouth, showing off toned arms. The tiny pause of anticipation, then the slow parting of full, pink lips. The slide of fork into mouth, of cake off fork. The slow, sensual chewing and the pure pleasure on her striking face.

Yeah, watching her eat cake was maybe even sexier than actually having sex with the last woman he'd hooked up with. When had that been? Four, five months back? Marion, an outgoing redhead he'd met in a sports bar, spent a couple of nights with. The sex had been uncomplicated and fun. Yet remembering it wasn't half the turn-on of watching Karen's sensual, methodical attack on that piece of cake. If she paid that kind of attention to a guy in bed . . .

His cock pressed painfully against his fly. Trying to distract himself, he concentrated on Brooke, who was talking proudly about her granddaughter's cowgirl skills. The attractive blonde sure didn't look old enough to have a ten-year-old grandchild. Though he didn't know Brooke well, he'd quickly realized that she was a woman to respect. He got why Jake seemed so smitten.

Karen reached for her coffee mug, drawing his attention back to her.

He liked Karen. Everything about her. She looked as good as any woman could in the unflattering RCMP uniform, but tonight, in a tee and jeans that hugged sleek curves, she was killer. Tall—he put her at five ten—she moved like an athlete and looked like a model. High cheekbones, straight nose, full mouth, long-lashed eyes, shoulder-length hair now free of the uniform hat that had confined it all day. In a police report, her hair and eyes would be noted as brown and brown. In reality, her gleaming hair was a dozen different shades, from chestnut to mahogany to bittersweet chocolate, and her eyes were a tawny golden brown.

Oh yeah, there was lots to keep a guy looking.

But there was more to her than killer looks. Corporal MacLean was a damned fine cop. A cop who, at her best, operated by that special combination of intellect and instinct that you either had or didn't have. Because she had it, she'd busted Jake's cover. Because she didn't fully trust her instincts, she hadn't caught on to Henry Miller's criminal activities.

She set high standards for herself and others, which he respected. And she hated bad cops.

If she knew how badly Jamal had fucked up, she'd write him off. Bottom line: his drinking had gotten out of control on one U/C assignment and Jake had taken a bullet because of it. It was sheer luck that the shot had merely winged him. Yeah, shit happened, as Jake had said earlier, and if you had any brains and decency, you learned.

Jamal had been sober for two years now.

They should have reported the incident, but Jake had covered for him. Jamal's alcoholism was their secret. A dirty, painful secret that, along with his guilt, ate at Jamal. All his life, he'd survived by being the tough guy who could handle whatever shit life threw his way. It rankled that he'd let alcohol get the better of him. That he'd put his partner's life in jeopardy. He'd been a fucking failure and he fought the booze craving every day, determined not to fail again.

Those were ugly truths he sure as hell wasn't about to share with Corporal MacLean. Didn't want to lose the respect he saw in her golden-brown eyes.

She licked the last bit of icing from her fork, drawing him back from the dark place his thoughts had taken him.

Yeah, she was sexy. She was also a strong woman and a good cop. Not someone to be taken lightly. Jamal had only hung out with women like Marion. Fun women, nice women, women who weren't looking for more than he could offer. Karen struck him as a person who wanted and deserved permanence.

He shouldn't be so attracted to her.

Her body language said she was attracted too. A lot of women—including RCMP members—thought U/C guys were sexy bad boys. Sleeping with one was brushing up against danger without getting too close. Was that what Karen wanted? A night's worth of hot sex to remember after she settled down with the kind of man who deserved her?

His body urged him to go for it.

"Yes or no, Jamal?"

"Huh?" Brooke had asked a question that uncannily echoed his thoughts. "Sorry, I was, uh . . ." A glance at his plate showed that, while he'd been musing and watching Karen, he'd finished his dessert. "Just enjoying the cake." Taking a deep breath, he willed his body to chill.

"I asked if you'd like seconds."

"Couldn't hold another bite. That was the best meal I've had in . . ." He considered. "Maybe forever."

He glanced at Jake. Brooke was pretty, strong, capable, warmhearted, and a great cook. She put the kind of smile on Jake's face that Jamal hadn't seen in . . . maybe forever.

Tomorrow, Jake and Jamal would head back to Vancouver. Would Jake and Brooke keep seeing each other? The guy'd be a fool not to, and yet Jake had always been as much of a loner as Jamal.

"It was a wonderful dinner," Karen said. "A great celebration."

Jamal nodded. There hadn't been many evenings like this in his life.

"But I think it's time for me to head home." Karen shoved back her chair, rose, and glanced at him from under long lashes. "Jamal, can I give you a ride to your motel?"

It was only eight-thirty. Either she wanted to be alone with him, or she figured they should give Brooke and Jake some private time. Maybe both. He stood up. "Thanks."

Brooke said, "Karen, let me give you some cake to take home. I'd give you lasagna too, but we ate it all."

While Brooke packaged up the cake, Jamal helped Jake clear the table. His buddy seemed preoccupied. It'd be his last night with Brooke, either for a while or for forever.

Jamal felt antsy too, thinking about being alone with Karen. What did she want? Things would be so much easier if she was a woman like Marion. But if she was, he wouldn't be so strongly attracted.

Finally, they all moved toward the front door, where Brooke and Karen hugged.

Jake held out his hand to Karen. "It's been good working with you."

"You too." They shook.

Brooke said to Jamal, "I'm glad I had this chance to get to know you."

"Goes both ways." He kissed her soft cheek, noting a surprisingly exotic flowery scent. You had to love women.

Wondering what Karen smelled like up close, he followed her out the door.

The sun was thinking about setting and a slight briskness in the air reminded him it was still May. Brooke's front yard was full of flowers, laid out all neat and tidy the way his aunt used to do. But generous, warmhearted Brooke had little else in common with Auntie Celeste.

Hell, why was he thinking of his aunt tonight, when years could go by without her popping into his head? Maybe because Brooke's house felt like a home and she'd made him welcome the way his dad's sister and her husband never had.

Home? What the fuck? He wasn't a "home" kind of guy. Never had been, never—hmm. Never would be? That was what he'd always assumed and yet tonight had given him a glimpse of something that—

"Expecting me to open the door for you, Sergeant?" Karen's amused voice broke into his thoughts.

"Huh?" They'd reached her truck and he was staring at the passenger door. He shook his head to clear it and climbed into the vehicle, a burgundy Dodge Dakota with a canopy.

She got in the driver's side and stowed the cake container behind her seat. The truck had bucket seats. Karen wasn't close enough that he could catch her scent nor, accidentally on purpose, brush his arm against hers.

As she pulled onto the road, they waved good-bye to Brooke and Jake, who stood on the porch, arms around each other.

"Brooke's good people," he said.

"She is. A nurturer."

A word he'd never spoken in his life, but it fit. "What about you, Corporal MacLean?"

"I'm, hmm, a fixer."

"You gonna fix Caribou Crossing?"

"I'm doing the best I can."

He studied her as she steered down the narrow country road bordered by fenced fields. "You like it here? Seems like you fit, with your truck, the country music." He was more of a rock guy, but he recognized Garth Brooks's "The Dance"—one of those achy-breaky western songs—playing on the radio.

"Yes, Caribou Crossing suits me." She glanced toward him, then back at the road. "I grew up in a small town in Ontario, then went to Regina to study justice and policing. When I got accepted into the RCMP, of course I trained at Depot." She used the common term for the RCMP Academy in Regina. "My first job was in a small town in northern Saskatchewan; then I was sent to Edmonton, and then to Caribou Crossing."

Driving with her left hand, she used her right to gesture out the truck window. The sun was setting in shades of pink and purple over rolling, grassy hills dotted with a few trees. "Great scenery, friendly people, problems that almost, sometimes, seem solvable."

"Huh." Problems that seemed solvable. That was way different from what he did, where the moment you took one drug supplier off the street, another stepped in to replace him.

"Can't relate? Trucks and horses and country music aren't your thing? You like Vancouver better?"

"I like Vancouver." As much as he liked any place he'd ever lived.

"What do you like about it?"

"Uh, it's scenic." The mountains and ocean were spectacular. "And, you know, it's a city." People left a guy alone, not like in a small town.

She gave an amused chuckle. "Let me guess, you've always lived in cities?"

"Chicago, Toronto, Edmonton, Vancouver."

"You're American?" she asked with surprise.

"Not anymore." His past was a subject he never discussed. Noting that they'd reached the outskirts of town, he grinned at a "Caribou Crossing" road sign—like a pedestrian-crossing one but with the silhouette of a caribou—and said, "It's early. Feel like getting a drink? Cup of coffee?" Wherever tonight might lead, he wasn't ready to say good night yet.

She glanced over, either making up her mind or just making him wait, then said, "Yes."

"Pick a place."

"The Wild Rose has a nice pub, but there'll be rumors going around about what's happening with Sergeant Miller. We're making an official statement tomorrow, so I don't want to spend the night fending off questions."

Nor, he guessed, spend the next day fending off questions about her relationship with Jamal. "In Vancouver, people wouldn't even recognize you."

"Small-town curiosity means that someone notices when their elderly neighbor hasn't picked up his newspaper because he's fallen and broken his hip."

"Yeah," he admitted. "In Vancouver, he'd have to be well into decomp before anyone would notice."

"Charming," she said dryly, then darted him a glance from under her eyelashes. "I'm sure your girlfriend loves your dinner conversation." The words came out in a rush, confirming that she was interested in him and suggesting that she wasn't a pro at flirtation.

"No girlfriend. How about you? Any men in your life?"

A pause, then, "Men? Well, there's Harv and Dave."

His brows rose. "You're dating two guys?" He'd never

have figured her for a woman who'd do that. A twinge in his gut told him he didn't like the idea.

"Oh, you meant *dating*." She shot him a teasing glance. "Harv, the high school principal, is the husband of a friend of mine. I occasionally spend the evening with them and their kids. Dave's—"

"Let me guess," he broke in. "Ninety-five and has dementia."

"No, that'd pretty much be Mr. Morton. He escapes from the care home at least every couple months." She pulled the truck into a parking spot on the main street but didn't turn off the engine. Pointing to a beautifully restored historic inn called the Wild Rose, she said, "Dave owns this place. He's young, single, good-looking, and probably the nicest guy in town."

Another twinge. The guy sounded perfect, just the kind of man she deserved. Still, he remembered what she'd said. "But you're not dating him." He made it a statement, not a question.

She shook her head, sending that brown hair rippling. "We have dinner now and then, maybe go to a movie. Two single people just hanging out."

"Yeah, right." How could a man "just hang out" with a woman as sexy and appealing as Karen?

"It's true. There's no, you know, spark between us."

Did Dave feel the same way?

And why was he wasting time worrying about this Dave guy when Karen had just told him she wasn't attracted to him?

"I know spark," Jamal said. Deliberately, he leaned over and ran a finger down the back of her right hand, which now rested on the steering wheel. It was only the second time he'd touched her, the first being when Jake had introduced them this morning and they'd shook hands. This time he really did feel a spark, an electric charge leaping off her skin to fire up his blood.

"I figured you did." Her voice was low and breathy. Feminine, husky, sexy. It, too, climbed inside his blood and stirred him up.

Before he got a full-blown erection and maybe did something stupid, Jamal stopped stroking her hand. "So what about that drink? Willing to face the small-town gossips?"

She gave him a long, measuring look. "No. But I have beer in my fridge."

"Sounds good." And it did. The part about being alone at her place, and the part about the beer. A tall, frosty bottle, the long, chill slide down the back of his throat, the warmth as it settled in his stomach. But it wasn't going to happen.

Karen started driving again. A couple of turns and they'd left the center of the picturesque town and were in a residential area with rancher-style houses and double-wide trailers. She pulled up in front of a plain duplex with wire-mesh fencing around each half. "I rent."

"I hear you. No point putting down roots." When you joined the RCMP, you agreed to serve wherever they sent you.

They exited the truck, went through the gate, and headed to the front door. A German shepherd came running from the backyard and made a beeline for Karen, tail wagging. The dog pulled up in a hurry at the sight of Jamal.

"Hey, Tennison." Karen bent and patted her hand against her thigh, urging the dog forward. "It's okay, girl, this is Jamal. He's a friend."

Eying him, the dog ventured forward to head-butt Karen and accept her pats.

Jamal liked dogs, of the canine officer or the pet variety. He squatted down and held out his hand to be sniffed.

When he stroked the animal's brown and black coat, Karen straightened. "I found her two years ago at one of the campgrounds. She was just a pup, and she'd been left behind. No one got in touch so it probably was deliberate."

"And you took her home." He stood up too.

"By the time I drove her to the vet's, she'd won my heart." She led the way to the front door with Jamal and the German shepherd following.

"Tennison," he said as Karen unlocked the door and flicked a light switch, and the dog bounded inside. "That's a poet, right?" He hadn't figured her for the poetry type.

"Yeah, but that's not who she's named for." She toed off her leather sandals. "You know the British TV series *Prime Suspect*, with Helen Mirren? Her character's name was Jane Tennison. A very committed cop."

"Haven't seen it but I've heard of it." He took off his runners and socks and followed her into the living room. Plain, practical furniture, basic TV setup, neutral colors. Likely, she rented it furnished. She'd added personal touches: a multicolored quilt folded across the back of the couch; a couple of leafy green plants; half a dozen pieces of art ranging from a little-kid finger painting to a First Nations hummingbird watercolor to a photograph of a woman on a horse.

"Nice place." He walked toward the photo.

"You think?" She sounded surprised.

"Oughta see mine." His small rented apartment was bare bones. Used to be, he was away on U/C assignments much of the time. Even now that he mostly worked the desk, he hadn't fussed with the place. It had what he needed. He wasn't exactly the type for quilts and pictures.

He studied the photo. Karen, her hair loose past her shoulders, sat atop a horse with a coat roughly the shade of her own hair, and a black mane and tail. Tennison stood beside the horse. "You ride."

"Yes. That's my horse, Montana." She came up beside

him, not touching but close enough that his skin tingled. "He was already named when I got him."

"Huh. You own a horse."

"Let me guess—you've never been on one."

"Nope." Nor ever thought much about them.

"I rode as a kid and loved it. When I was assigned here, I started again. It's relaxing, great exercise, and it's also a way of keeping an eye on what folks are doing. Montana, Tennison, and I cover a fair bit of country."

"Cop on horseback. You really are a Mountie."

She chuckled. "Horses are a way of life in Caribou Crossing. If you want to fit in, you ride. Now let's get that drink."

He followed her to the kitchen. She took two classic brown bottles from the fridge and handed him one. His hand curved around the chilly, damp surface like it belonged there. The label read "Caribou Crossing Pale Ale" and had a stylized caribou on it. Saliva filled his mouth and he fought the powerful urge to raise that bottle to his mouth.

Here was the real reason he'd cut back on undercover work. Yeah, it was true that a U/C had to think about how many years he could push his luck, and Jamal, at thirty-five, had been pushing it for almost ten years. It was also true that he found challenges in running things rather than being the guy on the street. But, bottom line, he'd been working U/C when alcohol got the better of him and he sure as hell didn't want to fuck up again.

If only that damned craving would go away.

He swallowed and forced himself to hand the bottle back to Karen. "No, thanks. What else d'you have?"

When she opened the fridge door to put the bottle back, he leaned past her to gaze in. His cheek brushed her silky hair, and now he caught her subtle, intoxicating scent. Like lemons in the sun. For a moment he forgot what he was looking for, forgot even the craving for booze.

"Anything appeal to you?" she asked.

Hell, yeah. But that wasn't what she meant. He studied the contents of the fridge. "Orange juice, please."

"Sure." She extracted the carton and poured him a tall glass.

He took a long swallow. Yeah, it tasted good. And it was healthy. Nonaddictive. One day at a time; one nonalcoholic drink at a time. Brooke Kincaid had been sober closing in on five years. A big, tough U/C ought to be as strong as a pretty, blond grandma.

Karen poured her beer into a glass, admired it, then raised it to her lips.

Jamal's fingers tightened around his juice glass.

Maybe he looked envious, because she said, "You sure you don't want one? It's a new business, a local brewery. They make great beer."

He forced himself to shake his head. "I don't drink a lot. Doing U/C work, around booze and drugs so much of the time, it can get to be a bad habit." And that was as close to the truth as he'd ever share. Jake was the only one who knew the truth. Though Jamal had wondered about Brooke when she'd made a point of saying that the bubbly was nonalcoholic.

If she did know, she'd keep his secret. He was a good judge of character and he trusted her. She probably wouldn't think less of him either. Not the way she should. Not the way he did. Not like the rest of the world—the people who weren't alcoholics—would.

The RCMP was good about supporting members who were recovering alcoholics. However, if Jamal's superiors knew his secret, he might not be trusted with undercover work, and he did like the adrenaline rush every now and then. More than that, though, he didn't want anyone knowing how he'd let his drinking get out of control. He'd always drank, could always stop—until one day, he couldn't. That was his fucking weakness, a weakness that could have cost Jake his life. He hated that part of himself.

It sure as hell wasn't the way he wanted sexy Karen MacLean, with her high standards, to view him.

The dog came into the kitchen and gazed pleadingly up at Karen.

"I gave you dinner earlier." Karen took a bone-shaped treat from a box in a bottom cupboard.

Tennison accepted it neatly, walked over to the back door, and gazed over her shoulder.

"Yeah, it's a nice night out there. Go on, enjoy." Karen opened the door to let the animal out. "Indoor-outdoor dog," she explained, "depending on the weather and her mood."

After locking the door, she led Jamal back to the living room and sat down on one side of the couch. He sat beside her, leaving a few inches between their bodies. Being invited for a drink didn't mean an invitation to spend the night, much as that thought appealed. He'd enjoy hanging out with her and see where things went.

She drank some beer and put her glass on the coffee table. "You really like undercover work?"

"Yeah."

She rolled her eyes. "Expand."

"Uh, it's living on the edge and doing something worthwhile at the same time."

"Did you always want to do it?"

He nodded. He wanted to take down the kind of people who'd fucked up his parents' lives. Who fucked up so many lives. Besides, as a tough guy loner, it suited him. Just like it suited his buddy. "Jake and me, we met in training. Discovered we both had the same goal, to go undercover. We fast-tracked the system to get past the grind to the good stuff. Wrote the undercover exam when we were five years in, and we've been doing the work ever since."

"What I do is the grind?"

"Well . . ." Thank God she sounded more amused than offended. "Your work needs to be done. Sounds like you enjoy it."

She nodded firmly. "I do. And I like doing it in a small town."

"You said you're a fixer and some of the problems seem solvable."

"Exactly. It's not earth-shaking stuff like busting up drug gangs—well, at least not until this week." Her eyes sparkled and she took another pull of beer. "It's everyday policing like theft, vandalism, domestic violence, drunk driving, bar fights. Kids, drunks, and spouses getting in trouble. But it's bad stuff and it needs to be stopped." Her tone brooked no argument.

"That it does. And you stop it."

"When I can, and I try to really stop it, not just slap a perp in jail for the night."

"Yeah? Tell me more."

"I get people into counseling or community service, assist women who are leaving abusive situations, scare the shit out of teenagers so they straighten up."

"Sounds good." Curious, he studied her, a woman who was beautiful enough to be a model, smart enough to do whatever she wanted. "What made you choose police work, Karen?"

"My family."

"Your dad was a cop?"

She shook her head. "Social worker."

"Mom?"

"Environmental activist. They're both people with a social conscience. I take more after my dad."

"The social work stuff. Wanting to get people help so they won't reoffend."

She nodded. "My big brother's a firefighter. When we were growing up, he wanted to save lives. My interest was law and justice. I thought of being a lawyer but didn't want to spend my days in an office or a courtroom. I wanted to be out on the street."

"Or on the back roads on your horse." It was a pretty picture, so different from him infiltrating a drug-dealing biker gang.

"That too." She stacked her hands behind her neck and stretched, catlike, sensual. "It's a good life."

Her stretch pulled her T-shirt tight against firm breasts and a sleek rib cage. Man, but she was fine.

Jamal's groin tightened and he shifted position, reaching for his juice glass. What did Karen want tonight? Sometimes when she looked at him, the heat in her eyes said "sex." But everything else about her told him this wasn't a woman to be taken lightly.

Chapter Three

Jamal cocked his head. "A lot of women your age would be wanting marriage and kids to make a"—he did air quotes—"'good life.'"

Karen studied the extremely hot man sitting beside her. Generally, she was a forthright person. She figured it was better to be herself and find out up front if that put others off. Which, in her case, especially with men, it often did.

"I said good life," she reminded him. "Yes, for it to be great, there'd be a husband and kids. My ideal is the kind of family I grew up in."

A corner of his mouth kinked up. "Raising kids who aim to change the world."

Even though she knew he was teasing a little, she gave him the truth. "Exactly."

"So how come it hasn't happened yet? You have a lot going for you."

"Thank you. But a lot of men are put off by the cop thing."

"That's nuts."

"Tell me about it. But they're intimidated by me, or they don't think I'm feminine enough."

A slow grin lit his face and sparked his eyes. "I'm not

intimidated by you, Corporal MacLean. And anyone who doesn't think you're feminine doesn't have eyes, ears, or a nose."

"A nose?"

He leaned over until his face was only an inch from the hair that hung past her cheek. "Lemons in the sun."

"Lemongrass shampoo and soap." She wasn't into girly stuff like perfume or painting her nails, but she loved the fresh scent of lemongrass. She could also get used to the buzz from being close to Jamal, and to his own scent, which had both tang and spice.

"Lemongrass? Like in Thai food?"

"The same."

"I like Thai food." The suggestive gleam in his eyes hinted that he'd like to taste her.

Wishing she'd learned how to flirt, she didn't know how to respond except to take his words at face value. "So do I. That's one of the things I miss about a big city. We don't have a Thai restaurant here. Japanese, Chinese, and Indian, but that's about it." Great. Now she was babbling.

For a moment she imagined herself visiting Vancouver one weekend, dining at a Thai restaurant with Jamal. Dating. But even if the sex was stupendous, could a relationship lead anywhere? He was a city guy and she really did love the country. Besides, would a man who enjoyed undercover work even imagine marrying and having kids?

"How about you?" She tried to sound casual. "Do you see marriage and kids in your future?"

The question had him sitting back giving a quick shrug. "Never have."

"I kind of guessed that." She had a swallow of beer and noticed that he'd finished his juice. "Want another glass of juice? Or a beer? I've got vodka, tonic, Coke. I could make coffee or tea."

He swung to his feet. "I'll go look. Want another beer while I'm up?"

"No, thanks. I'm still working on this one." She watched him saunter toward the kitchen. Broad shoulders, back muscles rippling under his tee, great butt. Strong, powerful, but graceful too. Like an athlete. Unselfconscious about it.

She sighed. The one man who appeared to like her for who she was, who understood about her job, and who was totally hot in every way—and of course he wanted a different kind of future. Fine. It was what it was, and she was practical. She had two options, assuming she'd read that gleam in his eyes correctly. First, she could have a one-nighter. Tempting . . . Still, she'd never done that kind of thing. No matter how orgasmic the sex might be, would she feel happy about herself in the morning?

Another sigh, full of regret, as she faced reality. Nope, she wasn't the "casual sex" kind of woman.

Second option: enjoy some time together as colleagues and friends, and then say good-bye. Would she have regrets in the morning? Yes, of the superficial kind that would have her reaching for her vibrator, but not of the deep-down kind that tarnished her self-respect.

Okay, decision made. Pressure off. A colleague and friend. Just like Jake Brannon. Karen stretched back and lifted her bare feet to the lightly scarred wooden coffee table that had come with the rental unit.

Jamal returned, carrying a tall glass holding something that looked like orange juice and tonic. He seated himself beside her, glanced at her stretched-out legs, then raised his own feet to rest on the coffee table.

She stared at his strong, brown, very masculine feet. Tracked up the long stretch of faded denim and noted the way his firm thighs pressed against the worn fabric. Skimmed longingly over the strategically faded fly.

A hungry pulse throbbed between her legs.

Okay, he wasn't just like Jake. What a funny thing attraction was, that she could look at two stunning guys and feel nothing but respect and friendship for one, yet be totally in lust with the other.

"Tell me more about your family," Jamal said. "You guys still close?" There was something in his voice she couldn't define, perhaps envy or wistfulness. Was he not close to his own family? Later, she'd find out. For now, she'd happily talk about her parents and brother.

"Yes, we're very close. You know, my mom never expected to become a wife and mother. In her twenties, she was really into her work as an environmental activist. That was the 1970s. She traveled, protested, went out on boats to stop whalers, hugged trees to block clear-cut logging. Got arrested more than once. The causes were more important than her personal life. And then she met Dad."

"The social worker."

"Yes. They met at the courthouse. She'd been released after an arrest and he was there as a character witness for one of his clients. It was an instant attraction. Mom says her life turned around in the space of five minutes. When she and Dad got together, she realized that, while she cared deeply about the environment, she also wanted love, a personal life, a family. She and my dad have done a great job of balancing things."

"That can't be easy."

She shook her head, and settled in to share more family stories.

Jamal listened attentively and asked questions, like he was genuinely intrigued. Even while she was caught up in storytelling, she was intensely aware of each brush of his foot against hers on the coffee table, each touch of his hand on her arm when he reacted to something she said. Casual contact, but it had her constantly on the edge of arousal.

Despite that, she tried hard to not give him any misleading signals.

He didn't come on to her, and she told herself she was glad.

"Enough of my family," she said. "How about—"

"Caribou Crossing," he said.

Hmm. Did he genuinely want to know, or had he guessed that she was going to ask about his family? The man hadn't been very forthcoming about his own background. Maybe that was second nature for him, due to his many years of undercover work.

Still, she felt a little shut out. Oh well, she was a cop and she had ways of making a man talk. Right now, she'd try the chocolate method.

Rising, she said, "Brooke's chocolate-mint cake is calling to me. Ready for seconds?"

He gave her a slow, lazy smile. "An offer I can't turn down."

"Coffee? Tea? Milk?"

The quick glint in his eyes made her realize how close that was to the hokey old "coffee, tea, or me?" line. But all he said was, "Coffee sounds good."

She went into the kitchen, relieved to have a few minutes on her own. Jamal was just so *much*. Not only big and handsome, but he had a quiet, collected intensity. Sexual, definitely, but more than that.

Automatically, she flicked on the radio as she always did when she was alone in the kitchen. CXNG, the local country and western station, was playing Elvis Presley's "Suspicious Minds."

Humming along, she got the coffeemaker going and then flicked on the outside light to check the backyard. Tennison lay curled up outside the door of the doghouse in her normal summer sleeping spot. Her favorite winter location was the braided rug beside Karen's bed.

Karen turned off the outside light and took the container of leftover cake from the fridge. She was about to reach into the cupboard for plates when Jamal came up behind her.

He planted his hands on the counter on either side of her.

Her pulse jerked like it had been jump-started. She took quick, shallow breaths, wondering what would happen if she turned around. What if he kissed her? She wanted him to—oh God, she wanted him to—but it was such a bad idea.

He moved closer and his front touched her back. His heat and potent male sexual vibe pricked every cell of her body to tingling arousal. Bending his head, his voice a low rumble near her ear, he said, "Cake and coffee. Are those my only choices?"

She gulped, knowing he wasn't talking about milk or juice. He was saying he wanted her.

Brain whirling, arousal jolting through her, she tried to remember that she didn't want to wake up tomorrow feeling cheap. Empty. Lonely. "Yes," she forced herself to say. "That's all."

Immediately, he stepped back. "Got it."

Now she dared to turn and face him, where he stood a few feet away. Body still quivering with pure sexual craving, she said, "It's not that I don't want to, Jamal, but we barely know each other." Jake trusted this man, Brooke liked him, and Karen's instincts said he was a good guy. But that wasn't enough. "For me, sex has to mean something. I have to feel good about myself in the morning."

"Yeah," he said ruefully. "I kinda figured. But I wasn't sure."

She gave a shaky smile. "Never hurts to ask." And she'd bet that, when he did, he rarely got turned down.

"So. It's after midnight. I should probably go."

"No." The word jumped out of her mouth. She didn't want him to slip out of her life so soon. "I'm not tired, and I am having that cake and coffee. It'd be nice to have company."

Maybe it was a test. If all he wanted from her was sex, he'd go.

"Sounds good."

Pleased, she moved aside, her heart still racing too fast for comfort. "Why don't you cut the cake? Plates are in the cupboard above. I'll pour coffee."

A few minutes later they sat down across from each other at the kitchen table. She tasted Brooke's cake. Mmm, it was maybe even better the second time around. She took another bite. "I have to ask for her recipe."

Jamal was watching her, not eating his own cake.

"Are you okay?" she asked.

"If you're not into having sex, you shouldn't eat cake in front of me."

Hmm. Apparently she had feminine wiles she wasn't aware of. She stifled a smug grin.

He picked up his fork and began to eat.

Trying to quell the ache and pulse of unfulfilled arousal, she returned to her former agenda: finding out more about him. "You said you grew up in Chicago? What did your parents do?"

He froze in the act of raising his coffee mug toward his mouth.

Had she said something wrong? It seemed such an innocent question.

Jamal put down the mug with slow deliberation and squared his shoulders. Stone-faced, he said flatly, "Drugs."

Her lips parted but she didn't know how to respond. Still, he had answered her question, albeit succinctly. Cautiously, she said, "Your parents did drugs? That must have been, uh, tough."

He blinked. "Yeah." After a moment, more words came slowly out. "Inner city. Puerto Rican dad who was in a gang." His normally rich voice was cold, without inflection. "Sold drugs, did drugs, got killed in a gang war. Black mom who died of an overdose." His face was as expressionless as his voice.

"Oh my God, Jamal." She thought of her own wonderful childhood, and how her parents' social conscience had shaped her life and her brother's. "How old were you?"

"Six when he died. Seven when she did."

"So young." She reached over to rest her hand on his bare forearm, warm skin over tense muscles. "Any siblings?"

His Adam's apple rippled as he swallowed. "Baby sister. Four years younger. By then Mom was seriously into drugs and Alicia was born addicted. She had lots of problems and my parents didn't take her for treatment. She died before she was a year old."

"Oh, God." She took a deep breath, knowing he wasn't the kind of man who'd welcome gushy sympathy. "What happened when your parents died? Did you go into the system?"

Gazing down at his plate, he shook his head. "My dad's sister and her husband took me in. They lived in Toronto."

"How did it work out?"

When he didn't answer after a few seconds, Karen said, "I'm sorry. I don't mean to pry. I just . . . I want to get to know you."

He lifted his head and stared at her, his near-black eyes piercing. "Why's that?"

What an odd question. Why wouldn't someone want to get to know him? "Because I like you. Respect you." She pressed her lips together, reflecting on this fascinating man. "Undercover work is a tough job and takes a special kind of person. You have to be able to be a loner, to wear masks, to interact with evil people. Yet when I see you joke with Jake, kiss Brooke on the cheek, put your feet up on my coffee table, you're so . . . you know, human."

He gave a surprised snort of laughter. "No one's ever accused me of that before."

Realizing that her hand still rested on his arm, where it felt way too at home, she removed it and wrapped it around her coffee mug. "You must talk to girlfriends about this stuff."

Slowly, he shook his head. "Nope." A gleam lit his eyes. "Guess we don't talk all that much."

Again glad she wasn't a blusher, she accepted the change of subject. Curious, she asked, "You have hookups, not girlfriends?"

"Right."

She'd been wise to not have sex with him. No way did she want sex without an emotional connection, a relationship. As for Jamal, sure, she could understand a guy like him wanting no-strings sex now and then. But as a steady diet? "Don't you want more out of a relationship?"

"Like what?"

"Someone who understands you and cares about you." A role she might well volunteer for if he was looking for a serious girlfriend.

A long pause. She was aware of Glen Campbell singing in the background, asking his love if she was going away without a word of farewell.

In a rough-edged voice, Jamal said, "Guess I don't know what that's like."

She parted her lips on a silent "Oh." But, surely that wasn't true. Maybe he chose not to let women get close, but there was Jake. Tentatively, she said, "Jake cares about you."

Warmth flickered across his dark face. "My man's always got my back."

"And I'm sure you have his."

The warmth fled, replaced by tension lines that bracketed his mouth.

Again not sure what she'd said wrong, she stumbled

forward. "I know you've worked together a long time, you're partners. But you're friends too. There's a connection that's almost like brothers."

Slowly, as if he was weighing each word, Jamal said, "He's a good cop. A good guy. A buddy."

Karen resisted rolling her eyes. What was it with tough-guy cops, that they refused to acknowledge how deep their feelings for each other often ran?

"But we don't talk about this shit," Jamal said. "Our parents, how we grew up. It's the past. It doesn't matter."

"The past does matter," she protested. Pointedly, she said, "There's more to life than sex. Getting to know some-one matters. Normal conversation's a good thing." She savored the last bite of cake, then pushed aside her empty plate. "You seemed interested when I told you my family stories. Or were you just being polite?"

"No, it was nice." There it was again, that undertone of wistfulness.

"I get that you're a private guy, but I'd like to hear some of your stories too."

"They're not as nice as yours."

"They're yours, Jamal. I want to hear them."

He rose, cleared the plates, and refilled both their coffee mugs. When he sat down at the table again, he said, "Normal conversation, eh? Okay, I'll give it a try." He sipped coffee. "You asked how it worked out with my aunt and uncle. It was . . . strained. Auntie Celeste felt obligated to take me. It was one of the rare times she asserted herself with Uncle Conroy, though I'm sure she regretted it later. He never let her—or me—forget that he hated the idea."

"What a horrible man."

"A primo asshole."

"Tell me more," she urged.

Another sip of coffee. Then, speaking slowly as if he'd maybe never said these things before, he went on. "White guy. Thought he was way better than Puerto Rican Celestina. She had fairly pale skin and could pass for a white gal with a tan. He made her go by Celeste because her real name was too ethnic. She and Conroy had a son and daughter; both looked white. Then there was me." He raised a powerful dark hand, rotated it. "Couldn't exactly pass. He made folks think I was a very distant relative, a charity case they'd taken in."

"They didn't adopt you?"

He snorted. "Not hardly. And I never fit. The way I'd grown up, I didn't stand a chance. My aunt and uncle didn't include me in family stuff. Conroy Jr. and Elizabeth were snotty. Picked on me and got away with it." He shrugged. "But hey, I had food and shelter. In Chicago, I'd have had to join a gang. In Toronto, I lived to tell the story."

Karen clasped her hands on the table. "I've been told I can be too judgmental." She disagreed. Having high standards was a good thing. "But I have no patience with people like your aunt and uncle. There's no excuse for mistreating a child." She gazed into his eyes. "Jamal, you didn't just live to tell the story. Look how you turned out. A cop who puts gangs in prison. That's so impressive."

The tough cop actually looked flustered. "It's no big deal."

"You're wrong. It's huge."

His eyes warmed, and then the corners crinkled. "Okay, you can be impressed. Any chance that'll get you into bed with me?"

His tone was teasing, so she replied in kind. "No, but good try."

The truth was, it took all her willpower to resist him. She'd started out in awe of the man, and in lust. The more she learned about him, the more she respected and liked him. Too easily, she could see herself caring. Even falling for him. So, though she really, really wanted to have sex with him, she had even more reason not to. No way could she treat him as merely a hookup, and she'd hate to have him think of her that way.

If she was smart, she'd drive him back to the motel. Having the man around was just too much temptation.

And yet she might never see him again. How could she bear to cut the night short?

Chapter Four

Oh yeah, Karen MacLean *was* fine. Beautiful and sexy; a dedicated cop. A woman with intelligence, depth, and warmth. She was way too good for a guy like him.

Jamal had had sex with a number of women. Never had he experienced the same kind of intimacy as he did sitting with Karen at her kitchen table, talking about things he'd never before shared with anyone. Having her take his side, not like she pitied him but more like she respected him. He didn't deserve that respect. If she knew how he'd screwed up on the job and put his partner's life in jeopardy—

He jumped to his feet. "Want some more coffee?"

"Sure."

He took both their mugs and refilled them. She drank hers black, same as he did, and apparently didn't have a problem with caffeine. It was about the only thing they had in common, except for a fondness for Brooke Kincaid's cooking and a commitment to getting bad guys off the street.

Karen rose. "Let's go back to the living room, put our feet up."

He followed her and they resumed their previous seats, bare feet side by side on the coffee table. Her feet

were strong and capable like the rest of her, the toenails
unpainted. Those feet were way sexier than red-tipped ones
in fussy high-heeled sandals.

He wanted to rub his foot against hers, brush his fingers
against her cheek, press his lips to hers. Hell, he wanted to
strip off her clothes and explore those toned curves, to
thrust his swollen cock deep inside her. The craving was
even stronger than the desire to drink, a burning need that
he still battled daily.

But she didn't want that, and she was right. She deserved
more from a man.

Almost as if she'd read his mind, Karen said, "You don't
see yourself getting married and having kids. I imagine that
has something to do with your parents, and your aunt and
uncle?"

He'd never thought about it. "I've just never pictured it,
me with a wife, kids."

"And I've always pictured having a family. Being with a
great guy, creating a home together, raising children. Teaching them about values, helping them with homework. Going
riding, playing with the dog, swimming in the lake, having
picnics."

He could see her doing it too. Living a normal, happy
life, the kind he'd never contemplated. "Riding? D'you see
yourself staying in Caribou Crossing?"

A quick smile flashed. "You caught me. I know I could
be transferred anywhere, but I do like it here. The beautiful
country, the horses. It feels like *me*, if you know what I
mean."

"Uh, not really."

"Oh come on, Jamal. Off the top of your head, what
feels like *you*?"

To his surprise, an answer popped into his mind. "Basketball."

She cocked her head. "Yeah?"

"Played it in school. I was good at it. Got some respect."

When she nodded, he figured she was connecting the dots. A teenager with a lot of physical stuff happening: growth, hormones, rage that he barely managed to suppress. Finding a legitimate physical outlet to blow off steam. A kid who didn't fit and got picked on at home, becoming part of a team, even a bit of a star. Having hot girls chase after him. Yeah, he'd liked basketball.

"Do you still play?"

"Sometimes a few members shoot some hoops." After, they'd go out for a drink, talk sports. It was nice. Except that the others got to drink their beer. He'd pour his out in the john and refill the bottle with water.

"If you had kids, you'd hang a basketball hoop off the garage, play with them in the driveway."

And, just that quickly, her words conjured an image in his mind. Him and a couple of kids—a boy and a girl— tossing the ball around. Crazy dog getting in the way. A woman sticking her head out the back door, laughing at the sight, and darting down the steps to join in the game. A woman with gleaming brown hair and strong, practical feet that could tear up the makeshift court.

"Jamal?"

"Yeah," he said slowly, stunned at that weird vision. "Guess I would hang that hoop."

"You'd be a good father because you know how it hurts kids when their parents don't do right by them." She gazed at him with conviction in her tawny eyes.

If he had kids, of course he'd do right by them. And by his woman. But he wasn't going there. Was he? Why did he feel an odd yearning for something he'd never imagined having?

Karen rested her hand on his arm. "I've met some people who are true loners, who really don't want close relationships."

"Guess that's me." The words came out brusque and, despite the heat of her hand, a chill rippled through him.

"It's not how I see you. There's warmth in you and—"

He snorted.

Undeterred, she finished. "You connect with people."

"I do? I mean, yeah, when I'm undercover. Playing a role. But it's like there are two of me, the guy in the role and the cop who's always aware that he's there to take down the bad guys."

"You weren't playing a role at dinner tonight, or here with me."

"Uh, no."

"Which means you do connect. Just you, being yourself. But I'd guess you haven't had too many chances to do that. Fast-tracking your career, spending so much time undercover." Her mouth twisted and she took her hand off his arm. "Treating women as hookups, not girlfriends."

Okay, that didn't impress her. He wasn't surprised, because she was so different from the women he'd hooked up with. Most of them babbled on about silly stuff like movie stars and singers, or tried to persuade him to tell undercover stories even when he said those were classified. Some, like Marion, just wanted to have sex. Those were the ones he liked best.

As for Karen . . . Yeah, of course he'd like to go to bed with her, but he enjoyed her stories. She didn't push him to talk about dangerous assignments, but instead wanted to know about him. The man, not the cop. Earlier, she'd asked if he wouldn't like to be with a woman who understood and cared about him. Now, he kind of saw what she meant. "You make me think," he admitted.

A surprised laugh jolted out of her. "Should I say 'thank you' or apologize?"

"Not sure." He rubbed his head, grinned ruefully. "It's confusing. But maybe it's a good thing. You make me see . . ."

He swallowed, and then a word slipped out, soft as a sigh. "Possibilities."

"I do? Tell me."

Did he dare think about possibilities? "Oh shit, woman. I never talk about stuff like this."

"It's time you started. Jamal, you decided to take a promotion and do less undercover work. Weren't you thinking that you could have more of a life now?"

Not consciously. But maybe, somewhere buried deep. That image flickered into his mind again: the basketball hoop, the kids, the dog. The woman. Possibilities. Seductive and dangerous. He shoved them aside and said gruffly, "Don't think I'm suited for all that home and family stuff. Yeah, it sounds nice, like those stories about your family sounded nice. But hell, I don't think it's something I could do."

"You could if you wanted to. It's good to have dreams and goals to guide us." Then she grimaced. "Not that having them is any guarantee of achieving them. I'm proof of that." A sigh. "Even if by some miracle I did find a man who was interested in me, not everyone can handle being married to a cop. The divorce rate in the RCMP is pretty high."

He hated seeing discouragement on her pretty face. "Don't give up on the dream. Not all cop marriages fail, and not all guys are crazy. One's going to come along who realizes how special you are." Whether that man would measure up to her high standards was another issue.

"You're good for my ego," she said softly.

Oh hell, she was too damned irresistible, from the warm glow in her golden-brown eyes, to the interest she'd shown in him, to that touch of insecurity about her own attractiveness. "I could be good for more than that."

She pressed her lips together.

"No sex," he said quickly. "I get it, Karen. But one kiss . . ." He leaned toward her slowly.

Her eyes widened, but she didn't move away.

And when his lips touched hers, they were soft, warm, and giving.

He smoothed back a silky strand of hair that had fallen forward, then slid his fingers through her hair to the nape of her neck. He'd touched women's necks before, yet the skin had never before felt so soft and feminine.

Karen, the cop who cared fiercely about her job, was also one hundred percent woman. One hundred percent desirable.

Pulse hammering, he struggled for control as his tongue teased the crease between her lips until she opened. Her sweet, warm breath sighed against his face. The tip of her tongue met his, tentative at first, but quickly engaging in a dance of exploration and desire.

In the back of her throat, a whimper and moan combined to make a wordless sound that spoke of pleasure, hunger, need. To him, it said "more." As lust slammed through him, that was exactly what he wanted.

He explored her mouth thoroughly, then let her taste his. His lips sucked the ripe center of her bottom lip, teasing it, laving it, doing to it what he longed to do to her nipple. Then to her clit.

He'd never been really big on kissing. It was okay, depending on the woman, but mostly just a means to an end. The end being sex. Tonight was different. Karen had said no sex, and he wouldn't push. He wouldn't reach for her breast or slide his hand between her thighs. No matter how badly he wanted to. Hell, resisting touching this woman was maybe even as hard as resisting a drink, but he'd respect her boundaries if it killed him.

So he sank deep into the kiss, enjoying it for exactly what it was: a special, sensual moment. Possibly the only kiss he and Karen would ever share. And that thought chilled his heated blood.

Slowly, he drew back. "Oh, man."

Her cheeks glowed and her pink lips were damp and swollen. But then she pressed her lips together and a frown line creased her forehead. "Jamal, I believe in being forthright."

He nodded. "Okay. Good."

"I like you, I'm attracted to you, and I think I could care for you."

Care? This amazing woman could care for him? "I don't know what to say."

"But I can't go there, I can't head down that path. Not if you're only looking for a hookup." Her lashes lowered. "I'd only get hurt." They flicked up again and she gazed steadily at him. "I'm only interested in a relationship with a possibility of a future."

"A future . . ."

"I know we've only recently met, but I just mean that, uh . . . What I'm trying to say is, if you're only looking for casual sex, if you're sure you never want to settle down with a woman, or if you can't imagine me being that woman, then—" She broke off with a self-deprecating laugh. "Crap. I may be forthright, but I'm not exactly articulate."

"No, I get it." Until tonight, he'd never thought about having a future with a woman. But in that basketball vision, the woman darting down the steps to join the game had looked a lot like Karen MacLean. "Tonight has been, uh, a lot." Telling this woman emotional shit he'd never told a soul. Feeling things for her that he'd never felt before.

But hell, if she knew who he really was, this woman with her high standards would write him off as the fuckup he'd proven to be. Though . . . That was the past. He was sober and he would stay sober. No more fuckups. He could stick his dirty secret in a box, lock it, and throw away the key.

She nodded. "It has been a lot."

He reached for her hand and clasped it in his. "I'd never want to hurt you."

"I believe you."

"I need to go now. Guess I need to do some thinking."

She gave him a tremulous smile. "Let me know how it goes."

Chapter Five

A month after the night he'd spent talking to Karen MacLean, Jamal sat across from Jake in a seedy bar in Winnipeg. They both had scruffy facial hair and fake tattoos. Initially, another member had been assigned to go undercover with Jake, but when he was stricken with appendicitis, Jamal had filled in. They were trying to bust a new gang, the Black Devils, who were dealing drugs to local kids.

Eying Jake's beer enviously, Jamal took a sip of his tomato juice and bitters. "One hell of a job for an alcoholic."

"You need any motivation to stay sober, just take a look over there." Jake nodded toward a guy in the corner whose shaky hands, even cupped around his glass, could barely lift it to his mouth.

The grungy wino was way less motivation than the knowledge of how Jamal had let Jake down. "Hard to believe that's the route I was on."

"Harder to believe Brooke was doing it too."

"Amen. That's one hell of a lady." Five years sober. For him, that seemed a very long way off. He only hoped that, as other recovering alcoholics told him, the cravings diminished over time.

"Yeah." Though Jake said he and Brooke had broken things off, it was obvious she was on his mind.

"There you go, all mushy faced again," Jamal ribbed him. As they spoke, he kept an eye on the pool table. The group of students were playing a half-assed game, looking jittery, like they were more interested in scoring drugs.

"Don't tell me you haven't been thinking about Karen MacLean."

Of course he had.

Jake gave a wicked grin. "The two of you seemed to be getting on pretty well that night you left Brooke's so early. Almost makes a guy think . . ."

"Don't go there. Believe it or not, we sat up all night talking." He took a sip of his drink, still keeping an eye on the students. No action yet.

"Talking? What did you find to talk about all night?"

"You know. Her job, my job. Parents, schooling. What she wants out of life. What I want out of life."

Jake gaped. "Hell, I've known you almost fifteen years and we've never talked about that shit."

"That's a woman for you." No, that was Karen. She'd told him that her mom's life turned around in five minutes when she met Karen's dad. Jamal was coming to think that maybe his own life had turned around, talking to Karen that evening.

"Yeah, I guess." A pause. Then, "So, what the hell do you want out of life?"

The picture that had popped into Jamal's mind that night was seeming more and more solid. He'd float it by his buddy, see how Jake reacted. "The usual, I guess." He tried to sound casual. "Good woman, couple of kids. Job I enjoy." No alcohol; no cravings; no weakness. "House, maybe a dog. Did you know Karen has a German shepherd?"

"Well, hell." Jake's tone said that Jamal had given away more than he'd meant to.

When the other man didn't say anything else for a few minutes, Jamal had to ask. "You thinking I'm crazy? You can't see me teaching some little boy or girl how to play basketball?" Staying sober, being in a loving relationship, having a family. Being normal.

"Huh. Yeah, I can." He sounded surprised. "You'd go for staff sergeant, and it'd really be a desk job?"

"Likely." This assignment had come at a good time. It helped Jamal test his feelings about undercover work. As much as he enjoyed excitement and challenge, this wasn't the right job for an alcoholic, nor for a guy who had personal commitments. "Figure priorities gotta change when you hook up with someone special."

When this job was done, he'd give Karen a call. See if she'd like to come down to Vancouver and let him buy her a Thai dinner. Or, since she'd have a pile of work cleaning up Miller's mess, he'd offer to go up to Caribou Crossing.

The bar door opened and two suspected Black Devils entered. "Action," he muttered.

Jake raised his beer glass and flicked them a glance. "So you're going to see Karen again?"

One of the pool players made eye contact with one of the gang members.

"Thought I might head up that way when we get back. How 'bout you and Brooke?"

Slowly, Jake shook his head. The light had gone out of his gray eyes. "Don't see it happening. She's got a good life going for her. Doesn't need me."

"Yeah, but do you need her?"

"Don't need anyone."

No, a man shouldn't need anyone. Jamal didn't. But that wasn't really what he was asking. Karen would know the right way to phrase the question, to make Jake dig deeper.

Casually, he raised his smartphone, holding it like he was checking texts or scrolling through contacts. Instead, he had its camera at the ready.

The college kid left the pool table and headed toward the men's room. Jamal clicked shots as the gang member sauntered down the hallway after him, then put the phone to his ear. Pretending he was on a call, he said, "You two got pretty strong chemistry."

"Yeah, that's for sure. And I care about her. But it wouldn't be fair to her. I can't come and go in her life. She's not that kind of woman. She wants stability, peace. She doesn't want some guy who spends his life like this." He gestured around the grungy bar.

"You plan on doing this for the rest of your life?"

"Don't know what else I'd do."

"Don't see the basketball thing working for you?"

Jake snorted. "Guess I don't see myself as a parent. Most parents fuck up their kids' lives. Don't want any part of that."

Nor did Jamal. Karen seemed to think he'd be an okay dad, but Jake had known him way longer. "You think I'd fuck up my kid's life?" he asked, still pretending to be on the phone.

Jake pondered. "You'd try not to. Besides, seems to me Karen's got her head on pretty straight."

Jamal couldn't hold back a grin. "So you're seeing me and Karen?"

"Aren't you?"

"White gal," he pointed out.

"Didn't seem to bother her. Does it bother you?"

"Nah. Poor mongrel kids, though. White, black, and Latino."

"Could be pretty." Jake grinned. "If they take after Karen, not you."

And that was the truth. Noting the college kid returning, Jamal lowered his phone and pretended to find another number as he surreptitiously snapped more shots. Kid was sniffing like he'd tried out a sample. He joined his friends, said something, and they abandoned their pool game and headed for the door. Mission accomplished. The two gang members took a corner table.

Jamal put his phone away. "Free table. Shoot some pool?" It'd keep them occupied while they kept an eye on the Black Devils.

"Why not?" Jake rose. Then he leaned over and muttered, "When you go to Caribou Crossing, get Karen to take you line dancing."

"Line dancing?" Now that, he had some trouble with. Basketball, yeah; line dancing, not so much. "Brooke do that?"

"She's good."

"Bet she's good at most anything she chooses to do."

"That's the truth." Jake finished his beer.

"Never saw you like that with anyone before."

"Like what?"

Jamal searched for words. Unfamiliar ones. "Relaxed. Happy."

Jake frowned, then said, "Get us some more drinks, will ya? I'll grab the table before someone else gets it."

Chapter Six

Karen walked back to the detachment on a Thursday morning after a quick coffee break with Brooke Kincaid. She was glad the two of them had become friends, but they needed to stop talking about Jamal and Jake. In more than a month, there'd been no contact from either man. Though Brooke asserted that she and Jake had enjoyed a good time and agreed to end it, he was clearly still on her mind. As for Jamal, that night Karen and he had talked and kissed had obviously meant more to her than it had to him.

Vowing to put him out of her mind, Karen strode into the detachment. *Her* detachment, until a replacement for Miller was put in place. The phone on her desk was ringing. "Corporal MacLean."

"Karen MacLean." A male voice, molasses rich, caressed the four syllables.

Jamal! His name almost burst out on a gush of excitement but she managed to hold back. Likely this was a business call. Briskly, she said, "Jamal? What can I do for you?"

"Say that you'll see me."

"I, uh . . ." She'd made it clear she was only interested in a real relationship and he'd said he had some thinking to do. If he wanted to see her . . . Her heart skipped.

"Jake and I are in Winnipeg. Been doing a U/C assignment."

"Oh?" Was that why he hadn't called?

"We're tidying things up today, then flying home."

"And?" Would he ever get to the point? Her heart would go into fibrillation if he didn't.

"I've been thinking. Want to see you and talk about it."

Did that mean he *did* see a possible future for them, or what? "Could you give me a clue?" she asked warily.

A low chuckle met her ear. "Maybe one. Been thinking about a basketball hoop in the driveway."

Her heart clutched. A home, kids. A wife. He wouldn't tell her this if he didn't think she might be part of that picture. "A basketball hoop is good." Her voice came out shaky; then she laughed. "It's very good, Jamal."

"I wondered if you'd like to come down to Vancouver for Thai food or—"

"Oh God, I'd love to, but there's so much going on here."

"Figured there might be. How 'bout I come up tomorrow? Spend the weekend. Whatever spare time you get, we can see each other. Talk." He paused, then said seductively, "Or, you know, whatever."

The tone said *sex*. And oh yes, she wanted that *whatever* so badly. "Yes, come. Come as soon as you can. I'll free up some time." Did she sound overeager?

"Be there as soon as I can."

She smiled into the phone. He sounded pretty damned eager too.

Friday afternoon, Karen left the detachment early, at five o'clock. At home, she showered, brushed her hair to a sheen, and rubbed lemongrass lotion into her skin. Her sage green sundress wasn't exactly sexy—she didn't own "sexy" because she figured it wasn't appropriate for a small-town cop—but the dress did have a short skirt and thin shoulder straps, baring more skin than she typically showed. Her ears weren't pierced and she never wore earrings, but she did add a gold chain necklace.

Anxiously, she paced around the house. Jamal had said he'd fly up and rent a vehicle at the airport in Williams Lake, an hour and a half away.

She'd organized the evening in her mind. A drink here and a private chance to talk, then dinner at the Wild Rose because she wasn't confident enough to try out her cooking skills on him. After, if everything was going well, coffee back here and . . . that remained to be seen. But the bed had fresh sheets and she'd shaved her legs.

Caribou Crossing would have eyes on her. Dinner in public, Jamal's rental car parked outside her place. She had to find out, right off the top, why he was here. If they were entering into a real relationship, then she was fine with people knowing.

Tennison, out in the yard, barked excitedly.

Karen flew to the front window. A black Jeep Wrangler had pulled up behind her truck, and Jamal stepped out. Oh my, he looked good, dressed in jeans and a cream-colored shirt with the sleeves rolled up his dark forearms. He took a padded rectangular bag—a cooler?—out of the Jeep and opened the front gate. Inside, he gave Tennison a quick pat and then strode up the walk.

Heart racing, Karen waited. She didn't want to greet him outside, where nosy neighbors could watch.

As soon as he stepped onto the porch, she swung the door open. Though she meant to say "hi," the word stuck in her throat. All she could do was stare at him.

A big grin split his face and his eyes widened as he took

her in, from head to bare, unpainted toes. "Even better than I remember," he murmured. He nudged Tennison, who'd followed him and was sniffing at the bag, away, strode into the house, and closed the door. The bag went on the table by the door and then Jamal was in front of her. His hands grasped her shoulders.

Karen trembled at the surge of heat that rushed through her, and gazed into his dark, shining eyes. As he leaned in for a kiss, her legs flexed and she went up on her toes—an automatic movement as she was drawn inevitably toward him. Her lips parted on a soft gasp of pure *want*, and then his mouth claimed hers.

She answered with an equal demand as her arms went around his waist and his around her shoulders.

Mmm, the kiss was hot. Tender yet demanding. Questing tongues, tiny nips. Soft, throaty moans. Her needy whimper as arousal arced through her, straight to her sex. Her pelvis pressed against his fly, where, already, a rigid erection met her. The knowledge of how badly he wanted her made her even hotter.

God, this was so good. Even better than their first amazing kiss because now they knew. They knew. . . .

Wait a minute.

As her heart tried to thud its way out of her chest, she forced herself to pull away and step back. Panting for air, she hunted for the right words.

"Too fast?" he asked, his voice as ragged as her breathing. "I didn't mean—"

"I know. We got carried away." By passion. She'd never had that happen before. "Jamal, I need to know . . ." Know that she could trust him the way her instincts—and her lustful body—urged her to. "When you said 'basketball hoop,' what did you mean?" Intently, nerves taut with hope, she watched his face.

He gave a rueful grin. "That wasn't enough words? Uh, it means . . . that I have a dream of a future now."

His frown of concentration told her he was struggling to express himself. As she'd seen before, talking about feelings and dreams didn't come easily to this very private, independent man. But he did look totally sincere and her anxiety eased.

"The kind of future I never saw for myself before," he said. "Like, with a family. A home. A regular job, no more undercover assignments." He gave a rather shaky laugh. "Guess you'd call it a normal life." His words flowed more freely now, and the expression in his eyes was warm and caring. "You're the one who made me see it, want it, believe maybe I could have it. You're the woman in the dream, Karen. I can't make promises, but . . ." He shrugged, apparently out of words now.

"No, of course you can't, and nor can I." Her heart sang and, totally uncharacteristically, her eyes were damp. "It's too soon. But you've told me what I need to know. And I have that same dream."

"Doesn't bother you, you being white and me being brown?"

Huh? In this day and age? "Seriously? Are you saying it bothers you?"

"Hell no. I like your pretty white skin."

She gave a teasing huff. "I am *not* white. At least no parts of me that you've seen so far. I have a nice outdoorsy tan."

"I'm looking forward to seeing the parts that aren't tanned."

"Mmm," she purred in anticipation. "I'm looking forward to seeing *all* your parts."

"Guess you want to do some more talking first?" He sounded resigned.

That was what she'd planned for tonight. But now, what

she needed wasn't more words. It was physical and emotional intimacy. Lovemaking. "I do. After."

"After?"

It gave her a delicious sense of feminine power to keep the undercover cop off balance. "There's a time for talk and a time for—" Leaving the word *action* unsaid, she stepped forward, clasped her hands behind his neck, and tugged his head toward her.

His eyes gleamed. "Hell yeah."

This time, Karen gave herself fully to the kiss, her heart full of hope, her body ripe with desire. She stroked down his back, so powerful under the soft cotton of his shirt. Hooking one leg around his, she pressed close to him, reveling in the hard, tantalizing thrust against her belly as his erection sprang to life again. Impatient to touch bare skin, she tugged his shirttail from his belted jeans, then greedily ran her hands over ripped muscles that flexed under her touch.

His fingers were busy with the back zipper of her sundress. "I like this dress," he muttered. Then he stepped back, freeing himself from her grip.

Impatiently she shrugged her shoulders to send her dress sliding to the floor. She was about to step back into his arms when he said, "Mmm, I like that even more." He studied her appreciatively. Clad only in a silky peach-colored bra and panties, she straightened her shoulders and delighted in his gaze.

"What happened?" He gestured to the scar on one hip, above the top band of her skimpy panties.

She ran a hand over the puckered flesh. "I was arresting a husband for domestic violence. His battered wife hauled herself up off the floor and grabbed a kitchen knife. She got in a swipe before I could stop her." She studied his face, wondering if he found the scar ugly.

Instead, his hand cupped her hip in a warm caress. "Yeah, shit happens."

A cop respecting her as another cop even when the thing most on their minds was lovemaking. Yes, she liked it.

And she liked it even more when his caress moved up to her breast. His large, dark hand was so masculine compared to her soft curves and the peach silk. She was a tall, fit woman who prided herself on her strength, yet how lovely to revel in her femininity, her sexuality. Her nipples tightened and he caressed one bud through her bra with a slow, circling fingertip.

Eager to see him naked, she unbuttoned his shirt. He stopped teasing her breast long enough to pull off his shirt and toss it on the floor. Even as he did, she was at work on his jeans, and soon they slid to the floor too.

Oh God, Jamal in nothing but black boxers. Boxers tented by an impressive erection. Dusky skin gleaming in the late afternoon light that slanted in the window. Muscles any athlete would envy and any woman would drool over. He was beautiful—and he, too, was flawed by scars. She touched one on his side above his waist, guessing from the shape that he'd been creased by a bullet. One day she'd ask. Now, she was just glad, so glad, that he'd survived all those years of undercover work and was ready to move to something less dangerous.

"Bedroom down the hall?" He hoisted her into his arms.

She let out a startled squeak. "Yes, but I can walk."

"This is more fun."

And it was, being carried as if she weighed next to nothing. This was the first time in her adult life except for training exercises that a man had carried her. She snuggled against Jamal's hot, naked chest as one powerful arm curved around her shoulders and the other hooked under her bare legs. Leaning her cheek against him, she breathed in his scent, slightly musky and totally male. Seductive, addictive.

Her bedroom was plain and functional, only a few family photos for décor, but Jamal didn't glance at anything other than the bed. He laid her down, her head on stacked pillows. A moment later he was on the bed too, leaning over her, unfastening the front closure of her bra and sucking her nipple.

Pleasure arced through her and she pressed into him, demanding more. Her fingers stroked through his wavy hair, its texture springy and slightly rough, as masculine as everything else about him.

He licked around her areola, flicked the tip of her nipple with his tongue, took the bud between his lips, and alternated sucks and licks.

Gripping his head, she moaned, arched, and her hips twisted as need hummed between her legs.

His erection was sandwiched against her thigh, thick and hard. She wanted to touch him, lick and suck him, explore every inch of his body. But even more than that, she wanted him inside her. Later, there'd be time to do everything. Right now she wanted to merge their bodies, to seal the deal so there was no going back. God knows, her body, celibate for over a year, was primed and crying out for release.

"Jamal, now. I want you now." She stretched out a hand to open the drawer of the bedside table, where she'd stashed a brand new package of condoms.

He raised his head, studied her face, then glanced at the box she'd pulled from the drawer. "What happened to foreplay?"

"We'll do that later."

"Thank you, God." Deftly he sheathed himself, then kneeled between her spread legs.

She gazed up at him, dark and powerful, muscular and gorgeous, that thick erection all hers. Their first time. Another woman might have wanted it tender and romantic, but tender wasn't the way she felt right now. She wanted him;

he wanted her; they belonged together. It was that simple, that primal.

"Kiss me," she demanded.

When he moved forward to comply, she reached between their bodies to grasp his penis. It jerked in her hand and she firmed her grip.

As Jamal's lips took hers in a fiery kiss, she eased the tip of his erection between her damp folds, guiding him inside her. She gasped with shock—it had been so long since she'd felt a man enter her, and he was so big—and with pleasure as her sensitive flesh responded to his touch.

He thrust in and out in small movements, working his way deeper as her body loosened to accommodate him. Had anything ever felt so good? The sensations, combined with the fact that this was Jamal, had her wrapping her arms around him, holding him like she never wanted to let him go.

Their kiss was frantic now, a mix of tongue thrusts, nips, and moans. Much of her attention was focused elsewhere, on the quick, irresistible build of arousal that intensified with his every thrust. Sexual tension and need coiled, a tightly wound spring that begged for release.

"Faster," she panted. "Jamal, I'm so close and I need—"

She broke off as he obeyed her command, driving into her. If she'd been a smaller, less strong woman, his thrusts might have hurt. As it was, she rose eagerly to meet them, reaching down to grab the taut curves of his butt and urge him even deeper.

Tilting her hips to increase the pressure of his shaft against her aching clit, she said, "Oh yes! There, like that. More! Oh God, Jamal, that's—" And she cried out with the pure, sharp pleasure of orgasm as he took her over the edge in a fierce crash, followed by throbbing waves of aftershock.

She'd barely started to breathe again when his hips jerked

harder, he groaned, and his climax poured into her. His sharp thrusts crashed her into another orgasm of her own.

Vaguely, she was aware of her heart beating like she'd raced up ten flights of stairs. Of Jamal collapsing in slow-mo on top of her. They lay, sealed together by sweat, chests heaving.

Finally he blew out a noisy sigh and managed to roll off to lie beside her.

She lay flat, arms and legs flung out, limp and used up. Grinning with utter satisfaction. How perfect was that, for a first-time memory?

Jamal reached for her hand and gave a throaty chuckle. "Guess I'm better at taking orders than I thought I was."

She turned her head on the pillow and gazed at him. Naked and gorgeous, he looked as used up as she felt. "Did it bother you, me telling you what I needed?"

"Hell no. I like it. It's better than trying to guess what you want."

"You, Jamal Estevez. That's what I want."

His eyes twinkled with humor. "Again? Now? I'm a little—"

"Idiot. You know what I mean."

"Oh." The humor faded as comprehension dawned. "Well, uh, yeah. That's . . . good." He shoved himself off the bed and headed toward the bathroom.

She rolled her eyes. His communication skills definitely needed work. His sex skills, though, were outstanding. Stretching luxuriously, she ogled his rear view, noting another scar but mostly just appreciating all those firm muscles flexing.

When Jamal came back, he sat on the edge of the bed and offered her a glass of icy cold water. "You know you're too good for me, right?" His expression was surprisingly serious.

Still, he had to be joking. Tongue in cheek, she said,

"Totally." Pushing herself up to a sitting position, she felt the pleasant ache of muscles, inside and out, that hadn't been used for a long time. Muscles that had never been so thoroughly exercised. She took the glass and had a long, refreshing swallow of water.

"Okay then." He still looked serious. "Just as long as you realize I'm not exactly perfect."

He was probably thinking about how his two crappy families and his undercover work didn't give him much of a foundation for knowing how to build a relationship. A family. She put the glass on the bedside table and captured his hand. "No one's perfect."

"You have high standards."

"And you'll measure up. We need to keep talking, keep trying. Be honest with each other."

He freed his hand and reached for the glass. "Want to think about dinner?"

"I thought we could go to the Wild Rose."

"Tomorrow."

Her brows rose. On the job, he outranked her. If he thought he could boss her around in their personal lives, he had a lesson to learn.

"I brought Thai food," he said.

"The cooler bag," she remembered.

"You said you like Thai and can't get it here."

Okay, not bossy. Considerate. "I love Thai. Jamal, that's so sweet of you."

He winced, which made her chuckle.

Chapter Seven

Half an hour later, after Jamal and Karen had shared a shower and a steamy quickie, he sat at her kitchen table. He could get used to this: having great sex; spending time with a beautiful, strong woman; contemplating a future he'd never before imagined. Didn't hurt, either, that the kitchen smelled of spicy Thai food.

They'd heated the tom kha gai soup and spooned it into two large bowls. The rest of the food—chicken with red curry and bamboo shoots, ginger beef with onions and mushrooms, pad Thai, and a big container of jasmine rice— sat on the counter waiting to be nuked.

Karen, again clad in that sexy green sundress, leaned into the fridge. "Beer?"

"No, thanks. I'm good with water."

"Seriously?" She poured a bottle of Caribou Crossing Pale Ale into a glass for herself and came to sit across from him. "Beer's perfect with Thai food."

"You think? I like water." He swallowed, imagining the taste of beer, the way he'd done millions of times in two years of sobriety. Hurriedly, he spooned up some soup. The flavors of chicken, coconut milk, mushrooms, lemongrass, and spices mingled on his tongue.

This was going to get tough, finding reasons to avoid drinking. He couldn't do the empty-the-bottle thing in Karen's kitchen, like he did in the bar after shooting hoops. On the job, he sometimes used that trick, but had other pretenses as well, depending on the circumstances. He might say he was into drugs, and booze was too lightweight. Or he'd pretend to be "above" the pitiful people who needed drugs and booze.

"I'm not much for drinking these days," he said. "Like I said before, when you work undercover, it can get to be a bad habit. Besides, the last couple times I had a drink, it didn't agree with me." Back in the bedroom, she'd told him they had to be honest, and every word he'd spoken was true.

"Hmm. Maybe you've developed an allergy. You should see a doctor." She lifted her glass. "Not that I'm a big drinker, but it's nice to have a beer or a glass of wine when you feel like it."

"Yeah." She could say that again. Maybe it'd be okay now—now that he wasn't doing undercover work, now that he'd gotten his life under control—to have the occasional beer.

His fingers itched to reach across the table and curl around that sweating glass of golden brew. Under control? Hah! He was an addict. That meant no more drinking. Ever. He wouldn't give in to weakness, wouldn't fuck up again.

Karen was way too good for him. She thought he was a better man than he was, and damn it, he was going to be that man. No need to tell her about the loser he used to be. This was a fresh start.

She raised another spoonful of soup to her lips. "Mmm. Delicious. Thank you so much."

"Perks of the big city."

A nod, then she leveled him with a steady gaze from those tawny eyes. "We've got a long-distance problem in this relationship. If we got serious . . ."

"Commuting between Vancouver and Caribou Crossing would get old pretty quick," he agreed.

"You really plan to give up undercover work?"

"I do." A pang of loss, of regret made him pause and reflect. But he knew the decision was right. "On this last assignment, I was thinking there are things I'd rather be doing."

Her lips curved. "Basketball hoop?"

He nodded. "Eating Thai food with you." A grin snuck up on him. "Or doing what we were doing before this."

"Making love with me was more fun than stalking drug gangs? Gosh, I'm flattered."

They both chuckled.

Karen cleared the empty soup bowls and put the rest of the food in the microwave. Turning to face him, leaning back against the counter, she asked, "D'you hate small towns? All the country stuff?"

He'd put some thought into that, knowing how fond she was of this place. "Don't have enough experience to say for sure. But you know that if we got together, we probably couldn't both work in the Caribou Crossing detachment. It'd be different if it was bigger, but—"

"I know. If you took Miller's place, you'd be my boss. A member can't date her supervisor."

"Or even work the same shift as someone she's dating. With only a handful of members here, it'd make for a logistical nightmare."

"Williams Lake is a bigger detachment." Again with that steady gaze. "The staff sergeant there is retiring in a couple of months."

"Huh. It's an hour and a half drive. Nice scenery along the way, but it's a long commute," he mused.

"There are nice places to live between here and Williams Lake. If we wanted to split the difference." She gave a soft laugh. "And we're getting way ahead of ourselves."

Funny how it didn't scare him. At least not much. "Well, this weekend we're both here. How about you show me Caribou Crossing, Karen?"

A grin flickered. "Sell you on it, you mean?"

"Hadn't thought of it that way, but . . ."

She flicked her head. That multicolored dark brown hair slipped and slid over her bare shoulders, making him want to plunge his fingers through it and caress the skin below. Then her chin went up and her eyes sparkled. "I'll accept that challenge, Sergeant Estevez. I bet I can make you love Caribou Crossing."

Right then, looking at tall, toned, curvy Karen in that little green dress, Jamal figured she could make him love pretty much anything. Including her.

He should've known there'd be horses.

It was Saturday afternoon and Jamal was in the passenger seat of Karen's truck, on his way to go riding for the first time in his life. A female voice on the radio sang that she knew some guy was trouble from the moment he walked in. Outside the window, the sun shone in a clear blue sky and the scenery unfolded. They'd passed some craggy hills and a low-key tourist attraction called Gold Rush Days Park. Karen told him that the town had its origins in the 1860s gold rush. When the gold died out, a few enterprising men turned from mining to ranching.

They were definitely in ranching country now. Split-rail fences lined the two-lane country road, marking off rolling hills with grazing cattle and fields with horses. Here and there a farmhouse, often with a barn and outbuildings, gave evidence of the humans who tended the livestock.

The morning had started the best way possible, with great sex. After, Karen had gone into the detachment and he'd caught up on rest. Sleep had been scarce the last few days, as he and Jake had tidied up the Black Devils case.

Now, he was glad to feel more rested. He might not have cowboy boots and a Stetson, but if he could ride a motorbike on challenging roads at high speed, he could stay on top of a horse.

On their left, a wooden sign with a couple of stylized horses said "Ryland Riding." Karen turned. "This is where I keep Montana. Sally is a widow who boards horses and teaches riding. She was a barrel racer when she was younger. I called her, so she knows we're coming."

The white fence alongside the narrow road could use fresh paint. So could the house and outbuildings, which included a large barn and what he guessed was an indoor ring. It seemed the widow was having trouble keeping up with things after her husband died.

Karen parked in the barnyard beside a Ford truck with a horse trailer attached. Closer to the barn, eight horses sporting Western saddles and bridles were tied to a couple of hitching rails. They gazed curiously as he and Karen exited her vehicle.

She opened the canopy and Tennison jumped out, panting with excitement. With the German shepherd at her heels, Karen strode across to the barn door.

Jamal hung back a moment to watch. Snug-fitting jeans on a good-looking woman. One of life's pleasures. With them, she wore cowboy boots, a Stetson, and a blue-and-green plaid flannel shirt with the sleeves rolled up her forearms. Jamal, used to blending in on undercover jobs, felt out of place wearing Nikes and a black tee with his jeans.

When he entered the barn, he paused to let his eyes adjust to the dim light. On the ground floor, horse stalls lined a wide center aisle. Karen stood halfway up the aisle talking to a woman clad in Western garb who was squatting to stroke the dog.

As Jamal joined them, the woman straightened with a smile. A couple inches shorter than Karen, she was attractive, with short, curly strawberry blond hair framing an oval-shaped face under her Stetson. Freckles sprinkled her nose and cheeks, as well as the top of her chest, revealed by the round neckline of the gray tee she wore under an unbuttoned blue denim shirt.

Karen made the introductions and he learned that this was Sally Ryland. When she'd said "widow," he had expected gray hair, but Sally looked to be in her midthirties, like him. Lines of tiredness did no favors to her greenish gray eyes and full, chapped lips. Her well-worn clothing was a size too big on her thin, muscular body.

"I brought Montana in," Sally told Karen. "For you, Jamal, we'll go with Smoke Trail. He's an appaloosa gelding."

Gelding, he understood. Appaloosa, he found out when Sally led the way to one of the roomy stalls, meant spotted. Smoke Trail was mostly a dark charcoal gray, but his hindquarters were white with a sprinkling of dark spots. Even Jamal could tell that this animal had good lines.

When he told Sally that, she nodded. "Yes, he does. And nice smooth gaits, and a bit of spirit. You don't look like a man who wants a wussy horse."

"Nope," he agreed, wondering what "a bit of spirit" meant.

"I'll get him ready while Karen tacks up Montana."

And that, he found as he stood patting Tennison and watching Karen, meant putting a pad on the horse's back, followed by a saddle and bridle.

Karen led her horse, with its glossy dark brown coat and black mane and tail, out of its stall. Sally brought Smoke Trail to join them. The two animals made friendly sounds as they greeted each other. Neither seemed bothered by Tennison, who stayed close to Karen's left side.

The two women led the horses out of the barn into the yard, where a silver Honda CR-V was parking. "The first half of my two o'clock class," Sally said.

Four kids around seven or eight years old, three girls and a boy, poured out. The children, dressed in jeans, cowboy boots, and helmets, headed over to the horses tied to the rails.

"You teach little kids?" Jamal asked. "Or all ages?"

"All ages, but I admit to having a soft spot for the little ones." A fond smile touched her lips.

He was about to ask if she had kids of her own, but stopped when that smile flickered out and the corners of her mouth turned down.

Briskly, she said, "I need to talk to the carpool mom. I'll leave you in Karen's capable hands." She handed Smoke Trail's reins to Jamal and headed over to greet the stocky brunette who had exited the driver's side.

Jamal turned back to Karen. "What now?"

"Mount up. Reins in the left hand, grip here and here, left foot in the stirrup, and swing the right leg over." As she spoke, she demonstrated. Quick and agile, she made it look easy.

He clambered aboard with less grace. As he settled into the heavy leather saddle, something tugged on the bottom of his jeans leg. "Mister," a piping female voice said, "you're supposed to wear boots." A pint-sized blonde frowned up at him.

"I don't have boots," he told her.

The frown turned to a scowl. "Real cowboys wear boots," she announced, then stalked back to the other kids and the horses.

To Karen, he said, "I guess that puts me in my place."

"That's okay." Her eyes, more gold than brown in the sunlight, danced. "I still like you."

The two horses set out, walking side by side across the

barnyard, then onto a dirt road. The animals strode along like they were happy to be outside on a sunny June day, getting some exercise. Their mood was contagious. Particularly when he glanced to his left and saw Karen, her lithe body swaying gently with her horse's movements. Beside her, her well-trained dog kept pace, nose raised to scent the air.

The road ran along the side of the Ryland property. "There's a network of roads and trails going for miles," Karen said. "Many of the locals give public access to portions of their spreads."

"That's generous. But I have to wonder, why aren't some of those generous people helping out Sally? She looks worn out and her place could use some work."

Karen turned concerned eyes on him. "I ask her and she assures me everything's fine. She's proud, a bit of a loner."

Hard to criticize someone for that, since he was the same way. "Any kids?"

She shook her head. "She and her husband put a lot of work into getting Ryland Riding going. She loves kids and I'm sure they planned to have them, but then he died. He wasn't much more than thirty. The poor guy had a serious heart condition that no one knew about. One day he had a massive heart attack and that was it."

"Doesn't seem right." He and Jake had worked undercover for almost ten years and except for an occasional bullet hole or knife wound, they'd survived just fine.

He and Karen rode in silence for a while. This had a lot going for it, compared to city streets. The scenery was spectacular yet peaceful: rolling grassland, low hills, patches of trees, and wild rosebushes in bloom. Birds sang from fence posts; squirrels chattered in tree branches. Occasionally they passed someone else, either on horseback on the trail or out working on their ranches. Friendly words were exchanged, which was kind of nice compared to a city full of strangers. Tennison ranged more freely now, but stayed within sight and responded immediately when Karen called.

It was all pretty impressive, but best was the sight of Karen in her well-worn jeans, flannel shirt, cowboy boots, and Stetson, graceful and at home on her horse's back.

A dedicated, skilled cop; a sexy, surprising lover; a natural horsewoman. He had the feeling that anything Karen chose to do, she did well. She'd be a great mom, raising responsible kids who would also know how to have fun. To play and picnic; to ride and maybe shoot hoops.

Could he see himself fitting into her life here? Hell, he'd blended into the roughest gangs and he'd once infiltrated an evangelical church to prove that the leader was a pedophile. Despite the little blond girl's censure over his footwear, he could fit in in the country. If he wanted to.

"How are you liking it?" Karen's voice drew him from his thoughts.

"Not bad, but do these horses have only one speed?"

"I've been taking it easy on you, letting you adjust."

"Adjust to a horse walking? Oh yeah, big challenge."

"All right, tough guy, we'll kick it up to a trot and then try a lope. Plant your butt deep in the saddle, keep your back straight, heels down in the stirrups—which is one reason for wearing boots. Don't be afraid to grab on to the horn or the cantle." She patted the back part of her saddle.

"Got it."

Her horse sped up, with his following along. The first gait, the trot, was a bone shaker, but he kept his balance without grabbing on to the saddle. Then, when the horses loped, he quickly caught on to Smoke Trail's rocking motion.

Karen tossed him a smile. "Okay?"

"Okay!" Though they weren't going all that fast, it was exciting. In its own way, even more exciting than riding a motorbike. It was more primitive and raw, just man and beast. He smothered a chuckle. Here he was, going all Wild West. Next thing he knew, he'd be buying cowboy boots.

As the horses ran side by side through a patch of sparse trees, Karen said, "We need to pull up because this trail crosses another up ahead." She called, "Tennison! Come!"

The horses slowed, heads tossing as if to make it clear they weren't happy about it, until they were walking again. The dog bounded up and fell in beside them. Ahead, through the final few trees, Jamal saw another country road with a parade of maybe ten riders approaching. "Man, it's a crowd." These were adults, not kids, and they all wore riding helmets except for the leader, a pretty woman with glossy chestnut hair pulled back in a ponytail, riding a near-white horse.

"That's the group from Riders Boot Camp, coming back from their Saturday trail ride."

"Another riding school?"

"An intensive residential one. Students sign up for one or two weeks, and come from all over Canada and the States. Whereas Sally gives lessons to local kids and adults."

On reaching the spot where the roads intersected, Karen stopped Montana. Smoke Trail and Tennison halted on either side.

The ponytailed woman stopped her group too. Moving her horse a few paces ahead of them, she said, "Hey, Karen. Who's your friend?" Her gaze rested on Jamal with open curiosity.

"Hi, Jess. Jessica Kincaid, meet Jamal Estevez. Jamal, Jess is the owner of Riders Boot Camp and she's also Brooke's daughter-in-law. Jess, Jamal is—"

"You're Cousin Arnold's—I mean Corporal Brannon's—RCMP colleague," Jess finished. Her eyes sparkled. "You're in Caribou Crossing tidying up details on the Miller arrest?"

He glanced at Karen, looking for a cue. Did she worry about people gossiping?

"No," she said, "this is purely a social visit."

"Nice." A smile widened on Jess's face. "Very nice. I hope you have a wonderful time, Jamal."

"So far, so good."

"Karen, you gonna bring him to the Wild Rose tomorrow night?" Her smile tilted into a grin.

Karen grinned back. "I'll do my best."

"See you then." Jess waved them on, to proceed ahead of her group.

When they were out of earshot, Jamal asked, "What's at the Wild Rose tomorrow?"

"Line dancing."

He winced. "Did I mention, I think I'm coming down with the flu?"

"Ha ha." She slanted him a seductive gaze from under the brim of her hat. "There'll be slow dancing too."

"Hmm."

"Slow dancing can be a lot like foreplay, don't you think?"

He threw back his head and laughed. "Okay, you win."

She grinned. "I like a man who can admit when he's wrong." Then the smile faded and she gazed at him with an expression he couldn't read.

Next thing he knew, she'd stopped Montana. When Smoke Trail halted too, Karen shifted her horse closer so that her leg brushed Jamal's. "I like you, Jamal." She leaned toward him in a clear invitation to kiss.

He stretched over to meet her lips with his. The kiss went deep, fast. His body's response was fast too, tightening, swelling.

Smoke Trail moved restlessly, jarring them apart.

"Have mercy, Karen. A Western saddle's not designed to accommodate a hard-on."

She gave him a saucy, pleased look, then got their horses going again. How did she do that, with no obvious signals?

Riding clearly took skill. And, as he was learning, strong thigh muscles. His own, which had no problem running ten miles, felt a little sore.

"So that was Brooke's daughter-in-law," he said.

"As of a year ago. Brooke acquired a granddaughter, and now Jess is pregnant again. Hard to believe Brooke's a grandma, isn't it?"

"Yeah, she's so young and pretty." And she'd survived an amazing amount of shit—bipolar disorder and alcoholism—and come out strong.

"She and Jake seemed pretty close," Karen mused. "And yet she said they agreed it was just short term."

"Yeah. He's a loner."

"Just like you were," she pointed out.

"You know how you said your mom's life changed in five minutes? Well, that night you and I stayed up talking, you got me thinking. Seeing possibilities. Jake's not thinking that way."

"Then Brooke's better off without him," she said sadly. "It just seemed like they really cared about each other." She shook her head bemusedly. "Listen to me. I'm turning into a romantic." She shot him a wink. "Words guaranteed to scare off any guy, right?"

"I don't scare easy, Corporal MacLean."

The only thing that terrified him was how she'd react if she ever found out his guilty secret.

But she wouldn't. Only he and Jake knew what had happened on that assignment two years ago. Jake would never tell anyone. It was the past, and it would remain dead and buried. It had nothing to do with Jamal's relationship with Karen. She was his fresh start.

As Jamal and Karen left the dance floor at the Wild Rose pub, he, breathing hard, said, "Does this prove I'd do anything for you?" He still had trouble believing she'd talked him into line dancing.

Not appearing the least bit winded, she said, "Oh come on, you love it. And you're good at it."

"You said there'd be slow songs. Foreplay songs."

"We've had a couple. They'll play another one soon."

"No dancing with anyone else this time," he warned. For one number, she'd wanted to swap partners with Brooke and a sandy-haired guy a few years younger than him. Brooke looked particularly pretty, almost glowing, and a secretive smile played around her lips. She didn't ask about Jake. Maybe she'd already moved on. Jake was a dickhead, letting her get away.

"Deal." Karen bumped her shoulder against his. "I need to hit the ladies' room. Get me a beer?"

"Sure."

He watched her walk across the room, exchanging greetings as she went. At least forty people crowded the Western-style pub, many still dancing, most clearly regulars. A white-haired couple, Jimmy B and his wife, Bets, were the line dance instructors. They'd kept the group hopping— and Jamal's feet tangled up—for much of the last hour.

As he headed toward the bar, he was aware of being the only guy in the room who wasn't wearing boots and a Western shirt. His jeans fit in fine, but his tee and Nikes made him stand out. Not that there was any chance of him blending in here, not with everyone knowing everyone. And each one as curious as hell about his relationship with Karen.

A couple of men watched him approach the bar. Karen had introduced him to one of them already: Evan Kincaid, Brooke's son, who was there with his wife, Jess. The other was the swap-partners guy.

Evan introduced the two men. "This is Dave Cousins, the owner of the Wild Rose. Dave, Jamal Estevez."

So this was the friend Karen shared dinner and movies

with. Tall and fit, he was good-looking in an all-Canadian-
guy kind of way. Karen had said there were no sparks
between them, yet she'd wanted to dance with this guy and
they'd looked pretty comfortable in each other's arms.

Dave's gaze wasn't exactly unfriendly, but it was definitely assessing. "Came up to see Karen?"

"I did."

"She's a terrific woman." There was a warning note in
his voice. Maybe a hint of possessiveness or jealousy?

"I know she is."

"She's done a lot of good for this community," Dave
went on. "We'd hate to lose her."

Or did he mean *he'd* hate to lose her? Jamal felt a jealous
twinge of his own. What, exactly, was Karen's relationship
with this man?

"On the other hand," Evan said lightly, "Caribou Crossing could use another good cop."

Jamal figured this wasn't the time to explain why he and
Karen couldn't work together here.

The female bartender, a slender, attractive young Native
Canadian woman with a rippling sheet of black hair, came
their way. "What can I get you?"

"A bottle of Caribou Crossing Pale Ale for me, Madisun,"
Evan said, "and a ginger ale for my pregnant wife."

She served up the ginger ale in a tall glass with ice,
handed Evan a beer bottle, and gave another beer to Dave.
Those lightly sweating brown bottles looked so damned
good, Jamal's breath quickened with need. He intended to
order a beer for Karen and a tomato juice for himself, but
somehow heard himself say, "Another couple of ales."

"Coming up," she said cheerfully.

Okay, no problem. He'd do his dump-and-refill trick.

The bartender handed him two bottles, and damn, they
felt good in his hands.

Dave hoisted his drink. "To Caribou Crossing."

Jamal and Evan clicked their bottles against his, and then all three men raised their bottles to their lips.

Jamal breathed in a crisp, hoppy scent. Irresistible. What difference would one sip make?

It would mean he'd failed again. Fuck, it shouldn't have to be this hard.

Muscles screaming in protest, he forced his hand to lower the bottle, the beer untasted. There. He was sober. A minute at a time. He was in control and he wasn't going to violate Karen's trust, or Jake's.

"I grew up in Caribou Crossing," Evan said.

"Oh yeah?" Big surprise. And who cared about Evan anyhow? The bottle felt so damn *right* in his hands, like an old friend. Jamal needed to dump the beer quick, before habit—or fierce craving—overcame two years of hard-won sobriety.

"To me, it was a hick town," the other man went on. "I couldn't wait to get out. I lived in New York and loved it."

"And then you came back," Dave said. He and Evan exchanged a meaningful glance that Jamal, in his distracted state, couldn't hope to read.

"It was a shock to my system," Evan said. "But I soon realized how much Caribou Crossing has going for it. It's a healthy life. Perfect if you plan to raise a family."

"Karen sure likes it here," Dave put in.

Both men gazed at him, neither hiding his curiosity.

Yeah, "Mind your own business" did not apply in Caribou Crossing.

He glanced away, across the room, and saw Karen talking to another woman. A moment later, she headed in his direction. Relieved to escape the conversation, he went to meet her. When he handed her a bottle of beer, she glanced at the bottle in his other hand. "You're drinking?"

Panic froze him in place. Had she figured out that he was an alcoholic?

"You're not worried about feeling sick?" she went on.

Relief whooshed through him, along with annoyance at himself. He *never* forgot a cover story. But tonight the craving for a drink had made him forget what he'd told her. He cleared his throat. "Damn, that was stupid. Habit. Yeah, I'd better not. Want mine?"

She shook her head. "I'm a lightweight. Besides, the last thing I want is for the community to think I'm a drinker. That was something I hated about Sergeant Miller. The way he'd hold down the bar, be such a poor role model."

"Yeah. Right. I'll go dump this out."

"And then we can slow dance," she purred. "A little foreplay, but not too much. I don't want you destroying my reputation."

He forced himself to joke back, "Babe, I'll do wonders for your reputation."

Unless Caribou Crossing ever found out the truth about him.

Chapter Eight

On Thursday afternoon, Karen took a break to meet Brooke for coffee. Or, rather, peppermint tea for Brooke and a tall iced mocha with whipped cream and chocolate syrup for Karen. Thanks to her metabolism and her active life, she never worried about calories.

Sitting across from the blonde in the Gold Rush Coffee Shop, Karen thought how good Brooke looked. In the first weeks after Jake left town, she had seemed subdued. Later, she'd acted anxious and been absentminded. Recently, something had changed again, for the better. The glow on Brooke's cheeks and the sparkle in her lovely blue-green eyes owed nothing to make-up.

"You look fantastic," Karen said. "You haven't by chance heard from Jake?" She took a long sip of the rich, delicious icy mocha.

Those glowing cheeks flushed. "Karen, let it go. Jake is, will always be, a wonderful part of my life." Her eyes warmed with an emotion that looked an awful lot like love. "He's an amazing, good-hearted man, but we're too different to have a future together. I'm fine with that. Totally. The kind of work he does"—her face sobered and she shivered—"I couldn't live with it."

"What if he gave it up?"

Something flared in her friend's eyes. Hope? It was gone in an instant. Brooke smiled gently and shook her head. "I would never ask that of him." She lifted her mug of steaming tea and the scent of mint drifted across the table.

Brooke wasn't as pushy as Karen. No, she'd never ask. But Jake could choose to change his career.

"Even if he had a job like yours," Brooke said, "it would be too much for me."

"I know it's hard being in a relationship with a cop," Karen admitted. Her friend had been through a lot: an abusive ex, ten years of estrangement from her son, dealing with bipolar disorder, getting and staying sober. Brooke had become a strong woman, but a strong woman knew her limitations and didn't set herself up for failure.

"That's one of the great things about you and Jamal, that you understand each other's work." Brooke put her mug down. Studying its contents, she said, "You both looked like you were having fun on Sunday."

Karen wiped her napkin across her upper lip to get rid of her whipped-cream-and-chocolate mustache. "We had a fantastic weekend. I'm trying to turn him into a fan of Caribou Crossing. The scenery, riding, line dancing."

Brooke moistened her lips. "Even our local brew."

"Hmm?"

The blonde glanced at Karen. "You introduced him to Caribou Crossing beer."

"Oh, right." She chuckled, remembering. "Poor Jamal. He ended up chucking his out."

"Oh? What a waste."

"He says alcohol hasn't been agreeing with him lately. I told him he may have developed an allergy, and he should see a doctor."

"Oh?" Brooke said again. Tiny muscles between her

eyebrows pulled together slightly. If Karen hadn't been gazing straight into her face, she'd have missed it.

Body language often spoke more loudly and accurately than words, but she couldn't read this small, probably involuntary, message. "Brooke? What's on your mind? Is it hard for you, talking about beer when you don't drink anymore?"

"No, it's not—" She broke off, glanced away, picked up her mug again. Staring into it, she said, "Well, maybe a little." Her voice sounded strained, and then it hardened as she went on. "I remember what it felt like holding a chilled bottle. Raising it to my lips." She swallowed. "It's a hard thing to beat, addiction."

"But you've done it." Karen studied her with concern. "Almost five years, right?"

Brooke's tense expression softened. "Right." A smile, a rather secretive one, touched her lips. "There's no danger I'm going to drink again." Then that tiny frown returned. "I really need to get back."

"So soon?"

They exchanged good-byes and Brooke left, her mug of tea still half full.

Odd. Odd behavior following an odd conversation. Brooke's explanation rang true but instinct told Karen there was something more, something troubling, on her friend's mind. If she was uncomfortable thinking about people drinking, why had she even raised the subject of seeing Karen and Jamal with bottles of beer?

Karen sipped her own drink, barely tasting it as she let random thoughts drift through her mind.

Brooke was an alcoholic yet she was fine with Jake drinking in front of her.

When Karen had brought nonalcoholic bubbly to their celebration party, Brooke had mentioned to Jamal that it was nonalcoholic.

Karen had never seen Jamal drink alcohol.

Alcoholics kept each other's secret.

Undercover cops were subjected to a lot of temptation. Drugs, booze, prostitutes, gambling. Jamal had said that drinking could get to be a bad habit—

No! Karen pressed both hands firmly against the table, rejecting that train of thought. Jamal had meant that he avoided drinking so it *couldn't* become a bad habit. He was a good cop. And he wouldn't keep this kind of secret from her. She trusted him.

Karen left the detachment just after seven on Friday evening. She stopped at the Japanese restaurant to pick up Caribou rainbow sushi—a local specialty using rainbow trout—and ate it as she walked to a meeting of the board of directors of the women's shelter.

During the board discussion, she tried to concentrate but anticipation filled her with a happy buzz. Tonight she'd see Jamal. This week he'd been back at his desk in Vancouver, working regular hours. Preferring to have his own wheels, he'd decided to make the six-hour drive rather than fly. He'd get in around midnight.

That meant it didn't matter how long the meeting lasted. Still, she fidgeted, impatient with the others' inefficiency— particularly that of the President who was chairing the meeting. Volunteering was great, but people should volunteer for jobs where they had some actual competence. She could do more on her own than it took this five-person board to accomplish in twice as long, but if she tried to take over and run the meeting, the others would be offended.

Was she being judgmental again? A high school girl-friend had teased her that all would be well if the world would only appoint Karen as Queen of the Universe, so she could whip everyone else into shape. Although Karen had given the obligatory "Ha ha," privately she'd thought it wouldn't be a bad idea.

When the meeting finally ended, Karen drove home, took a leisurely shower, and slipped into new lingerie—a cami and shorts set. Used to wearing a uniform or practical casual clothes, she admired her reflection in the bathroom mirror and luxuriated in the silky slide of the rose-pink fabric against her lotioned skin. So much for the guys who looked at her uniform and wrote her off as butch. Jamal had the sense to see, and admire, all sides of her.

As she did with him, she thought when the rumble of an engine sounded outside. Peering out the front window, she grinned. It figured that Jamal's "wheels" were on a motorcycle. A big black BMW built for speed, endurance, and style. Just like the man who climbed off it, dressed in a gray tee, jeans, and black boots.

Aware of her skimpy outfit and the proximity of neighbors on this warm summer night, she didn't rush down the steps but opened the door and stood back.

He took a small duffel from a pannier and sauntered toward her. A white grin widened on his dark face as he came up the steps. "Look at you," he said in that rich molasses voice.

"It was a toss-up between this and my gun belt and handcuffs," she joked.

As he bent to put down his bag and take off his boots, he said, "It's only civilians who like to play with handcuffs." He reached out and big hands framed her face, holding her steady.

Well, not so steady, because her breath caught and her pulse jerked. "That's true."

"Cops have to find other forms of kink."

Such as? The thought evaporated as his lips met hers. The kiss was the sensual equivalent of his saunter, lazy and confident as his lips caressed hers and his tongue slid into her mouth. She sighed with pleasure. Waiting to see him had been tough, but now he was here, hers for the next couple of days. They had time. Time for lots of sex, lots of talk, lots of getting to know each other better.

When she could talk again, she said, "I'm glad you're here."

"Me too."

"Did you stop for dinner? Are you hungry?"

"Grabbed a snack on the way. It's you I'm hungry for. Is it rude to show up and want to go straight to bed?"

"Not when I feel the same way." She took his hand and they headed for the bedroom.

She'd never been into fancy décor or girly touches. Yet this week she'd bought candles and now she lit them. Jamal had stirred up new instincts. He'd also revived her long-held dream of creating a home like the one she'd grown up in.

And right now he made her long for spectacular, intimate lovemaking.

He glanced around the room, then said, "I need a quick shower."

"What? I thought you had sex on your mind."

"Oh yeah. But look at this. The candles, you in that sexy outfit. I've been working, riding, haven't seen a shower since dawn."

Before she could say she'd gladly take him now, sweat and all, he'd grabbed his duffel and headed into the bathroom. Last weekend they'd showered together, but tonight the closed door told her she wasn't invited. When the shower came on, she went to the kitchen and poured a glass of orange juice. He'd likely be thirsty after the long ride.

She'd just set the glass on the bedside table when the bathroom door opened and Jamal stepped through. Naked. And already semiaroused. Candlelight burnished his dark skin and glinted off drops of water that his hasty toweling hadn't caught. Behind him, lemon-scented steam puffed out the bathroom door.

"Okay, maybe the shower was worth the wait," she said appreciatively.

"Figure a woman who looks like you at least deserves clean." When he kissed her, she discovered that he'd brushed his teeth and tasted of peppermint.

She explored his mouth thoroughly, then teased, "Hmm. One big peppermint patty. Do I get to nibble?"

"As long as you watch where you sink those teeth."

"Maybe I'll satisfy myself with licking. Makes the treat last longer."

"Or not," he muttered as she suited action to words and leaned forward to lap a drip from the base of his throat. She followed a trail of droplets down the indentation between his firm pecs. His chest was smooth, almost hairless, under her exploring lips and tongue. She teased his nipples and gave them gentle nips.

Their first few times together, she'd made it clear that sometimes she wanted to be in charge, and he'd better not argue. She'd told him it was a turn-on for her to enjoy his fine body and to arouse him. Now her nipples tightened to buds and her sex throbbed with the heavy pulse of lust.

Lowering herself to her knees, she kissed her way down his six-pack. His erection rose out of a nest of wiry black curls, straight up his belly to his navel. She brushed her breast against his shaft, feeding a tingly ache in her nipple and making him moan.

His hands gripped her shoulders and he widened his stance. She guessed his legs were a little shaky. Her big tough cop, rendered weak by her seductive caresses.

She licked up and down his shaft, moistening it with saliva until it gleamed, then grasped it in one hand and slid the head between her lips. One arm went around him to squeeze his firm butt and the other hand slipped down to fondle his balls.

His fingers dug more tightly into her shoulders and his voice rumbled as he said, "The treat's gonna explode if you do that much longer."

Tonight, she wanted him deep inside her. So she let him slide free of her mouth. "It's tough being with a rookie who has no staying power."

He chuckled and released her shoulders. "Then you'll need to train me better, because you're sure as hell not trading me in for another partner."

"You got that right." She rose and wrapped her arms around him, trapping his erection between them.

He kissed her long and hard, his tongue thrusting in and out to mimic sex. Then he reached down and peeled the cami over her head. Leaving the brief shorts on, he led her over to the bed and laid her down.

In leisurely fashion, he kissed the spot where her neck met her shoulder, the scar on her arm from where she'd fallen out of a tree as a kid, the triangle of freckles on her tummy, the puckered flesh where the knife had slashed her. Each sensual touch heightened her arousal until she squirmed with needy pleasure. Finally, he moved to her breast, toying with her nipple until a slow, rippling climax shuddered through her.

He worked his way down again, peeling off her shorts in the process. Putting his mouth to her center, he licked across folds that were already slick. Gently he worked two fingers into her and her sheath gripped them, clung, until he started to tease her—sliding his fingers in and out, circling them inside her, using one to tap her sweet spot. Out, in, circle, tap, and repeat. The pattern sent sensual charges darting through her. And when his thumb firmly pressed her clit, another climax, this one sharper, more powerful, jolted her.

She was still riding the lovely waves when he sheathed himself and entered her.

Sighing, stretching, she said, "You're so good at this."

"Takes the right inspiration." He stroked her cheek, smoothed back sweat-dampened hair. "Takes being with someone who's special," he added, his voice soft and a little rough.

Oh God, she was falling for this man. Fast and hard. It was early, their relationship still so young, issues yet to be worked out, but this felt so right. So inevitable.

"Rumor has it," he said, "that you like riding." Before she could answer, he'd rolled their interlocked bodies so she was on top.

Accepting the invitation, she pushed herself up to crouch astride him. Reaching up to pull her hair back from her face, she thrust her breasts out proudly.

And that was an invitation he accepted, cupping them as she glided up and down.

Sex, yes. Great sex. But so much more. As she gazed down at Jamal's intent face, his dark eyes watching her with what looked like wonder, she knew that this was so much more.

Early Saturday evening, chopping a cucumber in her kitchen, Karen paused to enjoy the sight of Jamal. His fine body was nicely displayed by cargo shorts and a tee with the sleeves ripped out; his muscles flexed as he sliced a purple onion.

End-of-the day sunshine slanted through the window and CXNG played Tammy Wynette's "Stand by Your Man." From the oven came the tantalizing scent of Greek chicken casserole.

Jamal tossed the slivers of onion into the salad bowl. "Something wrong with the cucumber?"

She shook her head and returned to her task. "Just admiring the view."

"Can't complain about the view from here either." He winked.

She wasn't wearing anything special, just a blue tank top over tan shorts, and that made the compliment even more special. Real life wasn't all about cute sundresses and sexy lingerie; it was mostly T-shirts and jeans and practicality. She liked that it didn't take fancy trappings for the two of them to feel the attraction.

"Any sore muscles after this afternoon's ride?" She'd taken him farther this time, and they'd loped and galloped more.

"Not that I'll admit to. But if we're going to keep doing this, I need my own cowboy boots."

"The ones I borrowed from Dave are his old ones. He said no rush getting them back."

"Isn't that nice of him?" There was a snide tone in his voice that she hadn't heard before. Could he be jealous?

"I told you Dave's just a friend, right?"

"That's what you said."

If he was jealous, would she be amused, flattered, or pissed off? She'd never been in that position before. Deciding to leave it alone, she took the feta cheese from the fridge and crumbled it into chunks.

The Greek salad was finished just as the oven timer went off.

Karen took the ceramic casserole dish from the oven. She turned the heat way down and slipped in the loaf of Italian bread they'd bought from the bakery. "What would you like to drink? Oh, did you see the doctor about the alcohol problem? Is it an allergy?"

"Uh . . ." He opened the fridge and seemed absorbed in studying the contents. "You want a beer? Or some of that white wine?"

"White wine. Thanks." She studied his back. Wasn't he going to answer her question? Likely he was the type of guy who avoided doctors unless he was pretty much dying.

He pulled out the wine bottle, along with a can of Coke, then opened the wine and poured her a glass.

She took the bread from the oven and she and Jamal sat down at the table. "You didn't tell me if you saw the doctor."

"Oh, right. It's not an allergy, just, uh, an intolerance thing. It's best if I avoid alcohol."

"Too bad, but I'm glad it's nothing serious."

"Yeah." He didn't look so happy himself.

"Would you rather I didn't drink when—"

"No." He shook his head. "Have whatever you want. It's no big deal."

He'd tell her if it was. She trusted him.

"Try the chicken and tell me what you think." She was a little nervous since it was the first time she'd cooked a real meal for him. When they'd shopped for groceries, she'd given him his choice of steak on the barbecue—as they'd done last weekend—or her Greek chicken dish. His choice of the casserole had surprised her. Catching her expression, he'd teased that she shouldn't stereotype him.

It was true that in the beginning she'd seen him as a dark and dangerous, rather mysterious, undercover cop. But she was long past that now. He was Jamal. A man who was undoubtedly strong but who could also be tender. A man with a teasing sense of humor. A man who drank Coke rather than beer.

"Tastes great," he said after his first bite. "When I saw you put this together, I wondered how it'd come out. The cinnamon works."

"Thanks." She forked up a mouthful for herself. The casserole had chicken, onions, feta cheese, tomatoes, and black olives, and the main seasonings were oregano and cinnamon. It tasted good the first night and it made excellent leftovers. Not that, given the enthusiasm with which Jamal devoured it, there were likely to be leftovers this time.

If they did get together and start a family, they'd need a bigger casserole dish.

Off and on today, they had played an "I see" game. As in, "In my dream of the future, I see . . ." By making it a game, they could say things without pressure. They could each float their ideas and see how well they matched up.

Now she said, "I see a house with a big kitchen. A wooden table with plenty of room to lay out a hearty dinner for four. And after dinner, the kids wouldn't go to their rooms to do homework. They'd work at the table, with their computers and books spread out."

A smile had grown on his face as she spoke. "Man, that sounds nice. That how you did it at your house?"

"Yes. Though I admit, when I hit my teens I craved the privacy of my bedroom."

"To gossip with your girlfriends about boys?"

"A bit. But I was a pretty serious kid. I was more involved in activities like organizing an antibullying club and lobbying the school board to provide more assistants for special-needs kids. I didn't hang out with the kids who just wanted to have fun."

"High standards even back then."

"I expected more of myself than of anyone else," she defended herself.

"Not saying there's anything wrong with high standards." He offered her the salad bowl and held it while she scooped out seconds; then he dished the rest onto his own plate.

Gazing at Jamal across the table, Karen felt a deep certainty that this was right. The two of them had a lot of things to work out and they needed time to explore and develop their relationship, but her heart told her they were perfect for each other.

Chapter Nine

Jamal would have liked to spend Sunday morning lazing in bed—okay, making love—with Karen. But as acting commander, she wanted to go into the detachment for a few hours and he respected that. He used the time to cruise the countryside on his bike, eying it as a possible future home.

Different. So different from Chicago, Toronto, Winnipeg, Vancouver, and all the places where he'd done undercover work. So open, so clean, so fresh. Here, he felt like a cleaner, better version of himself.

Yeah, he could see it.

Maybe here the craving for alcohol wouldn't be so strong.

He rode back to Karen's to meet her for a late lunch; she was taking the afternoon off. Later in the day he'd ride back to Vancouver and catch some sleep before showing up at work Monday morning.

Working easily together in her kitchen, debating the merits of French's mustard (him) versus Dijon (her), they put together ham and Swiss cheese sandwiches. They took lunch out to the front porch and sat side by side on webbed folding chairs. Tennison tried to beg for scraps, but Karen banished her to the backyard.

Jamal stretched, thinking how rare it was to feel so relaxed. "This is nice."

"My place is pathetic compared to Brooke's."

The view was of a scrub grass yard, a wire fence, a street, and a virtually identical house across the way. He shrugged.

She went on. "I see in my future a proper house with proper porch furniture and a proper yard. How about you?"

Their "I see" game was fun. A low-pressure way of sharing visions. This time he gave a mock groan. "I see a lot of lawn mowing in my future."

She leaned over to bump her shoulder against his. "Got anything better to do with your spare time?"

He bumped back. "Sex."

"Get a place that's private enough, there could be sex in the garden," she bargained.

They were both chuckling when a battered Honda Civic parked across the street. A middle-aged woman and man climbed out of the front as an adolescent boy and girl erupted from the back and tore into the house. All wore nice clothes.

"Church, then Sunday lunch with her parents," Karen murmured. As the other woman gazed in their direction, Karen waved and called, "Hi, Janet, Harry. Lovely day, isn't it?"

"Hi, Karen," the woman called. "Yes, just beautiful. You and your boyfriend make the most of it. You work too hard, girl." She and her husband headed toward the house.

Yeah, Caribou Crossing had labeled Jamal as Karen MacLean's boyfriend. After all his years as a loner, it felt weird but also made him damned proud.

Inside her open front door, the landline rang.

She groaned as she rose. "Please tell me that's not a work emergency."

A moment later, she came out with the phone in her hand. "It's Jake, for you."

Jake? Yeah, his buddy had known Jamal would be here with Karen this weekend, but why would he call on a Sunday? And why not on Jamal's cell?

Jamal took the phone. "Hey, Jake."

"Hey. Guess what?" There was a weird, exhilarated note in Jake's voice, like he had great news he was bursting to tell.

Were he and Brooke back together? Wary about asking, Jamal instead said, "No idea."

"I'm in Caribou Crossing."

Jamal grinned. There was only one reason Jake would be here *and* sound happy. "Visiting a certain blonde?"

Karen's eyebrows shot up, her face lighting with curiosity and excitement.

"Yeah, visiting." A pause, and then, "And getting engaged!"

"Engaged?!" The word burst out of Jamal, so loud it would've woken any neighbors having a Sunday nap.

"Engaged?" Karen cried. "They're engaged?"

"Shh, let me listen."

Jake said, "I rode up yesterday and told her I'd been an asshole—"

"Like she didn't already know." Jamal put his arm around Karen, who squatted down by his chair so she could listen too.

"Yeah, yeah. Anyhow, she forgave me because she's"— Jake paused and Jamal heard Brooke's teasing voice in the background saying "a bighearted, generous, wonderful woman." Jake said, apparently to Brooke, "Which was exactly what I was going to say." And then, speaking into the phone again, "You heard all of that?"

"We got it," Jamal said.

Karen whooped, the sound ringing in Jamal's ear. "I'm so happy for you guys."

"Yeah, man," Jamal said. "Me too."

Karen grabbed the phone and spoke into it. "Jake, I want to talk to Brooke."

"Hang on a sec," Jamal heard him say. "There's something I want to ask you, Karen." The rest was lost as she straightened, the phone to her ear.

Jamal sat back, smiling. Jake and Brooke. That felt right. As right as him and the pretty woman who listened intently to whatever his buddy was saying. She started nodding, clearly impatient for Jake to finish.

Then she said, "Yes! I think that's a great idea. We work really well together. You're just what the detachment needs."

Hah. So Jake was going to apply for Miller's job.

If Jamal got that staff sergeant job in Williams Lake, they'd all live in the same neck of the woods. Hell, they could have Sunday night barbecues and go line dancing together.

He and Jake had come one hell of a long way from that dive bar in Winnipeg. And damn it felt good.

On Wednesday evening, heavy thumping on Jamal's apartment door in Vancouver cut through the noise of the basketball game on TV. Muttering a curse, he was ready to ream out whichever drunk had stumbled his way to the wrong apartment.

Through the peephole, he saw Jake.

He swung open the door. "How'd you get into the building?" The question was rhetorical; all Jake would've had to do was flash his badge. The real question was, why hadn't he buzzed from the ground floor? Or called first?

Jake got right up in his face. The man who'd been wearing a goofy grin since he came back from getting engaged now looked as pissed off as Jamal had ever seen him. What the hell was going on?

Harshly, Jake said, "You haven't told Karen you're an alcoholic."

Oh. Jamal's mouth formed the word but no sound came out. Then he blustered, "What makes you say that?"

"Brooke figured it out. Brooke knows about you."

He'd guessed that, but still . . . "Fuck. You said you wouldn't tell anyone."

"I didn't. She guessed."

Fear suddenly lanced through Jamal. "What did she say to Karen?"

"She didn't tell her you're an alcoholic. But she mentioned to Karen that she saw you with a beer—"

"What?" Then he recalled the night he'd ordered a beer but dumped it out. "I didn't drink it."

Jake gave him a long, slitty-eyed look, then said grudgingly, "I figured. Karen told Brooke that you said alcohol hadn't been agreeing with you and you might be allergic."

"Well it's not like she was going to tell Brooke I'm an alcoholic," he hedged.

His buddy knew him too well to fall for that. "You didn't tell Karen."

Jamal flicked the remote, shutting down the basketball game. "Okay, fine, I didn't tell her I'm an alcoholic. Why should I?" he defended himself. "I said alcohol didn't agree with me and it was best if I avoided it. That's true, damn it. My drinking's in the past. It's not gonna happen again. She doesn't need to know I had a problem."

"*Have* a problem. Alcoholism doesn't go away. Don't tell me you don't still crave a drink."

"But I don't give in." Did Jake think he was still that guy who let booze control him? "Look at Brooke. You don't think she's going to drink again, right?"

"No, but it's been five years and she's stronger and smarter than you."

"Ouch." That hurt. Because it was true, which Jamal

hated. Always, until his battle with alcohol, he'd prided himself on being the toughest. He gazed steadily at his long-time buddy. "Look, I know what my drinking resulted in." Though dragging the words out hurt like a son of a bitch, he forced them from his mouth. "I screwed up on the job. I got you shot. I won't drink again." He swallowed against the barbed wire in his throat. "Karen's a good cop with high standards. If she knew what I did, she'd write me off."

Jake's accusing glare had softened as Jamal spoke. "I hear you. But what are you gonna tell her when you go to meetings? Make up some excuse? I may not know much about relationships, but I'm pretty sure that lies get in the way."

Jamal swallowed again.

Jake's eyes widened in disbelief. "You're not planning to go to meetings?"

"Small town. Eyes everywhere."

"And alcoholics keep each other's secret."

"As long as they're sober. Someone slips off the wagon, they can get loose lips. Don't need that happening if I get that staff sergeant job in Williams Lake."

Jake shook his head. "I don't buy that. When you were undercover, I got why you wanted to keep it a secret. But if you're a staff sergeant and you're sober, the RCMP will support you. It won't cost you the promotion."

"It'll cost me credibility. Respect. Don't need people knowing I couldn't keep my shit together." Under his breath, he muttered, "Don't want to lose Karen's respect."

Jake glared at him. "You're rapidly losing mine."

That cut deep, and it was damned unfair. "Look, I don't need to go to meetings. I've only been to a couple in the past few months." He hated standing up in those meetings as a self-confessed failure. "All that God, higher power, spirituality stuff rubs me wrong."

"I'm not so big on that myself," Jake admitted. "But you

can get past that and focus on the message behind it. What does your sponsor say?"

Jamal shrugged. His sponsor was into touchy-feely stuff like confessing your weaknesses and putting your faith in some higher power. It sucked. Jamal had always handled shit on his own. "We didn't get along."

"Then you need a new sponsor," he said uncompromisingly.

"I don't. I'm handling it." And hoping that one day it would get easier.

"Like hell you are," Jake said heatedly. "There's a woman you care about, and you're disrespecting her. What kind of future d'you think you can build on a giant lie?"

Rather than point out that he hadn't actually lied, Jamal went to the heart of the matter. "More of a future than if I tell her how badly I fucked up."

The expression in Jake's gray eyes was troubled. "I don't think you're giving Karen enough credit. And if you tell her and she doesn't understand, then she's not the right woman for you."

He stared at Jamal for a long moment. When Jamal didn't say anything, he strode to the door and exited the room. He didn't slam the door, but closed it with a solid thunk.

"Shit." Jamal scrubbed both hands across his face. "Shit, shit, shit."

Jake was the one person in the world who'd always had Jamal's back, who'd stood by him.

Jamal went over to the window and stared out. The sun had set and it was starting to rain. The streetlights illuminated Jake walking down the street, hands thrust in the pockets of his jeans. He appeared oblivious to the drops that hit his bare head and T-shirted shoulders.

A realization hit Jamal.

This was the man who hadn't told the RCMP that the

bullet he'd taken was due to Jamal's drunken screwup. Instead, Jake had given him a serious talking to and urged him into A.A. He'd helped him get sober. That was how he'd had Jamal's back two years ago.

Was tonight's confrontation Jake's way of standing by him now?

Chapter Ten

Saturday morning, Karen went to the detachment at dawn. Sadly, Jamal wasn't there to keep her in bed for some early morning lovemaking. Though he'd originally planned to ride his bike up on Friday evening, the way he'd done last week, he had phoned on Thursday saying something had come up and he wasn't sure when he could come. Then yesterday he'd phoned again, saying he'd ride up in the morning. Atypically, he'd been gruff and she couldn't draw him into chatting or sexy banter.

She hoped there wasn't a problem. And if there was, she was selfish enough to hope it was work related, not him having second thoughts about their relationship.

Late in the morning, Dave Cousins phoned to say that a Wild Rose Inn guest had not only given a fake credit card but skipped out with a couple of pieces of original art. She went over to take a report and dust for prints. After finishing, she poked her head into Dave's office. "I'll keep you posted on the investigation."

He lifted his hands from the keyboard and flexed his fingers. "Any chance you're free for lunch? I'm buying."

"Sounds good." Jamal wouldn't arrive for another two or three hours.

After notifying the detachment, she joined Dave in a booth in the inn's dining room. Whereas the pub was Western casual, this room was decorated like a saloon in an upscale gold-rush hotel. The décor featured glossy dark wood, leather, and gleaming brass. A waiter in 1860s garb came to greet them. "Hi, boss, Sergeant. Can I get you a drink?"

Karen ordered a Coke, Dave went for Sprite, and they both chose one of the daily specials, a field greens salad with grilled chicken and dried cranberries.

"Jamal's not in town?" Dave asked.

"He's riding up now. ETA midafternoon."

He gave a rueful half smile. "You two are getting serious. Looks like I may lose my gal pal."

The sadness in his eyes jolted her. She'd been so sure he didn't have feelings for her. "Uh, Dave, you didn't think, uh . . ."

He held up a hand, humor now warming his eyes. "No. God no, Karen. I mean, you're terrific, but . . ." He paused, and now the sadness was back, a double shot of it. "Anita's the only woman in my heart. I don't see that changing."

That was exactly what she'd thought, and it broke her heart. He'd barely found the love of his life when Anita had been diagnosed with terminal brain cancer. When she died, she took Dave's heart with her. He was still kind, generous, and hardworking, but his vibrancy, his joy in life was gone.

Hmm, Karen mused as the waiter served their salads. She knew another Caribou Crossing resident who was a lot like Dave.

She took a bite of salad and mmmed approval. "Of course I still want to be your friend. But there's someone else who could use a friend. You know Sally Ryland, who owns Ryland Riding?"

"I've met her once or twice."

"She's having trouble keeping up with the place since her husband died."

"Folks would help her. She just needs to ask."

"I know. But she's proud. Shy, I think. Isolated. Her only social contact is with the people who board horses, the riders who take lessons, and kids' parents. She's never become part of the community."

"No, she hasn't. Any idea why?"

"When she and her husband bought the place and moved here, it was their own little world. Now he's gone and she's just . . . sad. I figure it's like you and Anita and he was the love of her life. She's alone out there, lonely, busting her butt to keep the place going."

Dave eyed her skeptically. "You're not matchmaking?"

Was she? Two lonely souls who didn't believe they'd ever have another chance at love? Now that she'd found Jamal, she wanted everyone she cared about to be happy. With her and Jamal, things had moved fast. Not as fast as with her mom and dad, but really fast. It was partly due to the strength of their attraction but also because they were both ready to move to the next stage in their lives, even if Jamal hadn't initially recognized it.

If Dave and Sally ever fell for each other, it would happen with baby steps. Pressure from outside wouldn't help. "I'm not matchmaking. She could use some help and you could find a tactful way of getting it for her. And I think the two of you might enjoy each other's company." And then she changed the subject.

When Jamal climbed off his bike and walked to her front door, his expression was grim and each step looked forced, as if he'd rather be anywhere other than there.

Karen's heart clunked in her chest. Oh God, what had gone wrong? Had he found out that he couldn't get the job in Williams Lake? Or had he changed his mind about her? About them? About that basketball hoop?

She squared her shoulders and firmed her jaw as she stepped back from the door so he could enter. Needing to know, and know now, she said, "Are you breaking up with me?"

His lips pressed tight together, his Adam's apple rippled, but he didn't answer.

He was, and he couldn't bring himself to tell her. What had she done? What had gone wrong? And why, why had she let herself hope, let herself care?

When he did speak, his voice wasn't rich molasses this time; it sounded rusty and painful. "More likely you're going to break up with me."

She frowned. "What are you talking about?" On legs that had gone rubbery, she led the way into the living room and sat down, not on the couch but in one of the two chairs.

He paced over to the window. Facing it rather than her, he said, "I'm an alcoholic."

Slowly, those words sank in. Oh shit. Karen's lungs burned and she realized she'd forgotten to breathe. She sucked in air, shallow breaths through her mouth. Finally able to speak, though it was to his back rather than to his face, she said accusingly, "You said you had alcohol intolerance."

"Yeah." He turned slowly but didn't come toward her. "I've been sober for two years. I'm not gonna drink again."

"And I'm supposed to believe that?" If that was true, why had he lied to her?

"Yeah, you are." He dragged a hand through his hair with fingers that shook. "I have a really good reason for staying sober." He swallowed. Swallowed again.

Her? Did he mean their relationship was the good reason? "What reason?" she asked, wanting to trust him but feeling betrayed.

Slowly, with obvious pain, he said, "The drinking got out of hand. When I was undercover a couple of years ago, I screwed up."

Her mouth opened. But he was a *good* cop. He wouldn't drink on the job. Would he?

"Jake took a bullet because of it." He swallowed again and stared at her, his usual larger-than-life vibe vanquished.

"Oh my God," she breathed.

"After that, I got sober. And I'll stay sober."

Heart racing so fast she could barely breathe, she managed to say, "I'm supposed to trust you? After you lied to me?"

"I didn't exactly lie. I just didn't tell you everything."

A quick surge of anger brought her to her feet. Hands on her hips, she glared at him. "You deceived me. It was a lie by omission. And now you won't even acknowledge it. Alcoholics are deceptive, Jamal. You say you're sober, yet you're still being deceptive."

"I won't do it again."

"Do what? Drink? Lie? Deceive me?" He wasn't the man she'd believed him to be. She took a breath and tried to think. Maybe he was strong enough to become sober and stay sober, which earned her respect, but she needed a man she could trust. "Why didn't you tell me before?"

He rolled his shoulders in an awkward shrug. "I hate that part of myself. Hate how I let alcohol get the best of me, how I endangered Jake's life. I didn't want you to know about that part of me."

Okay, she could kind of understand all of that, but . . . "What were you thinking? Did you never intend to tell me?"

"Uh . . ."

He hadn't. "Why did you change your mind?"

"Jake. He made me see that you can't base a relationship on a—" He broke off.

"Lie," she finished.

This time, he didn't protest that he hadn't really lied.

Now it was her turn to pace across the room as she worked this through. "You told the RCMP, right?" Deceiving her was bad enough; concealing something so crucial from his employer would be unconscionable.

He shook his head. "Jake's the only person who knows. Well, and Brooke knows I'm an alcoholic, because she figured it out."

"No, Jamal." She shook her head, long hair flying every which way. "That's not acceptable. The RCMP has progressive policies. You're not going to be fired or demoted as long as you stay sober, go to your A.A. meetings, and—" Something in his face brought her to a stop. "You don't go to meetings?"

"I've gone to some. Lots in the beginning. But I don't need to. Do you know those Twelve Steps? It's all preachy stuff about God."

"If you're not religious, you don't have to take it literally."

He groaned. "Shit, Karen, alcoholics can stay sober without A.A."

"I know that." She went to stand in front of him, staring up into his face. "But did you *get* sober without A.A.?"

"Uh, well, no, but I could have. I was just in a bad place back then and—"

Interrupting what sounded like rationalizing, she asked, "How about now? When you hold a beer, is it easy to put it down or do you feel a strong craving to drink?"

His guilty expression told her the answer.

"It's only been two years, Jamal. Is it getting easier or is it still really hard? Do you have any kind of support? Your sponsor?"

"I don't need a sponsor." He sounded angry now. "I don't need anyone. I can do this on my own."

"Listen to yourself. Most recovering alcoholics realize

they need help and are grateful for it. But not Jamal. Oh no, he still has to be the independent tough guy." She raised her hands to cover her face. How could she have so misjudged him? How could she have trusted him? She almost never cried, but now tears threatened. Forcing them back, she struggled for control.

When she found it, she lowered her hands and again gazed into his face. "You could be a man to admire. A man who conquered alcoholism and won that battle every day."

"I *am* that man," he protested.

"Today. But maybe you're going to slip because you're too arrogant to understand that you need help staying sober. If you don't relate to A.A., then find some other kind of support group or person. Jamal, if you really are a man to admire, then stop hiding and be proud. Acknowledge who you are."

His mouth was a grim line.

"Look at Brooke," Karen said. "She's a recovering alcoholic, she has bipolar disorder, and she did some awful things in her past. Things that hurt her son, that made him leave town, leave her, for ten whole years. Now, every day, she faces the community where she was once the town drunk. She shows other people that it's possible to overcome your problems and redeem yourself."

Again, tears burned behind her eyes. She battled her emotions until she could speak without a quaver in her voice. "I respect and admire Brooke. As for you, Jamal . . ." She shook her head, sad and confused. "I don't know what I think. What I feel. I don't even know you."

His face was stony. His eyes closed for a long moment. When he opened them, they were as black and cold as death. "You once told me that people say you can be too judgmental. Maybe you ought to listen to them."

When he strode toward the door, her body ached with the

desire to run after him. Her throat burned with the need to call out. But what could she say?

She'd been well on her way to falling in love with the man she'd believed Jamal to be. But he wasn't that man, and the dreams they'd shared would never come true.

The only reason Karen answered the phone later that afternoon was because she was acting commander. It wasn't the detachment, though. Thank God, because she'd have hated to go out on a call with her face red and swollen from crying.

Brooke's voice said cautiously, "Hi, Karen. How are you?"

That tone told her something was up. "Why do you ask?" Her voice was hoarse and croaky.

A sigh, then, "Jake had a fight with Jamal this week. I wondered if Jamal came to see you this weekend."

"Came this afternoon and left shortly thereafter," she said bitterly.

"Oh, Karen, I'm so sorry. Do you want to talk?"

That sounded awfully appealing. But . . . "Jake's there, isn't he?"

"No. He had to work this weekend. Want to come over? Or I could come to you."

This impersonal half-duplex, the place where she and Jamal had broken up, versus Brooke's cozy home? "I'll be right over."

Karen splashed cold water on her face until she looked semipresentable, yanked her hair into a ponytail, and made the fifteen-minute drive to her friend's.

Brooke greeted her with a warm hug, then sat her down on the porch on a slatted-wood couch with green-and-white-striped cushions. "Tea or beer?"

"Tea, please." In her state, alcohol would hit her too hard. And she did have to drive home eventually.

When Brooke went inside, her marmalade cat came outside, jumped onto the couch, and made his way onto Karen's lap. Stroking Sunny soothed her, as did the sound of Kenny Rogers singing "The Gambler" from somewhere inside the house. Brooke too was a CXNG fan.

A few minutes later, her hostess came back with a tray. On it were a teapot, two mugs, and a plate of chocolate chip cookies, obviously homemade. She handed a mug to Karen. "Peach-ginger. It's soothing. Now tell me everything." She curled up in a cushioned rattan chair and picked up her own mug. Her engagement ring, a vibrant opal surrounded by tiny diamonds, sparked fire as she moved her hand.

How serene she looked. Brooke's happiness was hard won, but still Karen felt a little envious. She sighed and dove straight in. "You know Jamal's an alcoholic."

Brooke nodded. "He hadn't told you, had he? I guessed that, and I . . . Well, it was bothering me, so I mentioned it to Jake on the phone. I gather he went roaring over and blasted Jamal. I didn't mean to interfere, but—"

"No." Karen held up a hand. "You were looking out for me." And so was Jake. They were people she really could trust. "Jamal told me today. Before that . . ." And now she started at the beginning. Once she got going, there was a sense of release in letting the words spill free: initial attraction, meals shared, dreams spun. As she spoke, she stroked Sunny, sipped tea, and nibbled a couple of cookies.

Brooke nodded, commented occasionally, refilled their tea mugs, and reached out to touch Karen's arm a couple of times.

Karen finished with a summary of Jamal's abbreviated visit today, leaving out only what he'd said about drinking on the job and Jake getting shot as a result. She guessed Jake would have kept Jamal's secret.

How good it felt to let down her hair and share her emotions. Or at least it felt good until Brooke said, "Jamal called you judgmental? Well, he was obviously angry, but I do think there's a grain of truth in that."

"Seriously?" So much for having a friend who'd take her side.

"Karen, a few minutes ago, you said you had thought Jamal was the perfect man. But those words don't go together. He is a man, which means he's human, which means he's imperfect, just like the rest of us."

She huffed impatiently. "Of course no one's perfect. But I don't see how I could ever trust him again."

Brooke reflected, then said, "When Jamal deceived you, was it to hurt you or to protect himself?"

"Huh?" And what difference did it make?

The blonde put down her mug and leaned forward, her blue-green eyes peering intently at Karen. "You told me his background. This is a man who has always, since infancy, had to protect himself because no one else in his life was doing it."

"That's true. But that doesn't excuse what he did."

For a moment, neither of them spoke. The only sounds were Sunny's purring and the music on the radio. Which, Karen now realized, was Tammy Wynette's "Stand by Your Man," a song that had been playing the night she and Jamal made dinner in her kitchen.

Brooke must have been listening too, because she said, "Like the song says, Jamal is just a man. Not a superhero. He's a man who has survived by being strong, tough, independent. In control. You don't know what alcoholism is like, Karen. You can't even imagine. You don't have control; this horrible craving takes over and it makes you do terrible things. I'm sure Jamal hates that part of himself. He wants to wish it away, to not acknowledge it. He wants to believe he's conquered it and can put it behind him."

"You can't do that with alcoholism."

"No." She closed her eyes briefly, then opened them

again. "I thought of leaving Caribou Crossing when I realized I was an alcoholic and was diagnosed as bipolar."

"Why didn't you? Wouldn't it have been easier?"

Brooke shook her head. "My sponsor helped me see that it could be a kind of denial. Running away. Pretending that if I got a fresh start somewhere else, I'd be a different person. If I was going to get sober and stay sober, better to do it in a place where I'd be accountable."

"That sounds wise."

"I think Jamal has his own form of denial. And it does take time to learn the lessons." A smile bloomed. "I've hit five years sober now."

"Brooke, that's wonderful." For a moment, Karen forgot her own misery. She raised her mug in a toast. "Congratulations."

"Thanks. It hasn't been an easy five years, but each year—each month, week, day—gets easier. Jamal's only at two years. He still has some learning to do."

Karen nodded firmly. "He has to learn to acknowledge who he is, including the weak parts. And he has to realize that he needs support to stay sober."

"Yes. And the people who care about him need to respect his strength rather than judge him for his weakness."

Karen bit her lip. "I respect that he's sober, but I don't respect that he won't admit he needs help." Nor did she respect his refusal to tell the RCMP that he was an alcoholic.

"So you want a man who's as close to perfect as possible, who's dealt with all his flaws and basically stopped learning and growing? A man who doesn't need any help from you?"

Her mouth opened but she couldn't answer. Was that true?

"Karen, you need to really examine your feelings. All these things you told me about Jamal, the physical attraction

Susan Fox

and great sex, these dreams you're sharing with your 'I see the future' game, well . . ."

Brooke frowned and pressed her lips together, worrying them against each other. "Is it all just new and exciting for both of you, spinning fairy tales? Each of you has a vision of the future, and wow, suddenly you meet someone who shares the vision, and it just happens you're both cops so you understand the demands of each other's work, and it also happens that the sex is amazing."

"I'm not quite following."

"Is it an endorphin high, like teenagers who think they've met that one Mr. or Ms. Right and they're going to live happily ever after? That's how I was with my ex, but it wasn't real. I don't think I ever truly loved Mo, and he didn't love me. Being with Jake, that's taught me what love really means."

"You're asking if I love Jamal?" Karen swallowed. "I thought I was heading in that direction, but he's not the man I thought he was." Sipping tea, she reflected on what Brooke had said. "My gosh, you're right. I was like a teenager, assuming that my boyfriend was totally perfect."

"But you're not a teenager, you're a woman. And you have feelings for a man who has many fine qualities, but definitely isn't perfect."

Slowly, Karen nodded.

Brooke went on. "Jake stood by me before he even realized he loved me. He does that with the people he cares about. He does it with Jamal, even when it's hard. It seems to me that Jake's been the only person who ever stood by Jamal. Those two have something special. And so, I think, do you and Jamal."

"Maybe." She used to believe that.

"You need to figure out what it is, Karen. And then decide what you're going to do about it."

"I guess."

"Life's never straightforward. It's how you handle the rough patches that shows you what you're made of, deep inside."

Karen studied Brooke's lovely face with the tiny lines around her eyes and mouth. This woman knew all about rough patches. "You're right."

"The man came to you and he trusted you with his deep, dark, very painful secret."

"He should have trusted me from the beginning." Even to her own ears, her tone lacked conviction.

"Maybe he was afraid you needed him to be perfect."

"Oh . . ." Karen wrinkled her nose. In the past, when people had said she was judgmental, she'd told herself that it was good to have high standards. And it was, but not if it made her self-righteous. "When he did come to me," she said slowly, "I got up on my high horse and reamed him out."

"You did."

"I owe him an apology for that."

Brooke nodded.

"But I still have trouble with his notion that he can stay sober without any support."

"Discuss it with him. Perhaps he'll let you support him. Or if he's looking for someone to talk to, who's been through what he's going through, I'd be happy to."

"Oh, Brooke, that's so kind of you." Karen reached over to capture her hand. "I'm so glad we've become friends."

"So am I." Brooke smiled. "Now, what would you say to some dinner? Chicken and veggie kabobs on the barbecue?"

"Sounds wonderful. I'll meet you in the kitchen in a sec. First, I need to leave a voice mail for Jamal." He'd still be on his bike, riding back to Vancouver, but when he had a chance to pick up messages, she wanted him to hear her apology.

"Oh, Brooke, what if he doesn't give me a second chance?"

The blonde paused in the doorway. "You're giving him one. If he doesn't do the same, you're better off without him."

Chapter Eleven

Karen felt considerably better a couple of hours later, driving home from Brooke's. Her tummy was full of good, healthy food, and she'd heard all about how Jake had proposed and Brooke had accepted. Her phone hadn't rung once, but she told herself that Jamal might not be home yet. And if he was, he might not have checked messages.

He'd call. She knew he would.

She sang along to the radio: Sheryl Crow, Kenny Chesney, Taylor Swift, Johnny Cash. CXNG played a nice mix of old and new songs. Before she'd come to Caribou Crossing, she'd hardly ever listened to country music. Now she knew most of the words to most of the songs.

Belting out "Ring of Fire" along with Johnny Cash, she turned onto the street to her house. And there, parked in front, was a BMW motorbike.

She barely managed to stop the truck and wrench the keys out of the ignition. Jamal sat on her top step with Tennison beside him. Karen flung open the gate and raced toward the house, ignoring the dog who bounded to greet her.

Karen stopped at the base of the half-dozen steps, suddenly nervous. "You got my voice mail?"

"A couple hours ago, when I got here." He rose. He hadn't turned on the porch light and the glow of the street-lights didn't reach his face. She couldn't see his expression.

"Here? You mean . . ."

"I'd already come back. Not much to do on the back of a bike but think." He came down a step toward her. Now she could see his face, for all the good it did her. He looked tired, strained, anxious.

"Think?" Think that he never wanted to see her again, or that . . . ?

"That I was being an asshole." Another step.

A grin tugged at the corners of her mouth. Oh, yes! "So was I." She climbed the bottom step.

"You had a damned good reason to be pissed off." He came down again, one step above her now.

"Yes. But I was self-righteous and didn't give you a chance. Jamal, I want to give you—give us—another chance."

As she took that final step, he moved aside so she could come up beside him. And then they were in each other's arms, hanging on tight. He was hot and hard and smelled faintly of vehicle exhaust and sweat, but she didn't mind one bit.

He kissed her, quick and fierce, then said, "Sit down. There are things I need to say. I've been practicing on your dog."

She gave a soft laugh. "Brooke's been talking some sense into me."

"Jake tried, but I wasn't listening. I owe him an apology too."

"He'll accept it." She sat on the top step and tugged him down beside her.

He put an arm around her shoulders and drew her close.

She snuggled there, wishing things were that easy, that two quick apologies could solve all their issues. But then, as Brooke had pointed out, real relationships weren't all sunshine and basketball hoops and line dancing. There were disagreements and tough problems to work through. Maybe this was a test for her and Jamal. Did they, as individuals and as a couple, have the . . . whatever—the internal strength, the flexibility, the genuine caring—to make it long term?

She sure hoped so. This man made her feel things she'd never felt before. Yes, she'd been spinning dreams, but when she examined those dreams with her practical, analytical eye, she couldn't imagine any other man in the picture but Jamal.

Tennison, tired of being ignored, head-butted their legs. Jamal told the dog, "You sit down too, and make sure I get this right."

To Karen, he said, "I always thought I was so tough. Alcohol got the better of me and that pissed me off. I want to believe I have it beat. But it's a battle, every day."

"Brooke says it gets easier. But she also recommends having support along the way."

"I get it. What you said about me being arrogant . . . Yeah, I hear you. I'll go to meetings, get another sponsor, do whatever it takes. I'll keep winning the battle. I won't let you down, or let myself down."

"I believe that, Jamal. You have that kind of strength." And she knew how important it was to him to not let alcohol beat him again.

"Every time I stood up in A.A. and said, 'My name is Jamal and I'm an alcoholic,' it felt like a knife was stabbing me in the gut. Everyone else in the room was an alcoholic too, and misery loves company, but I still felt like a loser. But now I realize I've got to focus on the positive. 'My name is Jamal and I'm an alcoholic. I haven't had a drink in seven hundred and forty-eight days.'"

"Congratulations, Jamal," she said softly, resting her hand on his thigh and squeezing. "I'm proud of you." Then, because he needed to hear her truth, she said, "I'm not so comfortable with you keeping your alcoholism a secret from the RCMP. I'm not saying you have to tell them about what happened two years ago, but . . ." She paused, not sure how to continue. Jamal was a private man, a proud and independent one.

He sighed. "I shouldn't deceive my woman and I shouldn't deceive my employer. That's what you're saying."

She nodded.

Another long sigh. "Yeah. I need to have the guts to come clean."

Relief flooded through her.

His arm tightened around her. "Hell, it's gonna be hard, Karen."

She could only imagine what it would cost him to do it. She reached for his free hand and threaded their fingers together. "I know. I'll help in every way I possibly can."

"Shit, you thought the worst you were getting was a tough old undercover cop," he said gruffly.

She eased back in the curve of his arm so she could smile up at him. "You think Jake would love Brooke more if she didn't have bipolar disorder and wasn't an alcoholic?"

He tilted his head, an expression of discovery on his face. "Hell no. She wouldn't be the same woman."

"Exactly. She's strong and wise because of the ways she's been tested. So are you." She squeezed his hand. "Jamal, I'd be so proud of you. In my dream of the future, I see you like Brooke, five years sober, then ten. Strong and healthy, out shooting hoops in the driveway with those two cute kids."

"Basketball dreams," he said softly. "A family, a home. A fine woman to love. I never thought I'd have those things."

He pushed up to his feet and brought her with him. Placing his hands on her shoulders, he said, "But now I'm really starting to believe it."

"So am I," she said as he lowered his head to kiss her. No, he wasn't the man she'd first believed him to be. He was far more complex, more fascinating, more lovable.

But then she remembered something else Brooke had said, and eased away from the kiss. Again, nerves fluttered. There was one more thing she needed to know before she could relax and truly be happy.

He took a step back. "What's wrong now?"

"Brooke asked me if we're really serious about each other or if we're, well, in love with the dream. If we're like infatuated teenagers, spinning glittery fantasies about happily ever after. If we're so carried away by all the 'I see in the future' visions that we're just, you know, slotting each other into those visions because the timing's right."

He frowned. "You think you're doing that?"

"No. I thought it through, and no, I'm not. This afternoon, the fight we had, that's definitely not my dream. Being with a man who's an alcoholic isn't my dream. Well, not my old dream. You're not a perfect fit for that old dream, but . . . you're you. You're Jamal, the man I've come to—" She broke off, because the word that leaped to her lips was *love*. And yes, that was how she felt. It was just the beginning of love, a fragile and tentative love, but if it was nurtured, it would grow into something strong and true.

"Yes?" he prompted.

"I've come to care for you," she said quietly. "You, with your strengths and your flaws. You're unique, exciting, frustrating, amazing." She gazed into his eyes, black and unreadable in the dim light. "But how about you? When we met, you hadn't even thought of being in a relationship, and within days we were talking about kids and a basketball hoop. I don't want to push you into a future that isn't what you truly want for yourself."

He nodded slowly. "I hear you. I hadn't consciously thought about settling down. I think that's because I couldn't believe I'd ever have a real home and family. When I was a kid and I wanted them, I got shit."

"I'm sorry."

"I know. Me too. But that's long past. Anyhow, there was something that started pushing me away from undercover work. Yeah, in part it was the drinking, the fear that I'd screw up again. And a feeling that I might be using up my luck. But I think deep down, this need, this hope for something more in life, was resurfacing."

"Then you met me, and we felt an attraction, and suddenly the possibility was in front of you and you grabbed at it because it was easy." Her heart sank. That sounded like the teen thing, endorphins rather than true emotion.

"Easy?" His rich voice rolled the word around with a certain humor. "A woman who wouldn't sleep with me until I figured out what I wanted out of life. A woman who got me up on a horse and made me go line dancing." He touched her cheek, smoothed back a messy curl that had escaped her ponytail, tweaked the curve of her ear.

A hopeful smile trembled on her lips.

"A woman who made me talk about stuff I'd stopped even thinking about years ago because it hurt too much. A woman who calls me on my shit." He let out a slow, lazy chuckle. "Oh yeah, Karen MacLean, that's been real easy."

"If it was so hard, why did you stick around?" Tension quivered her nerve endings.

"Hey, you forgetting who you're talking to? The tough undercover cop?" Then the joking tone faded and he said, "I stuck around because I was falling for you."

Her heart skipped. Oh, yes!

"Earlier today," he went on, "I left because it cut me to

the core that you didn't respect me, didn't trust me. I thought, I don't need this shit, don't need to be disrespected."

When she started to speak, to apologize again, he hushed her and went on. "But that was a hurt kid getting defensive. Three or four hours down the highway, the grown man kicked the little kid's butt and told him to get over himself. To focus on what's important." He bent and rested his forehead against hers. "And that's you, Karen. It's you, my feelings for you, and your feelings for me. It's how you expect me to be better than I am, and I want to do it. It's the fun we have together, the good we can do in the world, the life we can build together." A twinkle lit his dark eyes. "And then there's the sex."

"Sex? Hmm." She gazed into those deep eyes and teased, "Don't you mean lovemaking?"

"Yeah. That's exactly what I mean. Speaking of which, seems to me we left off right about here."

When he leaned down she came up on the balls of her feet to meet his kiss. His lips were tender and caressing. They cherished her mouth, letting her know how much he cared.

She poured her own emotions into that kiss too: relief, joy, hope. Love.

Epilogue

Eight months later

Because they were in uniform, Karen didn't hold Jamal's hand as they walked down the long corridor at Caribou Crossing Secondary, where kids poured out of classroom doors. She did, however, move closer on the pretext of avoiding students, and let her shoulder slide against his upper arm.

"How are you feeling?" she murmured. Today was the first of his public speeches as the new staff sergeant of Williams Lake RCMP. Here, speaking to students and faculty, he wanted to make his presence known, instill a respect for law and order, and maybe get a few kids thinking about a career in the justice system.

"Nervous as hell," he muttered.

"Tough undercover cop," she reminded him.

"I was trained to do that work. This is different. It's . . ." He broke off, shaking his head like he didn't know how to explain it.

"You're not playing a role. You're being you."

"Yeah." He grimaced.

"I happen to think *you* are pretty terrific."

"You have to. You're going to marry me."

The principal, Karen's friend Harv Granger, strode toward them. A balding man, he always looked a little rumpled even when, like now, he wore a suit and tie. He shook Karen's hand, then Jamal's. "Thanks again for doing this, Staff Sergeant." Harv and his wife had shared a couple of dinners with Karen and Jamal, but today, at school, he acted more formal.

"No problem."

Together the three of them walked toward the auditorium.

"After I introduce you," Harv said, "you'll have fifty minutes. It would be great if you allowed time for questions."

Jamal nodded.

"Right, then, we're set." Leaving Karen and Jamal in the stage wings, Harv walked out to face the audience of three hundred students and a couple dozen teachers and staff. The stage was bare but for a podium with a microphone and a glass of water, and a tall stool. The principal called for order and launched into some administrative announcements.

Karen gazed into Jamal's eyes. "I'm proud of you."

"Hope you'll say that after I'm finished."

"I will. Remember, they don't need you to be perfect, they need you to be human. And so do I." Over the past eight months, she'd learned that the imperfect, occasionally vulnerable Jamal was a man who truly deserved her respect, trust, and love. She'd also learned to lighten up on her tendency to judge others.

"Give it my best shot." He bent to give her a quick kiss. Then, as Harv said, "And now please welcome Staff Sergeant Estevez," he strode onto the stage.

He was so handsome in his uniform, so distinguished. His demeanor was powerful and confident, belying his nerves.

Harv joined her and whispered, "Want to sit down?"

She shook her head. Her own anxiety had her shifting from foot to foot and twisting her engagement ring around her finger.

Jamal didn't rush as he pulled the stool from behind the podium, unhooked the mike, and sat down with nothing between him and his audience except a few feet of empty stage. "Good afternoon. I'm new to your area, and this is my first time being in charge of an RCMP detachment. I'll be working closely with Sergeant Brannon and his team here in Caribou Crossing. I want to learn about you folks and your community, and I want to tell you a bit about the kind of work we do in the RCMP."

Although she always wrote a speech and rehearsed before making a presentation, he hadn't written a speech and had turned down her offer to help him rehearse. She had resisted the urge to push, and trusted him to do this his own way.

As he went on, he sounded relaxed and knowledgeable. All the same, he had a tough crowd. A lot of the teens, even a few of the adults, were muttering to each other or texting.

"Well, that's policing one-oh-one," Jamal said. "Now I'll tell you something about me." He paused and cleared his throat.

What was he going to say? Perhaps he'd talk about his undercover days, to spice things up.

Holding the microphone close to his lips, he said, "My name is Jamal and I'm an alcoholic."

Karen gasped. Yes, he'd told the RCMP, was attending a support group, and had private chats now and then with Brooke. He had come to understand that there was strength in admitting the truth and moving forward. But he was still a private man. She'd had no idea that he intended to share this information today. She gazed at his face, saw the tension on it.

Then she checked the audience. Most of the faces had now turned toward him.

"I've been sober for two years and two hundred and sixty-six days," Jamal went on.

Oh God, she was so proud of him.

"I'm not here today to lecture you about the dangers of having a beer or two, or a toke or two. I'm sure you get enough of that from your parents and teachers."

A few chuckles rose.

"What I want to talk about is strength and weakness, about knowing yourself." He spoke earnestly, his gaze moving around the audience, focusing on one face, then another. "About what it means to grow up. About responsibility to yourself, your family, your friends, your classmates. Your community. About knowing when you've screwed up, admitting it, and having the guts to get help."

Most of the kids were totally focused on him. Several nodded, but a few were obviously wisecracking with each other.

Jamal raised his voice. "Because you will screw up. Everyone does. Some worse than others. And looking out at all of you, I see some of you who like to think you're badasses. Well, guys, compared to some of the punks I met when I worked undercover for ten years, you're nothing but innocent little lambs. What I hope for you is that you will never turn into the kind of men and women I've arrested. The kind who get locked up in jail for years, who get beaten up and raped there. Day after day."

Some kids and teachers murmured in shock or protest, but Karen liked that Jamal didn't sugarcoat the truth. His words could be the catalyst that helped some of these kids turn their lives around, or gave the good ones the guts to stick on the right course.

"You all deserve a better life than that," he said. "But

you're the only ones who can make it happen. That's what I mean about responsibility, and growing up. Believe me, getting older isn't the same thing as growing up. Even doing stuff like working undercover, that doesn't make you an adult. You can still screw up. Still let down the people who matter to you. I'm living proof of that. And when you let down the people you love"—he glanced toward Karen— "that's the worst failure in the world."

She smiled, showing him all the love in her heart. Yes, they were two strong-minded people and there'd been some tough times, hurt feelings, angry words. But they were learning patience, flexibility, compromise. Communication, vulnerability, sharing. When they hit a rough spot, they took a step back and focused on their love for each other.

Last weekend, Jamal had proposed. She hadn't felt the slightest doubt before saying yes. Their future would hold children and basketball hoops, horses, a dog, and the ongoing struggle to make the world a better place. It would hold friends. A home. Love.

Whatever the future brought, she and Jamal would stand together, united not just by love but by courage, respect, and trust.

Books by Bestselling Author
Fern Michaels